Death of an American Family; In the Beginning

Joseph S. Hinshaw

The Hinshaw Saga
Four Generations Series Book One

TotalRecall Publications, Inc.
1103 Middlecreek
Friendswood, Texas 77546
281-992-3131 TEL
www.totalrecallpress.com

Library of Congress Control Number: 2020945667
Printed in the United States of America with simultaneous printings in Australia, Canada, and United Kingdom.

FIRST EDITION
1   2   3   4   5   6   7   8   9   10

This book is dedicated to My Father, William Lorraine Hinshaw, my mother Catherine Jean (Stewart) Hinshaw my Daughter Taryn Hillary Dawne Hinshaw Hauser, my Son Brent Edward Adam Hinshaw and my grandchildren Bradley Hayward Hauser II, Barrett Brahm Hauser and Jocelyn Mae Hinshaw.

To all of my brave and honest ancestors who make the framework for these stories so enjoyable and real.

I thank my immediate family for providing the time, opportunity and the understanding to let an old man pursue his dreams and to support him in his efforts while forgiving him for all of life's pitfalls.

Author Joe Hinshaw

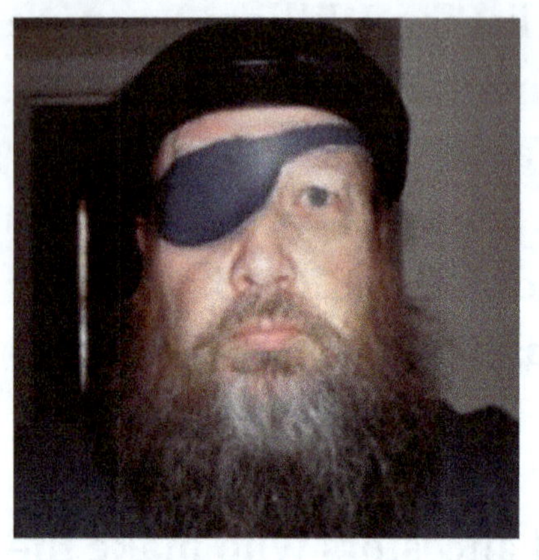

Joe Hinshaw grew up in Indianapolis Indiana. Born during the civil rights period of our nation and living through the turbulent 60s has put its mark on his thoughts and the way that he sees humanity. He was introduced slowly to the family history. His earliest memory of it goes back to a family reunion in his prepubescent yeaours in a City Park in Lebanon Indiana. The memories of this event are very cloudy. The vision of a hand drawn large tree on a big peace of white cardboard is that was hand drawn is the clear surviving memory. He remembers tracing through its limbs until he could find his own name and see just what a large family it truly was. He remembers playing with family members who were mostly strange to him. Other than this one event he vaguely remembers going to his great Grandparents house one time while they were alive but at such a young age that he could not knew now if it was real. He remembers meeting a great Aunt in Hendricks County Indiana that was purported to be over 100 years at that time. She had a small home in the country outside of North Salem. She spent their time together watching professional wrestling and yelling "Get Him" for this entire visit. In his teens his father received a letter offering a coat of arms and a book on the family. His father ordered one and about one month later it was received. The Arms were plastic but correct in its form. The book was not professional but had a lot of information in it. Out of boredom heHe picked it up and started to read it andto follow the family tree once more.

This began his interest and he decided then that he wanted to do this project of writing an historical fiction series based on the real stories of the family genealogy. His own family had been such a disappointment to him that he knew there would be some redeeming value to this process. His parents had been good people. There were dark areas with his siblings and some of the family that he would know. Through this he found that there were the characters that repeated themselves in each generation of his family. There were also those that interacted with the family that he would find in his own life from in each generation. The stories are told with as much detail to history that he would find available to him. He would stay true to the stories themselves and choose his own path where multiple and differing possibilities would appear. The stories then have a fictional base to them to try to explain the possibilities of the events or reasons for some of these behaviors or migrations. The other element of the stories is pure fiction.Some fiction is necessary however. This was added to make the stories cohesive and interesting. Even the fiction is based on possible scenarios that could be deduced or fabricated from the facts of the story. Either way, the reader should keep in mind that some of the stories are historically correct, some are from logical conclusions and some are pure fiction.

ACKNOWLEDGEMENT

I would like to acknowledge my parents, children and those that wrote down the history of the family from generations ago that gave me the basis and impetus to put these words and ideas to paper

This section could not be complete without acknowledging my publisher, Bruce Moran of Total Recall Publications and all of those he had reading and critiquing the content. It is a difficult thing for a writer to stay within their own parameters and an even more difficult thing for someone to tell you that you missed your targets in some of these areas. It is necessary to the process and helpful to me. Thank you all for getting and keeping me on track!

PROLOGUE

The story begins at its natural origins. The family history has been traced back to the fourth century. There were obviously family members prior to that but it was around this time that surnames came into use thereby identifying the relatives in a historically traceable manner through stories, government files, religious records, family accounts, family records, genealogy and heraldry. Before we begin the story of Sir Thomas Henshaw it is necessary to understand the history of England and the three kingdoms of Ireland, Scotland and England. We will look at a snapshot of the history of the Three Kingdoms prior to our story of Sir Thomas Henshaw and prior to the 1600s where our story is set.

World History
General Historical Background of the Three Kingdoms
100 BC to 1066 AD to 1276 AD to Present

The United Kingdom of the current day has a rich history. There is evidence of settlement as far back as 700,000 BC. It was under constant settlement from the Bronze Age. It was invaded multiple times over the early years depositing diverse gene pools and cultural, religious and ethnic backgrounds in the area.

It had various names. In the early ages it was known as Albion. Later it was called Britannia and then England and Great Britain. It is now part of the United Kingdom reflecting the joining of the Kingdoms of England, Ireland and Scotland under one government

Early settlements were of warrior clans or invaders and this like many things I have discovered in my family history and current events set a pattern that would simply be repeated from that time and most likely into the future.

Celts and Britons

During the Bronze Age (700 to 400 BC) the British Isles were populated by the Celts along with western and central Europe. The Celts were also in Ireland and Asia Minor. They ruled the area prior to the Roman period. The Celts were called many names:

To the Greeks—Keltoi, To the Romans—Gauls or Galli Gauls: France, Galicia: Spain, Galatians

The Celts were split into tribes and never became an empire. In Scotland and Ireland they were called clans. Below are some of the known names.

__Names of some of the Celtic Tribes/Clans in Britain/Ireland/__
__Scotland:__
Caledonii, Boresti, (Northern Scotland); Damonii, Novantae, Selgovae, Votadini (Southern Scotland); Carvetii, Brigantes, Parisi--old Gauls (Cumbria, Yorkshire, Durham & Lancashire);

Deceangli/Ceangi (north coastal area of Wales), Ordovices, Silures, Demetae (Wales); Cornovii, (Staffordshire, Shropshire, Cheshire); Celts: Well established tribes, but never joined together to form an empire: Corieltauvi/Coritani (Lincolnshire, Leicestershire, Nottinghamshire, Derbyshire, Northhamptonshire); Dobunni (Cotswolds); Durotriges (Dorset, parts of Wiltshire & Somerset); Dumnonii (south west peninsula--Chysauster & Carn Euny); Iceni, Catuvellauni, Trinovantes--north of the Thames--& Cantiaci (Norforlk, Essex, Sulfolk, Cambridgeshire, London, Hertfordshire, Bedfordshire, Oxfordshire, probably Buckinghamshire, & Canterbury);

Atrebates--associated with the Gauls & pro-Roman--(Sussex, Hampshire, Berkshire, West Surrey, north east Wiltshire); Regnenses/Regni (also Sussex; Hampshire); Cantium (Kent, part of Sussex); Belgae--migrated from Belgium? (Winchester, Bath).

Britons and Roman Britons

The Roman Empire became interested in the Islands around 300 to 400 BC. Aristotle had used the term "Albion" to describe the area and this is what it was known as during this time. The Romans were aware of the large tin deposits on these lands and deemed it to be worth their interest around 55 BC. Rome had a passing interest until around 31 AD when they returned to conquer the area and bring it into the Roman Empire.

The Britons, under Roman rule, formed into the Roman Britons and emerged onto this time. This period lasted from 78 to 441 AD. The Islands were now known as "Brittania" and it became one of the forty-five provinces of the Roman Empire. During the Roman times there were many improvements made to the areas infrastructure such as roads, buildings, cathedrals and baths.

Many of their methods of transportation, manufacturing, farming and culture were absorbed by those living through the times.

Anglo-Saxons

The next invaders were the Angles. Described as a Germanic Tribe they combined forces with the Jutes and the Saxons to invade England in force in the 5th century AD. Their invasions began during the Roman occupation around 376 to 441 AD through around 800 AD.

The current name of "England" came from these people who spoke a language called "Englisc". There was a mass migration of these people from northern Germany that settled the area. This in turn caused a migration of the Britons/Roman Britons into the mountains or the Brittany and were now called Bretons or Roman Bretons.

The Anglo Saxon period is considered to be roughly 400 to 800 AD. They were savage warriors. According to Winston Churchill in his writings he described them as thus "The invaders themselves were not without their yearnings for settled security.

The Saxon was moreover a valley-settler. His notion of an economic holding was a meadow for hay near the stream, the lower slopes under the plough, the upper slopes kept for pasture". The Saxons that settled into the area were known as the 'Old Saxons' to distinguish them from the Saxons on the European continent that had stayed behind much like the English who came to the new world became Americans. The evolution of the Anglo Saxon was complete when their designation changed after the Norman Conquest and Anglo-Saxon simply came to designate the term English. Many believe that this migration is the starting place for the Henshaw Family on the Islands.

Vikings & Anglo-Normans

The remains of a Viking Ship which conducted raids on The Three Kingdoms

Around 789 AD the Vikings began to raid. These raids came in earnest around 835 AD. They ruled the area for two hundred and fifty years. The Vikings were seaman and warriors from Norway, Denmark and Sweden. The Vikings settled in England and France. The Vikings used the ancient Runic (Futhark) alphabet made up of symbols and was deemed 'Magical Writing'.

These groups that settled in England and particularly in France (Normandy) were called Normans. It was a derivation of

Norsemen meaning men of the north. These Normans, especially those that settled in France, were made up of the remnants of other invaders including the Vikings, Saxons, and old Roman Bretons. The group in France was considered more advanced and culturally developed than the group that settled in England. The French group had developed their own dialect and customs. The Germanic and Scandinavian based Normans came back across the channel and invaded the Saxons in 1066 AD. These Normans now became the new English Aristocracy.

Modern English was a mixture of Old English and Anglo-Norman. ("Old English" was Saxon-low German; "Anglo-Norman" was Scandinavian and Romanic--a Roman Latin and Germanic blend.)

As this history is described one thing becomes apparent. From the earliest times the area, like most populated areas of this age, was under a state of constant conflict from one enemy or another. Several cultures acclimated to the area and when they were driven out some of the soldiers and civilians stayed behind and settled into the land. Indeed, the people that we now know and the people of the sixteenth century were undoubtedly of a bloodline from one or many of these conquerors or invaders that came into the area and failed to leave.

Family History

Henshaws before the use of Surnames

Surnames were a product of a time when populations in certain areas began to expand to the point that there needed to be a designation to identify individuals using the same name within a particular region. For example, the name William would have been easy to remember. But it was a popular name and many families named their children William. Indeed, in some families, two to three generations of sons could have been named William within the same household----thus William I, William II, William III, etc was a designation developed to specify the specific individual. When the names were not in the same family but within a community or region---surnames were developed. Early names such as William the Red, for example, could be used for the William who had red hair. Eventually surnames developed such as Williamson for the son of William or Stratford for being from the area near the ford across a particular river or stream. In the times before this we indeed and obviously had family members. Some were not identified in a distinct enough manner to enable us to track them through existing records or history. It is likely that some or all of the bloodlines listed above run through the family itself. In a visit to a small Heraldry shop in the Shambles, an older section of York, England, I was told by the proprietor, when we found our Scottish Coat of Arms, that the family almost definitely had Viking blood from earlier times. Indeed, there exists a family name in the Scandinavian Countries of Hanshus which translated means the same as Henshaw in English. Upon further investigation it is clear that Viking strongholds were established in the area around Liverpool where our family history begins adding credence to this idea. With this information, we go forward, rather than backwards, as our detective work would not be fruitful beyond this period. We know that the first Coat of Arms was issued to a William Henshaw in 936 AD. He was described as a gentleman of wealth and influence. There is another entry of Arms on December 20, 1565 during the reign of Elizabeth I. A further entry during the reign of James I stated that the arms had been restored to Thomas Henshaw of Toxteth Park and that he was knighted. This search into the past beyond Sir Thomas Henshaw could be done at a later time to endeavor to put some of the earlier pieces into place and would start with an examination of the Hanshus.

It should be noted that Arms were awarded to an individual and not the family. There were rules of passing and who could wear the arms. Usually different branches of a family would alter the arms in simple ways to identify each branch. The Henshaw

Families chose not to `alter the arms and they were kept and worn identically by each branch. Because of fraud in the wearing of arms in the time of James I a heraldry commission was established whose mission was to certify and approve each set of arms in use. Sir Thomas Henshaw was certified from the commission as the proper wearer of the arms. Sir Thomas was personally knighted by the King.

Some Examples of the English Coat of Arms

HENSHAWE
1611

Hinshaw

A REPORT ON RESEARCH
IN THE OFFICIAL RECORDS
OF HER MAJESTY'S COLLEGE OF ARMS

Prepared by
H. E. Paston-Bedingfeld Esq.
Rouge Croix Pursuivant of Arms
The College of Arms
Queen Victoria Street
London EC4V 4BT

14th October 1988
Dear Mr. Hinshaw,

I write to give you my report on research carried out amongst our Official Records of the College of Arms for the name and Arms of Hinshaw/Henshaw and variants.

Research amongst our Official Records of Grants of Arms, made by the English King of Arms from approximately 1530 until 1880, produced no references for Hinshaw, but two for variant spellings as follows:

1) Misc. Grants VIII-47.

This refers to the Confirmation to John Heynshaw of Chichester in 1565 of the following Arms and Crest:

Arms: Quarterly Argent and Azure a cross charged wth [sic] five crescents all countercharged in the dexter chief and sinister base a dolphin embowed of the first.

Crest: A griffin's head couped per pale Argent and Azure charged on the neck with three bars countercharged, in the beak an olive branch Vert, fructed Or.

2) Grants 2-657. This was a grant to Thomas Henshawe of London son of Robert Henshawe of Prestbury in Chester son of Edward of the same county of the following Arms and Crest:

Arms: Argent a chevron Ermine between three Moore cocks Sable beaked and legged Gules.

Crest: A falcon seasing on a wing Gold with a crown about the neck Gules beak and legs Sable with bells of the first.

The above Armrial [sic] Bearings were granted on 26 June 1611 and were to be borne by Thomas Henshawe and his descendants.

A separate series of Grants made since 1800 was checked for Hinshaw but without result.

Our official Records of the Herald's Visitations were then examined. These records cover the period between 1530 and 1686 and were compiled by the heralds as they visited each county checking that the Arms being used by the gentry were correct and also recording their pedigrees. Once again I was unable to find any entries for Hinshaw but the following were found for Henshaw(e):-

1) C21-14 (Essex 1634). This entry shows a three-generation pedigree headed by Thomas Henshawe of London who died 11th January 1611. He had three sons, Nathaniell, Benjamin and Thomas. The Arms shown with this entry are similar to those in Grants 2-657.

2) C27-18b (Sussex 1634). A four-generation pedigree headed by Thomas Henshaw, who had sons Thomas, William, Michael and Edward. No issue is shown for William and no mention is made of any members of the family having emigrated to Ireland.

3) C38-44b (Chesshire 1663). A six-generation pedigree of Henshaw of Henshaw, headed by Thomas Henshaw of Henshaw. His grandson Thomas is described as "Thomas Henshaw of Henshaw a Captain in Ireland. Slaine there.". This Thomas is shown as having a son Lea who died in 1661. This Lea is not described as Thomas's only son, so there could have been others. The arms depicted are slightly different - Argent a chevron between three birds Sable beaked and legged Gules.

For the next phase of research our Official Pedigrees, placed upon official record since the end of the Visitation period were examined and the following pedigrees found:

1) NII-141. A three-generation pedigree headed by Benjamin Henshaw of Dorset who died in 1631.

2) NXII-74. A two-generation pedigree (connected to NII) headed by Thomas Henshaw who was Envoy Extraordinary to Christian V, King of Denmark, and was born in 1618. No arms are shown for Henshaw.

3) NXIII-12. A two-generation pedigree headed by Charles Henshaw of London.

4) 14 D14-255. This entry shows a six-generation pedigree headed by Thomas Henshaw eldest son of William Henshaw, whose own son William died in 1676. Arms are as in Grants 46 (Fraser Bradshaw Smith appears on this pedigree).

Our Irish Records were then consulted and an entry found for Hinshaw. This entry concerns a narrative pedigree contained in the Visitation of Ireland 1607 and which shows the marriage of Nicholas Welsh of Dondrumme to Ursula daughter of Captain Hinshaw of Hinshaw Hall. No arms are shown.

As I expect you realise, in order to bear Arms legally, one has to be able to prove legitimate descent in the male line from an ancestor who was legally granted or allowed Arms in the past, and to place the proven pedigree upon official record here at the College of Arms. In order for you to legally bear and use any of the coats of arms referred to in my report you would need to prove such a descent from the grantee in the case of Grants references or from the person heading the pedigree in Visitation references.

It would be possible to provide you with a painting, for display purposes, of any of the coats of arms described in my report for which I would be pleased to obtain a quotation. Such a painting, commissioned from one of our own heraldic artists, would be of the highest standard of heraldic art.

I hope that the information I have given os [sic] of interest, although I am sorry not to have been able to find any references amongst our pedigrees relating to Hinshaws having emigrated to America.

Yours sincerely,
Mrs. B. Pendley
Assistant to Rouge Croix Pursuivant of Arms.

Some Henshaw Family History

Family History: History of the Henshaw, Hinshaw, Hanshaw Surname

Origin: According to the Deliquest's "Three Names of Ours", Hinshaw, Henshaw and Hanshaw are believed to be a variant of Hernshaw, and signifies "ancient wood" derived from the Old English "Hen", meaning "Old or Ancient", and "Shaw" meaning "a Wood". The name Hernshaw is abbreviated from Heronshaw; a woodland abounding in herons, or a heronry where long-legged wading birds were bred. Henshaw is also a local or place name derived from a locality in County Chester, England by the name of Henshaw.

From Bardsley's "English and Welsh Surnames" we learn that a "Shaw or Schaw" was a small woody shade or covert. As a shelter for game and the wilder animals, it is found in such compounds as Bagshaw, Hindshaw, Ramshaw, Henshaw and Earnshaw.

Below are other spellings and their likely origins

Hensha found in the records of Joshua Henshaw in Dorchester MA after abduction by Peter Ambrose and Robert Mathers.

Hinchy/Henchy found in various records in Ireland

Henschaw Various spellings of the name using the ending "Schaw"

Hinschaw Various spellings of the name using the ending "Schaw"

Hanschaw Various spellings of the name using the ending "Schaw"

Hinshaw- considered a spelling error which would reverse itself on different records. There is a story that it was from the family who settled in Northern Ireland and a product of the Irish lilt in speaking the name

Henshawe Other radical spellings considered errors in transcription of spelling

Hineshaw Other radical spellings considered errors in transcription of spelling

Hindshaw Other radical spellings considered errors in transcription of spelling

Hanshaw   Other radical spellings considered errors in transcription of spelling

Hincher   Other radical spellings considered errors in transcription of spelling

Hinshall   Other radical spellings considered errors in transcription of spelling

Henshall   Other radical spellings considered errors in transcription of spelling

Hinchow derived from a gravestone in Franklin Co. TN. The deceased lady pronounced her name Henshaw.

Hofinchel A spelling appearing in the Domesday Book

Hanshus   Variations of the name from the Norsemen or Saxons

Hansus Variations of the name from the Norsemen or Saxons

Hanshaw   Other radical spellings considered errors in transcription of spelling

Hingeshaw from research of Wade Henshaw of Celtic origins and meaning "Dweller at or near a tree grove frequented by wild birds. The bird would be the Moorhen or its other name Heronshaw.

Hernshaw same as Hingeshaw

Heronshaw same as Hingeshaw

Heronshawe same as Hingeshaw

Hanshaugh As late as the 1500s the English Heraldry records show the name Henshaw, its accompanying coat of arms, the surname's origin from early English "Henshaugh" and before that the Saxon "Oldhaugh".

Oldhaugh same as Henshaugh

Richard de Henneshagh Earliest written reference to the Henshaw name in 1365 near Siddington

Hethingeshalt from the area known as Henshaw, near Hadrian's Wall, makes its first appearance in records as 'Hethingeshalt' and could be another spelling of the name Henshaw from more ancient or Roman roots.

Holmes' in his "Ancestral Heads of New England Families" tells us that Henshaw, Hinshaw, Hindshaw or Hanshaw is derived from "hein" meaning "a kind of fowl" and "shaw" signifies "a shady enclosure".

The surname Hinshaw is a very rare name comparatively speaking and appears to be locational in origin. Research indicates that it can be associated with the English, meaning, "dweller at or near the grove frequented by wild birds". At the turn of the century there were an estimated 4000 Henshaw/Hinshaw households in America.

The surname Henshaw is found throughout England (and some in Scotland and Ireland). Henshaw is noted in the Domesday Book as "Hofinchel". Other spellings found in England are "Henshaw", "Henshall", and "Hanshaw". Other known spellings are "Hinshaw", "Hindshaw" and "Henschaw"

There are several "Henshaw" place names in England:

- There is a small village named "Henshaw" in Northumberland, near Hadrian's Wall, east of Newcastle-upon-Tyne, off A69 or B6319.
- There is a "place" near Siddington, in the parish of Prestbury, county Chester, named "Henshaw".
- There was also a family homestead/manor, "Henshaw Hall", in the township of Siddington, County Cheshire.

The Henshaw Family Story

1600 England

It is believed that William and Marjorie Henshaw were associated to Henshaw Hall in Siddington, Cheshire County, England. They were also listed in records of William Henshall and Marjorie Gyll. They actually lived in Toxteth Park after their marriage just outside of Liverpool to the southeast. To them was born Sir Thomas Henshaw who was the father of William Henshaw of Wavertree Hall.

Liverpool at the time had about 1500 inhabitants and was a port city on the Irish Sea, and gateway to the Atlantic, but in this time and the time immediately preceding our story, it was a gateway for the armies that invaded England and a port for moving troops and military equipment to Ireland to support England's conflicts there. The port was also used to move Irish troops to England to fight in English conflicts. Indeed in an earlier time the Vikings used the port as one of the Viking strongholds. It was located directly across from Liverpool on the Wirral Peninsula. In the time of this story Liverpool found itself growing and by the 1640s would have around two thousand five hundred inhabitants. It was a trade port as detailed in the information on Liverpool that follows. It is important to understand the community and its history as a snapshot in time where this story finds its backdrop. In this way it will be easier to understand the saga as a whole. We must put ourselves into the times and live the life as it was lived by the characters in the story.

Sir Thomas and Marjorie Henshaw were considered to be well off by the standards of the time. They were landowners, which throughout the ages, stipulated a membership in the higher class of British or World society as it may be.

World History

Land through all civilization was the measure of standing in society back to the earliest times, except in the times of the "hunter/gatherers" who lived off of the land and moved from place to place in rhythm with the seasons and food supplies for their people's survival. Under this lifestyle land ownership would have been unnecessary and unwanted. Land ownership as a measure of wealth began when man started to learn to plant seed, farm and domesticate animals that would bear the heaviest of the work burdens. These people would grow and raise their own food, hunt in the local forest and fish the local streams which meant the difference between survival and death. The need to move locations from season to season was thus eliminated and man stayed tied to the land he worked. The basic needs of food, housing, clothing and defense would be satisfied in this manner. A more permanent and substantial housing unit would be a benefit for protection and keeping out the weather elements throughout the seasonal changes. The landowner, once established, would then allow others to live on his land. In exchange for their housing the landowner received the labors of these tenants and would share portions of the food and build small shelters for these people. They were under the protection and dependent on the landowner. It was to their ultimate benefit that the land owner was prosperous. Their survival depended on it. History progressed and larger numbers of people crowded onto these lands. Because other landowners would attack and absorb weaker ones the need for armed forces became a necessity. A societal structure was developed from need. This would result in the strongest landowner being able to force their will on smaller landowners and those subservient to them. In England the most powerful would be the Royal Family. The Royal Family, knowing that their vast holdings were too large for them to manage would grant land to political cronies, The Church and others who had earned their rewards through military, social or religious service. These people would still have to pay the Royal Family under their charter in the form of fees and taxes levied against the land. It should be noted that the

Royal family did not rule over the entire domain of the United Kingdom for most of the times like it is today. There were times where several Kings claimed kingdoms in various parts of the country and England, Ireland and Scotland were separate from each other.

There was one other established way to gain land holdings and this was by arranged marriage. A daughter of legal age then became a business holding. A family could bargain with a prominent or wealthy family to strengthen their social status and combine inheritances to improve the family's holdings and finances. Any real feelings of love between the bride and groom were secondary and rarely considered. Some marriages would even involve pre-teen brides to older men. It would hardly be accepted in our time and culture in America.

Family History:

The Beginning: Sir Thomas Henshaw
Sir Thomas had four children:
William, b. circa 1612 who went to Ireland and had two sons

1. *John, born circa 1614, who went to Ireland and died with one child*
2. *Henry (fictional name), born circa 1615, a son who died unmarried*
3. *Ellen, born circa 1616, who married a Mr. Harrison of Toxteth Park and died in 1699.*

A Brief History of Liverpool

In 2007 Liverpool celebrated its 800th birthday. King John founded the city and port in 1207. It was a strategic port throughout history located at the mouth of the Mersey River as it empties into the Irish Sea. It was likely named for the term lifer pol meaning 'muddy pool' for the muddy tidal pool which formed the bay and port.

In the Doomsday Book there was no mention of Liverpool

when it was published in 1086. It did mention the current suburb of Liverpool, West Derby, attesting to the fact that there was settlement in this area at that time.

Liverpool was a port city and had various uses and successes and failures over time.

There was civil planning in Liverpool in its infancy and King John had the city divided up into lots or "Burgages". These "Burgages" were awarded by invitation of the King for its inhabitants to build their houses. This attracted a sufficient number of people to the area to operate the port and supply the needed services to sustain its existence. By the 1400s there were about 1000 living in the city and it would grow to around 2500 at the time if the English Civil War in 1642. In the Middle Ages Liverpool imported wine from France and skins and animal hides from Ireland. Iron, tin, salt, sugar cane, textiles and wool were the main exports to these areas and around the world.

The Middle Ages

William de Ferrers, the 4th Earl of Derby built a Castle on the high ground of Liverpool overlooking the tidal pool, Mersey River and surrounding areas between 1232 and 1235. This provided protection for the port. Ferrers went to nearby West Derby and took the long-standing castle at that site in 1232 to coincide with the Liverpool Castle. This castle had a short life and it was in ruins by 1296.

The Muddy Pool   Liverpool Castle

The castle is important to the story as you will later discover and is central to one of the major events in early family history and certainly had a great impact on the future of the Henshaw family. Were it not for the events on this site the family might have moved in a completely different direction and maintained its holdings in England and Ireland and not migrated to America. There is today a scaled down version of the castle in the Village of Rivington at Rivington Dyke on the West Pennine Moors near Choley.

The 16th and 17th Centuries

Liverpool was a natural deep-water port and supported the largest of the shipping vessels of the time. With England's colonial holdings growing in North America and the West Indies among others the need for a port city became a priority and Liverpool was growing accordingly.

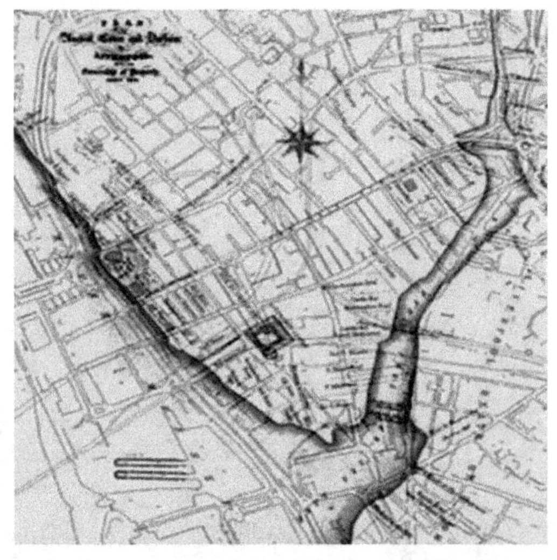

Its geographic location made it a natural trading port for these purposes. At the end of the 17th century a writer named Celia Fiennes visited Liverpool giving a glowing report, writing:

Liverpool is built on the River Mersey. It is mostly newly built, of brick and stone after the London fashion. The original town was a few fishermen's houses. It has now grown into a large, fine town. It is but one parish with one church though there be 24 streets in it, there is indeed a little chapel and there are a great many dissenters in the town - Protestants who did not belong to the Church of England. It's a very rich trading town, the houses are of brick and stone, built high and even so that a street looks very handsome. The streets are well paved. There is an abundance of persons who are well dressed and fashionable. The streets are fair and long. It's London in miniature as much as I ever saw anything.

England and Ireland

Areas of Interest to Our Story

Lancashire: A county in mid-western England, just south of Cheshire and north of Derbyshire. It is also sometimes spelled "Lancastershire" or "Lancaster" and incorporates the city of Lancaster.

Liverpool: A major seaport city in the County of Lancashire, England.

Toxteth Park: A township near Liverpool, in Lancashire. William Henshaw, son of ("Sir") Sir Thomas Henshaw and father of many/most U.S. Henshaws, inherited estates at Toxteth Park and Wavertree ("Wavertree Hall") from his marriage to Katherine Haughton. Toxteth Park, adjoining on the S. and S.E. of Liverpool, is in the parish of Walton, under which it has a chapel of ease: Patron; the rector of Walton. There is also a dissenting chapel in this township.

Wavertree: A village near Liverpool, in Lancashire. The village of Wavertree, often mentioned for its beauty and delightful situation, is in the parish of Childwall, 3 miles E. of Liverpool. Wavertree Hall is 2 miles E. of Liverpool. Also see Toxteth Park above.

Siddington: A tiny village, the home of "Henshaw Hall", in Lancashire. East of Liverpool, and West of Macclesfield, S of Manchester.

Cheshire: A county in mid-western England, just north of Lancashire. It is also sometimes spelled "Chester", "Chesshire" or "Chestershire" and incorporates the city of Chester.

Chester: Either the city Chester, or sometimes meaning the county Cheshire.

Derbyshire: A County in mid-western England, just south of Lancashire. It is also sometimes spelled simply "Derby" and incorporates the city of Derby.

Derby: There is a city of Derby in the County Derbyshire, but Henshaw history refers to the Derby of Lancashire. Derby, commonly called West Derby, to distinguish it from the county town of Derbyshire, gives name to the hundred in which it is situated and the title of Earl to the noble family of Stanley. It is in the parish of Walton, under which it has a chapel of ease, called Derby Chapel, 4 miles N.E. of Liverpool; patron, the rector of Walton.

Henshaw/Henshaw: A "place" name (either a tiny village or a family hall), variously reputed to be either:

- A family hall in the township of Siddington, county Cheshire. Below is a picture of the farm house still standing at Henshaw Hall
- A place near Siddington, in the parish of Prestbury, county Chester.

Henshaw Hall

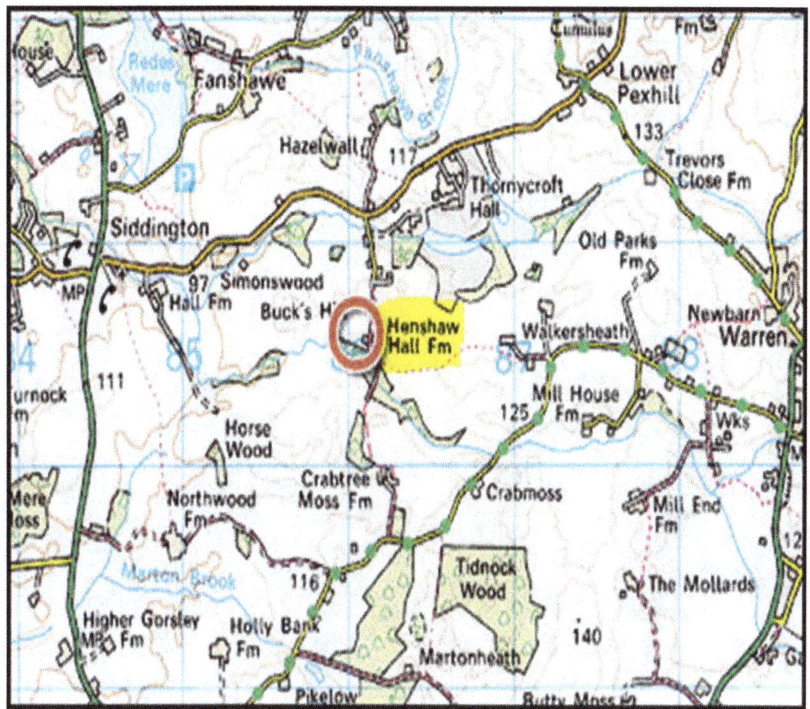

A Map to Henshaw Hall

The Entrance to Henshaw Hall

A description of Henshaw Hall of Siddington, which passed into the hands of the Thornycroft family in 1712 by marriage can be found in the recorded pedigree "Thornycroft of Thornycroft and Henshaw of Henshaw" by George King, R.D. 1687, ordered to be entered by Henry, Duke of Norfolk, Nov 28, 1687. It describes it as follows: "Henshaw Hall is a stone building which has been modernized. It was surrounded by a square moat, some portions of which are still visible. Over the entrance doorway is a large stone slab bearing the following inscription, in capitals:

They Heirs | Of This Land | William Henshaw | Hugh Henshaw |Adam Henshaw | Hugh Henshaw | Hugh Henshaw | Sir Thomas Henshaw | Edward Henshaw | Sir Thomas Henshaw | Lea Henshaw | And Sir Thomas Henshaw | Who Dyed The 9 | Day Of Febr Ano | Domi 1674

Map of Henshaw

This was the home of the Henshaws of Henshaw - see William Henshaw. Henshaw is also noticed in the Doomsday book as Hofinchel, under the same head with Henbury, q.v. pg 351, col 1.

- A small village in Northumberland, near Hadrian's Wall, east of Newcastle-upon-Tyne, off A69 or B6319. (See: "Keys to the Past").

Hadrian's Wall near Henshaw

The area known as Henshaw makes its first appearance as 'Hethingeshalt' and could be another spelling of the name Henshaw from more ancient or Roman roots.

Henshaw (Northumberland)

Henshaw civil parish lies in west Northumberland, on the border with Cumbria. It stretches from the banks of the River South Tyne northward into the remote lands of Wark Forest and the banks of the River Irthing. For the most part, only the southern part of the parish has any settlement in it today and this is largely concentrated along the very southern edge in the Tyne Valley. Archaeological remains date from the Bronze Age onwards but the most famous are probably those of Hadrian's Wall.

Ireland

**Tyrone:** A county in what is now Northern Ireland, in the province of Ulster.

**This was identified as Henshaw Castle.
It is unclear of its location.**

Armagh: A county in what is now Northern Ireland, in the province of Ulster.

Antrim: A county in what is now Northern Ireland, in the province of Ulster.

The Story of Joshua and Daniel Henshaw
The Henshaws (Henshalls), Houghtons and Ambroses

Early records of the family should give a grave precursor of the footprints that the family would take throughout its history. Sir Thomas, William's father, was most likely raised at Henshaw Hall in Siddington which was located east of Liverpool and South of Manchester. There was an estate at Toxteth Park about three miles east of Liverpool where he later lived with his wife and family until his death around 1631.

World History

England had just finished the Seven Years War and rule had changed upon the death of Elizabeth I to James VI of Scotland. He took the moniker of James I of England in 1603. This was the death bell of the House of Tudor and the beginning of the reign of the House of Stuart in the Kingdoms. James wished to combine the three Kingdoms or England, Ireland and Scotland into a single Kingdom. This, in his time, caused some trouble but generally was accepted.

England saw itself as a Protestant nation, however Roman Catholicism had deeps roots in England as early as the 1500s. Ireland and most of Western Europe were still in Catholic hands. Scotland and England were both interspersed with the religion and it would be an infinite problem into the future. England had been tied to Rome and Catholicism through the 1500s. It was during the reign of Henry VIII that the Church of England was established. This was not because of religious upheavals but because the Church refused Henry his request to divorce Catherine of Aragon. With the establishment of the Church of England the Roman Catholic faith was forbidden. Once this door was opened it would never be closed. Many now separated would not return to the Catholic Faith. After Henry VIIIs reign came to a close Queen Mary returned England to Rome and the Pope. She forbid the Anglican Church and punished those that held onto the Church of England. There were many arrests, mutilations and executions over the refusal to rejoin the Roman Catholic Church. She gained the Moniker of "Bloody Mary" because of her iron hand on the issue.

Because of the ongoing conflicts with the European Nations of France, Spain and Italy, who were Roman Catholic nations of long history, anyone belonging to the faith was thought of as an enemy in the England of the 1600s. With the Crusades and the close ties of Scotland and England to the Knights Templar it was a time of mistrust of the Pope and Catholicism in general. The conflicts that arose in this time period are partially from these

  religious issues. This was not only the division between Protestant and Catholic but the division between the King and his subjects over religious issues. These issues were centered on whether the monarch would dictate the religion followed by his subjects or if the subjects themselves could follow their individual paths to their faith and God. The monarchy of this time wanted to control all religion in the Kingdoms including the books, songs and rituals used in the churches and ceremonies. In Ireland the King enforced several new taxes on the Roman Catholics and at the same time denied them full rights as subjects of the United Kingdom. In Scotland religious and political upheaval continued and the events between the Coronation of King Charles I in 1625 signaled a downward spiral at the death of King James I.

1625 to 1627

King Charles I had taken the throne in 1625 from his Father James I of England (James VI of Scotland). Along with his coronation he had married Henrietta-Marie de Bourbon of France who was a Roman Catholic. This did not set well with Protestant England.

Charles I, painted by Van Dyck
Henrietta Maria, painted by Peter Lely, 1660
The threat that Charles and Henrietta's children would be

raised Roman Catholic was at the forefront of these fears. Thus the royal ascension of these children would put a Roman Catholic on the throne of England in the near future if they were raised in the Catholic Church.

House of Tudor:
Elizabeth I 1533-1603; reigned 1558-1603
House of Stuart:
James I (King of Scotland & England); 1566-1625; reigned 1603-25; Charles I 1600-1649; reigned 1625-49

Charles, like his father, wanted to unite the three kingdoms of Ireland, Scotland and England under one rule. Trouble was brewing in Parliament over the unification of these independent nations and Charles choice for a wife.

Our Story
As far as English society is considered Sir Thomas Henshaw was in the upper ranks. Being a landowner had brought him into the best social circles where he was able to mix and associate with British society and aristocracy. This became an important cog in the Henshaw family fortunes. The children of Sir Thomas were born into this society. Sir Thomas had three sons and a daughter. Ellen was the youngest of the four children. The third son in our records was unnamed but for the purpose of this story we will call him Henry. Sir Thomas's second son was named John. William was the first born and being first born he became the mantle of the family name. In William's birth record his surname was listed as Henshall. This was not uncommon as the root of the name had identical meaning as the name of Henshaw. When William was married his surname had evolved to Henshaw and was most likely used because the family name under Sir Thomas was awarded a "Coat of Arms". This decision stamped the family name to the "Coat of Arms" and clarified any misconceived

notions that the family was the one associated with it. At this time there were three branches of the Henshaw Family. The first was from the county of Chester and were known as Henshaws of Henshaw. It is assumed that this is the Siddington place where Henshaw Hall stood. It is said that in the church of Saint Sylvester in the city of Chester that this family's Arms still stand as well as other places. Another part of the family went north to Lancashire and were then known as Henshaws of Derby or Toxter (Toxteth) Park. It is from this branch of the family that our family migrated to the Colonies. The third branch migrated to the south to Sussex and London. The following excerpt from the book "Our Family, A Little History of it for my Descendants" by Sarah Edwards Henshaw from the Mid 1800s states the following:

In 1587 William Henshaw, of this branch, was buried in Worth, in the County of Sussex. "His funeral was attended by the Heralds, and after the ceremony the hatchments were hung up in the church. His ancestors "Were of Cheshire." I quote from the official documents spoken of. Some of this ("Southern) branch were admitted to the Inner Temple; some went into the Church. One, Joseph Henshaw, was a Canon of Chichester Cathedral, and Lord Bishop of Peterborough. Some lived in Devon: some in London.

It was important in these times to groom the eldest son to represent the family and carry the family name in honor. It was imperative to marry well within society. This then was the mission of Sir Thomas and Margerie to carry the family name and heritage forward to establish its legacy.

Another family of prominence in this time and place crossed paths with Sir Thomas and Margerie. This was a family of high society with a pedigree that traced back to King Edward III and Queen Philippa of Hainault. A family with Royal linkage held a high place in English society and this did not go unnoticed by Margerie. Evan and Helen (Parker) Houghton (Pronounced Hocton) were high society. In addition to joining British society through lineage, Evan Houghton was a military man who held his own Coat of Arms. The Houghton family had solid ties to their position through both acceptable paths to societal standing. Evan's grandfather had once been the Mayor of Liverpool. Helen was the only child of Richard Houghton and Margaret Stanley. The "Stanley" name reveals royal blood from its association with the Earl of Derby.

Edward Geoffrey Smith Stanley Derby,
14th Earl of Derby | Hulton

Noble link: Earl of Derby

Finally, the last name "Stanley" on your family tree could reveal some royal blood, thanks to its association with the Earl of Derby. The title dates back to 1139. It actually merged with the Crown upon Henry IV's coronation.

The Surname Database characterizes the name Stanley as

"one of the oldest and noblest of all English surnames, with the Stanley family who hold the earldom of Derby tracing their descent from a companion of Wilham the Conqueror, Adam de Aldithley."

https://www.cheatsheet.com/culture/last-names-that-reveal-you-have-royal-blood.html/18/

The title traces its origins to 1139 and merged with the Crown upon Henry IV's coronation. It is "one of the oldest and noblest of all English surnames". The Stanley family hold the earldom of Derby that follows their descent from a companion of William the Conqueror, Adam de Aldithley. The Stanley family is mentioned because of an odd clause in the Last Will and Testament of Margeret Stanley. In essence this clause stated that upon her death the Stanley lands would be returned to the rightful heirs. With the marriage of Katherine Houghton the rightful heirs would be Katherine and William as husband and wife and then their issue or children. This would be an important document in the future. It would impact the family and its heirs in unthinkable ways.

It was then the duty of Helen Houghton to find their daughter, Katherine, a marriage at the right station in society. To this end both families were on a familiar mission for their children's future. It was a matter of finding a family with a good pedigree or settle for what was termed a commoner -- and a commoner simply would not do.

A third family of interest at this time was the Ambrose family. The Ambrose family was a society family but had not risen to the level of the Houghton Family. They were related to the Stanley family also albeit not the close ties of the Houghton family nor were they considered an heir to any of the family holdings unless there were no rightful heirs through the Houghton line. It was said that Peter Ambrose was a relation, possibly a cousin, to the family. Peter's parents, James and Ann Ambrose, were considered below the station of the Sir Thomas Henshaw family yet still active in the societal affairs of the time.

Sir Thomas was awarded a Coat of Arms for his service to the crown. These arms were reaffirmed during the reign of James I at which time Thomas was knighted. The Houghton and Henshaw families had both achieved their standing through a service path to the crown but the Houghton's had royal lineage. Both families moved in the same social circles.

The Matchmaking of Katherine Houghton

To the happiness of the maternal entities Sir Thomas had an elder son and Evan had an eligible daughter. It was long thought that these two would inevitably marry to the pleasure of both families. It was a good match. From very young ages the children were placed together for play, schooling and upbringing although William had three years of age on Katherine. As the years went forward natural changes occurred that altered their relationship but led them into formal courtship. This would have played out unhindered except for one additional player in the mix. James Ambrose had a son, Peter, born between William and Katherine. It was James's contention that his son Peter was a better match for Katherine. Maybe it is better described as James's wife, Ann, had decided that Peter was a better match and imprinted that position on James. Ann was a powerful woman and ruled the Ambrose family with an iron hand.

James did not challenge Ann. This same imprint was indelibly put on young Peter. Peter had no borders on what he would do to please Ann. He felt obliged to follow her directions. He knew well the consequences of failing to not only follow the directions but to complete them successfully. Peter Ambrose and Katherine Houghton were closer in age, both held social standing and it was very beneficial to James, Ann and Peter to make this match to the benefit of the Ambrose family. This was an obsession with Ann but was not so important to James and Peter. In reality it was not a possibility at all but Ann would not abandon her mission at any cost. Ann's family had been in the gray area of the stratum: not quite low enough to be considered a commoner and not quite high enough to be in the best company. Ann's mother promoted this right of entitlement to her by marrying her to advantage. This same compulsive behavior was now inherited by Ann.

Peter had been friendly with William in their childhood even though there was an age difference. It was a relationship of "friends" and proximity. There was a hidden dark side to the relationship. The Ambrose family had a more difficult road in society. It was easy enough that inheritance was their path but their social graces were awkward at best and they found it hard to fit in at the regular gatherings. Peter was handsome in his own right, but was always in William's shadow. Peter was a good student but was a bookworm and spent much of his time alone. He was lacking in social skills. He was uneasy around friends and faded into the woodwork at dances and could ultimately be found alone. He did not join in the activities unless he was urged to do so by the host or hostess or his overbearing mother who pushed him past his comfort zone to administer her own goals and wishes. In this, she alienated herself and family from mainstream families. She was not well liked.

William was a bright, spirited boy and had the kind of looks that attracted the opposite sex. Mostly it was just hidden glances or whispers as he passed. Peter fostered a jealousy for William that was of the most dangerous kind. It lay inside and festered until later it would become an open sore and lead Peter down a dark path in his life. It would not only affect himself but also his own progeny. Additionally his mother would fertilize this jealousy in the hope of pushing Peter outside his boundaries to compete for a win the hand of Katherine Houghton. It ultimately would affect his families standing in the coveted societal order. Peter had set his attention on Katherine in direct competition with William and that could only end badly for Peter. Failure would come with dire consequences.

Katherine Houghton

William Henshaw

As William came of age it was decided that he would be sent away to boarding school. The schooling consisted of all of the basic subjects: English, mathematics, science, social studies, history, economics, athletics, arts and military training which was obligatory due to the honor of carrying the family Arms. William went away when he was twelve years old and completed his training by the age of seventeen. He did well in school and was involved in theatre and sporting events. He was outstanding in his military training and earned rank during his tenure at school. Some ranks were purchased and some earned. The latter carried much more weight with his peers and future commanders. After he left school he would be required to perform military service with his commission for a period of time. This seemed to be a formality as William had looked upon the military as an honor and a vocation. William loved the discipline and order that the military ranks demanded.

While he was away, Katherine had gone through her childhood and had grown to a fourteen-year-old beauty. When William returned home in his seventeenth year prior to his graduation she had blossomed. She had shining blonde hair that was like spun golden thread. Her eyes were a crystal blue color and the color alone pulled ones attention directly to her face. Her features were wonderfully proportioned and contained all of those small intricacies that made it interesting and overwhelmingly sexual. Her lips were full and heart-shaped. Overall, they were very inviting. Her nose was small and had a childlike turn to it. In addition to the dazzling color her eyes were large and alert but sensual. After being hypnotized with her face her figure was striking and men could not break their stare from her person until she had passed out of sight. She was not aware of this yet and her innocence made her even more desirable. Her heart was steadfast and true. She had an outgoing personality and her friends seemed to worship her. Although she was young and did not have a keen interest in boys just yet, this would soon change. Because of her true innocence many of the boys seeking her attention would mistake her friendliness as a sign of affection towards them. This included Peter Ambrose. She felt no such emotions towards them. She would be introduced to boys at the events and holidays. She would be polite but she knew that the path set for her life was for her to be betrothed to William. She had no interest in meeting other boys and the introductions became less frequent as it was becoming understood that these attempts were for naught. Some boys finally accepted it for what it was and others did not.

William would have several years of military obligation ahead of him but he would be able to come home from time to time on furlough during his training. When this was complete he could be home most of the time unless a conflict would arise. This was a relative time of peace in the Kingdom so none was expected in the near future. William was very impressive and handsome in his Lieutenants uniform. Katherine, entering puberty, did not let Williams' sudden and impressive appearance pass by her unnoticed and tucked it away in her mind as a memorable image. It was at this time that Katherine felt her first quick heartbeats and nervousness when in William's presence. William, for his part, noticed Katherine but did not act on it at this time because of her age and his heavy burden of upcoming commitments. She would like to tell him that she would be pleased to help him but it was not proper.

He was aware of the things to come later in his life were most likely woven into the cloth of his future by the two mothers who were doggedly on the prowl for the correct match for their offspring. In this time marriages came early in life and Katherine was coming within the window of being considered of a marriageable age. William too was aware of the custom of this time and knew that discussion would soon turn in earnest to this subject by the maternal elements of the families.

It was during this period of William's absence while he was at school that Peter made his presence known to Katherine. At first he would shyly work his way around her. Later he would say hello and after time engage in short conversations. All of these actions were at the prodding of his mother and with his father's blessing. Katherine was polite but showed no interest in Peter in a romantic way. Ann would interrogate Peter as to his progress and Peter would shy away from the subject or avoid it altogether if he could. James would sometimes take his defense but there was always a cost for confronting Ann at any level especially on this subject on which she was hereditarily obsessed. Peter would eventually acknowledge some efforts to appease Ann and save himself from further inquiry or worse. Peter was averse to this pursuit as it made him uneasy and nervous.

The Future Begins to Evolve

It was a warm summer day when William returned from school. It was the occasion of his eighteenth year and his graduation and commission into the military. On his return he passed the Houghton home and Katherine was strolling on the estate near the Liverpool Road. Katherine was in her fifteenth year and soon would turn sixteen. It had been over a year since she had last seen William but had fond memories of her last encounter. As he trotted by Katherine he recognized her and tipped his hat. Katherine did not immediately recognize him until he stopped and formally introduced himself. Katherine was struck. She found him very handsome in uniform and he had grown so much since their last encounter. She could make out some whiskers on his chin not shaven from his long journey home. It made him more manly to her and caused a swoon. She was thrilled that a boy of his age and looks would acknowledge her and she became somewhat dizzy and chatty in his presence highlighting her attraction to him. William was aware of the meaning of her behavior and found it to his liking. He acutely noticed that Katherine was now developing her womanly figure and found her to be a beauty in her own right. He excused himself with a small smile and continued on his way home for his visit. Before his return to school there would be a formal birthday celebration and a homecoming. It would be a community event with some of the more prominent families attending. He would see Katherine again on a more advantageous field. An announcement of his military assignment and rank would be made at the gathering. Evan Houghton, a ranking officer in the East Anglia Unit would perform this duty. William would be stationed with Evan and fight in battle beside his future father-in-law.

Katherine was transfixed on William as he rode off down the Liverpool Road. William had not gone far down the road when Katherine broke from her longing stare at him as he moved farther away from her.   As the reality of her surroundings returned to her and her senses enveloped them she had an eerie feeling that she was being watched. Her consciousness completely returned now from her daydreaming she decided to walk back to her home to report her encounter with William and discuss the strange feelings she had experienced in his presence. Hopefully she would be able to overcome this paranoia that her senses were screaming to her. The uneasiness was palatable. Katherine tried to dismiss it because of her strong reaction to William but the warning signs were too strong. The times were not safe and there were those who would prey on a girl of her age and standing. There were highwaymen, thieves and murderers that traveled these roads to take advantage of the people's good will, take easy pickings or to just find an advantage over the unlucky soul that crossed their paths. As Katherine walked she heard a twig snap in the woods to her right. She stopped and looked into the woods but saw nothing. She hurried her steps to draw her close to the house where the threat would disappear. She thought she was being foolish. Maybe she had truly heard something! It could have been a wild animal or a limb dislodging from the tree in the breeze. For some time she had felt the sensation of an unseen presence around her when she came to these woods. Now there was a rustle in the bushes just ahead and she could see some movement of the undergrowth. She picked up her speed and decided that even if it was a wild animal she could still be in danger not knowing what kind of animal it might be. The noises to the right increased in frequency and intensity as she accelerated her pace. Something or someone was trying to mirror her steps but were clumsy in their manner and gait. She now started to jog ahead but it was awkward in her girl's clothing. There was a point ahead where the path would turn and enter the wooded area before it passed through to the clearing on the other side. It was imperative that she got there before the intruder to her right. She began to run towards that point and a view of her house would reward her when she arrived. It would be likely that some family member or worker would be in the area to hear her shouts if she determined that the noise in the woods presented a real danger. For now, she would continue her run. Just up ahead the trail entered the woods for a short time and then opened into the clearing surrounding the house and outbuildings. Katherine began to slow her pace as the familiar surroundings came into her vision. At a sharp turn of the trail before the opening was a large and inviting hickory tree with limbs opening their arms and providing shelter to many of the forest animals and birds. Katherine had made this a favorite tree and often climbed its branches when in a reflective or happy mood to get away and make her world right itself before the universe that surrounded her. A feeling of safety accompanied this ancient and Katherine was being lulled into this feeling of security. She slowed to a jog as she came to the tree. She leaned with her back against its strong trunk to get her wind and listen for the forest noises. All was quiet for now.

From the road William, on his horse, spied movement in the trees at the point that he had separated from Katherine. He saw a flash of motion through the thick foliage and could see that Katherine had picked up speed from walk to jog and jog to full run. His concern grew from seeing the motion in the forest and decided to turn and investigate the movement. His horse was now at full gallop as he recognized the well-known path. He had used the path many times in his youth and knew of the old hickory with its safe haven. He too had gone to the tree on many occasions in his life to ponder the universe just as Katherine did now. At times they would share its limbs. As he approached the woods he was moving fast. Katherine heard the noise of the approaching rider and knew that it was not the noise she had been hearing to her right. She quickly decided that the woods would not be a place for her to be if there was someone chasing her and broke from the tree at a run for the clearing. As she made the initial turn from the tree a shadow bolted from the foliage into Katherine's path.   The person was taller and larger than Katherine and wore a hooded cloak disguising his identity. Katherine ran headlong into the shadow and collided with much force before she could stop. She careened off of him and took a nasty fall to the right and into a small ravine lined with boulders. She screamed in shock and pain and tried to attract the attention of those in the house up ahead. The second noise was coming closer and faster and Katherine identified it as the horse and rider on the path. The shadow stood in the path motionless and staring at Katherine. There was a hesitation in the shadow's demeanor as if deciding what to do next. It was then that William made the turn and spied the potential threat. Katherine was now trying to escape the ravine with her disheveled look and some blood visible from the scrapes and abrasions from her fall. The shadow turned on the horseman but froze on the path. William pulled his sword and rushed to put himself between the shadow and Katherine. As he passed the horse brushed the shadow knocking him sideways and spinning him to the ground. Having achieved the strategic position sheltering Katherine from further harm he turned and heard a whimpering. The hood had fallen away exposing Peter's identity as the shadow. It was clear that he had been stalking Katherine on her walk and his odd behavior had reached a point of concern for her. Peter regained his feet and scurried back into the woods at a run. William dismounted and tended to Katherine who was shaken but was a girl of substantial independence and recovered quickly so as not to appear to William as being weak.

Although this seemed like an insignificant event it was meaningful in the way their lives would unfold in the future. William asserted himself as the strong one who went to Katherine's defense. He would be the knight in shining armor coming to the rescue of the damsel and in doing so cementing his future bond with Katherine. Katherine for her part had made her emotional and physical connection to William. In their shared adventure, she had clearly defined her traits of being cool, intelligent and independent. She had given to William a flash of the beauty that lay within. William was already aware of Katherine's external beauty that had not yet reached its zenith. Most important between the two an unspoken bond had appeared and a mutual support and respect developed in the minutes that passed. Peter had brought his strange behavior to William's attention. After William determined Katherine's state and escorted her back to her home he sought out Peter for an explanation of his behavior to determine what actions should be pursued. English society had its own gossip current and once a tidbit entered this unofficial torrent it was never forgotten and attached to the person as if it were tattooed on their body. It could ruin a young boy's life. William certainly did not want this for Peter and of course did not want any fallout from such a thing to tarnish Katherine in any way. For now he would conduct his own investigation and keep silent about Peter. Katherine was unaware of the identity of her stalker and William felt that it was best to keep it that way for now so she would not develop a bad impression of Peter. There could be a logical and harmless explanation to his actions after all.

William searched the woods and possible paths back to the Ambrose estate to no avail. Failing this, he rode directly to the Ambrose house and asked to speak with Peter. He was rebuffed first by the doorman and then by Peter's mother saying that Peter was in ill health and unable to have visitors. William knew that this was not true but would not argue the point at this time. He was expected home and running late. William would only be home a short time on this trip and felt that he needed to confront Peter before his return to school. Graduation would be soon enough and a return home afterwards for a period of time would accompany his graduation before his deployment for his military obligation or career. That is if he decided to pursue the soldier vocation. This would provide another opportunity to put the events to rest if it was not possible on his time here this trip. William felt that the situation needed to be disposed of in some way as soon as possible to avoid any misunderstanding or escalation in Peter's behavior towards Katherine. He was in a quandary. The deception that came from the Ambrose family and servants did much to heighten his concern. During his stay he regularly hiked and rode the trails and roads around the Ambrose home but did not see Peter during these outings. Peter was nowhere to be found in the following days. William was perplexed. In the past he would site Peter performing his chores, studies and moving about regularly over the course of the day. The only conclusions that could be drawn is that he was indeed in ill health as stated by his mother and the doorman or he was being kept in the house to avoid William's inquiries. Although it was usually proper etiquette to accept the explanation given by an adult; there were undisputable facts that Peter was seen on the path shortly before the illness explanation was proffered and his demeanor and physical appearance were not in line with a person in poor health. If this logic was used, then the only other explanation was that Peter was being isolated to avoid William. The only reason for this would be that Peter had indeed been stalking Katherine and worse----his family apparently knew of it and condoned the actions. William could only deduce that there was something dark in Peter's actions. He had to seek advice.

Flashback: Peter Ambrose

James and Ann Ambrose were married in an arranged fashion. James carried the family name and therefore a suitable marriage had to be found. This marriage was based entirely on the needs of the families and James and Ann were not likely to have married if it were left to them to meet, start a courtship and make the decision themselves. They were not compatible and love never entered the equation. It was simply a marriage to create an heir and to bind two families together in their quest to be of importance. James was brought up in a strict home with a dominant maternal figure. Peter's father was away on travels a large amount of the time and when he was home he was involved in society and stayed with the other men of the community as much as possible. Secretly, James felt emasculated by Ann. She ran the household heavy handedly and any challenge to her authority by Peter, James, the servants or their acquaintances was dealt with in loud, overbearing and sometimes by violent means. James spent little time at home to avoid the environment and spent little time with Peter.

Peter, being of a young age, had no such escape except to his bed quarters and his books and studies. Even in this sanctuary he was not safe from the demands of his mother. Peter was two years younger than William. As such, this put him at a disadvantage in this relationship as well. In fact, in most interactions he was disadvantaged by his own shortcomings. Peter found himself to be the follower rather than the leader. In younger ages he looked up to William and wanted to be like him. When signs of independence or individuality made their way to the surface Ann was there to squelch them and keep Peter under her thumb. This was critical to Ann to be in charge and control and she would stop at nothing to maintain her position in the household.

Peter retreated into his studies, books and school. His awkwardness around Katherine and in social interactions was a direct result of his mother's controlling behavior and left him no measure of self-esteem. He was always trying to fit in or to simply avoid embarrassment to himself or his family which could carry severe repercussions from Ann. This is not to say that under different circumstances that Peter could not have been a leader. This ability had been abruptly and convincingly retarded by Ann to promote her own goals.

Peter, for his part, was content to be a loner and to immerse himself in his studies, books and hobbies. Peter suffered from severe depression from his surroundings and the large amounts of stress he felt to appease his mother. He felt he was a failure at that and was embarrassed by this. He found safety in his isolation. Of course there were the obligatory events that required his attendance, and these would not have been so overwhelming if it were not for the demands of his mother. The hardest demand for Peter was the pursuit of Katherine Houghton. Peter had not had a keen interest in members of the opposite sex. Although biologically this inevitable event would occur Peter was considered a late bloomer. He alone realized that he had no chance of loosening the grip that William had on Katherine. He knew that Katherine and William were unofficially matched through gossip, talk and the unending badgering by his mother to be more aggressive in this pursuit. Peter had no desire to do this but like many things in his life his mother demanded her will be obeyed. He was keenly aware that the stress of competing in an arena with no skills or attributes had the makings of a devastating failure to him at this age. He did attempt to keep his mother appeased and would venture forward into this abyss and much to his detriment and public humiliation.

For several months now Peter had been spying on Katherine. He would take a book into the woods and find the hiding places he had built on the paths that he knew would be used by Katherine. Before long he had developed knowledge of her routines and where and when she would appear and roughly what she would be doing on a day to day basis. Even when there were deviations in her schedule he had learned enough of her routines that he could easily find her if he needed to during these changes of schedule.

On this day Peter had been in the woods. At first he had perched in his favorite tree that overlooked the brook. Here he would have stayed indefinitely were it not for the pressures exerted on him. This tree was Peter's version of his own respite.

It roughly had the same purpose for Peter as his father's disappearances from his mother had for him. As the day unwound he dutifully put his book in his book bag and descended from the tree to meet up with Katherine on her walk. He was feeling good today and was immersed in a story from his reading that had awakened a confidence in him. These visits into fantasy would sometimes carry over into reality emboldening Peter for short periods of time. It was his intent to approach Katherine today and try to talk with her. This was his plan until he heard the steady hoof beats of an unknown rider and horse approaching on the road. He recognized William and was surprised to see him. William's absence had given Peter an opportunity to try to make his mother happy and to bond with Katherine without William, his primary competitor, in the field. Peter was not a brave boy and even though he had sighted Katherine and begun to make his approach he slithered back into the bushes when the rider approached. He had tried several times to make himself known to Katherine on her walk this day but each time his shyness overcame him and he would go back into hiding and out of sight. He was wearing a cloak with a hood and had put the hood over his head to camouflage himself in the bushes. It had worked well for him in the past and had already worked for him today. He was not aware that Katherine had heard his movements around her or that he had startled or scared her. He would do nothing to hurt or annoy her. As this scenario played itself out, Peter had noticed that Katherine was walking faster, then jogging and then running hard to get to the cut back in the woods by her favorite tree. He had sped his pace to intercept her knowing that he had decided to approach her and that if he did not do this he would have had to explain his failure to his mother yet again and the punishment would be severe. He rushed to meet her before his confidence and bravado from his reading that day would desert him. Finally, he noticed Katherine slowing as she neared the tree. He decided that this was his time to approach her and he needed to do it quickly before it was again too late. It was this problem that made Peter seem awkward and strange to Katherine and once more the encounter did not go as planned. In Peter's haste he had forgotten that he still had the hood over his head concealing himself. As Katherine continued forward from the Hickory tree she was looking back and as she turned Peter had timed his approach badly and Katherine collided with him solidly and the force of the collision knocked her over and down the ravine. Peter felt badly but remained glued to his spot not knowing what to do or how to explain his behavior. A state of panic set in. Peter could not think or clear his thoughts from the panic. He was pondering what to do to extricate himself from this situation in the best light. Then there was a noise of a fast-moving horse and rider coming towards them. Peter's instincts told him to run and he found himself following this course of action even before he could remember making a conscious decision do it. As he turned the horse and rider were upon him and he turned directly into the horse's path. The horse sideswiped him and he was spun to the ground violently. In the melee he lost the cover of his hood. The rider could clearly see him now and Peter could see that the rider was William. Their eyes locked and there was no doubt that William recognized him in this moment. Embarrassed and scared Peter picked himself up and shot into the woods and back down the path that brought him there. William knew the path well and would come looking for him once he had ascertained that Katherine was safe and healthy. Peter hid several times on his flight home but arrived there without being found by William. He was pale, perspiring and crying when his mother greeted him at the door. She noticed some bruises and scrapes on Peter and immediately took him into her arms and spoke to him like a small child. When Peter calmed she asked what happened and Peter explained the whole story. Ann was displeased and upset that William had witnessed the whole event and could identify Peter.

She was a changed woman now that she knew that Peter had again failed to connect with Katherine and he had again embarrassed himself in her presence and continued his socially awkward phase. She became irate and screamed like a banshee. She sent Peter to his room and told him to stay there until he grew old. He was a failure and an embarrassment in her and in the family's eyes. She screamed aloud that she did not know what would become of him and that the Ambrose family was better off without him. She blamed Peter's inabilities for destroying their family. When she got this way there was no calming her or appeasing her. This rant would go on now for days. She instructed the servants that Peter was to stay in his room and no one was to see him. She went to her room and took her medicine to calm her own nerves but it rarely did anything but agitate her more or render her unconscious. In the latter circumstance, when she awoke the ranting was renewed until it ran its course. She blamed William for Peter's problems and as the years went by this turned into an internal hatred that would eventually ruin the lives of many people. She sent a servant to bring James home immediately to discuss the situation. James knew better than to refuse.

Ann was in a state of rage at William for interfering in the relationship of Peter and Katherine. In her mind it was a real relationship even though neither Peter nor Katherine if queried would have acknowledged it as anything above an acquaintance. She was irate with Peter for his demeanor and failures in courting Katherine properly. It did not stop there. James shared this blame for not spending more time at home with Peter and grooming him into manhood. She believed that he should use his own pedigree to influence the Houghtons to promote the joining of Peter and Katherine. She greatly overestimated what this influence actually was. She felt that her life was threatened by the potential failure of this match. Her greed and envy was all encompassing. Over time it became the driving force in her life from sunrise to sunset. The obsession began to affect her relationships with others in the community and more times than not they would avoid inviting the Ambroses to gatherings or hide out of sight of her gaze until Ann passed on the streets so they did not have to hear the aging diatribe about Peter having his destiny stolen from him by William. Ann said terrible things about William and his family hoping to change the opinions of the town. In short, she became so obsessed with this issue that it was argued secretly that she had lost her mind. This was not just an idle thought----it most likely over time was exposing both Peter and James to stranger and stranger behaviors. James was known to spend too much time at the pub. It was rumored that he frequented the local houses to find the companionship missing in his bed at home. Business travel increased to the point that James became an apparition at the estate.

Peter retreated to his places in the forest during good weather and his room in the bad weather. In addition he had developed several hiding places within the Ambrose estate that he could go to and not be found unless this was his desire in both good and bad weather. If Ann was in search of him and could not find him she would dole out vicious physical punishment to him when he appeared and to those that she felt had abetted him in his seclusion. She used all of the psychological ploys that she could think of to break him down into absolute obedience.

She was in one of her classic manic moods when James returned home from her summons. As James entered the foyer he was greeted by the doorman who whispered his warnings about her mental state. James would have much preferred remounting his carriage and riding off into the evening. However, he was here now and felt that it was his duty to attend to the family situation. He knew of the terrible beatings and punishments that she inflicted on Peter. He also knew that even if he was present there was little he could do to stop them. If he managed to stop the punishment for the moment it would only then be delayed until he was absent again. Ann would watch for a time when she was isolated with Peter and the punishment would come at the earliest opportunity when there was no interference. The punishment she would dish out on these occasions would be much worse than if it would have been administered immediately and not delayed. The longer she waited the more vicious she would respond. In this way, James for the most part had deserted Peter and his safety for his own.

The doorman continued with a warning of the pattern of behavior and the facts of what had happened as he knew them. James knew that this would not be a good day at the Ambrose house. He began to formulate ideas that would require his immediate presence far away from there. James whispered to the doorman to wait twenty minutes and then knock on the study door and deliver the message that James had prepared. This self-penned message said he was being called away on urgent business that could not be delayed. James then proceeded into the study where Ann was pacing the floor and muttering to herself in a state of agitation.

James gingerly walked across the room to one of the chairs by the fireplace. He poured himself a stiff drink of expensive whiskey and sunk into the chair by the fireplace and a distance from Ann. It would be a stretch of the truth to say that it was a comfortable chair because in the history of this room, since Ann had resided with James, there was no comfortable place to sit or stand in her presence during these times. This had nothing to do with the craftsmanship or aesthetics of the chair; it had more to do with the environment and mood of the room. It took Ann several minutes to recognize James's presence in the room. As so often lately, Ann seemed to move from reality to fantasy and back in a matter of minutes. She did not notice her surroundings or those in it until her mind focused away from the obsession. She would then become aware once again.

Ann was still pacing and agitated when she noticed that James had entered the room. This had become such a routine that the expensive rugs on the floor had wear patterns reflecting her trail during her many manic episodes. James did not know what to expect and would certainly not have the advantage of being enlightened from Peter of the happenings before this meeting. "James!" Ann said. "Something must be done. This Henshaw boy has gone too far this time. He attacked Peter in a fit of jealousy while he was in the presence of Katherine Houghton!" "This cannot be allowed to go unchallenged" she said.

James asked "Did Peter tell you that this happened?"

"He did not have to tell me all of it. He told me that William near ran him down with his horse and he has the marks to show for it. He is in his room and I believe we should call for the Sheriff and a doctor. William must pay for this! He cannot interfere with Peter's courtship of Katherine. It means too much to us as a family. Why does William think he is better than Peter anyway? I am sure that with time and William out of the way that Katherine would have no choice but to accept Peter!" Ann screeched.

James replied "Ann, I am sure there is an explanation of the events that we are overlooking. The Henshaw boy is away at school most times and only home occasionally now. I know that there is talk of William and Katherine being matched, but these things take time and many things can change before it is time for the match to take place. With all of the turmoil in the kingdom at this time and William attached to the military this whole incident could be mute before it comes to fruition! He could be assigned to some foreign land or even killed if hostilities broke loose"

Hearing this, Ann now worked herself into a high state of irritation. Not only about William but now she also focused on James himself. She spoke in a low voice full of brimstone and told James "If you will do nothing then you force me to take action. The Sheriff will be notified that the Ambrose family will want formal charges of assault brought against William at the earliest possible date. I am sending a messenger to fetch the Sheriff now!"

James knew that this was going to happen and he also knew

that the repercussions in the community would be severe and doubted that the allegations being made by Ann would be taken lightly. Ann would wrap herself around this issue and continue to harp on the Sheriff and family friends to support her position---even to the point of slander and defaming William's character. He knew that the community would rally around the Houghtons and Henshaws to the detriment of the Ambrose family if this was allowed to go forward. James had to get to Peter quickly to find out what had happened on that day. It was at this time that the doorman quietly knocked on the door of the study. He whispered in James's ear and handed him the note as they had prearranged and he was precisely on cue. Ann was still ranting and fading back into the fantasy world that she had erected for herself. He excused himself from Ann explaining that he had been called away on urgent business and would be leaving immediately. His departure was barely noticed as she continued her rant and her repetitive march around the room following the ever-thinning carpet trails. James headed straight to Peter's room. On his retreat James heard one disturbing thing as he moved from the room. Ann made it clear that if he was not taking an immediate action that she would do so herself and began making plans to contact the Sheriff.

James entered Peter's room without knocking. At first glance Peter was nowhere to be found. James called for Peter but received no answer. Then he heard it. It was a low sound like a forest animal whimpering and he could not trace its origin. He checked around the room in all of the normal hiding places but could not locate Peter or the noise. He closed out all of the outside noises and again tried to find the sound. As he neared the wall to the left of the fireplace in Peter's room he believed that the noise became clearer and louder. He put his ear to the wall and moved slowly to the left. Again, the noise became clearer. He called out in a low voice for Peter and the noise stopped. Slowly, and quieter the whimpering began again. James could now pinpoint the origin of the sound as coming from behind the wall where he was standing. He called to the maid from the hallway. She quickly responded. James asked her if she could hear the noise which had again gone silent.

She listened and said "No, sir I do not hear a thing." James waited a few seconds and heard no further noise.

"Have there been rodents in this part of the house?" James asked.

"Not to my knowledge sir, but it is possible" she replied. He asked her to make arrangements to have this infestation addressed. He told her that he had been called away on business and would be away for a period of time. The maid seemed hesitant and uneasy about the questioning and James felt the uneasiness. In truth the maid knew of the problems with Ann and her fear of her was much deeper than her fear of misleading James. After all she had no such escape as James or Peter from Ann and often received her ire when James was gone or Peter could not be found. She knew where Peter was and had discovered the hiding place behind the wall while cleaning. In her heart she knew that Peter needed this place during poor weather or other times when he could not escape the house and she would not reveal it to anyone except the doorman, Charles, who had a good connection with Peter. Charles was the only true father figure that Peter had known. She felt that Charles might need to know of this secret place if she were ever dismissed from the house which was a common occurrence with Ann as the Mistress of the staff.

James packed quickly and left the house in haste. He had his carriage delivered within the hour and it steered up the path away from the madness as it had many times before. He took some time to look for Peter along the road and path. He followed the trail on foot to the big tree. Peter was nowhere to be found. James ended his search and told the driver to take him into Liverpool and to his secret life.

Peter had found the entrance to his hideaway several years ago. He could enter through a movable piece of woodwork and enter a space in the wall. He had outfitted it with padding and bedding and candlesticks for light. Being close to the fireplace it stayed warm in the cold weather and cool in the hot weather when the fireplace was not used. A breeze came down the flue if the damper was left open and Peter had rigged it to blow into the wall space. When things were particularly bad at the house he would enter the space to escape Ann's wrath and ranting. Sometimes he would stay there for days venturing out only at night to raid the kitchen for food. When Ann was in her manic states time passed without her knowledge of it so she was unaware of the longer durations of Peter's isolationist behavior.

James found Liverpool to his liking and had many different distractions at this place. Unknown to Ann, James kept a room in the nicer part of town and conducted not only business there but also pleasure. Upon his arrival he sent for his woman and upon her arrival retired with her to his bed to live the life that he knew he could never have at home. It was not that he did not love his son. It was that he could not have access to him without access to Ann. He had never loved Ann but he did not have the option of divorcing her. His word was his honor and to James staying married kept that promise and maintained his honor even though his life was lived in a dishonorable manner to achieve the end result. The other issues he looked on as unavoidable damages. Even if he did overcome this issue the church would never approve of leaving his wife and family through divorce. James was away so much that he had not developed the father and son relationship that would have been so beneficial to Peter. He had failed to recognize the damage that Ann's condition had wreaked on his son. James in essence had developed his fantasy world away from Ann and in his own way followed her path of madness. This left Peter alone and vulnerable at a formative time of his life and the seeds of his future deeds were being deeply sown into his psyche. Like all of these scenarios, they would be passed from generation to generation growing stronger and more obsessive as generations passed. The only true parental figure in Peter's life was Charles the doorman.

The Aftermath of the Forest Incident
The Henshaw Household:

William had finally given up the search for Peter and ridden on to the Henshaw estate. He was greeted warmly by Sir Thomas and Marjorie and his brothers and sister. It had been a little over a year since William had been able to return home. This trip was a true occasion with the celebration of William's birthday, graduation and enlistment into the military highlighting the upcoming party in his honor. After the greetings were complete William retired to his room to freshen up and rest for a while. This gave him time to think on the course of action that he would take resulting from the incident with Peter. He was in a quandary but he could not quite grasp as to who he was concerned about the most: Peter or Katherine. He knew both of them and their families well. He was aware, even from far away, of the talk about Peter's mother's potential mental deficiencies and the push for Peter to court Katherine. He was aware that the public talk had turned to the match between himself and Katherine in the near future which likely added stress to Peter's situation. William was nervous about this and felt for the first time a little awkward about meeting Katherine again under these new circumstances. He was feeling the butterflies in his stomach about Katherine for the first time just as Katherine had felt that way about him earlier that day. Katherine was now of marriageable age and he knew his absences over the past few years and the demands on his time in the upcoming years would play a large role in the plans being made. He also felt for the first time that these plans were real. Before this they had just seemed to be something waiting and untended in the future. Peter added another consideration to these plans and it would have to be dealt with just right. William had other good feelings about the upcoming relationship with Katherine and wistfully thought back to a mental picture of their meeting earlier in the day, fondly remembering how well she had grown.

The Ambrose Estate:

James had been gone for two days when the Sheriff answered Ann's summons. He was met at the door by Ann herself, which seemed very odd knowing that Ann tried to keep up appearances for her self-perceived social station. She invited him into the study and had the servants serve tea and sandwiches presenting the appearance of a powerful family which the Ambrose's were in their own right. For this occasion it was simply used to remind the Sheriff of who he was dealing with and to add an element of intimidation to the meeting. The Sheriff knew that there had been an incident and that he was being drawn into a politically charged quagmire involving the local societal politics. He wished to be anywhere but here with Ann.

Ann began the meeting cordially and followed all of the parlor etiquettes of a proper hostess. She was ladylike and polite. Her dress was impeccable and her manners precise. At regular intervals the servants made their appearances and Ann gave her orders establishing her position of authority graphically for the Sheriff. After tea and sandwiches Ann began her work in earnest.

Ann began "Sheriff, I have summoned you today to discuss a criminal act by a member of one of our finer families in the area although I believe that their standing is greatly overrated. There are stories of improprieties in the family's past that I have heard. These current circumstances bear out these …uh… stories in my opinion. The boy I speak of in particular has taken residence away from our community for many years now and has currently returned. During his absence I am afraid he acquired some bad habits and morals. Now he has visited upon my son a violent side sir. He has attacked Peter in the forest path not two days ago. Peter returned home with visible injuries and had to be seen by our family physician. The whole instance has greatly disturbed Peter. I have interviewed him extensively on the events and here is what I have learned. Peter and Katherine were walking on the forest path between the Liverpool Road and the woods adjoining the estates. The children have used these paths and found their solitude there for most of their lives. As you know Peter and Katherine are being spoken of as a match in our circles and this walk was a part of their courtship. They have taken these courtship walks for several years now. During their walk, they were accosted by a rider on horseback: A rider so cowardly that he concealed himself in a hood. Peter took a stance upon the rider's approach to defend Katherine and was struck down by the rider's horse. As this occurred the hood was lifted revealing that the rider as none other than William Henshaw who had also been courting Katherine prior to his abandoning the area and moving on to another city where he learned his bad habits. William in a fit of jealousy drew his sword and attacked Peter although missing him with several thrusts and jabs. He used his horse to batter Peter just as he has been trained to do at his military school. Peter was able to defend himself and run the coward off with nothing but his bare hands but in doing so he sustained some injuries. Katherine was able to escape to her home during this confrontation which was Peter's intent to see to her safety. What I want of you is for formal charges of assault to be brought on William Henshaw at the earliest possible time. I am aware that there is a party at the Henshaw Estate in William's honor this next evening and he will be available at this event in his home for your arrest. The Ambrose family has some standing and we will see this through so that justice is done. Make no mistake about that." During her conversation Ann had risen and started to pace the floor her agitation growing. Ann was an intimidating presence in this state and the Sheriff, even though he confronted and subdued criminals from all walks of life in all sizes, shapes and dispositions, felt this intimidation. It was not at all her physical presence—it was her ability to get under peoples skins, pester them until she achieved her goal and keep a threat of social and political repercussions solidly available to her that backed the intimidation and made it effective. The Sheriff knew that he was in a no-win situation. If he did as Ann wished he would be at odds with the Henshaw family and possibly the Houghton family. The Sheriff had no idea if Peter and Katherine were engaged in courtship but had no choice but to believe Ann's account. To his knowledge Peter had never been in trouble or involved in anything that the Sheriff needed to investigate in his past. He did not know much about William in the past half-decade because as Ann had pointed out—he had been away in the city. The Sheriff was unaware of what business William might have had while he was away. He now felt that further inquiry was in order beginning with Peter.

The Sheriff asked Ann, "Is Peter here so that I can speak to him about the attack? I will need to interview him to get all of the facts."

Ann was irritated. She said "Peter is ill and cannot speak to you. I have told you the facts, are you calling me a liar?"

The Sheriff did not know how to answer. He was uneasy and was now backed into a corner. He could not afford to upset Ann: It could cause him an untold number of problems. He said "No My lady, I am not calling you a liar, however it is my duty to verify the facts and complete a full investigation of the events."

"You can do that after you have arrested William Henshaw and put him in the stockade. You owe that to Peter and Katherine for their safety. This boy should be arrested. If you refuse I will go to my husband's uncle for relief. If you recall he is a Duke and of substantial importance and contacts! You may conduct your investigation after the arrest!" The Sheriff balked and Katherine was ready. She followed the teaching of her mother and her mother's mother in their ways in these situations and would get her way at any cost to maintain dominance on those around her. She said to the Sheriff, "It is said that your position as Sheriff is in jeopardy. If you do not arrest William the issues that you will face will multiply. You live a very good life as Sheriff and I am sure that you wish to remain in that position. With the arrest and prosecution of William you will have the Ambrose family support to eliminate that threat. In addition the Ambrose family would be willing to fund many men to help you with your duties and there would be a generous amount exceeding your needs that could be spent in any way you see fit. These are your choices and it does not take a wise man to clearly see what path should be taken! I will expect the arrest at the party tomorrow evening! Good day! The doorman will see you out!" With that Ann haughtily dismissed the Sheriff and retired into the hallway and ascended the stairs to her medication and to her rest.

The Sheriff's Investigation

The Sheriff was in a conundrum. How could he possibly make an arrest without an investigation of the events? How could he possibly make the arrest at such a publicly attended event? How could he risk upsetting the Henshaw family and possibly the Houghton family?   He knew from Ann's demeanor and evasiveness that there was much more to this demand than met the eye. He knew that inaction could also damage him personally just as taking the wrong action could damage him on the other side of the coin and either could negatively affect his future. His day would be busy. It was imperative to find James and discuss this with him. He would ride out to the Liverpool Road and path looking for evidence and hope to have a chance encounter with Peter or a witness to the events. Saving one of these things happening; he would have to make the arrest to satisfy Ann Ambrose.

Inquiries were made that eve about James's whereabouts and the Sheriff learned that he had been called away on urgent business. The Sheriff was aware of James's frequent travels and that it was rumored that these were simply a way to avoid the problems at home. He asked if they knew where James had gone for his business and was told that he never discussed his itinerary. Having this avenue of reprieve eliminated the Sheriff mounted early and went to the road adjacent to the estates. He saw many travelers on his journey but did not see Peter at any of his normal places. He did see Katherine but knew that if he made his inquiries to her it could upset the Houghton's and alert William of the accusations. It was his hope to have verified the information before bringing the Henshaw's into the fray. His investigation was going nowhere and all of the relief he had sought to avoid the ugly affair had failed. He collected his deputies and rode to the Henshaw house in the early evening hours.

The Ambrose Estate:

Ann had now awakened. The effects of the medication were fresh and she felt rested and somewhat proud of herself. All of the pieces fell into place. With this one event she could discredit the Henshaw family, have William arrested and charged with assault and launch Peter a new identity as a brave young man who saved Katherine Houghton from a hooded rider. It would make William look like a weakling and a coward and cast him in a bad light with the Houghtons and the community. This would allow Peter to court Katherine unimpeded and by default. James leaving town was another stroke of good luck as that weak man might have a rush of conscience and interfere with this wonderful plan. Ann summoned the servants to dress her for the party. Peter would not attend tonight due to his recovery from his injuries while protecting Katherine. He would also not attend because Ann did not believe that Peter could stand up to the scrutiny or the interrogation by the Sheriff if the arrest was called into question. It was with great satisfaction and the secret of the surprise events that would occur at the Henshaw party that evening that put one of the rare smiles on Ann's face. The servants and Peter were very uneasy at Ann's behavior. Some thought that the craziness had finally overtaken her and that she had overmedicated herself. They did not know what treachery she had hatched that very afternoon.

The Henshaw Household:
The preparations were going well for the event. There were several types of meat being prepared. Unique and traditional dishes made from the large homegrown vegetables that were raised at the estate. Servants were sent to market to buy delicacies. Baked goods were in the oven and several varieties of deserts were being prepared. For William this would be a sort of coming out party for his eighteenth birthday and his graduation. He would put his stamp on manhood this very evening.

William was still disturbed by the events with Peter Ambrose after his sleep. He sought Sir Thomas for advice. Sir Thomas was working in the stables when William located him. Sir Thomas, being a military man, worked first hand with his horses knowing that the military mount could be the difference between life and death in the cavalry. He had acquired a very good cavalry horse and had been training him to present to William at his graduation ceremony. William approached Sir Thomas and asked if he could trouble him with a problem. Sir Thomas was glad to be consulted by William and thought it to be an emblem of mutual respect between a son and his father. William related the story of the afternoon and what he had done to try to resolve it. Sir Thomas had been a part of many conversations with James about the situation in the Ambrose household so the story was not a total surprise to him nor the actions of James and Ann. Although Katherine's name had not been brought into the conversation the two men skirted the ramifications of William's upcoming courtship. This was a discussion best left to the women of the families; however the implications were understood by both. James was aware of the reality of the situation. While speaking to Sir Thomas about this subject he always invoked an imaginary scenario as if they were talking about his cousin and her son to mirror the situation. Sir Thomas followed the ruse and offered James sound advice about the handling of the situation. Sir Thomas for his part advised William that he had handled the situation in the way that any good man could and had taken care to protect both Peter's and Katherine's reputation. He told William that when James returned from his travels that he would broach the subject with him. Until then, Sir Thomas would discuss the situation with the Houghton's in private and in strictest confidence so they could monitor the situation from their side of the potential problem.

William thanked his father and tried to put it out of his mind for now, after all, this was to be his night. It was a celebration after all. He sought out his mother and siblings and had a wonderful time catching up from his time away. He was genuinely amazed at the changes in his brothers and sister since he had been away. His mother was older now than he remembered her but she had grown intellectually and William saw a different connection with her now that his education had been completed. He was surprised and delighted at his mother's knowledge of the stage, literature and even the military history of the three kingdoms. Evan Houghton was an officer in one of the local units and discussions had been undertaken to have William attached to this unit. All of the pieces of William's young life were coming together and his future looked bright. His discussions and interactions with John, Henry and Ellen were mature and of substance. It was quite a departure from their time together prior to his going off to school. Several years of their lives had been a vacuum to William due to his distance, but he was eager to re-establish his connections with them. The reunion lasted until the late afternoon at which time the family retired to their rooms to bathe and dress for the festivities of the evening.

The preparations were complete. The family gathered in the main room off of the kitchen to review the upcoming events of the evening and to review their duties and obligations to the festivities. The food was cooking on schedule to coincide with the planned dining time. The Henshaw house staff was considered to be most excellent cooks and planners of these events. They were the envy of the household staffs in the area. The decorations were in place, carriage staff and livery boys stationed to help guests dismount their horses and carriages and tether the horses and carriages for the evening. The doorman was stationed at the portico to announce the guests as they arrived at the reception. The guests began to arrive. These were the most important families of the area. They included government and military officials, the Church, businessmen and their families. One of the early arrivals was Ann Ambrose. She arrived alone explaining that Peter was ill and James was away on important business. Ann wanted to arrive early so that she did not miss one minute of the evil that she had set into motion the day before.

The guests were arriving at a brisk pace. The food was being finished and the hors d'œuvres were served along with cocktails. Ann was making herself at home. She would blend into the most influential groups she could identify and attach herself to them. Eventually she would take over the conversation to be the center of attention just as she fantasized. These were the times that she could not reconcile reality with fantasy. She had several drinks. After all, this was to be a coup for her and her family. She would eliminate Peter's competition and pull a dark shadow over the Henshaw family. She was elated but knew that she had to play down her role in the events and be ready to leave quickly after the Sheriff made his appearance. She wanted badly to stay long enough to hear and see the effects of her work and the calamity it would cause. Unfortunately for Ann, her consumption of alcohol mixed with the medication she had taken earlier had two effects. It loosened her lips so that she spouted her venomous attacks on the Henshaw family prematurely and she was becoming somewhat immobile hindering her ability to make her getaway at the proper time. Her behavior had started driving away the groups of people that she was able to penetrate. At first they would excuse themselves politely and one by one left the group until Ann found herself standing alone. She would then move to another unfortunate group. Over a short period of time her behavior became boorish and the groups broke up quicker and with a look of disgust. Eventually, she became a pariah and the groups would disband at the sight of her moving their way. Most found it distasteful and unacceptable to use the hospitality of the host and behave so rudely. This was especially rude when her attack was aimed at that very person who had offered her the hospitality and more specifically aimed at the event's guest of honor. At the appointed time William was announced and appeared at the top of the stairway to a warm welcome from the guests, except Ann. Katherine was front and center at the entrance and was overcome by William's appearance and demeanor. He was in his military dress uniform and looked so much like a man of honor, bravery and integrity that it made her light-headed. Katherine had seen this demonstrated by William's quick defense of her in the woods from the hooded stranger. There was a reception line and each of the guests had an opportunity to congratulate and speak with William on this occasion. As the line dwindled the bell was sounded announcing the serving of the feast. William was seated to the right of his father at the head of the table. To William's surprise, Katherine was seated to his right. Although this was awkward at first the wall soon began to dissolve into easy conversation and small talk. Neither mentioned the incident in the woods. Katherine was not aware that William knew the identity of the hooded figure but it was a matter of time that evening before these events would come to the front and be revealed in their full disclosure.

Ann for her part moved through the reception line and shook hands with William. She kept the smile on her face all the way through the line. There were whispers from the assembled guests discussing Ann's behavior and drunkenness as she proceeded through the line. Evan Houghton was right in front of Ann and she overheard his well wishes and his hopes for the future---whatever they were. Ann secretly thought that those wishes would most likely end badly now that William would be in prison in a short time. She did not know or understand the connection that Evan and William would soon have in the military and as part of his family. Ann retired to her seat for dinner and found the environment uncomfortable. None of the guests were willing to sit with her and she was left alone at her table. This was odd because like everything Ann did she had picked a prestigious table in the middle of the event to highlight herself. She had maneuvered the place cards by removing some at the best table and placed hers on the table in their place to be right in the center of the room where all eyes would normally be drawn. To her disgust many simply looked away. The other name tags remained at the table but the seats sat empty and Ann could see these people sitting at other tables in deference to their assigned seats. This started to irritate her but she was able to control it with the thought that soon these snobs would be enlightened as to the type of people the hosts and guest of honor were ---nothing but common criminals. It was ironic that her anger was directed at these people for breaking the seating rules of the event when she had done exactly the same thing to move to the center table. Her drinking and arranging herself at one of the premier tables made her stand out in the room since no one would sit with her now. It also made it hard for her to slip out of the room once she had seen that her plan had been carried out by the Sheriff that night as she was quite in the spotlight at her location in the room.

Dinner was going into its main course when the doorman entered the room and walked to the head of the table. He bent low and whispered to Sir Thomas "Sir, the Sheriff is here with two deputies. They wish to speak with you and Mr. William at the front portico."

Sir Thomas replied "Did they indicate what their business was here tonight?"

The doorman whispered, "No, Sir, but they seem awfully nervous." Sir Thomas leaned to William and asked him to accompany him and they rose, excused themselves and walked from the room. As they reached the front doors they found the Sheriff standing there flanked by two deputies. In his hand he held a paper which he extended to Sir Thomas. Sir Thomas opened the paper and read its contents as follows:

Acting as Sheriff of the County of Lancashire and on evidence presented to me this past day I am hereby ordered by the court to place into my custody William Henshaw on the charge of assault. I am to transport him to the jail with his appearance in court the following morning to answer these charges with the Judge. A preliminary hearing will be held at that time to frame the charges and the offense or offenses.
Signed Walter Stratford, Sheriff
The honorable Henry Wickford, Judge

Sir Thomas read the paper and handed it to William. William read the paper and turned pale. He said, "Sheriff, I have just returned here yesterday and have been in no confrontation. Can you give us any information on the substance of these accusations?"

The Sheriff was nervous and said 'Your accuser is currently on the premises and I would feel uneasy about disclosing the information, however he said I can tell you that it has to do with Miss Katherine Houghton.

Sir Thomas turned to William and asked, "Do you know anything about an assault on Katherine, William?"

William replied "No, Sir, unless it is in the context of the incident we discussed privately earlier in the evening." The Sheriff looked baffled. It was not likely that a guilty man would discuss an incident in front of him.

The Sheriff asked Sir Thomas "Could I inquire as to the facts of the incident? You are under no obligation to tell me, however for the matter of clarity of the accusations it would be helpful"

Sir Thomas started to relay the story but the Sheriff wished to hear it directly from William. A crowd had started to gather around the men and the substance of the visit was becoming clear. There was a buzz generating about the house that William had assaulted someone and he was being arrested. Henry Brisby, who was in attendance and was legal counsel to the Henshaw family stepped forward from the crowd and identified himself to the Sheriff, which was hardly necessary as the two men were well acquainted by their duties.

He suggested, "Sir, I will represent William in this matter and I believe it is in all of our best interests to retire to a more private place for this discussion."

Ann was ecstatic and was enjoying herself immensely. Now the "people" would believe her and they would remember that she was the one warning them that the Henshaw family was not what they seemed. She was up and moving across the room and making the rounds. Strangely, she was no more popular now than before and several of the visitors were openly rude with her. She began her appeals to the guests denigrating the Henshaw family and her reception was icy to say the least. Ann had greatly underestimated the standing of the Henshaw family and the loyalty of their friends and acquaintances or she had greatly overestimated the negative feelings towards herself and the Ambrose family.

Sheriff Stratford began the meeting by outlining the charges. "Sir Thomas: William, I am going to tell you the charges that have been brought against you. I am doing this as a courtesy and it must be kept in strict confidence. Frankly, I find the way these charges came about questionable and since they have been hurried along there has been no time to investigate them further or to speak with key witnesses. In some cases these witnesses have not been made available to me. I have not spoken to the Houghton's because I wanted the statement from the victim to be spoken to me first. He is not to be found and any attempt to reach him at his residence has been met with interference. Obviously, I find myself in a very bad predicament as each person in this scenario comes from very important families and I feel that I have to handle this in a way that appeases each of them. Now, here are the charges. William, you are charged with assault on the person of Peter Ambrose. The facts of the case as related are this. Peter Ambrose was walking with Katherine Houghton, the girl he has been courting for a substantial time, which was their habit. There purports to be a rivalry of such, between Peter Ambrose and you involving Katherine Houghton. Although, it is alleged that Katherine and Peter are the legitimate couple. William carries a jealousy over their relationship and his failure in it. As William traversed the Liverpool Road he chanced seeing Peter and Katherine on their walk and was overcome with the jealousy mentioned. He then charged into Peter Ambrose with his horse and threatened him with his sword causing bodily injury to both Peter Ambrose and Katherine Houghton. This is the sworn statement from which the charges arise. Do you have any questions?" asked the Sheriff.

Barrister Brisby asked the Sheriff for a few minutes to consult with Sir Thomas and William who the Sheriff readily granted. It was his hope that this could be resolved and ease the delicate situation in which he now found himself. Brisby sought conference with Sir Thomas and William in the corner of the room. Brisby whispered "William, these are serious charges. Can you shed any light on this incident?"

Sir Thomas intervened, "Brisby, William came to me upon his

return for advice on this situation, albeit the facts are greatly different than presented here. It was my intent to speak with Evan Houghton and James Ambrose about the situation, however James is away on business and I felt that the subject must be broached with him prior to a discussion with Evan to determine a resolution."

Brisby thought for a while and then asked William for his version of the story. William related the story in detail and answered Brisby's questions to clarify any points that he needed detailed for his discussion with the Sheriff. Brisby was a good Barrister and had some questions of his own.

"Sheriff Stratford, can you please state for us the party who registered the complaint?" asked Brisby

"Well, Brisby, you know that this is a touchy subject and I don't know how much I am at liberty to disclose about that information." countered Sheriff Stratford.

"Let me make it simple then. Master William has the right to know his accuser and to question them directly if this issue should go to court. I will make this easy for you. We know that you have not spoken to Sir Thomas or William ---- Has the Sheriff spoken to either of you?" asked Brisby

Sir Thomas replied, "No Sir, neither of us has spoken to the Sheriff on this matter."

Brisby continued, "We know that you have not spoken to Evan or Katherine Houghton on this matter as you have stated, have you Sheriff?"

The Sheriff responded, "That would be correct."

Brisby reasoned, "We also know that Peter Ambrose has not been questioned and that James Ambrose is out of town on business. Are there any other witnesses to the incident outside of the family members Sheriff?

The Sheriff was being backed into a corner and he was aware of it. He also knew there was nothing that he could do to stop it. "No Brisby, no one outside of the family."

"Then we can deduce that the complaining party is none other than Ann Ambrose----correct Sheriff?" stated Brisby

"Sir, In the interest of this meeting I cannot deny that this would be the complaining party nor confirm her as the one who provided all of the statement that resulted in this action." admitted Sheriff Stratford.

"All of the parties are present tonight except Peter and James Ambrose. I would suggest that we convene in this room to get to the truth of these allegations. Would this be acceptable?" asked Brisby

"It would be acceptable to me, however I do not know if Judge Wickford would allow such as thing." stated the Sheriff.

"Judge Wickford is in attendance tonight." Brisby stated as he walked to the door of the study, opened it and told the people outside to locate Judge Wickford and ask for him to come to the study. The message was passed but it was not necessary because the Judge had migrated just outside the door in anticipation of his presence being needed due to his signature appearing on the warrant.

"Brisby, I am here!" stated the judge and made his way into the study. "I am sorry for this Sir Thomas. We tried to get to the facts before it came to this but apparently great pressures were exerted on the Sheriff to resolve this here tonight.

"Judge Wickford, we believe that the issuance of a warrant under these circumstances was premature. No witnesses have been questioned, no evidence has been collected and the entire story is predicated from one person who has no direct knowledge of the events. In fact she, by reputation alone, is not a credible witness due to her apparent issues with the family. One of the principles in the events, Peter Ambrose has not been seen since the incident and there seems to be an intentional attempt to keep him from being questioned. Many of the allegations as presented are easily verified or dismissed as all of the parties are present tonight except Peter and James Ambrose. We suggest that to clarify the facts that we interview those present here in the study. Do you have any objection to this plan Judge?" stated Brisby.

"I have no objection and in the matter of expediency this is an efficient way to proceed!" stated the Judge

Ann Ambrose was expecting that when the gossip started about the arrest of William the attendees of the party would flock to her for information on the issue and that her popularity would soar. Ann expected that the impact would catapult her popularity instantaneously. This did not seem to be the way events were developing. Ann could find no friends and as she tried to join a gathering they would disband. Some of the groups even rebuked her and spoke harshly to her. It was now very clear to her that she had indeed greatly underestimated the loyalty of the community to the Henshaw family. Ann decided that she should get her exit strategy in order as things were not to her liking and she did not want to be present any longer than necessary as the circumstances were now unfolding and turning ugly. Ann heard loud voices across the house calling for Judge Wickford to join the Sheriff, Sir Thomas and William in the study with Bannister Henry Brisby, the Henshaw legal counsel. She found her anger had started to boil and knew that she needed to get away to keep it under control. If these fools did not recognize the reality of the situation then she wanted nothing more to do with them tonight or until the situation had cooled somewhat. Ann saw the Judge and approached him. "Judge Wickford, I understand that you have been called to the study. Please remember that these people will lie to save their son and that my family has suffered much pain from this crime." Ann said.

Judge Wickford said, "Ann Ambrose, our duty as officers of the court is to get to the truth. We will be proceeding in that direction momentarily. If we find that parties have given false statements or misled us in any way there will be consequences. This is an affront to the court and the King and the good citizens of Lancashire and will not be tolerated. You are to remain on the premises and make yourself available to tell your story and answer any pertinent questions--- do you understand this?"

"Yes Sir!" Ann replied "but I must return to my home to care for poor Peter!" Her exit strategy was no longer an issue and she was aware that she had waited too long to leave and that it had put her in an unexpected predicament requiring her to support and defend her statements. Originally, she had believed, from her naive view point, that her statements would be not only believed at face value but go unchallenged simply because she had made them. Judge Wickford gave her a stern look and reiterated, "You are not to leave these premises until I grant your leave Madam! Do you understand?"

Judge Wickford entered the study. He turned to the deputies and said "You are to isolate Ann Ambrose and make sure she does not leave the premises. Also, one of you go to the Ambrose house and check on the condition of Peter Ambrose. If he is in good health bring him here to me. While at the Ambrose house find out where James Ambrose is staying on his business trip and summon him to return immediately? We can verify each fact in evidence here in this room tonight before there is any damage to William or his family if the allegations are untrue. William, please begin by telling us your version of the events that took place in this incident."

William began, "I was riding towards home from my school for a visit on the Liverpool Road. I was along the main road and noticed Katherine Houghton standing near the road. We acknowledged each other and I rode off towards home. I had not gone far when I sighted a movement in the woods but I could not tell of its nature. I stopped and continued to watch and noticed other small movements in the area where Katherine was walking. When I looked in that direction to check on Katherine she had begun to run and I thought that she had noticed the movements or heard the noise and was in fear of her safety. I felt it was my duty to ride back to make sure of her safety. If it was an animal I could run it off and if it were a person I could determine their intentions and identification and defend her if necessary. She was running to the bend in the road near the old Hickory tree there which has long been a place that we go to for many reasons. Temporarily, I lost sight of her so I accelerated my approach to catch up and intercept her. As I rounded the turn Katherine was climbing up from the ravine and had visible scrapes and blood was visible from her fall. From the right a hooded person appeared in my path and spun directly into my horse as if to run off. I pulled up but struck the figure spinning him around and landing him on the ground on his buttocks. He quickly recovered and I dismounted my horse and drew my sword placing myself between the intruder and Katherine. No further action was necessary however. The fall had shaken the cloak loose and I identified the figure as Peter Ambrose. He stood for a moment with a befuddled look but when he recognized me he ran back into the woods. Peter and I have borne no animosities in the past. I checked on Katherine's condition and escorted her to her house. I then searched for Peter in the woods to talk with him about the incident but could not find him. I went to his house and was told he was ill and could not see anyone, first by the doorman and then by Mrs. Ambrose herself. I felt concerned about the incident and discussed it with my father this afternoon. He was going to speak with the Houghton's after he spoke with James Ambrose upon his return."

Sir Thomas joined in and said "This is to my knowledge the proper chronology of the events and we indeed did discuss the issue this afternoon, however the plans for the events tonight and James Ambrose's absence had made it impossible to pursue the issue further at this time!"

"Sheriff, does this roughly follow the time line and structure of the events related to you by Mrs. Ambrose, except for the facts of the story?" queried the Judge.

"Yes Sir, however, Mrs. Ambrose stated that Peter and

Katherine were in a relationship that would lead to marriage and that William attacked him because he was jealous of that fact." said Sheriff Stratford.

Sir Thomas broke in, "Judge, these are things best left to the womenfolk of our families. However, it is my understanding that for some time now Mrs. Houghton and my wife have been planning the marriage of William and Katherine. This could be verified by speaking to them to clarify this issue."

Judge Wickford asked the doorman to locate Evan and Helen Houghton and Marjorie Henshaw and escort them to the study. "We will soon be able to verify who is telling the truth on this issue." replied the Judge.

The Houghton's and Marjorie Henshaw were quickly located and they made their way into the study. None of the activity was lost on Ann Ambrose who remained outside and under watch by not only the deputy but most of the contingent of guests who were having their own court of public opinion in reference to Ann including her behavior at the party and now in her personal life. It was becoming clear to Ann that her climb up the social ladder was at an end. It was also clear that she would be banished from the social calendar and invitations would be few and far between. They would be isolated to only those events to which the entire community was invited. She did not consider that the outcome could be much worse.

"Mr. and Mrs. Houghton, Mrs. Henshaw, I have asked that you join us because there are allegations that William Henshaw assaulted Peter Ambrose yesterday. These allegations include statements that Peter and Katherine have been promised to each other for a future marriage and that they are currently in proper courtship. Could you clarify this issue for us please?" asked the Judge.

Marjorie and Helen glanced at each other in surprise. Neither one knew what to say. Had Helen guided Katherine to Peter in William's absence unbeknownst to Marjorie? Helen spoke up and said, "Judge, this had not been discussed for quite some time with William away at school. It has always been the hope of Evan and I that Katherine be matched with William. There have never been any discussions with the Ambrose family about Peter and Katherine. I have been aware of the desire of Ann Ambrose for such a match but it was never in consideration. Of course, we should consult with Katherine to see if anything has developed beyond our knowledge."

Marjorie spoke next saying "It is the wish of Sir Thomas and I that William would be matched with Katherine. There has never been anyone other than Katherine in our consideration from either family to my knowledge. Peter, Katherine and William have always been friendly, but those who know Peter would find that this courtship, if it exists, has never been in the open and would have been considered from our view as a one-sided relationship unless Katherine has developed different feelings for Peter outside of our knowledge."

The Judge considered this and then asked the Houghton's to bring Katherine to the study. "I am bringing Katherine to the study and I will ask all of you to wait outside while I have a discussion with her. She would be one of three people to witness the event first hand. She would also be able to clarify the issue just discussed. Now, would you all step outside please?" asked the Judge.

The door opened and the Henshaws, the Houghton's and the Sheriff stepped outside. Ann Ambrose looked around wondering if the meeting had adjourned, then she saw Katherine Houghton coming forward and entering the room. For the first time she felt that her plotting and planning for all of these years would now come to her own ruination. Those leaving the room spied Ann and gave her a look of disbelief.

"My name is Katherine Houghton sir, you have asked to have a discussion with me?" said Katherine

"Yes ma'am, we did need to discuss the events on the road

with you, William and Peter Ambrose yesterday. Is that agreeable with you?" asked the judge.

"Yes Sir, however, William and I were on the road and there was a third person. I do not know the identity of the third person. If you say it was Peter I would have no knowledge of that and would except you at your word. William protected me from him but he was wearing a hood and I could not see his face or identify him." said Katherine. Katherine retold the story matching William's story to the details, except that she did not know that the intruder was Peter Ambrose.

"Miss Houghton---Katherine, I must ask you another question that might cause you to be uncomfortable, but I must ask it. Were you and Peter in courtship?" asked the Judge.

"No Sir, that has never been discussed or wanted by me or my family!" she said shocked. "My mother and I have always had our focus on a match with William and our last two meetings have made me feel this in a real way, but I know that my attraction and loyalty lies only in that direction!" she finished

"Thank you Katherine! You may go now. Please do not discuss this outside of this room except with your parents please. Could you tell the others to rejoin me here?" said the Judge.

As the entourage returned to the room it was becoming apparent that Ann Ambrose had been found out. There were a few more questions and discussions to be had to clarify points. The truth of the issue was materializing. "I have determined that there are significant differences between the allegation received by Sheriff Stratford and the accounts of two of the three people involved in the incident. I also believe that the unavailability of the third party has a bearing upon the truthfulness of the original accuser. I have sent a deputy to collect Peter Ambrose and I suspect that there is nothing wrong with his health----at least not from this incident and that his illness is conjured up to manipulate these proceedings against William. I have sent a deputy to summon James Ambrose to this location although I believe his appearance is several days off from now if he can be located at all. It is my intention to bring Ann Ambrose into the room to answer questions on her statement. I am aware of various derogatory statements that she has made tonight in your hospitality that she should answer to in this study. You are welcome to stay in the room and I request that you do so, but if any of you would prefer to leave it will have no bearing on our meeting." declared the Judge.

Outside Ann was feeling uneasy and wished nothing more to call for her carriage and go to her home and take her medications. She wished that she had not imbibed so much alcohol because she did not feel sharp and clear in her mind as this unfolded. Peter had once again failed her and she placed none of the blame on herself. James was just as bad by being away all of the time. It was a wonder that they had any children at all for all the good it had done her. The words came across the room as a jolt. Ann was struck down to her soul. Her name was being called to come to the study. She knew this would not be pleasant and that her years of deception and vile talk would be called out in this meeting and she would have to answer for it. She felt panic and feigned illness. She was being moved towards the study like a whirlpool sucking her in against her will.

Ann felt the eyes on her and heard whispered comments about her as she entered the room. None of the comments were becoming. The Judge asked her to sit down in a chair across from him. He said "Mrs. Ambrose, I have reviewed a statement that you gave to Sheriff Stratford. I am aware that you pushed the issue to a quick resolution. We have spoken to the Henshaws, Houghtons and two of the three people involved in the incident—namely Katherine and William. I would like to ask now if you would like to amend your statement.

Ann replied "No, I do not! You don't understand how hard it has been for me living in all of these lies for so long. This family is not what everyone thinks. Peter and Katherine should be married as soon as they are old enough. The Henshaws do not need this marriage. Then there is the attack on Peter, how can you ignore it---Peter has injuries!

The Judge paused "Mrs. Ambrose, Katherine also has injuries that were caused by Peter. What do you say to that?"

Ann said "Peter was not the cause of her injuries, if she was injured it was at the hand of William or through her own clumsiness!"

The Judge again paused, "Mrs. Ambrose, I have sent a deputy to your house to check on the well-being of Peter and ordered him brought here if he is well enough to travel. We have summoned James as soon as we can locate him. As I have told you, we have interviewed William, Katherine and both families. None of the evidence backs up your allegations in any way. First, Peter and Katherine are not courting nor has there ever been any idea of there being a marriage between the two. I have spoken to both mothers who verify that for a long time now the match has been made between William and Katherine: indeed Katherine approves of the match to William. Second Peter was not with Katherine on the road, rather he was following her in the woods out of sight. Since we have been unable to speak to Peter we do not know what he was doing there. Peter came onto the trail into the path of William's horse and was struck a glancing blow by the horse. William did not ever touch him in any manner. Peter's injuries were slight as he ran back through the woods after his hood came off and he was identified by William. To his credit, William did not tell Katherine who it was under the hood that had collided with her sending her down the ravine and causing her injuries. Instead, like the gentleman he is, he withheld the identity from Katherine and tried to speak with Peter about the incident. He protected both Katherine and Peter. You have spouted your vile comments all evening and to my knowledge in the community about this family for many years now and all of your charges are unfounded and untrue."

Ann's anger was growing. She did not like to sit in the room and be told these things. She felt that she was better than all of the people here but circumstances and bad luck had held her back. The truth was that she was simply not a very likable or intelligent person. Regardless of her luck or circumstances she would never be accepted in the upper circles nor even liked by many people in her life. This too was about to be made clear to her. "Judge, do you expect me to sit here and listen to these vile lies and hearsay? They are joining in a campaign against my family and their only wish is to destroy me!" said Ann.

Ann was off on one of her tirades and rose from her seat to start her pacing when the Judge said, "Sit down Ann!" This was too much and she was talking in a loud voice but so fast and slurred that no one could make out what she was saying. Again the judge told her to sit down and again she ignored him.

The Judge stood and said, "Deputy, escort Mrs. Ambrose from the room and keep an eye on her!"

At this precise moment there was a murmur in the hallway and a deputy entered the room with Peter Ambrose at his side. Peter looked gaunt and shaky. He was pale and scared. The Judge rose and asked Peter if he was ill. Peter replied, "No Sir!"

"Peter, you do not look well. Your mother said you were ill. If you are not ill then what is wrong with you?" asked the Sheriff

"I was injured sir!" replied Peter

Ann broke loose from the deputy and screamed, "There Judge, I told you that Peter was injured from the assault. Now maybe you will believe me!"

The Judge quickly reacted by having the deputy remove Ann from the room. There was something about the way Peter was looking at her that made the Judge uneasy. "Peter, were you injured in the incident with William? " asked the Judge.

Peter said, "Just a little from the horse. William and I have no quarrel."

"What caused your injuries then Peter?" asked the Judge

Peter went silent. He did not want to talk but was pressed for an answer from both the Judge and the Sheriff. Peter said he did not want to answer them but they were not going to stop until they got their answer. The doorman from the Ambrose house, Charles, had accompanied Peter and stood up and said, "Stop! Mr. Peter will not tell you the answer. For all of these years he has told nobody, not even his father, although James had to know. Peter's injuries came from his mother who whipped him for not making a match with Miss Katherine as she had commanded and it was not the first time. She does other things to him too!"

The room went silent. Peter broke into a sob and buried his face in his shirt. The doorman risked much to stand up for Peter and would most likely be punished severely for talking about the household secrets. Peter was escorted to a room upstairs away from the commotion. The doorman would now be questioned at length about the behavior at the Ambrose house. They would find many horrors at the hands of Ann Ambrose and the behavior described led those in attendance to feel that Ann was mentally ill. They would incarcerate her until James could be reached and then decide what proper steps to take. The abuse included being whipped, locked in small dark areas without food or water for long periods and the mental abuse of living with Ann. James was not immune to the scrutiny either. There would be an investigation as to his trips and whereabouts during this abuse and the findings would uncover his unfaithfulness and his abandonment of the family to Ann's will.

The Judge now turned his attention to Sheriff Stratford. "Sheriff," he said "why would you bring this case to me when you had not completed any investigation or verified any of the facts presented to you? As you can see it was a simple matter to get to the truth of the event."

"Judge Wickford, I would prefer to discuss this matter in private." said the Sheriff.

"We will discuss it here and now in front of the citizens that you so inconvenienced sir!" declared the Judge.

Sheriff Stratford knew that his career and job had just taken a major setback. "Judge, Ann Ambrose threatened to go to the Duke if I did not follow her instructions in this matter! I had no choice!" he said.

"No choice! You had no other choice but to do your job and investigate the allegations fully and completely no matter what the time frame or the threats made against you before bringing charges that could ruin a young man's life. You could have come to me with this and I would have supported you completely. Instead you breached your responsibility to the crown and these citizens in an apparent attempt to save yourself. Is there anything else I should know before I make my report?" asked the judge.

"Well…. There is uh….. one other thing. Ann Ambrose wished to donate large sums of money to the Sheriff's office and she said it would be a very generous amount and I could do as I pleased with the money but of course all of it would have been used for the office in the service of the King and none of it for myself." stated the Sheriff.

"Sir, the fact that you found it necessary to state that you were not going to use the funds for personal use speaks to me that you had contemplated just that!" said the Judge. "This will be included in my report to the proper authorities! Deputy, take Mrs. Ambrose into custody and place her in our jail until we determine what actions will be taken. Find James Ambrose and bring him to me immediately.

The Judge, Sheriff, Sir Thomas and Marjorie Henshaw and Evan and Helen Houghton remained in the room to discuss the welfare of Peter Ambrose. There were sufficient numbers of people at the Ambrose house to oversee Peter. Peter was not of legal age as of yet and as such the Judge appointed Henry Brisby as a guardian of Peter's interests. This was agreeable in the interim with all of the people in attendance. Peter's legacy had to be protected as King Charles had suddenly enforced some out dated laws that confiscated property from orphans or wards of the court and sold it with the proceeds going to the crown. The Judge was tiptoeing around this problem to make sure that Peter would be able to retain the family holdings if it would require that he be made a ward of the crown. His uncertainty of the whereabouts and intentions of James Ambrose required no less from him. Ann would not be returning to the home and James behavior was a question mark in the future of the estate and Peter's birth right. The search was on for James; however it would be a short one and another shocking revelation to the community. It would have a devastating effect on Peter who was now sixteen years old.

Through information gathered from the doorman, Judge Wickford sent two deputies into Liverpool to determine the whereabouts of James Ambrose. The normal investigation procedures were followed and James could not be found through his business contacts. The deputies then retired to the pub near the docks. In British life the pub was the center of activity and information. The deputies bought a few rounds and steered the conversation to the Ambrose family. Within the hour they had found that James had kept a woman in Liverpool for many years and that he had his own rooms in the city. His drinking habit and carousing was well known in the cities gossip pool. These things were amazing. James lived only about three miles east of town and none of this information had made its way back to Ann. It was another testament to the loathing that Ann had bred against her with her neighbors and acquaintances. The fact that they would fail to tell her this information on the public behavior of James was testament to this. They found James ensconced at his rooms and summoned him to the Judges quarters.

"James Ambrose, a difficult man to find!" stated the Judge.

"Not so hard if you know where to look!" replied James. "Why have I been called here sir, I have done nothing wrong?

"That is a matter of opinion sir!" the Judge stated in a stern voice. "Our information is that you have abandoned your duties as a husband and father to your son, Peter. We have your wife in custody for abusing Peter and possibly other charges relating to making false allegations against William Henshaw. Certain facts have come to light about your behavior also. First and foremost that you are away from home for 'business' purposes quite a bit under false pretenses. We are aware that you use business as an excuse to leave home. We are aware that you keep separate residence in secret in Liverpool. We are aware of your 'life' in Liverpool and the deprecation that it involves. We are aware that while you are away in this 'life' you ignored the state of affairs at your own home. This dereliction has allowed your wife, Ann, who we believe to be dangerously mentally ill to abuse Peter both physically and emotionally in your absence. What we are here to decide is what role your behavior has played in these occurrences. What do you have to say for yourself on these matters?" asked the Judge.

"Sir, I was away on business much of the time. At times things became so unbearable with Ann that I had to get away from her. I am sorry about Peter but taking him with me would have alerted Ann that I was not away on business. I had long ago stopped loving Ann; that is if I ever did. She was impossible to live with so I fled to Liverpool and set up my rooms so I could get some peace." replied James.

"Well sir, this explains a part of the incident. It does not explain how you expected Peter to find peace and security in his own home. Now would you like to explain the woman who has shared your bed, your abandonment of your fatherly duties to your son and your lies to your family, friends and community to keep your alternate life a secret?" asked the Judge.

James was silent for a moment. "Sir, I know that this looks very bad for me. You just do not understand how the many years of living with a woman like Ann can wear you down and bring about a desperation that has to be appeased. To some extent my life in Liverpool was known by many but kept secret nonetheless. These things were wrong-I admit, but all of them replaced the things lacking at home. Peter is the victim here and there was nothing I could do to protect him. When I would step in between Peter and Ann I was only delaying the inevitable. Ann would simply wait until I was absent and settle her score with Peter. She was becoming increasingly angry and irrational over this last few months and the only thing I knew was that I had to get away from her. Her obsession focused on the Houghton girl and I was afraid that there would be drastic consequences to anyone standing in her way. I feared for my life at times. I feared sleep because I could not know of her plans or of my own safety if I put myself in this exposed state!" said James.

The Judge stated that he did not believe charging James with a crime and incarcerating him would be in the best interest of Peter who was already losing his mother for at least a long period of time if not forever. "James, Peter must be protected. If what you say is true then there is no reason for your behavior to continue. You may go back to your home and refocus your attention on raising your son. My deputies will be monitoring you to make sure this is happening. I order you to submit to me an itinerary and documentation of any time you will be spending away from your home so you can be held accountable to the obligations you have to your family. Is that understood?" demanded the Judge.

"Yes Sir!" replied James.

"You may go, remember that you will be monitored and if I find that you are not keeping your oath to me the consequences will be swift and harsh!" commanded the Judge. "Additionally I will need for you to sign the letters of commitment placing Ann in the Asylum if and until she recovers! Your Doorman, Charles I believe, is the closest relationship that Peter has and he will be an integral part of Peter's care and life now!"

World History 1631 to 1640

In medieval times it was custom that coastal towns pay a tax for maintaining and building a strong navy in times of emergency. The Dunkirk Pirates were sailing in the Channel and the Barbary Pirates were raiding Ireland for slaves both on land and at sea. In 1634, Charles decided to declare an emergency and again levy the tax. The next year Charles taxed the inland counties. The funds were to be spent to build the English Navy and add new ships and men to defend the coast. This did not seem to be the issue at hand. The issue was that Charles had raised and instituted a new tax without the consent of Parliament. The tax money was being used to support the King and his campaigns rather than being used to build the defenses against the pirates. There was an organized campaign of non-payment of this tax in protest of the King's omission of Parliaments oversight. The protest was led by Viscount Saye and Sele, whose associate John Hampden was prosecuted before the Court of Exchequer in 1637. Hampden challenged the legality of the tax. The twelve judges split their decision seven to five in favor of the King. The case was ruled in the Kings favor, but it was still somewhat of a victory for Parliament as the court was substantially split on the point of law. It was not such a victory for Mr. Hampden who was imprisoned.

The citizens were aroused and indignant about the way Charles was subverting the authority of Parliament, but this was not the worst of this period. By the time Lord Weston, Charles savior of the Royal Economy, died in 1635, the Crown was solvent. Government expenditure could not be further reduced.

With one of the two major elements at the heart of conflicts, namely greed, ego and power creating upheaval and protest temporarily appeased, the second element, religion, was brought to the front. These two volatile issues would almost guarantee new hostilities. Charles believed in High Anglicanism. This was a sacramental version of the Church of England and made it more closely resemble the services and accouterments of the Roman Catholic Church and its traditions and services. This played right into the English fear of Charles's heirs being born into the Roman Catholic faith, no matter how it was disguised.

The Henshaw Family fell on both sides of the religious question over many years. Joseph Henshaw was eventually appointed to Bishop of Peterborough. This path had him assigned as first chaplain to John Digby, Earl of Bristol. He then came to the same position with George Villiers, the Duke of Buckingham and close advisor to Charles I who was assassinated. He was appointed to a canon's office at Chichester Cathedral. In this period Archbishop Laud would bestow on him the benefices of East Lavant and Stedham-cum-Heyshot in Sussex. He maintained all of these positions until 1644. With the rise of Cromwell the church went through upheaval and those of the old order were stripped of their titles, land, banished from England or executed. Joseph had a lot to lose if Charles was dethroned. During the Restoration under Charles II he was returned to his titles and rose to his position as Bishop of Peterborough Cathedral. With this he earned a seat in the House of Lords. He served in these Offices during the reigns of James I, Charles I and Charles II. He was living in exile during the rule of Cromwell.

In 1557 a young man named Thomas Henshaw was arrested with 21 others who were devout Protestants under the rule of Queen Mary. They were placed in the stockades for 10 days hoping that this would gain their compliance. After the ten days Thomas was taken to be tortured to force him to recant his allegiance to the Protestant faith. He did not recant. The torture continued until he became ill with "Ague" (A febrile condition in which there are alternating periods of chills, fever, and sweating. Used chiefly in reference to the fevers associated with malaria.) They felt that this would be his death and they left him to die ending his torture. To his advantage "Bloody Mary" died during this period and Thomas and his fellow prisoners were released. Amazingly Thomas recovered from the disease. The story of Thomas and this group was chronicled in a book by John Foxe titled "Book of Martyrs" published in 1835.

During this time a Blacksmith, Jesse Henshaw and his wife Mary were burned at the stake for their refusal to abandon their Protestant beliefs and return to the fold of Catholicism. This fight was deeply embedded in to family history and tore both ways.

With the assassination of George Villiers, the Duke of Buckingham, after his failures in France, there were changes in relations between former opponents and the King. He now gave the favorable appointments that once belonged to Villiers to his most vocal of critics to silence their campaigns against him. They were contrite after receiving their new bribes and silenced their voices in opposition.

In addition to the earlier appointment of Sir Richard Weston, who was the wizard of Charles's financial recovery were the appointments of Sir Francis Cottington (1582-1646)-Chancellor of the Exchequer and Sir Francis Windebank (1582-1646)-Secretary of State. All of these men were former opponents of the King based on their dislike of Villiers. This ended when he was assassinated, but the appointments had a dark nature if it were to have been revealed to Protestant England and Scotland. All of these appointees were secretly Roman Catholics.

The Puritans suspected this to be the case but had no proof. The appointments invigorated the debate about which religion, under Charles, would be favored and what was the future of the Church of England. The Puritans and the Protestants generally were suspicious of the mounting evidence of support for the Catholics in England by the King and his ministers. Queen Henrietta was known to practice her Catholicism in the Royal Castle and in the Catholic Church. The religious situation was growing tense.

In 1633 Charles appointed William Laud as the Archbishop of

Canterbury. Like Villiers, Laud was a personal friend of Charles. Like Villiers his association would begin a flow of ill will throughout the three Kingdoms which would end in disaster for Charles. Laud brought with him a staunch belief in the Arminian Doctrines of the Church. In summary, Arminianism had its beginnings from a Dutch Reformed theologian named Jacobus Arminius (1560-1609) and his followers were called the Remonstrants. It should be noted that these doctrines were accepted by most Christian institutions and theologians of this time, however, they were suspect under the circumstances of being Catholic in origin by the Puritans and Protestants. The Protestants too accepted the doctrines. The problem then arose from the appearances of the grandiose churches and ornate services. Arminianism was inherently not Catholic but most closely related to Calvinism or what is called the "Reformed Theory". The Calvinists and the Arminians were considered rivals due to their differences in their ideas on divine predestination and salvation.

Laud had voiced his opinion that he believed the Puritans to be more threatening to the Church of England than the Catholics. He was instrumental in the persecution of the Puritans of this time. Laud's relationship with Charles progressed to the point that he had gained influence with Charles and sought to promote his own interests through the King. One instance of this was the appointment of Bishop William Juxon (1582-1663) as Lord Treasurer replacing Sir Richard Weston upon his death in 1636.

Laud was a zealot for his cause. Securing the appointment of Juxon reinforced to him that he had a great power of manipulating the monarchy to his will. Laud was aware of the great importance that the office of Lord Treasurer carried. One of Laud's desires was to hold wealth. To this end, he knew that the Church itself had seen better days. Its glory was diminished throughout the Reformation and much of the church's riches had been stripped during that period. Laud felt that the time was at hand to renew the Church to its previous standing and wealth. This he extended into Ireland and Scotland in the guise of having one unified Church of England in the three kingdoms. In the end it was his undoing.

Charles supported Laud in this endeavor but Charles had lost touch with public sentiment to the point that he was unaware of the negative effects this was having within his kingdom. There was open hostility and resentment over Laud's policies. The conflict and distrust between Laud and the Puritans was escalating.   The Puritans being of a simple philosophy towards religion were mistrustful of the Arminian order. It was at least a step closer to Catholicism as Puritanism was a step further away from it. The opposing forces were drawing their lines clearly at this point.

Laud was quick to squelch the opposition and called for the removal of Puritan and Non-conformist Preachers. Laud had the support of the Star Chamber and the High Commission through his position and used it as a tool to quell the unrest. In his hands it had the reverse affect. These religious opponents were arrested, pilloried, branded and mutilated in public. The arrest of a Puritan Preacher, Alexander Leighton, for the crime of circulating a petition for the abolition of the Episcopacy in 1630 was a benchmark in this battle. He was quickly tried in the Star Chamber.

**Episcopacy n., pl. -cies . A system of church government in which bishops are the chief clerics**

The trial was decided before it began as many of the trials were in the Star Chamber. Leighton was found guilty. His sentence included flogging, mutilation and life imprisonment. This became the pattern for future prosecutions and religious harassment at the hands of Laud in his transformation of the Church of England during the next decade.

Charles had a void in his life with the assassination of Georges

Villiers who was his friend and confidant. He could not find another and turned to his wife, Queen Henrietta. He confided in her as he had with Villiers and she became a policy adviser to him on all major decisions and appointments. It was unusual f for a woman to yield such power unless she was acting as the monarch. The early 1630s were off to a rocky start and Charles had done nothing to dispel the outcry from his subjects on the Catholic issues.

England had cut its ties to the Roman Catholic Church after the Reformation and there was a great amount of hatred from the common people of England and Parliament. Fueling the unrest on this subject was Charles himself entertaining an emissary from the Pope in 1634 for the first time in close to one hundred and fifty years. The timing could not have been worse.

In June of 1637 three prominent Puritans were arrested for publishing pamphlets that attacked the Episcopacy and directly criticized Laud's church practices of bowing towards the East, establishing crucifixes and turning the communion tables into altars. The three were found guilty and taken to the pillory. They were branded on their cheek, their ears were "cropped" and they were imprisoned for life. They immediately became martyrs to their cause and public demonstrations against Laud ensued. Laud paid no heed to the political and religious upheaval. Charles allowed it to proceed. In addition to the changes that Laud had made in the Churches he now ordered that the "Anglican Book of Common Prayer" be used in all Churches in England. The Puritans were again in the forefront of the protest.

Our Story: 1630 A Pivotal Year
January, February, March, April
Henshaws and Houghtons

The year or our Lord, 1630, had promised to be a great year for William. Katherine Houghton, through the issues of the Ambrose family had said that she was smitten with William and she was now almost sixteen years old. Eighteen was considered a good age and the people of the community accepted William as a man now. This was very much to his liking. He had a very good relationship with his father and mother. His siblings looked up to him and the family thrived with William home now. He had a developing relationship with Evan Houghton, his future father-in-law. The events with the Ambrose family were certainly unpleasant but these events were settled as far as the Houghtons and the Henshaws were concerned.

Peter Ambrose

Peter and James Ambrose had finally found some peace at their home. Ann was placed in an asylum and there was little hope of her ever getting out. Peter had mixed feelings. This was his mother and now he would be motherless. She was a strong female figure in his life and he knew no other. James was a stranger to his son due to his long absences. To his credit he tried to develop a relationship with Peter but it seemed that Peter always stayed an arm's length away from letting that occur. Peter had the issues that many abused children have. Peter had a need for forgiveness and love from the parent who had abused them. It was a dichotomy. Instead of one person they saw two people in this role----good and evil. Peter had trouble separating the reality of what Ann was from what he wished her to be. He was conflicted right now but was also angry that his life had been disrupted and that his mother had been taken from him. He did not know who to blame for this but old feelings were starting to stir from inside on that issue. James now became the keeper of Peter. The feelings that were bred into him by his mother were as a seed in the field that would sprout and grow. It was bearing the fruits of Ann's insanity. Its fruit was hatred and the irrational and illogical hate directed at the Henshaw family as a whole and William more specifically. These feelings were now cultivated by the interruption of James's secret life. This disruption further disrupted Peter's life with the insertion of his absentee father as the head of the household. They had germinated and began to grow like weeds in an untended field.

James Ambrose

James on the other hand felt a sense of relief but also a sense of embarrassment and entrapment. He felt a strangling loss of personal freedom that he had reveled in when he would desert the reality of the house in favor of his fantasy life. The failure to connect with Peter was not making the situation any more bearable for him and he could only wish to flee his obligation. James missed his lover and his life that he had made away from the Ambrose house. He simply wished to return to a life where he was accepted for who he was with no judgment and no responsibility. He had not wanted children but when Ann set her mind to this after the Henshaws were wed he knew it would happen whether he wanted it or not. There was even a rumor that Peter was a Bastard child conceived out of the sanctimony of the marriage by Ann. James found some appeasement in his actions from this gossip. Shortly thereafter Peter was born and named for Ann's grandfather. Under Ann's fantasy world she had achieved a rightful heir to the family and this was necessary to move on in her rise. He felt resentment and a hate for Ann. He rationalized his feelings for Peter but deep down he just wanted to flee and never come back. James was angry because the Henshaw family had brought this to a head. He failed to see that in actuality it was Ann and her obsession that had caused his situation. James needed somebody to blame. It was not natural to blame Peter so he blamed Sir Thomas and William. The seed that had been planted in Peter had also taken root in James and it bore the same fruit.

Today it is known that abuse in families will follow generations unless something is done to stop the cycle. In 1600 England with all of the cruelties of the time period from government and religious battles this type of abuse went largely unnoticed. These events would have followed that path except for Ann's plotting bringing it to the public eye and once there it was fodder for the community gossip. It would no longer be ignored in the case of the Ambrose family. James, like Ann before him, spoke unkindly of the Henshaws and continued imprinting this dislike on Peter as they grew. It was understood by Peter that whatever his feelings he needed to keep them to himself. The internalization of the emotions associated with the issues surrounding them would continue to develop and change over time, but for now Peter did what he had to do to appear as normal as possible in the public eye. Secretly, he hoped that someday the people involved in ruining his life, although a flawed one, would have their lives disrupted and turned upside down like he believed his had been.

May, June, July
Ann Ambrose

Ann had been incarcerated in the Asylum for close to three months at this point. She had been an unruly patient there and demanded attention. She continued to dispense orders and manipulate patients and staff. This approach did not work here because they dealt with many people with power and ego issues. The commitment papers took this power away and neutered Ann in that same way. The general treatment was to keep her sedated until the behavior improved. Ann was an intelligent woman, but flawed. She realized that she had to give her doctors some signs of recovery to ever have a chance to leave the asylum and return to her life. She would try to behave for short periods of time, but inevitably her temper would betray her. During these times she would focus her rage on the Henshaws and William in particular. She had not given up the idea that Katherine Houghton would be a match for Peter even after all that had transpired. This possibility would soon and forever cease to exist.

William Henshaw and Katherine Houghton; Williams Graduation

William looked handsome in his dress uniform. Sir Thomas had presented him with the Cavalry horse he had acquired and trained for William's use in his upcoming Military assignment. The horse was a standout and had developed physically and mentally during his growth and training. William had worked with the horse now for several months and the rhythm that develops between a horse and its rider had come into being. This would continue to develop and fine tune itself. On the parade ground today the two would be impressive. It was rare to find a horse that was such a good fit but Sir Thomas knew his horses and had the advantage of being in military action himself. He knew the criteria of a horse for these purposes and had not rushed his choice but looked around for some time to select what he considered the perfect horse for William. To all who knew about such things the mission was an overwhelming success. He would go through his formal graduation proceedings on this day. As part of the graduation he would be given his commission by Evan Houghton as a part of the Earl of Manchester's Eastern Association army from East Anglia at the rank of Colonel. It was a culmination of many goals that William had worked towards over the last seven years. He had achieved all of the things he had set out to do when he was sent away to school those many years ago. With Evan this day was Katherine Houghton. She had come to William's graduation as a guest. Over the last month the connection between the two had grown into more. William was proud and happy that Katherine would be a part of this day and share it with him. He was befuddled. It was still confusing to him as to why this would make him happy. The near future would help him to understand.

Graduation was all it was supposed to be. There were speeches, ceremonies, bands, food, drink, military parades and congratulations spread all around by the guests, faculty, students and classmates. The day was festive and William felt important. Having Katherine at his side made him feel even more fulfilled. For now that was enough. The dancing and gaiety lasted until late at night. The families were boarding at a local Inn so they would not have to travel at night. This could be quite dangerous. William was still in his dormitory at that time but would pack his things and move out the next morning. Katherine and William took a break in the early evening for a walk through the commons along the Mersey River path. As they walked their conversation came easy and Katherine was very impressed by the school and the events of the day. She looked beautiful in her formal dress and many of Williams friends had taken notice and commented to William and Katherine complimenting her beauty. William was proud to be with her.

William Henshaw and Katherine Houghton; Declarations of the Future

The path was lined with trees and a cool breeze blew along the river walk. The Mersey River was an important part of the area and its mouth to the Irish Sea created the basin for the port of Liverpool. The Vikings had used the port and more recently the English government had made it an important port for the ferrying of troops and supplies into conflicts in Ireland. In the fifteenth and sixteenth centuries the port was mostly used for trade with Ireland, in the near future it would be an important port to the new world and the Americas. As they walked they were quiet. William was feeling all of the good feelings that came with his age and accomplishments. His education now finished he had reached the age of emancipation. The world lay at his feet. Some of his future had been decided, some had been decided for him. There were still many major life choices that he now faced. It is a magic time in life where you face complete independence for the first time. William was not without advantage. His family was wealthy so his future was tied to their legacy and as a part of that legacy he would have all of his basic needs taken care of for the time being. As the oldest son he again had advantages and would carry the family mantel forward with pride. His father had discussed this with him along with all of the rights and responsibilities that go along with it from a young age. William knew that he was at the point in his life of many changes and the decisions that he made would be pivotal in planning his future. Katherine, being the only child of Evan and Helen Houghton, was also a future heir to a large estate and wealth. In this time it would pass to her husband. The estate was quite large. The two were now simply pinpoints located within the great expanse of the universe on this walk in the same parallel path in their lives. The immenseness of the universe and their insignificance did not escape them even now in this important time of their lives. William moved closer to Katherine and her to him. Finally, William cleared his throat and asked Katherine, "Are you cold? Would you like my coat?"

"Why William, there is a chill in the air along the water but there is warmth that radiates from being together with you on this stroll. I believe that I will use that warmth instead!" said Katherine.

"There are so many things happening right now, it is dizzying! Is it not?" said William.

"I believe that we are following the plan that was laid out for us many years ago by our families and even fate if you believe is such things. It has conspired to bring us to this time. I want you to know right here and right now that I do not now nor have I ever objected to such plans or future with you William. I wanted you to know that none of the events with the Ambrose family have changed that in any way." declared Katherine.

William paused for a minute, he was caught off guard. They had always tiptoed around the subject of their relationship but now Katherine was discussing it face to face and first person. William was a little embarrassed but happy that Katherine had felt the need to declare her feelings and let him know that she was loyal and committed to the future with him. "Katherine, I do not know what to say to you at this time in our lives. I have little experience in this area. I know that for many years we have been matched and I can tell you that I have never objected to this circumstance either. I find that you have grown into an intelligent, independent and beautiful woman that any man would be proud to call his wife." William replied. He reached for her hand and took it in his as the walk continued.

"I have heard the talk between my mother and yours recently. I am coming of age for marriage and I believe that they are discussing the timing of this. Do you have feelings on this?" asked Katherine.

"Katherine, fate is fate. I submit myself to that. If our families are ready for this commitment I too am ready to accept it. Let me declare openly, I feel that this is not simply a family commitment. We have recently been witness to the dark side of that type of blind match with Peter's parents. I believe that many years ago you, Katherine, and I, William, had a connection. This connection has continued to develop, even in my absence when away at school. I could think of no other besides you in my future. It has turned into a beautiful and natural thing. Much more than our parents could have hoped for from this type of thing. I hope you feel the same." said William.

"I agree with you about feeling some connection at a young age. I can tell you that the first time I saw you in your uniform almost a year ago you stirred feelings inside me that no person has ever been able to arouse. I do not understand all of these feelings, but speaking to my friends, they are the type of feelings that come with age and maturity and love. These feelings are the same feelings you describe, so yes I do feel the same in answer to your inquiry." said Katherine.

Without knowing it they had walked out onto the pier that overlooked the river hand in hand. They had now reached its end and stopped. They looked into the dark water swirling below and moving on its endless journey into the Irish Sea. They did not speak. They could each feel their hearts beating and feel the rush of dizziness in their heads. William and Katherine stared up into the clear and starry sky and felt enveloped by the universe in some mysteriously spiritual way. They found themselves in an embrace and their first kiss followed. They held each other for a long time after the kiss. Silently they turned and reversed their path back to the commons knowing that another life decision had just been made without the need for words being spoken to seal it. Of course there would be formal asking and answering, planning, permissions and all of the other formalities involved in the life plan for this important moment. William saw his life coming together in a very desirable way. Katherine saw her destiny in William and knew that this was all she had ever wanted from her life. It was perfect.

Margerie Henshaw and Ellen Houghton; The Match!

At dinner that very evening when the gentlemen had retired to the study to talk politics, current events and other manly pursuits while sipping their Brandy. Margerie and Helen had found themselves alone. As was inevitable the subject of William and Katherine would arise and became the main focus of their interaction. At this point in time it was rather redundant. It was the socially acceptable topic of choice even though it had been decided at least a decade prior. What the mothers did not know was what had just transpired on the Mersey Pier between William and Katherine. Katherine had spoken her wishes under questioning by the Judge in the Ambrose affair, but even though truthful, it did not seal the formal declaration to the mothers because of the unpleasant circumstances surrounding it.

Helen started the conversation this day by saying, "Marjorie, William is now eighteen years of age. His school is behind him. He has become a man under anyone's criteria. Katherine has turned sixteen and is of marriageable age. I bring this up because it worries me that Ann Ambrose could confuse the situation and publicly state that Katherine was a match for Peter once again. If that woman is released this issue will again raise itself from the ashes and become a problem unless James would try to make the claim himself in Ann's absence. He would stand to gain from it also. I wish to put any speculation to rest. I feel that it might be time to consider a marriage. How do you and Sir Thomas feel about this?"

Marjorie smiled, "Helen, nothing would please us more. We know Katherine's opinion and I will have a talk with William. He has not discussed this with me for some time. It is most likely of a shyness that prevents it and not from a lack of desire for it. I will discuss it with him tonight. It might be beneficial for you to discuss this with Katherine and make sure that this would not make her uncomfortable." said Marjorie.

"I am so pleased as a mother and as a family to have this marriage. Let us hope that all goes well and that we can make this a joyous occasion and a marriage filled with happiness and children!" exclaimed Helen.

With this, the future was set. The conversations were a formality but this was a good match from any standpoint. The fact that the bride and groom would have most likely possessed the proper attraction to discover their wishes on their own made it something more.

Marjorie and William Henshaw

Graduation and the events surrounding it had been a revelation to William. He came back to Toxteth Park with a bright new outlook on life. One door was closing and it seemed as though several doors were opening. He was full of vigor and embraced them all. He had many things on his mind now and was trying to wrap his mind around the necessary planning involved. The move from academia to real life requires planning.

William had received his commission and now would need to train and drill with his brigade. This would initially be time consuming but would lessen as the transition was made. William was not joining the militia from the lowest of rank. He was a Colonel and as such would need to be acclimated into the duties and responsibilities of his rank. This too would be a challenge. In many cases he would have command of men much older than himself. He would be based locally in times of peace and would live in the barracks but be able to be home much of the time after the early phases of his training. During this time he would work alongside his father to learn and understand the management of the family holdings and business affairs. This was critical because the oldest male sibling would be counted on to take control of the estate when the time was deemed necessary. The time spent with his mother now addressed a separate issue. One which he had not had much thought on with all of the other obligations demanding his time. It was the issue of his future with Katherine.

Marjorie was entering this discussion with knowledge that William had shown some signs of his fondness for Katherine. She was nervous as most parents would be discussing an issue of life changing importance with their children. This would be her first child contemplating matrimony and it had seemed like just a few years ago he was an infant. Time was passing on her days with her children and just as it is a sad time it is also a happy time. William had grown into a man and he had accomplished all that they had hoped for to this point in his life. Marjorie sat William down at the table and served tea. This had been a ritual growing up in England but it was now different somehow to both of them. Most noticeably they found themselves alone. Traditional tea time included the whole family. The tone of the room was serious and it made the interaction somewhat awkward which was not a common thing between Marjorie and William. "William," Marjorie finally spoke, "There are some things we need to discuss. As you know you are now considered a man by our community and you have proven yourself at school and now you will prove yourself in your career. We are all very proud of you!" With this declaration she went and hugged William. The hug lingered long past the normal type of hug she gave. It was as if she knew the ramifications of this talk and that nothing would be the same afterwards. "I have been speaking recently to Helen Houghton about her daughter Katherine."

William interrupted, "Mother, you have been doing that for years now! I think I know where this is headed, and I want to…"

Marjorie interrupted, "I know you are aware of this my son, but please let me get through this as I want to complete our talk before I find it too difficult to let you go! I have long thought that you have had feelings for Katherine, would I be correct?"

"Yes Mother, you would be correct!" answered William with a grin on his face.

"This is no small thing that we are discussing here! It will affect you and your family for many years to come and into history. Do you understand this?" asked Marjorie.

"Yes Mother, I do" answered William his grin growing.

"Katherine's mother and I have discussed Katherine declaring to be your fiancé. I have spoken with your father and we have decided that we would have no objections to that proposal. We want to hear from you that this is what you want also. Would you like to be married to Katherine and take her for your bride?" asked Marjorie.

"Mother, Katherine and I had a period of time at graduation together. On the evening of the party we took a walk. I am sure that you all missed us for that period because we were aware of being under much scrutiny. We walked the river walk to the pier. This was not any normal walk in my way of thinking you see. It was like a novel. As we started our walk we were still just two children. Our parents had long ago had the proper discussions and the planning for our futures for a long time before this walk. By the time we were on the river walk the plot had progressed and wordlessly we were walking hand in hand. On the pier your question was answered without it being asked. We had our first kiss on the pier and we both understood at that time what it meant and that we were ready for this wonderful event in both of our lives. You could not have made a better match for me and I am certain that I want to take Katherine for my bride at the earliest possible time that you and Mrs. Houghton can arrange that to happen!" declared William.

Marjorie felt a mix of emotion. The result was a feeling of fulfillment and happiness knowing that her obligation to the family and William had been an overwhelming success. Indeed all of the community would celebrate this union and wonder at how perfect it was for the bride and groom to be joined. Marjorie would start planning the wedding immediately with Helen and Katherine.

Katherine and Helen Houghton

The relationship between Katherine and Helen was a good one between mother and daughter.   They spoke easily, exchanged ideas, spent time together in work, social events, charity and recreational activities and knew each other's heart. Helen knew how the conversation would end before it began. She had watched her daughter as she changed and grew and how her relationship with William had begun, grown and now was reaching an inevitable crescendo that started long ago. Like Marjorie she was happy and sad at the same time. She knew that her daughter would make a good wife and William a good husband. Recently she had noticed the heightened tensions and behaviors when William was present and knew what it all meant.

"Katherine, it is time for a discussion on your future. Many mothers throughout history have had this talk and many have felt the emotions that accompany this pivotal point in their daughter's lives. Do you know what I am talking about?" asked Helen.

"Mother, we have already had this talk without really having it over many years. I know what we are to discuss and I would like to ease your suffering in this matter by telling you that I love William and he loves me. I know that it is time that we marry. As we move forward I am sure that there will be time for many discussions that a girl needs to have before entering into her marriage and we will certainly have those discussions and time together. But for now, I am very happy and I hope that you and father are also! William and I had come to this conclusion on the occasion of his graduation when we took our walk to the pier. It is a good thing and the desired match. It is in fact much more because we actually have grown together and have fallen in love. Thank you Mother and thank Father also!" replied Katherine. Helen was struck by the differences that she saw every day in Katherine. Her assertiveness in this momentous decision in such a strong way reassured her that Katherine was indeed ready for such a big change in her life and she was happy for this.

With that the stage was set---there would be a marriage and a celebration of two young lives as they undertook the institution of marriage.

There was a meeting called of the two families. The formalities were performed and affirmation accomplished. William formally asked Evan for his daughters hand in marriage. With his blessing he made his formal proposal on one knee to Katherine to be his wife. This being accepted the women were now in full planning for a large community wedding in August so that William and Katherine would be married before he was off to his initial training with the Brigade. They published a formal announcement of the engagement that quickly made its rounds in the community to much acclaim and congratulations except in one particular household.

The Ambrose House
The situation at the Ambrose house was not improving. Both

Peter and James had gone into isolation from outside contact and contact between themselves.   Peter felt secure in this environment but it gave him long periods of reminiscing and speculation of the events that had led to the total disruption of his life and family. He felt bitter and depressed. He was allowed to visit his mother on occasion but this had very negative effects. He could not bear to see his mother in the asylum. The conditions were deplorable and the other residents were of varying degrees of insanity. There were severe cases that upset and unnerved him. He wondered how his mother could exist under these conditions. He noticed Ann moving farther away from reality but at times seemed very astute and normal. Peter was not aware that the disassociation continued during these periods and these were the most damaging to him. Ann never stopped blaming the Henshaws or encouraging Peter to pursue Katherine Houghton. In her mind she was living in a time before her illness was exposed to all. Peter at first resisted but over time accepted these ramblings more and more. He knew that Katherine and William would be together. He had known it all along. It did not stop him from blaming all of the Henshaws, Houghtons and the community as a whole for his mother's condition. He blamed them for his and his father's conditions also. These feelings were tucked away inside and Peter did not acknowledge them publicly.

James was a different story. The longer he was in isolation the angrier he became. He outwardly blamed everyone for his problems but he had now targeted Sir Thomas Henshaw as the main villain for not controlling his family as the head of the household and now he had mirrored the diatribe so long preached by Ann. His drinking continued and anger and rage dominated at these times. He did not target Peter for his anger because he knew the Judge was monitoring him. He simply had no outlet other than a bottle of cheap rum that he could easily get on the docks of Liverpool or his pints in the pub. Judge Wickford and Sheriff Stratford kept an open eye on the situation with the Ambrose family and were aware that Ann's condition had worsened and there was little hope of recovery. Their follow up in Liverpool was a concern as they were very aware of James drinking habits and occasionally he would rendezvous with his old acquaintance. The Judge gave him some leeway because he knew James was involved in an internal struggle and felt it might help diffuse the situation in the short term with a long-term solution coming in time. James found these times of rebellion against the Judge's orders to be the happiest of his times in the present.

It was during one of these times that James saw notice of the engagement of William and Katherine. He was struck numb. Although this was long an accepted conclusion by the community James saw it as a final blow to his family and Peter. He had been drinking and carousing on this day and the anger rose through his being and pushed him to a breaking point. James returned home and called Peter to him. He told him of the upcoming marriage. He did not stop with the news. James worked himself into frenzy in his drunken state telling Peter that this was the final step of the destruction of the Ambrose family. He demanded that Peter go with him to tell Ann what was happening. They left immediately for the trip to the Asylum.

Ann was brought to the visiting area by a white coated attendant. She was surprised to see James and Peter together. They had only visited individually since she was brought here. James was irritated and without easing into the situation stated abruptly, "Ann, we are here to inform you that the marriage of William Henshaw and Katherine Houghton has been announced. It will take place next month!"

Ann sat silent for a moment. She knew the repercussions of what she had heard but it did not seem to register at once. The color left her face and she began to tremble. "James, this cannot happen, it is not fair to Peter! We must stop this from happening.

It is the end……..the end!!!" Ann began speaking softly but by the end she was shouting. She rose from her seat and rushed James striking at him with both hands rolled into fists. James stepped aside and tried to deflect the attack but Ann was on him driving her hands into his face with force. The attendant called for help but the barrage of fists continued. James was bleeding and trying to get out from under Ann who was on top of him. Peter was uncontrollably upset. James extracted himself from Ann and tried to reach the door. Ann lunged at him and James stepped aside. Ann careened into the door sill at full speed. There was a sickening thud and Ann dropped to the floor. Blood began to pool around her head where she lay. Her whole body convulsed and then went still. She was still breathing but her stare was blank and unyielding. Her pupils were fixed and dilated. A doctor was summoned and Ann was rushed off to an area that treated patient injuries. Her outcome was very much in question at this point. Hospital staff rushed to Peter and James. James was bleeding from his lip and nose and swelling was appearing on his face. There would be an investigation of the happenings and James in his state wanted no parts of an investigation. After all, the last investigation had torn him and his family apart. James ran from the room and mounted the carriage and fled the Asylum leaving Peter alone with no transportation home. Peter wanted to stay with his mother anyway. This was what would happen right now. All other options had been removed with James fleeing the scene. After several hours Ann had not awakened. The doctors said that she could be in a coma from her injuries but could not be certain. Medical knowledge of the brain was in its infancy during this period and treatments could be rather barbaric. Peter had been there two days when the doctors discussed the treatment that they would pursue. For the most part they would drill holes through the skull and perform a procedure called "Bloodletting". They simply drained a quantity of blood from the stricken person in the belief that this would remove the evil spirits inhabiting the body. In Ann's case the removal of blood from her skull had a basis in modern medicine. It relieved the pressure on her brain from the bleed. Ann finally stirred from unconsciousness. For a few minutes she seemed normal and Peter had hope that the blow had shaken her from her depths of insanity and returned her to her normal self. He hoped that not the evil self but the good mother that Peter so needed was what would appear. This was not to be. After a short pleasant conversation Ann was again staring at things and becoming less and less responsive. She was not unconscious. She simply was not there. Spoken words, acts of comfort, physical stimulation and mental response had simply left her being. She was now and would be until her death in a catatonic state which could not be reversed. Peter returned home.

James was on the run. He rushed back to the house and gathered his belongings. He mounted the carriage and rushed to Liverpool. The pub was his first stop. He drank a large amount of courage and developed a plan. Ann's last words to him echoed in his mind "We must stop this! It is the end .. the end!" He stripped anything of value from the house and loaded it into the carriage. He would sell these on the docks to gain traveling funds if necessary. First he sent an acquaintance to the asylum to interrogate the staff and discover what he was facing. Although there was an investigation it was incomplete. James knew the Sheriff and the Judge would be looking for him. He planned not to be found. He found a place to sleep with one of his pub friends. He spent time with his woman and his anger built. The days passed.

The Henshaw House

This was an era of good times at Toxteth Park. Just as in the bible there is a time to plant and a time to sew. The realization of Sir Thomas and Marjorie of their first born son brought many good memories and many hopes for the future. He had grown, finished school, found a vocation and now was marrying the girl of their choice and of his dreams it would seem. His life and their plans could not have gone better. The plans were in full swing by mid-July to have the wedding by August 15th. This was the date set. The wedding would be at the single church in Liverpool which lay in the shadow of the Liverpool Castle. The church was large and picturesque. It had been built around the same time as the Castle placing it around 1232 and 1235.

Liverpool (Anglican) Cathedral

It was a protestant church and the Henshaw family followed that faith at the time. Liverpool and the surrounding areas were abuzz with news of the wedding and the plans for the festivities. A wedding was one of the highest social events of the year and brought out all of the finery, society and the festive mood that would be expected and desired for a marriage of this magnitude. Exotic foods, fine clothing, colorful decorations, professional musicians, expert horsemen, various entertainers and extra staff were arranged and rehearsed according to the plans laid out by

Katherine, her mother and her soon to be mother-in-law. It was a grand event to say the least and no expense was spared. For the Henshaws the events highlighted the couple who would carry the family crest forward and into the future. For the Houghtons it was the marriage of their only child to one of the finest men in the area. It made them all very proud.

The Docks of Liverpool

James was very aware that the Sheriff and the Judge were on his trail. Indeed he had evaded them several times but the ring was closing in on him. He had developed an identity to use giving up his name and booked onto a merchant ship to escape the area. One thing he could not escape was the constant talk of the upcoming wedding which to him represented his failures as a husband, father and man. He had been in several brawls in the pubs as of late and this is what had almost been his undoing. His last scrape had allowed him to escape the local gendarme by mere seconds having to leave through a window to escape detection and arrest. James had developed a plan to avenge his manhood and it was clear to him that he had to implement it very soon or he would not be able to accomplish its goals before he was found and jailed. He stopped his drinking early this evening and went on board the ship for rest knowing that he would need to rise before dawn to get in position to fulfill his plan. As he found his bunk he fell asleep immediately; partially from exhaustion and partially from the effects of his drinking. James had not slept well and battled the demons in his sleep each night. He awoke around three a.m. and mounted his horse for the ride east. His ship was scheduled to leave dock around noon that day giving him plenty of time to finish his work and make sail. It was an advantage of living near a port that you could get out of town quickly and discreetly. Many sailors of this time were wanted criminals and they simply changed their names and hired onto ships bound for various points in the world rather than risk capture or incarceration for their crimes. This is the thought that was the keystone of his plan. James had excellent counsel on this from his nights in the Pubs while Ann was still residing at the Ambrose house. He contemplated with relish taking to the sea and abandoning Ann. He did not think that he would ever actually use this knowledge from fear of what Ann would do if he was found out but kept it stored away just the same. As the alcohol addled his mind and his perceived vengeance dominated his thoughts this knowledge rose to the surface and the plan almost made itself.

Henshaw Hall

Sir Thomas was a man of routine. Most likely he had developed this in his military days and on the long campaigns in which he earned his Arms. As a part of this routine Sir Thomas enjoyed getting up early and taking a ride on his horse through the property before tea was served. It was enjoyable, good exercise and a skill that needed to be practiced in case it was needed in the future. Sir Thomas was an excellent horseman and he passed this along to his children. William had been a stand out in his class at school in his riding abilities as a direct result of his tutelage. Sir Thomas was looking forward to the ride today. He had many things on his mind and as he achieved the rhythm of the ride he could clear his head and think precisely and deeply on the pressing issues of these days. He had ridden this course for so long it was a second nature to ride on his property with a horse that he had trained and ridden for many years now. He was a bit distracted as he went through the path and into the woods that morning. He was now in his forties but was showing no signs of age except for some old battle scars that eventually required that he retire from his military career. His course on his morning rides never varied and he struck out down the path to the river bank. The trees beyond were large and enveloping. Even in the daytime this part of the forest was dark and cool. It was one of the more pleasant sections of his ride. The horse and rider made the crossing slowly. Sir Thomas liked to watch the water flow down the river and today it mixed with his thoughts on William's future. Eventually he made land on the other side of the ford and made his way onto the path in the woods. This part of the ride would take somewhere around fifteen to twenty minutes to complete. Sir Thomas would exit the woods and cross a small clearing and then enter another forest on the other side. This is the place that he liked to run the horse and feel the speed and power underneath him. It also provided some excitement and stamina and an interlude from the deep thoughts he fostered on the ride. Sir Thomas felt content in his life. With William's marriage he felt that there was a natural force at work guiding him through a predetermined path in his own life as it inevitably wound down. He had two more sons to marry off and a daughter. When his parental duties were completed and he had trained his sons to run the estate and family businesses it was his intention to travel with Marjorie. He wished to share the sights of the world with her. There were many places on his list and he did not believe that he would possibly be able to see them all. Having the list made him feel that he was making progress on his goals though. Sir Thomas was coming to the clearing and looking forward to giving the horse his head to feel the mental and physical rush inherent in this exercise. As soon as they cleared the trees the horse knew his role as it had been repeated daily for many years. Sir Thomas tightened his grip and leaned over the horse's neck and kicked his flanks. The horse responded just as he knew he would and they were off on a gallop across the field. The wind was in the horse's mane and Sir Thomas could feel the muscles of the horse moving in unison under him and gave him the sense that he had become a part of the horse for this charge across the field. Sometimes he imagined he was in a horse race and others in a battle charge. His memories rushed at him during these times and they were always of pleasant and memorable times. Sir Thomas always felt that this sprint was never long enough but he started to reign in the horse as the tree line approached. The horse and rider were breathing hard but happy. Sir Thomas pulled up and sat up straight in the saddle as they entered the trees. Suddenly, Sir Thomas felt an impact. He knew that he had cleared the tree limb with his head and could not resolve what had hit him. He felt something warm, moist and wet on his forehead and put his hand up to find that he was bleeding profusely. He stopped the horse and dismounted. The impact had penetrated his scalp and he could feel some small bone shards in the wound. He began to mount the horse to return to the closest home for help when there was a second impact. Sir Thomas felt nothing and fell to the ground. He felt dizzy and sick. He had landed on his back and was staring into the sky. He was confused and could not understand what he had collided with to cause this amount of damage. He was unable to move and had no feeling in his extremities. He tried to get up finding it impossible and felt like he had to lie down as a wave of nausea swept through his body. There was a rustling to his side but he could not locate it. He knew someone was there. He called out but received no answer. He heard just a rustling in the leaves and finally footsteps coming his way. Someone had been in the tree above Sir Thomas as he had entered the forest. Sir Thomas thought that someone must have been nearby and saw his injury and had come to help. He turned his head a short way and glanced sideways. Standing there was James Ambrose. "James, I have had an accident. As I entered the woods I struck my head on something. I have injuries that will need attention. I was hit with a second impact and I don't know what it was. Did you see what it was?" asked Sir Thomas.

"Yes, I did!" replied James. "It was the backside of this ax that I am holding here in my hand."

"I don't understand James, if you were holding it how is it possible that the ax hit me?" asked Sir Thomas.

"Well, it is not so much as to how it is possible as to who hit you with it! I hit you with it----twice now you blithering old idiot!" stated James proudly.

"Why would you do that James?" asked Sir Thomas

"You have taken my life away from me. My wife is gone, my son is a failure and someone has to pay for that! It was you in that study with the Sheriff and Judge when my wife was taken from me. It is you that planned to rob Peter of his future by taking Katherine from him for William. It is you that have ruined my family and my life!" screamed James

"James, your wife is sick and Peter never would have married Katherine. The two of them were never compatible and Katherine had no interest in him other than friendship. You can ask him!" replied Sir Thomas.

"Peter had no chance because you never let him have a fair chance. You had all the advantages and your family saw to it to deprive Peter of his chances. Now, your family will feel a loss!" yelled James as he worked himself into frenzy. He brought a large boulder over his head and smashed in into Sir Thomas's head wound. Sir Thomas shook from the impact. He convulsed for several minutes. James was not sure that the desired result had been achieved. James picked up the boulder a second time and raised it over his head. Before he came down with it Sir Thomas stopped struggling and lay still. He took his last breath at his favorite spot at the end of his favorite run.

James staged the area to appear that Sir Thomas had fallen onto the boulder and took care to make sure that the impact area of the boulder and Sir Thomas's skull were in line. He cleaned up the footprints and sent Sir Thomas's horse off up the trail. He walked almost a mile to the dark woods where he had tied his horse. He was in no hurry because he knew it would be hours before the body was discovered. He rode at a normal gait back to Liverpool under disguise in case he was seen. James felt like he had satisfied his sense of justice in some way. He did not feel like he had evened the score with the Henshaws though. For now, he had to get aboard ship and make sail. James Ambrose was now James Ainsworth and he would live the rest of his life under this name. He had returned his horse to the livery stable to confuse the Sheriff and his deputies and boarded the ship just as they were pushing off from the pier. James would start a new life while leaving blood and murder behind him like so many others who he would keep company with over the years as a merchant sailor. Peter would be the sole Ambrose heir at the age of seventeen years.

Toxteth Park

It was mid-afternoon at Toxteth Park. The family was going about their business but Marjorie was the first to start feeling concerned. Sir Thomas normally would have returned from his ride before noon. He had occasionally taken longer rides but it was not a usual behavior. She thought that maybe he had some other business to attend to during the ride that she had forgotten or that he had crossed paths with someone and was delayed in talk as was his nature. It could just be that he had a lot on his mind to ponder due to all of the things going on in their lives currently. She would wait a while longer. There was no need to get upset and then feel silly later. William came into the kitchen for tea. He was quiet and studied his mother for a minute.

"Mother, is there something wrong, you do not act like yourself?" asked William.

"I do not want to raise concern just yet William. Your father has not returned from his ride. Do you know if he had any other business today that would keep him?" she asked.

"I do not know of any business mother. If you like I will go look for him on his regular trail." offered William.

"Not just yet. Let's give it a little while first. I would not want to be an alarmist! It would upset him so to know I sent you if nothing is wrong!" stated Marjorie.

Marjorie served the tea. William and his siblings joined Marjorie. Sir Thomas did not return. It was another unusual occurrence for him to miss the family tea!

After tea William went to his mother and whispered in her ear, "I am going for a ride, I will be back later. "He saddled and mounted his horse and set out for the path that his father had taught him to ride so many years ago. His father loved the path and so did William. He understood that each of his siblings probably had their own memories of sharing the path with Sir Thomas and while learning to ride.

William had ridden for a while and was in the same frame of mind that Sir Thomas had been in on his ride. He was moving consistently but thoughts were running through his mind about Katherine and his future and how all of the pieces would fit together. He wondered how she would fit into the life at Henshaw Hall. He could see the first leg of the forest up ahead and knew of the field beyond. He looked forward to stretching his horse out across the open field. William's father had named the horse when he acquired him. Knowing of William's upcoming commission he simply named him "Soldier". William felt that this was a fitting name and considered that he would have probably named him the same if it would have been his responsibility to name him. Soldier needed no encouragement to stretch out and run when they entered the clearing. Like Sir Thomas, William exercised the horse and rode this path many times alone and with his father. He felt very free in the race across the clearing and a feeling of exhilaration entered him. This was short lived as he reigned in and entered the forest on the other side. He knew immediately that something was amiss. He stopped Soldier and searched the area. A man of arms develops a sixth sense for danger through their training and there was something wrong with the scene. Just over the small rise coming into the forest he found it. At first in the darkness he could only see a body in the path. There was a noise to his left. He was shaken and jumpy and turned to face the noise only to find Sir Thomas's horse standing alone and waiting. William's mind raced and he did not want to believe what he knew to be the reality of what he would see. He quickly dismounted and ran to the body. The clothing was familiar and as he came upon him William knew that his father was dead. He saw the large bloody boulder and the severe damage to Sir Thomas's head. He was shaken but gathered his wits quickly not knowing if there was danger around him. It appeared that Sir Thomas had fallen and struck his head on the stone. William was having issues with believing that the amount of damage to his father's skull could have come from that type of impact. It was an ugly scene and one William wished he would have never had to confront. William covered the body of his father with his coat and rode back to Henshaw Hall for help.

Upon arrival he met his brothers in the barn where their chores would have them at this time. They knew something was wrong and William detailed what he had found to them. He sent Henry to the constables office and John to collect the Undertaker and the family doctor. He entered the house and went to the kitchen where he found his mother and his sister Ellen.

"Mother, Ellen, please sit with me!" commanded William.

"William! Did you find him?" asked his Mother

"Yes, Mother, I found him. He has had a terrible accident. I found him in the forest just past the opening where we run our horses. It appears he had a fall and struck his head." answered William.

"Where is he? Is he all right?" asked his Mother.

"I am sorry mother, his injuries were severe and he has passed!" replied William.

Marjorie collapsed and Ellen broke down into tears. William knew that he was now the head of the household and had to remain strong for his family. He went to the women and put his arms around them and they buried their faces into his chest and cried for a long time.

A short time later Henry arrived with the constable who had sent for Sheriff Stratford. The constable, a man by the name of John Westbury, went to the study with William and Henry.

"Mr. Henshaw, I am sorry for the circumstances under which we meet. Can you tell me what you know at this point?" asked John Westbury

"Sir, my father was out for his ride, as is his normal practice, and did not return at his normal time. We gave it a little more time so as not to create panic but he still did not return. After tea I rode out along his normal path. I came upon his horse and body just past the clearing as it enters the forest. He was lying face up on the ground and there was a large boulder with his blood on it lying beside him. I deduced that his horse stumbled as he was reigned in from his run in the clearing and Father fell from the horse striking the boulder." replied William.

"Yes, that would seem to be a reasonable theory. I am aware that Sheriff Stratford is in the area today to visit the Ambrose house. I have sent for him and would prefer his presence before going to the body if that is acceptable with you?" asked John.

"It would be prudent as I have sent for the Undertaker and our Dr. Anderson who should arrive momentarily, Ah, I believe I hear horses now!" replied William.

John Henshaw rode down the path at a gallop with the undertaker lorry behind him. Dr. Anderson was riding in the lorry with his horse tied behind. As they made their way up the path another single rider was coming onto the path from the road. It was Sheriff Stratford at a gallop completing the group.

He caught up to the lorry and they arrived in front of the barn. They dismounted and the stable boy took control of their horses. They entered the house and went to the study. Sheriff Stratford made introductions of all in attendance and asked to be informed of the details of what had happened. William updated the newcomers in the manner that he had updated Constable

Westbury and with that accomplished they made their plans to go to the body.

William said, "Sheriff, I have told you what appears to be at the scene of my father's death. What I cannot tell you is why I have a feeling that the evidence of his death seems out of place and in my heart I feel that there is simply more to it. My father was an excellent rider and knew the trail well. The horse is strong and sure footed and familiar with the path. It makes no sense to me how this could happen. My feeling is that something is amiss!

Sheriff Stratford took a minute to soak in the information that William had given him. He then had William send a courier to Judge Wickford to request his presence at the scene. The men mounted their horses and set out for the forest leaving one person behind who knew the way to bring the Judge upon his arrival.

As they came upon the forest across the clearing Sheriff Stratford asked the men to stop before entering the forest and dismount and tie their horses. The Sheriff and William entered the woods with the others waiting behind. Sheriff Stratford was good at his job but he was not good at politics which is what caused him trouble in dealing with Ann Ambrose.

"William, I want to walk onto the scene alone so I can get a better idea of what is there before anyone else comes forward. When you came here was there anyone with you or did you notice anyone in the area?" asked the Sheriff

"No, I was alone and other than my horse it should be the only tracks on the scene. Do you suspect something Sheriff?" asked William.

"I am not sure yet. Based on the feelings that you shared with me I would prefer to approach this in a cautious way rather than crash in on the scene haphazardly." stated the Sheriff. With that he slowly moved forward using his senses to absorb the scene around him. This took some time and William was anxious. The others in the field would call out to him wanting to come into the forest but William kept them at bay. After about twenty minutes two additional riders entered the clearing. It was the judge and the stable boy who had retrieved him.   Judge Wickford dismounted and approached William.   William related the details to the Judge along with his feelings and misgivings about the scene. The Judge started towards the woods and was met by Sheriff Stratford who spoke to the judge quietly and re-entered the woods with the Judge. They spent another twenty to thirty minutes on the scene before allowing the Undertaker and the others to enter to recover Sir Thomas's body. John and Henry broke into tears at the sight of their Father's broken and bloodied body. It was their first experience with death and this one was very close to home. It was strange to see the strongest man they had ever known reduced to a bloody heap of flesh. "William, the Sheriff and I would like to speak to you when you feel like it. Is that all right with you?" asked the Judge.

"Yes Sir, we can speak now if that is best for you!" replied William

"Let us recover the body and move it to the mortuary and we will sit down at your home to discuss our findings." said the Judge.

The mood was solemn and the men went into the forest and placed the body on a litter. They covered the body in sheets and packed the wounds to prevent further bleeding although it appeared that the body from its color and hue had hemorrhaged most of its contents. The litter was placed between two horses and they slowly made their way back to the lorry to transport the body to the mortuary for burial preparations. The Sheriff and Judge stayed behind to finish their investigation.

When they reached the house the doctor was on the porch. He had to sedate Marjorie and Ellen who were overcome with grief. He spoke with John, Henry and William and evaluated their states. The younger boys were shaken but strong and William had taken a strong leadership stand in the family at this point and was functioning at his new position in the family which neutered the effects of grief for him. The doctor said that he planned to stay the night barring some emergency to see to the family. The Undertaker had finished loading the body and the lorry moved slowly and morosely down the path to the Road heading for Liverpool. Everyone took a deep breath. John and Henry went into the house and began to deal with their own personal grief. The Sheriff and The Judge had now returned from their investigation and spotted William.

"William, may we retire to the study?" asked the Judge

"Yes Sir, this way please." replied William

William summoned the kitchen and asked for tea and some food to be served. He had forgotten that he had not eaten for some time and neither had the Sheriff or the Judge because of the time spent investigating the scene and recovering Sir Thomas's body in the forest. William closed the doors to the study and said "We may begin. I have taken the liberty to order us some tea and food from the kitchen!"

"We won't be evasive here William. The Sheriff is an excellent investigator. Your feelings of the scene are accurate. Several questions arose while we surveyed the scene. I will detail them here. If your father had fallen off his horse he most likely would have landed face down. While this would line up with the boulder, it is questionable that he would have died on his back unless he rolled over after the blow. If he would have fallen from the horse and struck the boulder the body should have carried beyond the boulder from the velocity of the fall, especially if the body rolled onto his back. We found that the boulder was not stationary at the point that we found it. It was not embedded into the dirt as a boulder would be if it had been there over a period of time. Dirt and debris would have filled in around its base and its base was clear of both. The boulder had been recently moved to the location. It was apparent that your father landed from his fall but there is no evidence of a print in the Earth from a fall in the dirt below where he was found. We know that in the area of your father's body there should be hoof prints and evidence of his struggle before dying in the dirt. For a perimeter of approximately thirty yards there were no hoof prints, footprints, or marks from him or his horse crawling or moving in any way. This simply could not have happened. We know that your father's horse at least would have left several hoof prints in the immediate area. Outside of this thirty-yard radius we found footprints of an individual that were fresh moving back through the woods. The Sheriff will go track those after we finish here but we surmise that it will yield no evidence. It is our conclusion that someone else was in the forest and obliterated all prints from this area. For what purpose we do not know. One thing is for sure. There was an attempt to hide the facts of what happened as your father entered the forest on this day! It is clear that someone attacked your father with the intent to kill him. The head wounds were not made solely by the boulder. We discovered a shape in the wound that suggested repeated blows by some sort of weapon. In my experience it was probably an axe. We will continue to investigate these circumstances and try to find some conclusions as to who was in the forest and why they acted as they did." declared the Judge. He did not tell William of the strange behaviors of James Ambrose nor did he tell him of the incident at the Asylum with Ann but he was sure that the gossip had born this knowledge to Henshaw Hall without need of him retelling it. Most important, he did not tell William that they had been pursuing James Ambrose for arrest since the incident in the Asylum. They did not tell of his returning to his drinking and erratic ways that the Judge had warned him against. Judge Wickford and Sheriff Stratford went directly to the Ambrose house when they left William.

The Ambrose House

Judge Wickford and Sheriff Stratford were not sure where the evidence pointed. They did know that James Ambrose had been seen running from the Asylum after Ann's injury and for the time being had deserted the Ambrose house and gone into hiding. They knew he was in Liverpool and that they had a close encounter with him at a Pub in the dock area. He had escaped and disappeared. In questioning some of the pub patrons they had learned that he was talking vehemently about his life and how unfair things had been for him. He was making threats against the Henshaw family and told these people that he would get his vengeance. This coupled with what they had just seen in the forest convinced them that it was likely that James Ambrose was at least a person to be considered as the culprit. They were cautious on their approach to the house as they did not know if James was around or what frame of mind they would find him in if he was. Peter came to the door and looked disheveled but healthy.

"Peter, the Sheriff and I would like to speak to your Father. Is he here?" asked the Judge.

Peter stood a minute and paused, "Sir, I have not seen my father for some days now and my mother is at the hospital. My Father left me at the hospital shortly after my mother was injured several days ago and I have not seen him since that time" he said.

"I am sorry Peter. I know things have been hard for you and your parents. But we must find your Father and talk to him!" said the Judge.

"I do not know where he is---I do not know if I will ever see him again. I am alone! He left the house. There are many things missing of value and I do not believe he plans to return here!" Peter choked out.

"We will not forget you Peter, I will send your guardian here to stay and help you with your financing, schooling and the management of your household. Charles and your staff can help you and I will speak to them." said the Judge.

"Mother had Father terminate Charles for speaking to you. I do not know where he is either I have nobody here that I can trust sir!" replied Peter.

Peter had been left many responsibilities with the disappearance of James. His mother's care had to be paid for and the maintenance and taxes for the Ambrose house had to be kept up. James had slowly drained the estate of its cash reserves and as it would come to be known over the next days he had been removing the valuables little by little over time so there was simply no value to the estate except the land, buildings, equipment and remaining livestock. Peter was only seventeen and much like William — the weight of the world had now fallen squarely on his shoulders. It was known that the Ambrose family was funded through inheritance from James's family and that would be in the form of a trust. It was difficult to know where the trust money was kept or who administered that money because James had kept this to himself and his personal affairs a secret.

The Judge told Peter that he would consult with Mr. Brisby and find Charles and send him back to the house. He was sure that Charles was still in the area and knew that he felt a loyalty to Peter and had said such during his talk with the Judge on the day Ann was incarcerated. Peter's needs would be cared for but the future of the Ambrose estate was unclear.

At this point James's trail had gone cold. Sheriff Stratford was sure that James had some role in the death of Sir Thomas but the proof was lacking to prosecute him even if he was found. It was likely, except from some stroke of luck, that James would never be found. He had heard the scuttlebutt on the docks that James had boarded a merchant ship on the fateful day and disappeared on the horizon out to sea to escape his crimes. Both the Sheriff and the Judge found it likely that this is exactly the plan James had followed. They knew James was unhappy in his role as a father and husband. His secret life had turned into his chosen life over time and there was no going back. The killing of Sir Thomas pointed to a very dark side that they had not anticipated. They found some of the same symptoms in James that had shown in

Ann. The concern was that if both parents had severe mental illness what effect this would have on Peter. He was raised in this insanity. It would have to be watched closely as mental illness was known to run through families and their offspring. Little was known of its causes or cures.

Henshaw Hall

A crowd had gathered as the news had spread across the community. The mortuary had come and was meeting with the family to make arrangements for Sir Thomas's funeral. There was a family plot and Sir Thomas would join his ancestors there as was the practice for centuries now. The rumors had swirled. The revelation of the injuries to Ann Ambrose and the flight of James Ambrose had struck close to home. This was a dagger to the heart of the community and many were concerned about what would happen with Peter at his age. It was decided that the services for Sir Thomas would be held at Henshaw Hall and it was left to the servants to plan the food, drink and coordinate with the church, mortuary and others to take the burden of it from Marjorie and the family. The family met and decided what things needed to be included in the services and who would deliver the eulogy. It was decided that Evan Houghton would be that person. He was a longtime friend of the family and a person who was as close to Sir Thomas as anyone in the community. These facts made him the logical choice. It was also decided that the wedding of Katherine and William would be moved back until the end of September to allow for a period of mourning. William applied for and was granted a delay in reporting to his unit to allow for him to settle the affairs of his father and conduct the business of the estate. Through all of this Katherine was by his side and they grew very close emotionally and spiritually which is the by-product of having intense shared life experiences whether they are happy or sad. The bond was growing. Sir Thomas would have been elated to see the progression of these two as a couple. Most of all he wanted to see his children happy and prosperous. Examining the slate on which his life was written, Sir Thomas left this world a better place for his being in it and with that mission accomplished William would now be the man of the house. Too soon it would be his house.

Sir Thomas was buried on a sunny day next to his father's grave. This was the way of the family and the tradition continued. There were now four generations of relatives in the family plot and room for future generations. The family made the long walk back to the house and reaching there were joined by many of the areas citizens. It was the largest funeral in the community's memory. Time marches on and waits for no one! Tomorrow would dawn another day and life would continue to move on like the water in the Mersey there was no pause.

August, September, October
The Ambrose House

Peter faced the same obstacles as William. He was suddenly the man of the house. In fact, he was the only person now living at the house. His father had disappeared and was a suspect in the death of Sir Thomas Henshaw. Peter had seen his father's behavior and could read between the lines. He was very unhappy at the circumstances forced on him when Ann was incarcerated. Peter was sure that he would never see his father again and if he did it would be a very awkward and short-term situation. Peter had gone from having a normal life, at least as normal as it could be living in Ann's care, to having no parents at all and in jeopardy of losing all that his family owned. Henry Brisby had stepped in as Peter's steward and immediately took inventory of the Ambrose assets. The estate on paper looked to be solvent. Before James had disappeared the liquid assets were either misplaced or simply taken to support James' new life. There were physical and immovable assets including the

Ambrose house, the flat in Liverpool where James spent much of his time, furnishings, heirlooms, livestock, carriages and various equipment and of course the family trust that were left behind. The trust would be the trickiest piece of work as it was in James's name and it was unknown where the assets and funds were kept or even who administered the trust. Brisby would need to contact James's parents or in their absence the keeper of the trust. This would require some time and detective work. Brisby would need to go through the papers at the Ambrose house and discuss the situation with Peter to gather the family information at his disposal. For now Peter would be the best source of information with the exception of Charles who had been with the family for many years before Peter was born. It was common knowledge that servants accumulated hidden family secrets and events that most people, not even other family members, would know. Charles was like an encyclopedia of information from James's and Ann's families.

Charles had not gone far. In fact he had taken on a job with the Houghton family. Under the circumstances, the Houghton's were more than willing to release Charles to help with Peter Ambrose. He had been with the family for so long and had demonstrated a compassion for Peter's situation when questioned about Ann's behavior that it was clearly in the best interest of Peter and the best fit to the situation the estate faced. He risked his job and livelihood for Peter's well-being and this is exactly what was needed now.

Judge Wickford, Henry Brisby and Sheriff Stratford met with Charles. The meeting would be to set up the structure for the care of Peter Ambrose until he came of legal age and to attempt to find the assets of the Ambrose estate. Charles was well educated and a quiet man. It was necessary in his job to hear many private things and keep them in confidence. This approach would tear at him during the conversation that was about to take place. Judge Wickford started things off and said "Charles, we are glad you could join us today to discuss the well-being of young Peter Ambrose. We believe that you have a fondness for the boy as you risked quite a bit in his defense during the ugly affair with his mother. Let me update you. Ann Ambrose is very ill. It is believed that she was attacked by James Ambrose at the institution where she resides. She is comatose and unlikely to awaken from that state. James Ambrose is a suspect in the murder of Sir Thomas Henshaw. We know that most people think it was an accidental death and we have not released this information to the public and we ask that you keep it in strict confidence yourself as I know you will. James has disappeared after the death of Sir Thomas and cannot be found. I know that there is speculation in the community as to his involvement. There are substantial funds missing from the Ambrose assets and we are trying to find some of these missing assets or some of the liquid assets. We need to have an accounting of them and know of their whereabouts so we can decide how to progress with the care of Peter. Do you understand us so far?"

"Yes Sir, I do" replied Charles.

Brisby interjected, "We feel that you are the person closest to Peter and with the loss of both parents he will need someone familiar to him and who knows the situation. We would like for you to be the caretaker to Peter. Would this be a situation that you could become involved with in that capacity?"

"Yes Sir, Mr. Peter will need my help and I am willing to give it!" replied Charles.

"Charles!" said Brisby, "We need some information on the Ambrose family and we think maybe you have overheard things while you were with them. Would you be able to shed some light on these questions?"

"Sir, I am sure that you understand that a gentleman of my station hears many things in the course of affairs. It is in conflict with my position to divulge this information!" answered Charles.

The judge spoke up and said, "Would you agree that your

loyalty lies with the Ambrose family?"

"Yes Sir" replied Charles

"So it would then be the current situation that the Ambrose family is in the hands of Peter Ambrose. It is also true that any information that you would have about that would benefit the Ambrose household and would be your duty to provide as needed. Is this your understanding Charles?" asked Brisby

"Yes Sir" replied Charles

"Then, we would not ask you anything that would breach your trust with the Ambrose family, only those issues that we have just framed. Could you tell us about James's and Ann's families?" asked Brisby

"Miss Ann's family was an odd sort. They did not start out that way. They wanted to be a part of the society affairs and Ann's mother pushed this on the family. She made it her job to try to marry Ann to a family that made them more important and raised them in the community. Her mother was much like Miss Ann. She never let Miss Ann forget that the goal in her life was to help her family by finding and marrying into the proper family and situation. This obsession is what I believe we saw drive Miss Ann to insanity. They did not get in James Ambrose what they had bargained for in the marriage.

The Ambrose family was a different circumstance all together. They started out as commoners. James's father, Robert Ambrose, was somewhat of a highwayman. He was a gambler, a gypsy of sorts, a thief when necessary and in the end he found one large enterprise that made him rich. He had enamored himself to a rich widow with no heirs. Although he had no feelings for her he did have feelings for her riches. He created a flurry of gossip but finally had a wedding to her in her later years. She was never a woman of good health and the end was in sight when Robert turned his attention to her. He was introduced to society as a part of his matrimonial duties and inherited all that she owned upon her death. Robert had other women secretly during his marriage while he was waiting for his inheritance and Marian, James's mother, was one of those women. Robert had to be smart though. Marian was a woman from a family in the social circles. The family had some standing but was in decline. Thus it was easy, after a proper time of mourning, to ask for and receive Marian's hand in marriage. From this entanglement came James as an offspring. Again, James behavior mirrored the behavior that we have most currently seen from him including any possible criminal behavior that he might be suspected of by you gentlemen." chronicled Charles. "James, himself was a handful and a headstrong child. He was a discipline problem in school and was asked to leave several establishments. He was thence home schooled, at least to the level that they could achieve his participation in this endeavor. He was not interested in education or work for that matter. On his eighteenth birthday Robert funded a trust, arranged a marriage to Ann and cast him off to this current estate, which was a part of the inheritance from Robert's first wife. The trust, although a way to rid their situation of James, was substantial and the property was deeded outright to James. At this point most ties to both families ended and the poor qualities of both families took center stage in the family of Ann and James. I think we all know the rest of this story. Ann's mother and father have both passed on. James mother has passed but his father still lives in ill health in London if the situation has not changed since my removal from the Ambrose's service!" he continued.

Brisby asked "Charles, we know of the physical assets of the Ambrose estate. What do you know of the trust and the administration of the funds and any other liquid assets that might be used for young Peter?"

"Sir, Mr. Robert Ambrose in London would have that information. I can tell you how to contact him. There was money at the house in a safe in the wall. I would not know if Mr. James would have taken that before his disappearance but I highly suspect that he would have." replied Charles.

"We have one last thing Charles! Will you be available to move immediately to the Ambrose house?" asked Judge Wickford.

"At the leave of the Houghton family, yes sir!" replied Charles. Charles duties would be much broader than they were when he was last at the Ambrose house. He would now be a sort of house manager and father figure there with some decision making authority over Peter. Major decisions would be made by Henry Brisby with the consult of Judge Wickford. It was learned through contact with Robert Ambrose that the trust was dried out for the most part with the purchase of the Ambrose house: the furnishings and livestock. He had placed a manager over the holdings in the trust for some time to get it on even footing and profitable so James would never need return to their care. This manager strangely disappeared one day. The secret rooms in Liverpool, the flamboyant lifestyle lived there and operating the estate for a number of years had drained the remaining funds and James was not earning any salary. His claims of his employment were for the most part false. The balance had been withdrawn recently closing the trust account. This created problems for Peter Ambrose. There were no operating funds available to run the Ambrose house or to pay the taxes. The group would meet and discuss the situation with the final decision decided by Henry Brisby. The property and furnishings had great value. The livestock was also top of the line and worth prime money in the market. It was becoming apparent that the assets would have to be sold to support Peter Ambrose. To this end a confidential buyer was sought for the property.

The search followed the normal inquiries. Investors, adjacent property owners, interested parties and then outsiders were sought. It was rare for such a property to come up for sale and many outsiders looking to join the community and society events would be pursuing Brisby to take this giant step if it were known.

The King would most certainly be heard from to collect his pound of flesh if the sale were made public. It was important that the property be sold quickly and discreetly as it was the policy of the King to confiscate property from orphans and place it into the King's treasury. It would deprive the rightful heirs of their legacy. This is why it was imperative to have a confidential sale so that the property passed if possible with no notoriety or embarrassment to Peter Ambrose. A buyer did not take long to find. Evan Houghton, owning property adjacent to the Ambrose house, had long ago decided to expand his holdings if the right piece of property presented itself and the Ambrose house was one that had been on the list of qualifying acquisitions. He believed that it would be one that would never pass hands. Evan inquired of Brisby of the price. Although it was within the range of what was determined fair market value it was considered a little above the value of common reckoning. Evan counter offered to buy the property at his own price and allow Peter Ambrose to live in the house as a tenant for one shilling per year. This particular deal met and solved many dilemmas for Brisby and was a benefit to Peter Ambrose so he was not uprooted from the only home he had ever known during this difficult time. The money could be used for his benefit and welfare while keeping the property and household running. Evan would staff the property including the house and the money entering Peter's trust from the sale would pay the salary to Charles as Peter's guardian and for his educational needs. It was a winning strategy for all concerned. The deal was accepted and the Ambrose property quietly changed hands. Peter was unaware of the sale of the property and at least for now it was decided that it was best kept in confidence. Since Peter would live in the house and be responsible for its upkeep with Charles help, he would not notice the change of deed to the Houghtons.

Peter Ambrose was now secure in his lodgings and care. Charles was a better parent figure than Peter had ever had in his life. To this end Charles and Brisby decided that Peter should go to school and get away from the area and the gossip brought on by the issues caused by Ann's health and James flight until these events left the community consciousness. Peter was sent to London to a boarding school. His interest was in business and accounting. He excelled in mathematics and the curriculum and career choice certainly seemed to be a good fit. Within a matter of weeks arrangements were made and Peter was moved to his dormitory at the School of Business. He would be there for three years and return to Toxteth Park at the age of nineteen to the lonely Ambrose house. Charles stayed behind to manage the house and business for Peter until his return. He would venture to London when needed or at regular intervals to observe Peter's efforts

The School of Business, London England

Peter was happy to be out of the spotlight during this time. He threw himself into his studies and excelled. His social awkwardness was intact and he spent many hours studying in the library or his dormitory room in isolation. He interacted with others only as necessary and did not mix or attend the social events. At night he thought about his mother and father. He also thought about the circumstances of their ill health and desertion. His father and mother had squarely placed blame for their troubles for the biggest part of Peter's life and Peter had to admit that he felt the rumblings of hatred in his heart. He knew that he must keep this under control. He had seen first-hand that it had driven his mother to insanity and caused, in a round a bout way, her impending doom. It had turned his father into a probable murderer and deserter. It drove him to his decadent lifestyle developed to create his alternate life while his mother ruled the household. Peter found that these events caused him great pain and fear that he would follow this path to either insanity or murder. It played with his psyche and emotions. He woke up many nights in sweats and nightmarish visions. Peter was a troubled boy and the world was closing in around him.

Henshaw Hall

It had been a month since Sir Thomas's funeral. The talk again turned to the nuptials of William and Katherine. Marjorie was still in shock and emotionally drained but pitched in with Helen to make the plans. Helen Houghton would carry the largest share of the duties being the maternal side and bride's mother as wedding tradition dictated. The original plans were scaled down to a tasteful event yet much reduced in scope. The large and festive wedding was overshadowed by the mourning Henshaw household. William was now running the estate and the affairs of the family. His approach was to be frugal and use his common sense. Katherine completely understood the situation and with a few concessions here and there planned a wedding that met all of her dreams and expectations. In Katherine's thinking it was better than the original plan because they would be surrounded by a smaller group of close friends rather than a larger group of casual acquaintances that would only have been invited to satisfy the social register. With all of the recent events these people would have focused the time on gossip rather than the celebration of their wedding. So the plan went forward with the guest list whittled down to family members, close friends and the highest of the high society. It was tasteful in its planning and stood up to the scrutiny of the situation under which it was held.

The wedding itself was a beautiful affair. The guests were warm, friendly and caring. It was a comfortable atmosphere and everyone was fed and happy. The business of the day, the wedding of William and Katherine, was completed without further complications. At the end of the day, Mr. William and Mrs. Katherine Henshaw were entering the world as a newlywed couple completing a cycle started long ago at their birth through the friendship of their parents and the approval of their close friends and society. It was indeed a good match. Both husband

and wife were happy and content moving forward into an unknown but promising future. Of course the mourning would continue for some time but on this day it was put aside in celebration of the young couple. The year of 1630 had been a pivotal year. William became eighteen years old, graduated from school, was commissioned into the military, married Katherine Houghton and became head of the Henshaw household at the death of his father Sir Thomas Henshaw. The Houghton's had married their daughter, Katherine, to William and acquired the Ambrose property into their assets. Peter Ambrose had lost both parents: one to insanity and one through abandonment. He too had become the head of the Ambrose household and at a younger age than William but under a much darker and stressful circumstance. He had begun his descent into the old Ambrose family tradition of blame, depression and hatred that would continue until his death.

Family History:

The earliest records show an ancestor, Sir Thomas, who was born in Derby, County of Lancashire in England and died in Toxteth Park near Liverpool in the Parish of Prescot, County Lancashire, England circa 1630.

William married the daughter of Evan and Helen Houghton who resided at Toxteth Park or Wavertre Hall. Sir Thomas must have been somewhat wealthy and held high social status, since his son William married into the family of Evan Houghton, a family with considerable wealth and noble blood. From this marriage, it is possible to reliably trace the lineage back to King Edward III and from there of course to many proceeding noble and royal generations.

Simplified, the lineage is as follows:

- *William Henshaw married Katherine Houghton, daughter of:*
- *Evan Houghton and Ellen Parker. Evan was the son of:*
- *Richard Houghton and Margaret Stanley. Margaret was the*

daughter of:

- *[Henry Stanley](#) of Aughton and Mary Stanley. Henry was the son and only heir of:*
- *[James Stanley](#), Marshall of Ireland, and Anne Hart. James was the son of:*
- *[Lord George Stanley](#) and Joan, 9th Baroness Strange. George was the son of:*
- *Lord Sir Thomas Stanley, 1ˢᵗ Earl of Derby, and [Eleanor Neville](#). Eleanor was the daughter of:*
- *[Richard Neville](#), Earl Salisbury, and Alice Montacute. Richard was the son of:*
- *Ralph Neville, 1ˢᵗ Earl of Westmoreland, and [Joan de Beaufort](#). Joan was the daughter of:*
- *[John of Gaunt](#), Duke of Lancashire, and Katherine Swynford Roet. John was the son of: [Edward III](#), King of England, and Philippa of Hainault.*

November, December

William and Katherine took a brief trip to London for their honeymoon. They did not stay there long because of the pressing responsibilities on William to settle the estate of Sir Thomas Henshaw, establish the living quarters for he and Katherine and receive a briefing on the operations and finances of Sir Thomas's estate. Although he could have delayed his reporting time to his military unit indefinitely he felt a sense of duty and loyalty to his unit and wanted to be versed in his duties as soon as possible. The London trip was in a way a time and a place for William and Katherine to take a deep breath, set their resolve and move bravely forward into their marriage responsibilities and making a new life not only planning for themselves but for William's mother, brothers and sister. He would repeat this education when he was taught by Evan of the operations of the Houghton's holdings. Here is an inventory of the real estate which they inherited from the Houghtons, not counting the property of Sir

Thomas. It comes from the Herald's College:

Wavertree Hall,	Lands in Liverpool,
Penketh Hall,	Lands in Ellell,
Lands in Penyngton,	Lands in Carltou,
Lands in Worsely,	Lands in Sowerby,
Newton in Mackinfield,	Lands in Warton,
Lands in Knowlsley,	Houses in Lancaster.

William's mother was having a hard time coming to terms with the loss of her husband. Time heals all wounds but time was right now the enemy. It was still within the flicker of time that was too close to the loss of her husband. It kept it fresh in her mind and yet not far enough away to have completed her grieving period. The horrible circumstances of his murder and the escape of his murderer made the situation much worse. She could not reconcile the evil that it took to end the life of Sir Thomas by James Ambrose. She knew of no reason that James should have accumulated that much hatred towards Sir Thomas and her family. She feared that they had not heard the last of him.

Christmas would be a somber affair this year and was right around the corner. Marjorie and Sir Thomas had been married at a young age similar to William and Katherine at their marriage. Watching them go about their lives inevitably made the memories of their courtship, marriage and their own transition a fixture in her mind. Their life had been very good at the time of the marriage and the transition was smooth. Sir Thomas and Marjorie were married in the time period of the death of Queen Elizabeth I in 1603. Following her death James I of England (James VI of Scotland) took the throne. During this beriod there was relative peace in England. Even the first part of Charles I reign continued this peace until the late 1630s with the exception of the Nine Years War and the continuous conflict in Ireland. Sir Thomas and Marjorie had built their lives around the Protestant church and lived in the beliefs taught there. They worked hard, lived an ethical and honest life, were well thought of in the community and carried the credentials to make the union a stalwart of the greater Liverpool area. The future was very bright. They were wed around the year of 1608. William, their first child was born in 1612 followed by his two brothers and his sister over the next five years with Ellen being born in 1616. Sir Thomas had been involved with the troubles in Ireland and during his service had been awarded the English Coat of Arms. Sir Thomas developed a business in cattle and livestock and had some of the premier breeding bulls in the three kingdoms. He maintained large herds of sheep and exported wool to Ireland, the West Indies and across England. The family ran various businesses in the Port of Liverpool in the import and export of goods and in textile industry converting a portion of their wool harvest into cloth. Sir Thomas and his ancestors came from the working class to own their own stable of businesses which had been under Sir Thomas's control until his death. Sir Thomas being a businessman had developed a structure of sub managers who oversaw the day to day operations of the businesses. These men were loyal and hardworking and would have laid their lives down to protect the companies or Sir Thomas's life and livelihood. The success of Sir Thomas was linked directly to their own well-being. These men felt betrayed by James Ambrose who associated with them during his time in Liverpool. They would be on watch for him if he ever returned to exact their own type of vengeance. In this time opportunities were rare and these men would protect theirs at all costs. Now they were to swear their allegiance to William and teach him the businesses and advise him on the industries, products, pricing and operations. Sir Thomas's brilliance as a business man, while most likely being criticized for developing these managers, could not have been foretold until a need like the one they were now facing was realized. Sir Thomas went to his grave knowing that these men would look out for his family and William in particular so the family, companies, managers, their families and all of the people employed within this structure would continue to operate, prosper and grow if the opportunities arose.

Marjorie would set in her room for hours just looking at the four walls that surrounded her. She lived inside her head now remembering the wonderful times with Sir Thomas: their first meeting, first kiss, birthdays, Christmas's, the birth of their children and all of those little things that left an indelible impression on the memories that live on long after death. These events form the basis of memory and the soul of the person that was lost. Death is much easier on the dying than those left behind and Marjorie had taken Sir Thomas's loss hard. Ellen and Katherine had taken the helm in the kitchen and running the household. Marjorie was normally stationed there and offering tea and conversation to anyone needing it before Sir Thomas's death. As the household settled in, the trees shed their leaves and the cold set in for the winter Marjorie's mood and demeanor matched the seasons. She had nightmares, little or no appetite, trouble sleeping, crying fits and was detached from those around her. It was hard to get closure when the facts of Sir Thomas's death were still being kept partially from the family. The true murder weapon had never been found but upon examining the head wound Sheriff Stratford was convinced, as was the Undertaker, that all of the damage could not have been caused by a single blow from falling downward onto the boulder. Both men had seen similar injuries from falls off of horses and they simply did not manifest themselves in the manner or the appearance of Sir Thomas's injuries. The wound resulted from a weapon. They had seen the damage many times in combat. William had been included in the discussions but even at those discussions some facts had not been disclosed. The remnants of blood had been found on the saddle of James's horse that he had abandoned in the local livery. They had also found some shed off clothes nearby that not only had blood on them that seemed to match the size and shape on the saddle but a fake beard and hooded cloak that appeared to be used as a disguise.

Marjorie spent less and less time out of bed. Her weight was becoming a concern. She had lost substantial body mass and her skin was pale and clammy most of the time. She found no joy. William would try to engage her on music and the theater like he had when he returned home from school. She would not engage with him and stared blankly into space. This continued. On Christmas day the festivities were planned and guests invited to share the table and the celebration. Marjorie stayed in her room. She stared at the drab walls and the rows of pictures staring back at her. The memories of brighter days reflecting through her mind became apparitions and transparencies as they began to fade. Time heals the wounds but it also degrades the memories that we so like to keep fresh. In reflection their lives had been wonderful. They met, fell in love, married and had a wonderful family. They did so in a rare time of relative peace in England. They were not poor, nor had they ever felt hunger, poverty, disease or infidelity. A wife and a mother could not ask for more. Yet, there was sadness that Sir Thomas was gone and the senselessness of his death. She felt cheated and wanted to make sense of a senseless act. She would never find the peace that came with this knowledge. She would live her life in sadness giving James Ambrose another victory over the Henshaw family that he would never know about. Finally she passed on to a better place to be with Sir Thomas and the Lord.

William's life was proceeding at a quick pace. He woke up in the mornings and met with Brisby to go over the family financial condition. He would ride into Liverpool for several days at a time to meet with his manager's and learn each business from the ground levels. He met and interacted with his brother's and sister to keep them apprised and begin their training in the family affairs and businesses. It was his hope that his brothers would take an interest in the family holdings and become a part of the operations lessening the work load on him. Of course he also had to become acclimated to married life including the duties that came with that.   Katherine and William were neither one experienced in the finer points of marital relations in their bedroom. Katherine had her mother to turn to for these talks. William had only heard the talk around the dormitory at college and the barracks at the regiment. Sir Thomas was not there to have these discussions with him and his mother was in no condition to take up that role before her death. It is likely that she would not have been comfortable in that role even if she was not having her own problems. Katherine was patient and tried to give William the benefit of her knowledge. At first it was awkward but with urging and guidance and filtering out all of the bravado of William's learning from those schoolhouse sources they settled into this part of life quite naturally and it was a very intimate relationship that developed. It was difficult in a crowded house and the opportunities were limited. When they arose they were full of passion and fire. William found it exhilarating and surprising that this wonderful woman that he met could bring such pleasure to him and him to her.

The School of Business, London England

Peter worked hard at school. His grades were exemplary and he came to the conclusion that the accounting profession he had chosen would suit him well. It allowed him to work on an individual basis relying on no one and not requiring him to mix in large groups of people. He could go to his room, get out his ledgers and work the numbers at his convenience and with no interference from the outside world. He, of course, knew that he would be required to deal with clients face to face in practice and to put on appearances at social events but he had already begun planning how to minimize the time he spent away from the ledgers. This time was like an escape from his personal demons. Like an alcoholic he craved that escape. He spent Christmas blissfully alone at the school and in his room with the ledgers.

1631 to 1634

William had taken to his duties with the regiment in full now. His initial training was behind him. There was still some settling in to do but his association with Evan Houghton had eased the transition. The men in the regiment knew his background and his story. Alexander the Great had led armies at this age and until he was tested in battle there would be no judgment of his abilities by those who would serve under him at such a time. William was respected in the quarters because he had studied hard, learned his job quickly and efficiently, excelled in horsemanship and tactics and was liked by his command. The peace of this time had lulled them into the acceptance of William even though he was unproven in battle. Many of the men here had not been in battle except a few who had fought in the Nine Years War and the skirmishes in Ireland.

William had kept regular schedules receiving his tutoring on each of the businesses in Liverpool. He had taken both of his brothers with him for much of the training so that there would be a solid future for the companies and a good understanding of the operations by the men of the family. William could envision a time when he could be called away and then Henry and John would have to oversee these operations.

Henshaw Hall

Time had passed and William and Katherine grew comfortable in their marriage. John and Henry, now of legal age had taken over duties at the Liverpool companies and reported to William and the council of managers to pass along information on the company. They studied the various industries, gained knowledge, stayed abreast of new methods of production, competitive pricing and domestic and international markets for their goods. William oversaw the overall operations of the estate and businesses. Recently he was looking into shipping as a natural addition to the import and export business. There had been and probably always would be a need to move freight, troops and supplies to Ireland and this need had a probability of growth and a continued need for shipping. Concentrating on shipping to Ireland would lessen the likelihood of being attacked by pirates and make possible the expansion of the businesses there.

On the High Seas

As the shipping business came into being it had several unforeseen outcomes: some good and some bad. William and Henry in particular found the ships much to their liking and spent time on them crewing and learning to be sea captains. There was always the magic of the seas during this time of settlement, exploration and adventure that attracted them and many men of the time bitten by the exploration and colonization bug. They were not able to go to sea full time as the other men had but spent much time on the ships going back and forth to their interests in Ireland and England. John had met and married an Irish Lass and had a child. John had become more of a homebody with the birth of their daughter Eleanor and structured his life around the businesses and their Irish home. He loved his family life and wished to never be far from it.

The King took notice of the family now that there was something of interest to him that could be of use. The shipping company provided transport for his troops between England and Ireland, revenue from customs collections on incoming goods and the possible use of the ships for defense against invasions from his enemies or the pirates active in the area. The ships were outfitted as Men of War and could put up a good fight. He felt he could simply commandeer the ships in an emergency for the use of the crown. This also freed him of the obligation to build the English fleet with the taxes he collected for that stated purpose and use that money as he wished.

The revenues from shipping had greatly exceeded the projections and vaulted the family name into prominence in London, York, Hull, Southampton, Scotland and Ireland. With this notoriety and wealth came the attraction of the less Desirables. On the docks there were thieves and saboteurs. At sea there were pirates. The pirates main cargos were slaves bound for ports around the world. Many that were taken from the Irish Sea and the coastal towns would be taken to the slave markets in Northern Africa. They would rifle the cargoes of these conquered ships and take anything of value and scuttle the rest. Although most believed that the pirates were in search of treasure it was much more a matter of survival and finding food, clothing and basic needs in these raids were of utmost importance to their survival. Of course treasure would always be welcomed but survival was the first priority. At times they would take the crews and passengers hostage and ransom them off to their families or the local church. The church in turn collected from their flocks for this solitary purpose. These outlaws did not run a normal business. They took what they wanted by force. The pirate life attracted the worst that the seas had to offer. It was a gathering place for thieves, murderers and other miscreants that would follow a charismatic leader. The pirates were democratic. They voted on their leader and could just as easily vote the leader out and replace him. Many of the beliefs of pirates and life at sea were simply stories made up to describe the life. In reality the life was very tough and short lived. Many of the pirates that sailed these waters came to the New World and plied their trade in the Caribbean Sea finding friendly ports in the Islands and along the Atlantic coast of the newly established American colonies. Some would find employment from countries such as England, France and Spain as Privateers that were basically employed to plunder the shipping of rival countries in these waters.

James Ambrose/Ainsworth, Ahoy!

James Ambrose/Ainsworth had just made it on board after his escape from his murderous mission when the ship left dock. He leaned on the rail watching for any signs of pursuit. He wished to make sure that the ship was well out of reach of the Sheriff or his deputies before he could feel at ease. This was not to happen and his focus was rudely interrupted by the first mate. "You there by the rail!" yelled the first mate, "Do you fancy yourself as a passenger on this ship---if so pay the fee and if not get your arse to your duties!" The first mates name was Hardy. He was a large man with a scar above his right eye. There were many other scars on his visible body sharply distinguishing him as a seasoned sailor. He did not take well to slackers or fancy boys and made it clear. This was not a good sign for James because he had arrived on board in his fancy attire as he did not have time to dress the part and develop a story and character to make life easier on board. He had jettisoned his disguise quickly to make it on board and was forced to wear what he had on underneath. It was too late now and he was exposed to this man who had the second highest authority on the ship. James had little to no experience on a ship and would have to learn his duties and routines. He could not allow the others to realize this weakness. He had told the Captain that he was an experienced sailor to get the job and had lied. He looked around the deck and found work that he could virtually disappear into as he observed the others to learn the duties. His malingering did not go unnoticed by Hardy. This was a man who operated off of first impressions. James was already finding this manual labor to his dislike and almost immediately started scheming to move his way into a position of authority. His conversations with shipmates would be geared to creating an allusion of importance and authority but it would have to wait as he was struggling mightily with the weight of his current duties. The faster he could learn the workings of the ship and the ladder of authority the quicker he could bring his plan together. He was aware that he had certainly got off to a poor start with Hardy and that this could be a hindrance to his plans. At this point he would settle in and learn and scheme--- and if it became necessary to eliminate anything or anyone that stood in his way. He knew he had killed before and that he was now capable of anything to reach his goals. James was to learn quickly that his plan had flaws. The life on the merchant ship was rife with perils. The reality of the life aboard a ship in this period was harsh, but a life through piracy could be worse.

James Ambrose/Ainsworth: Captured into Slavery

James had made his escape from Liverpool in the autumn of 1630. Working on the ship was hard work and very little reward. James in his entire life had never lived in such a low lifestyle but could not complain because the die had been cast when he signed on with the Captain and the crew. True to his belief Hardy was a bane to his existence. He watched James's every move and was quick on the discipline.   James watched his chances and continued to toady his way around the other officers and the Captain as the chances presented themselves. This had the effect of balancing the negative influence of Hardy on their opinions of James. The crew was now calling him Jimmy and he deduced that this would have the effect of blending him with the crew and making him look more like one of the boys to the Captain. He would then reduce his association with the deck hands. He was sure that at the proper time with his knowledge and above average intelligence that he would be ready to impress the right people as the opportunities presented to gain his freedom. In the short term he would have to do something to relieve himself of the negative influence of Hardy.   To this end he started volunteering for night watches. This having the effect of getting him off of some of the less desirable work during the day and isolating him in the dark with Hardy while most of the crew were sleeping and below decks. It was now 1632 and James had acquired his own weapons through ports of call. He gave no indication that he had money and gold of his own and lived frugally so no one would suspect that he had additional funds for fear of being robbed. When he could he simply stole what he could find to save his personal funds but to get what he needed some expenditure was necessary. He balanced the purchase of pistols, sabers and stilettos against reasonable gifts from the crew so there would be no suspicion. He had the best weapons on the ship and had stashed several of them in hiding so they would not be discovered. The night duties fit well with his ability to conceal these weapons and hatch a plan to rid himself of Hardy.

The day had finally come to him for his plan to be put in motion. After being on watch all night James was rudely awakened by Hardy and put on duty cleaning the hold of human waste and bilge. This was the work for the lowest of the low in the crew and James considered himself well above this work even though he was still technically of low rank. He knew that the unspoken war between himself and Hardy was coming to a head. Tonight would be the night. As the crew retired and James took his place in the crow's nest to keep the night watch he waited impatiently. Hardy would soon make his ship rounds. Normally Hardy would begin aft and move to the bow looking for anything out of place or unsafe along the way. He would be a second set of eyes on the watch. This night he was following his normal pattern. This allowed James to climb from the crow's nest and lie in wait in the hiding place he had prepared. He was armed with a large knife and short sword and would attempt to get behind Hardy. The man was large and strong and James was no match for him in a face to face battle. He crawled into the shadows and waited.

Hardy had been a sailor since the time he learned to walk. His father and his father's father had been sailors. He signed on to his first ship as a preteen after his parents had died of the plague. He knew they would put him in an orphanage and the policy of the King was to acquire the estate of the orphan and liquidate it to the crown's use. Hardy did not really care since the estate itself was meager and would not support him in any survivable manner. It was one of the issues causing a furor on land at this time. Hardy was operating on instinct. He had been up the last two nights watching James. He was called to duty during the day in his capacity and had little sleep. He had decided this day that if he had to be up that James would be up also. If you cannot trust your enemy at least put him on equal footing and the bilge duty would wear him down. It pleased the big man that he had this authority but knew to trust his intuition about James. He had seen many just like him in his day. He needed to convince the Captain of the situation. To date the Captain listened but he had no definitive evidence to convince him that his feelings were correct. He was making his way to the bow and had crossed the open deck beyond the wheel. It was pitch black in this area with no lighting. He had glanced upward but could not make out the crow's nest in the darkness with a hint of fog. He called to James to no avail. There was no reply. He moved forward again on alert but still could not tell if there was anyone in the lookout. Finally he moved to the mast and started to climb the rope ladder near the port side. He stretched his arms out and grabbed the rope with both hands and started to pull up. He felt a sharp burning pain in his side and a warm wet feeling. He turned only to find that movement caused the pain to become unbearable. He stopped to clear his head and looked down. Below was James with his sword out. Hardy came slowly to the realization of what was happening and felt the thrust of the sword for a second time in an upward motion through his rib cage. He was aware of the deceit and hate in James but could not sound an alert. He was slipping from consciousness and felt his grip on the rope ladder slipping. James moved under him to soften the fall and muffle the noise. He took Hardy over his shoulder as his feet reached the ground and spun him to the portside rail. He heaved him overboard and threw the sword after him. Nobody had ever seen this sword. It had been hidden near his nightly post. He stripped off his blood-soaked shirt and threw it overboard, washed the remnants of blood from himself and the deck and climbed the mast on his way to the crow's nest. He never made it there. He was tumbled to the ground by a fiery explosion and could hear multiple booms from cannon fire nearby. A Barbary Corsair was upon them and had been able to move in close while James was up to his evil. The watch had been vacated for that period of time. He ran to the wheel and clanged the bell to alert the ship but it was too late. They were being boarded by the pirates and any resistance that could be mounted was suicide at this late time. He threw down his pistol and surrendered. The pirate crew silently crept below decks and murdered any sailor that resisted in their bunks. Those that surrendered were brought above deck and detained. James kept silent and blended into the darkness. The Captain was brought to the deck and taken to the rail. The pirate Captain pulled his pistol and shot the Captain in the head and rolled him backwards over the rail. This was to demonstrate to the others that their authority meant nothing and they were now under the control of the pirate vessel. The Barbary Corsair was a sleek ship for its day. It was fast and heavily armed so in many cases there was no real battle once they came alongside a merchant vessel. There was no way that a merchant ship could defend against such an overwhelming display of guns and murderous pirates. It also had a galley of slaves chained to the oars to row the boat when they needed to maneuver or the wind failed them. It was a terrible fate to be a galley slave and many simply died chained below decks. They were fed bread and water and given little rest or care. If they died they were simply replaced like a worn out part. Many of the sailor captives would be sold to these duties upon their return to Africa in the slave markets. These pirates raided coastal villages and abducted its citizens for the same purposes. Mostly they would accept their fate and capitulate. The ship was sacked and a crew was chosen from the pirate's ship and put in place to raise the sail and follow. James knew that he had succeeded in his plan to get rid of Hardy but his inattention to his duties had caused the taking of the ship and the death of the Captain and some of his mates. He could only think of how this had changed his own life. He cared little for the others.

Slave Ship

James was fortunate not to be a big man in some ways. Those of size and strength were chosen for the galley work on the oars and some of those already on board were killed and thrown overboard if they were sickly or exhausted and replaced by fresh bodies. The women taken were often abused or raped. If they had value after this they were chained below. The children were evaluated for worth and those that were of little value were slain or cast into the sea. The rest of the crew was chained below for the trip to Africa and sale. There were others on board including women and children that were abducted by the pirates from villages and towns near the coast. The conditions below decks were deplorable and many died on the journey of dysentery, scurvy, pneumonia and other illnesses. It was of little concern to the pirates as they would simply fill their hold on subsequent raids.

James now worked with the pirates and informed them of any information he could extract from the other captives. Some of the information he just made up to make it seem needed. He was below decks for a portion of the day but had been put to work in the kitchen. Although this is not a duty James would have chosen in real life it was his savior in this situation. He was able to get additional food by stealing bites during food preparation and pocketing some additional reserves. The cook knew what he was up to but said nothing. James's salesman skills had taught him how to connect and make himself useful. These small and important relationships along with working his influence with the Captain of the pirates would be his savior later in the voyage and in the markets of Africa.

The Voyage for the captives from this area was much longer than those from the Mediterranean countries. They would have to sail around Europe and through Gibraltar then to the North African coast countries. This particular ship made its fortunes with its contacts in Algiers. On the average about one third of the captives aboard would die on a normal journey but with James deceit this number would rise much higher on this trip. It was critical to him for the entire crew of his old ship to meet their fates to assure that no one could associate him with his espionage on this ship or his murder of Hardy on the other. So far, with all of the turmoil no one had missed Hardy. On the long voyage with ample idle time below decks someone would eventually miss him and possibly come to the conclusion that the pirates could have not maneuvered so close to the ship if the lookout and

Hardy were on alert. They would recognize that there was a breach of security during the pirate assault which would be squarely placed on James's shoulders.

James was allowed to sleep on deck during good weather. At first he was tied to the mast but as time went on this was deemed not necessary by the officers of the ship. It was well known that James would toady to their needs and their will and was no threat to them. In truth he had nowhere to go in the middle of the sea with no land in sight. James hatched a plan and made a list of his enemies from his old crew. He would fashion wooden weapons when he was alone and some others that he had lifted from the crew in secret. He smuggled these weapons to the crew members that were on his list knowing that their fate was sealed if they were discovered with the weapons or harbored the thought of mutiny. James knew that if somehow the revolt was successful by his shipmates these men would not question his loyalty to them. He had provided them the weapons and was a major part of their victory. He was a danger to both sides but would position himself between them so that he would survive and prosper no matter what the outcome of his plot.

James had smuggled quite a cache of weapons to the crew from his ship and had singled out those he considered enemies or likely to do the most damage to him if they survived the mutiny. He showed them where to hide the weapons and provided them with tools to file through the chains. He had set the stage like a play and he was directing the action.

On his nights on deck he started to speak with the First Mate at length hinting that there was a plot by the prisoners to take the ship. He feigned his concern for the pirate crew's well-being and finally this made its way to the Captain. He had to choreograph the plot so the prisoners made the first move. He knew the time was short. On the fatal night he spent the day in the hold of the ship with his old shipmates telling them that the time to strike was coming that night when the crew had gone to bed and the watch had the least amount of men to repel the attack. He verified that all was in readiness and laid out the plan. Upon his signal the crew would shed their chains and arm themselves. Those without arms would follow the rest up to deck. They would immediately seek to overpower the watch and capture the arms of the first victims to complete arming their selves and complete the overthrow of the pirates. James would lure the lookout off of the mast and onto the deck for rum and some extra food which he had smuggled from the kitchen. As the crew made deck he would try to stop the sounding of the alarm so the element of surprise would last as long as possible and they could overwhelm and disarm the sleeping crew. It sounded like a legitimate plan and James would let it play itself out. He could not lose either way. However he would hinder the likelihood of success by his mates because they were in actuality a bigger threat to his future than the pirates. After laying out the plan below deck he took a tray of tea to the Captains quarters and alerted him to the attempted takeover of the ship by the prisoners on that very night. He told him a story about two of his own crew members being familiar with some of the sailors held captive and that they had armed them for the mutiny. Of course, these men he named were ones that saw through James and treated him harshly. James looked forward to them getting caught up in the whirlwind that would overtake the ship that night.

After dinner was served to the crew he had taken the bread and water rations to the prisoners; James made his way to the hold. He informed the leader of this action that the crew had been given unlimited rum this evening and many were inebriated beyond being able to assist in defense of the ship. They were to give him until they heard the watch bell ring twice and then make their assault. Each man knew the risk if they were not successful and were willing to pay that price for their freedom. James admired this in them but knew that it was the exact human quality that would make his plan work. He went back to the deck and sat by the rail near the watch bell.

In the crew quarters there was a rush of activity. The pirates loaded the pistols and sharpened there knives and swords. The Captain revealed the plan and all was ready for the watch bell. They stole from their bunks and packed their blankets to make it appear that they were still in deep sleep. They went to the deck and melted into the dark shadows out of sight.

James made his way to the watch bell when the reception was ready and rang it two times. There was a brief delay and then noises from the hold. Hushed voices and light steps were creeping to the deck for the assault. Half of the force would split off and move to the crew bunks to catch them by surprise just like they were caught by surprise on their own watch. The other half would take the wheel and eliminate the deck crew as light as it was on the night watch. As the first unit peeled off to make their assault in the bunks the pirates sprung their attack. The door to the bunks was quickly closed and locked trapping half of the force below decks. This divided the attackers and the pirates made short work of those left on deck. As the last of them were dispatched overboard the door from below was unlocked allowing the second force to storm onto the deck. It was a massacre. The last man was an officer of the ship and the leader of the attack. The Pirates tied him to the mast and began their fun. James was now with the pirates and the survivor saw him there. At first the officer was puzzled but a man like James was not a mystery and his treachery was no surprise. The man knew that putting his trust in this man had now cost him his life and considerable pain and torture before his death. James felt nothing. He sought out the Captain to negotiate the reward for his cooperation and his new and improved conditions for his current situation from his betrayal.

The voyage to Algiers was a long one. The pirates made several raids on unarmed shipping and coastal villages and towns to load their ships hold with captives and supplies for the crew. The captives that survived would be cleaned up, fattened up and sold in the slave markets. They would be chained to the oars or in the hold for the entire journey and be fed bread and water at subsistence levels. They would not see the open air for the entire voyage and if they did it was for a trip to the ships rail and then overboard because they had died or were dying with no hope of being of value to the pirates in the market. It was the same mentality as cattle farmers and the captives were looked on as no better than a commodity to be sold or bartered. The ships were at sea for almost twenty months before making port. It was now 1634 and the world that they had left behind in Europe and the British Isles was changing for the worse.

Peter Ambrose Graduation and Head of the Ambrose House

Peter was finishing his schooling in London in the spring of 1634 and knew that his life would take a drastic turn at its conclusion. Peter would have much preferred remaining in school or in London rather than return to Liverpool. He knew that his destiny would not allow for it. He graduated with honors and notified Charles of the impending event. Charles notified Judge Wickford. On graduation day Peter would not be alone. William and Katherine Henshaw, Judge Wickford and Charles traveled to London to attend and celebrate with Peter. William paid for the travel, accommodations, gifts and an endowment to help Peter get started in his new career. It was a somber occasion at times and did not compare to their common memories of William's graduation. Under the circumstances it was a wonderful celebration for Peter. For that brief moment in time Peter could have turned his life down a good path and pursued a normal life. He would choose the wrong path and struggle. In his defense some of the decisions were out of his hands. He was required to return to Liverpool. His depression dictated what he could and could not do and his social skills had not improved during these years. His path was plotted long ago but was greatly complicated by the acts of his parents. Initially these acts worked for Peter in a positive way as new clients came to Peter because they pitied his plight and wanted to help him get established. They were very tolerant of his moods and even his rudeness at times. He had developed a reputation for first rate work. Over the first few years he took on many new clients and made a living wage. Evan Houghton paid all of the servants and household expenses including the taxes on the properties. It was presented to Peter that the trust maintained the property. He was unaware that the property had not passed to him on the death of his mother. The failure to disclose this to Peter and the reasons behind it would be an error that would factor into future relations with Peter and all of those involved. Judge Wickford would tell him his story when he decided the time was right.

1635-1640

Throughout this period political turmoil was beginning to assert itself into the mix once again and hostilities would surely follow. William and his brothers, in counsel with his managers and trusted confidants, began making plans for the security of the Henshaw and Houghton assets and interests. The shipping company was established and outlays of cash were spent on acquiring a fleet of merchant ships. This included training and maintaining loyal crews to sail to Ireland and back. The company would initially handle local shipping with plans on expanding to world trade and settlement over the years. During this period the Irish connection would be of utmost importance.

With the two families holdings solidified in England, it was decided that each business would establish itself in Ireland and homes would be purchased for the families to enable them to relocate if hostilities broke out in the area and for the safety of the families and their children.

Henry and John had already relocated to Ireland and performed their duties from Ulster. Henry was the first to relocate. He had never married and this made him the logical one to go to Ireland to establish the new businesses and represent the family and business interests there.   John followed shortly thereafter because Henry's workload was very demanding with site selection, construction of the businesses, hiring of workers and establishing themselves with the local government officials. It was very important to present the companies to Ireland in a good light.   As mentioned earlier John had married a girl in Liverpool with Irish ties.   He had met her on board ship on one of his business trips while assisting Henry and fell quickly in love.   There were issues in this marriage that mirrored some of the strife in England.   Ireland was strongly Roman Catholic and John's wife was of this faith.   The Henshaw family was Protestant and the lines were drawn.   It was ironic that a century ago the Henshaw family was Roman Catholic and changed by edict of Henry VIII to the Protestant faith.   To accommodate this problem the Henshaws established their living quarters in county Antrim which included the port of Belfast in the Catholic area of the country.   They also established offices in Dublin which had an Irish Protestant presence. Both of the areas were easy crossings from the Liverpool docks and the short sail was somewhat of a defense against the piracy of the Barbary Corsairs. As the family established itself and its philanthropy in Ireland they were careful to support issues that were open to all in need and not associated with race, religion or national origins. It was hard for anyone to say that the Henshaw family and their holdings were not in the best interest of the areas where they located nor were they bigoted in any way. It was important that the family remained neutral in every way. English that settle in Ireland were looked on as usurpers of the lands and the birthright of the true Irish. This was mostly because of the King's actions to provoke the Irish and then strip them of the lands to punish the actions they took in defense of their lands. These lands would then be settled by the British that were relocated there.

The politics between the families were negotiated based on mutual interests and trust. In all other issues they agreed to disagree in a peaceful manner. John and Mary were married when he turned twenty-one (1635) and six years later in 1641 they had a daughter, Eleanor. Sister Ellen was also married in 1635. Similar to the courtship of William and Katherine—Ellen had met John Harrison in the social circles around Liverpool and was acquainted with him for some time through school, church, local events, charities and social gatherings. William was not as astute of a match maker as his mother. He did not really understand that side of the process. Marjorie had begun the matchmaking process before her death. The process had suffered after the death of Sir Thomas while she drifted in her sadness. It was evident that the Harrison and Henshaw match was a good one for the families and for Ellen. Upon the marriage of William and Katherine the pursuit of this match was taken up by Katherine as a surrogate for Marjorie. She was married in her nineteenth year to John Harrison and this wedding was truly the wedding that was originally planned for William and Katherine. Katherine enlisted the help of her mother in arranging the details of the wedding and there was finally a full societal event that had long been delayed in the Henshaw household. It was the only wedding of a daughter that would ever occur to the Henshaw household which made it unique. With all of the brothers looking over the festivities Ellen took the hand of John Harrison for better or worse. William walked Ellen down the aisle and gave the bride away to John as a surrogate to their father. Katherine substituted for Marjorie in the mother of the bride's role and reigning matriarch of the family. It was as close to the dream event for Ellen as could be had with the death of Sir Thomas and Marjorie. John and Ellen had decided to live in Toxteth Park and did not make the move to Ireland. John became an ally of Williams in the English based businesses and rose through the ranks to his place of importance. The companies were restructured at this point and the long-time managers were rewarded for their long-devoted services by receiving small interests in the companies. This smoothed the transition for John into the flow of day to day business and avoided any disenchantment from the long-trusted employees in these critical positions.

William and Katherine did not have children for several years. William's busy schedule and heavy load of responsibilities had kept him busy. Katherine fully understood that a family would have to wait. They never stopped wanting a family but put the matter of the weddings of Ellen and John and the businesses as a priority. They felt secure in their lives and they worked together at a blistering pace to meet the expectations and obligations to their families and associates. They gazed upon their niece with envy when John and Mary visited from Ireland and somewhere inside them both was a deep longing for a child of their own. William feared that the political climate in England, Scotland and Ireland was heating up and that his military obligations would soon be called upon to defend his home and country. Katherine was still in child bearing years and the decision for parenthood played heavily on her mind.

William had to deal with the legal, ethical and societal issues from King Charles and his demands for customs revenue on shipping tonnage. The east coast of England was leaning towards the Parliamentarian side of the issues between the King and Parliament. Charles was looked on as incompetent and uncaring. It was required for Parliament to grant the King the ability to collect this revenue and they had not done that for several years. In addition, Parliament had refused to collect taxes for the crown in this dispute to reduce the Kings power to mount an army. King Charles simply found creative ways to fleece his subjects using outdated and obsolete laws to raise revenue. This added fuel to the fire of distrust and dislike of him. He had surrounded himself by advisers and religious figures that seemed to be advancing their own programs and agendas.

Charles was blind to their greed and egos and how it affected the common man.

The pirate issue had indeed been another problem area for the family's holdings. The pirates had now commandeered five of the company ships and crews and abducted family members of some of his close managers in their criminal pursuits. Every ship that left port was unguarded and vulnerable to the Corsairs. Although one of the taxes that Charles had reinstated from the past was to raise revenues to increase and fund a navy to protect shipping. Those funds in actuality were being diverted to the Kings constant vengeance missions on Ireland and Scotland and his constant warring with Spain. Something would have to be done. William had a meeting this very day to discuss the problem with his board of managers, John Harrison, Henry and John. The idea had been put forward to build their own fleet of warships. These new ships would be fitted as battle ships and would be armed to provide escort and defense against attack on the seas. If successful they would stop or hinder the piracy in the Irish Sea and confiscate the pirate's own ships into their service if they were victorious. A second option to fill the void was to hire Privateers to battle the pirate ships but this would have to have the approval of the King. It could be done underground and this would most likely be pursued as a two pronged attack on their enemies. Henry was very excited by the ideas and had requested to be in charge of these efforts if they decided to move forward.

As the meeting convened William was at the head of the table with his brothers on his right and left. John Harrison was to Henry's right and the other managers of the various business interests were interspersed around the table. William had gone to the docks and sought the company of an acquaintance he had made several years before. This man was a boat captain. He in turn had recruited to this meeting a gentleman he knew that had questionable ethics when out to sea and was most likely a pirate himself. The idea was that their input would be invaluable in determining a plan and no minute detail would escape their knowledge.

"Good Day, sirs," said William. "I have taken it upon myself to research our options for the safety of our passengers, crews and cargoes. To date as some of you are aware we have lost five of our ships and crews but just a few miles out of port. In addition, our friend and company officer, Mr. Smith, seated at this table and known to us all has lost his family by abduction by these vermin. Our discussion today is to come to some consensus about how we will protect our interests and what means we will apply to this task. I have asked Captain Robertson and his friend to join us as experts on the subject so they can contribute their knowledge to finding a solution to this problem. Currently there are two probable solutions that are in consideration. First, we would develop or refit some of our own ships with guns and our own trained sailors to escort our ships while at sea and to seek out and attack any pirate ships in the area. Second, we would contract with ships of the same notion to act in our behalf to protect our ships. The payment for this service would be the captured ship's contents confiscated by the Captain who can successfully engage and defeat the pirates. There will be safe passage into the appointed ports for resupply, recruitment of extra or replacement crew members, repairs and recreation. One exception would be the release of any of the captives that would be found on board the captured ships that have been abducted from a ship or land by the pirates. We would also take possession of any confiscated ship and refit them into our fleet to expand this protection. I open the floor to discussion at this point." William finished.

Smith was to his feet. "Sir, my family is missing. What are we doing to recover those that have been taken against their will and return them to their families?" he shouted. "Can we not deal with these pirates as other countries do and pay for their release?"

William was introspective and measured his answer. "Sir, let me begin by saying how sorry I am for your loss. I believe that there is the occasion for this to possibly happen but the English crown has no interest in bargaining with the pirates. Most of the nations acting in this manner are Roman Catholic nations and represented by the church or its ministers in these negotiations. There is a significant length of time since your family was abducted and I would not know how we would be able to discover what ship or what Captain has taken them to begin negotiations. Make no mistake though, if it is money that would gain the release of any of our people or their families I would pay the amount from my personal funds to secure their freedom. It does not seem to be a solution available to us at this time however. Captain Robertson, would you care to address this situation?"

Captain Robertson stood and surveyed the room. He was a large weathered man with a full red beard and dark skin from being in the sun. He was heavily muscled and gave the impression that he was a Captain because there was no one to challenge him for his position in this room. He certainly commanded that type of respect and even fear as he began to speak. He gave Mr. Smith a direct stare and paused before he began. "Gentlemen, I have been at sea most of my adult life and some before that. I have been a sea Captain for almost twenty years now. I have dealt with many dangers and seen many things in my travels. I have seen the slave markets in the north of Africa where these captives will most likely land. I have witnessed and been attacked by the pirates in the open sea and fought them off. These are men with a very narrow and single mind. They take what they can get to sell for riches or power. They live a rowdy life and live in the moment and dangerously. Many are fugitives from the law where they have lived or grown. They know the tricks of the highwayman and the cheat. Their negotiations would be fraught with lies and false promises. The only option for purchasing a captive is the slim chance of finding them after they have landed at the slave port and been sold. It is then and only then that there can be negotiation for their safe return. Unfortunately, there are many of these ports and some slaves will never be sold if they become a favorite of their owner as a woman would. Many of the men will be used in the ships galleys and most will be dead in a matter of months. Children will be sold individually and a family could have different owners and even be taken to different locations in and out of the country where they were sold. As you can see, the likelihood of finding them once gone is minute. In the current time if a force can be put to sea armed equally and trained and disciplined as a good military unit in such force that pirates are sufficiently inconvenienced they will simply move to where their work is easier and less of a risk. You will not stop piracy, you can only hope to move it away from your area of influence by making it difficult or deadly to operate in your waters." stated Captain Robertson. "I have with me a man that I will simply identify as Roger. He, shall we say, has firsthand knowledge of life aboard a pirate ship. Please ask him all of the questions that you like---he will give you answers. You may not like the answers but he will be honest."

Smith rose and addressed the room, "I just want my family back and the others who were taken. Roger, how can we get this accomplished?"

"Sir, gentlemen, I would not want to tell ye' that this can be done. If they can be located----and if there can be civil contact made----and if you have large amounts of money---and if they have not been sold, died on route or have become attached to a harem or other sort----ye' could have a chance. Most likely though ye' would have your throat cut — your money stolen and off they would go with a good laugh!" replied Roger.

William stood and the room came to a pause. "Roger, knowing that you have intimate knowledge of the pirate life, what course of action would you recommend from the view of achieving our goals, which are to transport our goods and services and passengers unmolested at sea to their destinations safely?" asked William.

Roger sat silent for a while and the whole room was hanging on his reply. Finally he grunted, cleared his throat and said "You must meet force with force----an eye for an eye if you will. These fine gentlemen will continue their craft until it is inconvenient, unprofitable, or too dangerous. If the trade is easier practiced elsewhere that is where they will go. They will battle each other if they need to for territory. There will be blood spilled make no doubts. They enjoy a good fight, but after the first losses they will move on to easier work! I believe you have a good plan to get escorts out to sea and hire some of their own to go against them — Privateers you call them. I would be willing to sign my crew on with the right conditions as you first stated here.' said Roger.

The room was abuzz with whispers. William stood and asked what was on everyone's mind "... and what would those conditions be?"

Roger replied "simple---we keep what we take, except slaves and if you need us to help recruit others we get a fee for each Captain we bring to you of a hundred pounds. If you want me to teach you the pirate ways and their hideouts and forts there will be a fee for that also. I could bring another three captains to the cause now if you like and we will sail under our own flags."

"Could you gentlemen give us leave to discuss this in private sir? asked William.

Captain Robertson spoke, "We will retire to the pub, you know the one and you can come to us with your decision." With that they left.

"Gentlemen, you have heard some options but let's understand what we are up against here. There is no one type of pirate ship. They can be small carrying ten to twelve guns with a crew of forty to sixty sailors up to large galleon ships with thirty to forty guns and a crew of 100 to 150 sailors or a combination of multiple ships. They slip up on their unarmed prey with murderous intent overwhelming merchant sailors who are not accustomed to a sudden and vicious attack for no reason other than taking what they want. You may ask why a man like Roger would become a privateer in our cause. It is rather simple. They can now do their work in a legal manner. As an outlaw pirate they cannot come to port for repairs or to resupply as they are known and would be arrested and hung on sight. However, as Privateers they could now enter these ports and have access to these things. Many attacks on shipping by outlaw pirates are simply to resupply their necessities in addition to the abduction of crews and passengers. The theft of goods and the ship itself is considered bonuses to this function. The ship's supplies are used to restock their own ships. This is why they try to strike soon after ships leave port. Each sailor signs an agreement called the ships 'articles' agreeing to their share of the treasures and division of goods and of the money from their booty after it is sold. If they do not keep their agreement they will be put to death by the crew. Many times when the money is made from selling the cargoes or the slaves the pirates turn on themselves and kill each other for the shares. An active pirate will not live long but he will reap havoc on our ships, citizens and cities until that day he meets his maker. They have nothing to lose in their pursuits. The motion on the table is to move forward by hiring our own Privateers while we develop our own escort ships and learn the ways of the pirates to defend our interests. We will vote by acclimation----all for signify with a 'yea'----all against now signify with a 'nay'! The motion passes and we will follow the two paths in defending our ships, cargoes, crews and passengers." stated William.

"There is one final order of business today on this subject. Henry has asked to head up our efforts and will work with Captain Robertson and Roger towards this goal. We will temporarily replace him in his duties in Ireland." added William. "Now, we will move to matters of general business---may I have a report on our textile holdings?"

Captain Henry Henshaw

Henry was thrilled at the idea of taking to sea and running this daring operation. Being the youngest of the three boys he had been treated fairly, educated and given all of the advantages. However, William, the first born and the oldest had taken the family helm. Henry felt no ill feelings and knew that this was how families worked and honored and trusted William with his very life. Henry was unmarried and the woman who had stolen his heart had married another. This had broken Henry's spirit and he had decided that he would go through life as a bachelor. He was not worldly as of yet but this would certainly come with this endeavor. This was his opportunity to make his own name and have some adventure. Henry was a good-looking man--- built solidly, intelligent and a good and ethical person. The association that he was entering into would surely test his ethics and those of his family. He was to be the gatekeeper to their world and banish the stench of the pirates from his family, businesses and friends. He would not be able to control every detail of the Privateers, indeed not very many. It was business as usual for them except they could come into port to resupply. They could plunder their victims within legal bounds. He could only hope that they would surrender the captives as agreed. He was assured under the pirate code that this would be honored. The company would take the ships confiscated to rebuild their own fleet. Henry had taken fencing but the type of fighting that he would see in no way resembled the death thrusts and leaps of the pirates. It would be a base from which to learn shipboard fighting from Captain Robertson and Roger. He would sail with these men to learn the craft and then Captain his own ship against the raiders. This would be a quick study. It was now 1632 and a direct assault on the pirates would need to be mounted as soon as possible.

Henry took to sea with Captain Robertson two weeks after the meeting. His role was as an observer initially on a short run to the Isle of Man which lies in the northern middle of the Irish Sea.

Upon his return he purchased his personal weapons as the land based weapons used by soldiers would be too large and cumbersome for shipboard battle. Henry purchased a broadsword and a cutlass as his weapons along with an assortment of pistols and knives. They were used as side arms and when going into and assault would be tucked away in many places on his person so he could access them easily. Several would be tied by a string around the neck so they could be accessed when needed. We think of the pirate battles on ships in calm seas with a steady deck. This was rarely the case and most of the battles were on ships pitching in the waves making walking difficult let alone sword play. When they were thrown off balance or at the mercy of their enemy from being knocked down the pistols were a very effective defense. Unfortunately under these conditions the pistols were fired with gun-powder. It could get wet or damp and misfire—thus the need to have multiple pistols in a battle. These battles lasted a matter of minutes once the target ship was boarded. From the pirate's side most of their victims were not armed or able to defend themselves properly. Once the ship was breached they simply surrendered. This would not be so when Henry and his allies attacked the pirates or were attacked in turn. They would put up a fight for survival and fight to the last man. Most of these pirates, even if they survived the battle, would be hung when taken to land within a short period of time. Now with this knowledge at hand and properly outfitted and drilled Henry would sail with Roger against the pirates and look for battle. Henry was at sea for months at a time with either Roger or Captain Robertson and they had confronted and battled several pirate ships where they could find them. Each visit home Henry had changed. He was no longer naive and was much a man of the world. The impact of the death and carnage played on him. It whittled away at his vision and ideas that the world was a civilized place to live. He was finding the dark quarters where his God only visited occasionally or abandoned all together and where the inhabitants of his new world were without soul or conscience. Today we would call them sociopaths; unknowing and uncaring for anything but their own wants and needs with no concern for any others nor remorse for their evil deeds. No one was close to them and the closest thing that they knew to family was their mates. Even with this being the pirate's 'family' he would kill any one of them without a thought in a dispute on ship or off.

Henry had been at sea for two years. It was 1634 and there had been some confrontation with pirate ships in the Irish Sea. Henry was disappointed by most of them. The pirates in the fast moving sleek Corsairs would simply flee the field when confronted with equal power and avoid the battle looking for prey that would not fight back. There were a few successes and two ships had been captured. In these encounters as expected most of the crew fought to their death rather than be captured. Several captives had been returned to Liverpool and were being quartered by William at one of the factories until they could be returned to their families. None of the captives were from the families of employees or friends of the Henshaw family. Those who had their families and friends stolen from them were in better spirits knowing that progress was being made even if their loved ones were not returned they knew that those responsible were paying for the ill deeds.

James Ambrose Ainsworth

James spent his journey building relations with the pirates. His hope was to sign on as crew rather than be sold in the slave markets. These other poor devils would simply have to suffer their fate. James always had a second plan in mind if he could not weasel his way into the crew. He was not being watched and was no longer tied or chained. He would simply watch his opportunities and escape. He had allies in the crew but they would not take a risk of discovery to help him. James believed if he made his break that they would not shoot or pursue him and if they needed to fire at him to save themselves than it would be high or wide. The weapons of this time were not accurate at long distances and if he put some distance between himself and the shooter his odds were good of a miss. It was late 1633 now and James felt like it had been an eternity since he had left port on the merchant ship. He did not like to live a lifestyle where he was subservient to anyone. Being married had left a bad taste in his mouth for being under any ones control or dependency. He also had a burning need to mete out more punishment on William and his family. He had decided at this time that if he could not join the crew he would escape.

During the voyage to Algiers James had overheard talk on the night watch that the first mate would be taking over the ship that was confiscated from James and the crew. This of course would have to be outfitted and armed for piracy. James had spent many hours with the man since the mutiny and had developed a good relationship for a captive. Intuition told James that this man did not see him as a captive any longer as the amount of time spent together and shared experiences had bonded them in some way. It would be James cause to find out just how deep the connection ran. This option would be a considerably less dangerous option than escape. When they were two days sail from port in Algiers James forced the issue with this man.

The First Mate's name was Pete Rogers. He was muscular, weathered, hardened and under full beard and pirate regalia. He was a seasoned sailor and a man that you would be proud to stand next to in battle. He was feared by many due to his size, viciousness of and his abilities in a fight whether it was assaulting a ship, a fight at a pub or in a disagreement on board. It was rumored that in a port where pirates were allowed he once fought five sailors killing them all with little effort. He was not a person to challenge, unless there was a good plan and an advantage of some kind.

James moved across the deck to where Pete was sitting with his cups. At first he just sat without saying a word. He had hoped to get Pete talking and capitalize on his drunken state. Pete was more interested in his rum. After an interlude James said "I understand that you are to be congratulated!"

Pete looked at him and grunted "For what?"

"I understand that you are to be a Captain of your own ship after we land. My old ship at that!" replied James

"Aye, that I am!" grunted Pete

"That is a good ship, not as fast as the corsair but can carry many more guns and crew so there is a larger landing party for battle. I know that ship pretty well and I am from the area on the Irish Sea where you took us." replied James. "I could be a big help to someone like you with my knowledge and your skills."

"Why would I believe you, I have done well for me self without help!" roared Pete.

"I am sure that you have or you would not be able to take on your own ship but what I am saying is that you will need someone that has connections in the Irish Sea that can get you into ports and gather information to help target the richest of the vessels getting ready to sail so you can make the maximum profits. Do you have someone who can do that for you sir?" asked James.

"I reckon not." replied Pete.

"I will be sold as a slave in a few days, but I would much rather be on board your ship and provide you with these services." said James. "I don't want to cause you any trouble but if we can agree now that my service under your flag would be of benefit I would ask that you keep me from the slave block."

Pete sat silent for a moment then spoke "Even if I was inclined to take you up on your offer I would have to pay a premium price for you to set you free. I would come under scrutiny from the Captain and my crew for this. How can I be sure that you would be worth it?"

"I can only tell you that in my life I was able to be an asset to any endeavor that I have put to mind." declared James "You have no one else that can acquire access for you and your sailors in those ports. That alone would make me valuable to your mission!"

"We would be crossing the Cap'n to do this. We would have to look another way. Are you willing to go along with it?" said Pete.

"I have no choice in the matter sir." answered James.

"Here is what I have in mind---you are to be sold as a slave!" said Pete.

James was startled. He thought that the situation was going his way but it had taken an ugly turn. "I understand but you will be sorry for that decision!" James stated raising his voice.

Pete stared at him for a moment in disgust and then started again. "This is the type of thing I worry about with you. There is more to the plan but you jump to conclusions and insult me with your tone!" stated Pete. "You must learn patience and to keep your mouth closed or I dare say someone will end up closing it for you!"

James bowed to this anger. "I am sorry" he cowered.

"Once you are sold we will watch for your new owner to move you while the ship is resupplied and a crew is found. I assume that you are not using your real name and the name you give when you are sold should be different from that one so you cannot be found afterwards. I can arrange your new name on the log. It will be Charles Kingston after your King. When they move you we will wait in ambush and abduct you once again. You will work as a crew on the ship but until I say different will not receive a share of our takings. Do you understand?" stated Pete.

"But sir, If I work I should be paid" shouted James

"This is not a negotiation. It is your one and only chance and thus your debt is paid. Consider your freedom and your very life as pay!" Pete firmly stated. "If you do not like the deal then go die in slavery mate!"

James was silent. After a moment of thought he agreed to the plan and the deal but tucked this treatment away in his head for future purposes. The plot was set and in the next few days it would be in action.

The ship made it to port and the crew immediately took the captives to the baths and cleaned them up. They were quickly sorted and those that were healthy and had weight on them were separated from the sickly ones and the ones that were malnourished. They marched the latter group to a building where they would be healed, cleaned, and fattened before they were put on the slave block to bring the best price. James was put with the first group and they were taken straight to the slave block for sale. Pete kept an eye on the sale bill to see when the auction would be for James. He also went about finding a buyer for him that would be an easy target. He could not be too strong and must be relatively alone so there could be no retaliations before they broke back out to sea. Pete wandered the docks and the auctions looking for that special individual which ironically he found on the first night. The gentleman lived alone and was looking for a single slave or servant as he stated. He did not have much stomach for the slave market or at least the darker side of it. The slave he was interested in would be more of a butler than a slave and be treated with dignity. Obviously his set of skills and appearance would limit him severely in his search for a proper fit. Pete had engaged him in conversation on that first night and found his needs to be a proper fit. He was a wealthy merchant who was widowed when his wife had died from disease the year before. He did not feel proper bringing another woman into his household and came to the understanding that an educated, white man would be able to do the household duties and be a companion without the appearance of him moving too quickly to find another wife. Pete found him to be ideal. He lived alone, had few friends and no family in this part of the world and therefore no support for his defense. Pete said "My kind sir, I am aware of a slave that will be going on the block with just the qualifications that you are looking for in a servant. His name is Charles Kingston and he has a high level of education and is obedient, can cook and has many tales from his travels to be a good companion. I can find the auction bill and help you bid on him if you wish!"

The man was so pleased to have someone who would represent him in his search and stated "Sir; that would be a fine thing as I am of little experience in this area. Could you make the bid also?"

Pete felt the trap springing and with a sly smile told the man that he would act in his behalf at the auction.

The man was pleased. He would embrace the system but not the treatment of slavery. By doing so he would give one of these poor souls a good life and the very best that they could hope for under their circumstance while filling his own needs. Pete made arrangements to collect him the next afternoon to go to the auction block.

James was miserable. For two days now he was locked in a squalid cell with little food and much filth. Those going on the slave block were packed into this small area and there was no room to lay or sleep. Real estate in this space was at a premium and fights broke out to claim even an inch of extra space. The stronger took from the weaker and when the bread and water came the stronger ate well. James took solace in the fact that he would be out from under this lifestyle in a few days and beginning another one that promised to be much better. Fortunately he would not be locked in this place long enough to contract any diseases and if he could stay quiet and out of the glare of the larger predators in this social structure he would come from the ordeal with fewer scars. He curled into a ball to take the least amount of space and tried to sleep and think of better times in his flat in Liverpool. As much as he tried only hatred seeped through the cracks in his mind's door and that hatred was still focused on the Henshaw family.

As morning rose on the second day the guards came to the door of the cell and rattled it open. They ordered the men out in several languages but mostly by brute force. They were herded down to a water hole and stripped. They were ordered into the hole and told to wash. They were issues new clothes. They were not good clothes but all of the captives now were roughly dressed in identical attire marking them as a slave if there was to be any attempt to escape. Silently James was glad that his original plan was not taking place. He had not anticipated this procedure which would have made the escape plan more difficult. They were moved to holding pens in the heat and sun near the auction. They were given all the water they could drink so they would be fresh and hydrated for the block so they would look their very best for sale.

Pete had instructed him to not look his best and to cower down and stoop at the shoulders and not to speak while being auctioned. He did not want him to show any value at all to make the outcome of his bidding go higher. James was to play the role of a broken down, ignorant and useless slave driving any interest in him to the lowest levels. To this end James was moved into line for the auction chained to eleven other unfortunates who he knew would not have as good an outcome to their days as he would most certainly have today. Many of them would be dead within twelve months. The wait was over an hour and finally James was led onto the block.

Pete had arrived at the man's house in a borrowed suit and cleaned up with a haircut, bath and some lilac water for a pleasant scent which in his opinion made him look just like a high society man from England. Any outside observer could notice that there were many discrepancies to this theory but they went unnoticed to Pete. They enjoyed a cup of tea and then mounted the carriage that would take them to the auction. The man was uneasy to be participating in this barbaric practice. Pete enjoyed watching him squirm. Pete agreed to be the front man and do the bidding so that the man was not associated with the purchase of a human being. He was a Puritan who had himself left England with his wife to avoid the coming conflicts that would pit King Charles against the Puritans on the religious and political fronts. What he was doing was a total dichotomy. He read his bible and found passages that included slaves and even passages telling the slaves to behave for their masters. On a real level he was disgusted with the practice of buying and selling real people with families and souls. The selling of women for sex partners and harems was a level of depravation that he simply would not address and turned a blind eye to it. This too would be a difficult thing for him as they came upon the slave market and tied up the carriage. He was uncomfortable and felt himself under the eye of God for even being in this place of hell. He entered anyway and knew that his God would damn him for his participation. His need for a companion and servant overwhelmed him though and he hoped his God would understand.

Pete took up his bidding position. Pete was pleased to see that they had arrived shortly before James would be on the block so they would not have to spend too much time at this place of disgusting sights and smells.

"We have here a slave from of the English lands. Do not let his small stature fool you sirs, he is a strong worker and bright of mind!" barked the auctioneer. The bidders and audience chuckled at the sight of James. Pete shouted out "Is he full grown? Does he stand straight or is there something wrong with his back? Is he ill? Can he not speak or hear?" All of the bidders chimed in and the bidding chilled. Pete continued now passing rumors that made their way around the room about James being retarded and violent. He told others that he was diseased and carried the plague with him. The auctioneer continued his bark. "What will we have for this specimen of a man my dear sirs?"

There was silence. "Surely one of you could use a man like this. He is not large or strong but he could work in other areas." shouted the auctioneer knowing that the value of this slave was rapidly falling. Pete yelled "Just another mouth to feed as I see it and useless----move on to a real bargain!" Pete would make these comments and move to a different location on the floor. "Will anyone start the bidding on this man------anyone?" plead the auctioneer. He signaled for James to be led from the block and Pete yelled "I will give you five pounds for him --- take it or leave it!" The auctioneer looked up and yelled "Sold to the man down front for five pounds" James was led away to a table and he was marked as sold with information on who was to collect him. Pete and the man made their way to the table and the man paid the five pounds. They led James to the carriage in his chains. The ride to the man's house was not long. It took about thirty minutes by carriage and the house was fairly large and comfortable. Pete had never determined what business the man was involved in but the thought struck him that he had to have valuables. It was his plan to kill the man on the journey but that plan changed with this thought.

James was waiting for Pete to make his move on the man. He noticed Pete trying to get his attention and just played his role in this deception. The carriage was coming to a stop in front of a house and the man got down and said "Here we are, let us get ourselves inside and then we will get you settled and discuss your duties." James was confused but exited from the carriage. Pete held back behind the man and got close to Pete. He said "Just follow my lead I have a new plan!"

They went into the house and the man took James to his quarters. It was a nice room---much nicer than anything he would find on board a ship. The clothes were of a quality reminding him of his former life. The position the man was offering was a huge upgrade from his slave status or the positions that any of his fellow captives would ever hope to achieve. He was a very fortunate man. In James's life everything considered luck had gone his way. It was James that had eventually destroyed his life to his detriment and the detriment of others. Things came easy for James just as the current circumstance were presenting themselves. Being a servant was not a satisfactory conclusion to James. He wanted a position of power and most of all he wanted a position that led him back to Liverpool. This seemed to be a driving force that focused his decisions in life down one narrow and destructive path. There was a fog of obsession to it.

Pete moved close to James when the man was in the kitchen making tea. Pete said "Play along with the situation. Find out about the man over the next two days and find what valuables there might be. We will sail on the third day but if I must do away with this man we might as well find what gains we can make. I know you will need some means since you do not get a share on ship so I will give you one fourth of our gains in this endeavor!"

James thought to himself that he had no choice as he had to crew on this ship to get back to England. He did know that he could take many of the quick items for his own before Pete would know about them. If worst comes to worst he would simply end the man's life a little earlier than planned. James said to Pete "Got it! I will keep my eyes and ears open and investigate things when I can without being caught!"

Pete had his tea and retired for the evening. After his exit the man took James around the house and outlined to him what his duties would be and showed him the storage of the cleaning materials, his clothing, the food pantry and his bath/personal necessities. They set up a tentative schedule to go to market and what kinds of foods and items that the man enjoyed. Later that evening the man told James that his family had owned some mining interests in diamonds and gold and held some farming interests and an export business. He kept some inventory in the house and other inventory in a secure box at his office. The family was wealthy. The man's parents had died in an insurrection in the city and he was left alone. The north of Africa was a Muslim stronghold. Many of those enslaved could find their freedom by converting from Christianity. This freedom was really no freedom at all but carried some advantages over remaining Christian. He had no brothers or sisters and the aunts and uncles were far away and long forgotten. In fact it would most likely be a surprise to them if they knew of the man at all. The scene was shaping up to be the perfect situation for James. Diamonds could easily be hidden from Pete and transferred with him on his person. He would target the diamonds in advance of Pete's return and then focus on the gold. The Gold was much heavier and cumbersome. He would split with all of the other items they could take except the ones that could be hidden away. He knew that these smaller items were the most valuable. James knew that he must move quickly and waited for the man to get into deep sleep before rising from his bed and searching the house for information and the valuables hidden there.

The following morning James made sure that he was awake before the man. He went to the kitchen and started the tea and looked around for breakfast items. He found some bacon and eggs and made some corn meal muffins. There were some fruit preserves and butter to go with the biscuits. He cut up some fruit for a plate. This included melons, dates, and seasonal fruits from the area. Some were foreign to him but he put them on the plate anyway. The man came to the table and ate ravenously while chatting the whole time. It was apparent that the man had missed companionship and seemed to be making up for lost time. It is a weakness of this sort to begin to trust too early. The man was not an exception and gave trust because he wanted to bare his soul to have a friend. He felt the best way to promote that relationship was to open up and give his trust. This was a terrible move and would not have been recommended by anyone he knew---if indeed there were any acquaintances around. It made his victimization that much easier. After breakfast he announced that he would be going to his office. James would accompany him. The man knew that even though he had befriended him that James was a captive just one day before and could try to escape. The man dressed while James cleaned up the kitchen.

They made their way to town in the carriage. James was in his new suit and the man was dressed for business. When they arrived they were met by a black man who took the carriage and put it in the livery attached to the business. The office was impressive. The man had his own building close to the docks. It was far enough away from the docks that the foul odors of the slave and fish markets did not permeate his work world. He owned this building and was the only occupant. His offices were housed in it. They were finely appointed and there were several men and women earnestly at work when they arrived. Some were accountants and some were traders along with their support staff. There was an office of geologists who did the scientific work on the diamond and gold mines and measured their take for size, carat and value. James became excited because he knew that there would be treasure to be had here. The man made his rounds and introduced James to the others. For the most part James let the introductions go unnoticed except the names in the geologist's office and the accounting people. These he felt he could use over the next few days to determine the values assigned to the items here. The man did not fathom that James would understand the bookkeeping or any of the work being laid out before him. Those men of the sea that he knew were largely illiterate and centered on drinking, carousing and hard work requiring little intelligence. This assumption played right into James's plan. He had open access to all of the things in the office. This provided him with a detailed map towards his goals.

James had learned that the geology office kept large amounts of gold nuggets, ingots, and diamonds for grading and testing in the vaults. He indeed saw these items while he wondered through the office unattended and unnoticed. The scientists were busy going about their business. The man thought that it was good that James was showing an interest in his work. He did not suspect his actual motives.

The day progressed and the man left James at the office and went into the market for the evening meal. He was gone almost an hour and this gave James time to go through the drawers and materials in his office. During his search he found some papers and drawings of inventions the man had developed or was developing from the simple to the complex. One caught James eye. It was a simple walking stick. In one end, at the head, was a dagger and hollowed out in the middle was a storage area with a wood plug that could be opened and closed. The hollowed area ran the length of the walking stick minus the dagger area. James thought this to be a handy item for many purposes and looked around the room to see if there was anything there that would match the plans. He found nothing. He had a productive day and when the man returned it was time for the carriage ride to his home

James prepared the meal of chicken, vegetables, fruit and bread. He prepared it in the English style for which the man was very grateful. The cooks he had work for him locally had always cooked in the local way with different methods, spices and tastes. He longed for the food of his childhood and finally he was getting a taste of it. He felt the rushes of memories from his past. He thought to himself what a good idea it had been to buy James. James served a bottle of wine and some brandy after dinner. The man was satisfied with his meal. The alcohol and the heaviness of the meal made him sleepy. He retired early leaving James to roam the house. He searched high and low but could not locate diamonds or gold in the house. He had to search the man's room and waited until he was in deep sleep. He pushed in silently with a candle and quietly searched the wardrobe to no avail. He got down on the floor and looked under the bed and his mouth curved into a smile. There he found not one—but two strong boxes and upon further examination one was very heavy and the other of the same size but lighter. He knew they held a treasure but he would not be able to discover what it was for now as they were both locked. He made note of the key hole and slipped out of the room looking for keys. James looked through desks and drawers and the man's clothes but did not locate the keys to the boxes. It really did not matter as they could be opened by force after leaving the house and back on board the departing ship, however, James wanted them open to see what he could confiscate before he had to divide the booty with Pete. He felt that the keys were hidden in a clever space but would take his time and think about it and hope a solution would come to mind.

The following day he feigned illness and the man left him at the house by himself. It was a risk but the man knew if he was going to run he would and there was no stopping it----he could only have him caught. On the up side—the price paid was very low and would be a small loss. The man liked James though and felt that it would be hard to find someone from the auction like him. He gave his trust to him early and hoped for the best

James did an all-out search now that the man was away and he was alone in the house. The regular cook was at the market in town for most of the day. She was now only there to cook the main evening meal and help out as James assumed his long term duties. James went room to room and was down on the floor when he was startled by a loud voice saying "What are you doing there?"

It was Pete who had entered the house and he had a nose for something being amiss in the scene he had found.

James scrambled to his feet and said "Pete, you startled me! I was looking for the valuables like we discussed."

"Have you found any?" asked Pete

"No, not yet" lied James. In this he seemed convincing

enough but Pete dealt with all kinds of scoundrels and would have his ears and eyes wide open. "I have found some personal belongings that might be worth something but I have to take more time to find anything else. That is why I told him I was sick to get access to the house!" replied James.

"You best be straight with me mate—I have taken a risk and it would go very hard for you if I find otherwise?" declared Pete

James shuddered inside at the thought but knew that Pete was not a very intelligent person. Like many of his kind he used brute force to control his world instead. He would have to start making a plan to overthrow him if his long-term plans were to succeed. For right now he would not risk it until he had established himself on board ship out at sea. "I will find things for us before we go. The man has gold mines and there should be at least some around here or the office to take with us when we go." said James. James knew that the heavy trunk under the bed would satisfy Pete's desire and held it in reserve to be used as a negotiating tool if needed.

Pete said "I will help you look then"

James was quick "That cannot be done—the cook is due back and the man is working a short day. He could be home anytime---I was hurrying when you came in and have lost this time for searching. It is probably best that you not be seen here until the proper time." Pete hesitated but knew that it would be much more productive to wait and follow his plan then to move too fast. He begrudgingly said his goodbyes with another warning to James about crossing him on the deal and how bad things could happen to him if he considered being dishonest. He then left and promised to make contact the next day---the day that the plan was to be acted upon. He could wait a day.

James continued his search and finally found a treasure in its own right that contained the keys. It was under the chair where the man sat. Built into the front kick pad was a drawer. Visually it could not be detected but James discovered it while searching the undercarriage of the chair. He pulled open the drawer and there was a wooden box inside. Inside the wooden box he found a magnifying glass, scales, and some other utensils used to handle and view gemstones. He lifted the false bottom of the box and found approximately twenty small cloth bags bulging with contents. Several of the bags contained diamonds of various sizes and colors. Others contained opals, pearls, rubies, topaz, emeralds and others exotic stones that he had apparently collected through his mines or in trade for diamonds. They were to James's eye valuable and large stones. James realized immediately that these could be hidden away easily and would not be a part of the division with Pete. He closed the box and placed it back where it was to appear undisturbed. He sat down in the chair and stared across the room and what was there---- the walking stick. It appeared to be just as in the plan he had seen with the dagger top and the storage compartment in its body. Pete pulled out the dagger which was high quality steel and it shined in the light. It fit his hand nicely and he could see it as his companion on the ship for protection. He pried off the wood plug and was again pleased to find the walking stick full of diamonds of high quality. The man was very wealthy. He took the keys and opened the boxes under the bed and found as he anticipated a large store of gold in various forms. There were coins, ingots, gold dust and some gold figurines. The second box was heavy but not as heavy as the first. When he opened it he found more stones, gold and silver. He fashioned a pack and quickly placed his belongings in it. He would pass this off to Pete as his personal things and would use it to conceal and move the stones. Once on board he would go to his old hiding places and stash the stones so they could not be found. James finished just a few minutes before the cook came back from the market. He worked with the cook in preparing the meal and cleaning. The man returned to the residence about two hours later and the meal was ready. Again James served much alcohol to make the man sleepy and groggy so he would retire early. James needed some sleep too! After all tomorrow would be a big day.

The day dawned early. James had to move quickly around the house. The cook would not be arriving until the late afternoon. James feigned illness again to stay home and the man was bolstered by the fact the James had not ran away the day before. He felt he could trust him on that issue. James had fashioned his illness around the long voyage and the conditions at the slave market. The man was overwhelmed by guilt feelings about the market and probably did not question James's motives because of it. It was a hindrance to him to have him at his office and in his way during his work routine. He dressed and merrily went to work. As the carriage pulled away James moved quickly. He retrieved the keys to the boxes and quickly loaded as many of the jewels into the walking stick as possible. He then took his breeches and opened the lining quickly inserting the bags of gems into the pockets he had sewn there and then stitching the lining closed to conceal them. With what he had already concealed he would be a rich man but James was a greedy man and began making plans for the jewels and gold located at the office. He had anticipated Pete showing up and was not disappointed when he felt a presence off of his left shoulder and turned to find Pete standing there. Pete was in a foul mood and James actually felt fear of him in the initial confrontation of this day. It was short-lived as Pete demanded to see what he had found and James took him to the bed and opened what remained in the two boxes with the Keys. There were large amounts of gold in many forms, some jewels of lower quality and the keepsakes. James promised Pete more treasure when they would raid the office on the way to the ship as they made their escape from port. Pete's mood brightened noticeably and there was now camaraderie that developed between the two. Pete was becoming an ally of James in this period which was an unexpected consequence of the events. James knew it would be of use later as the events would play themselves out in time.

They ate and drank and waited for the cook and the man to come. Pete had brought with him two large trunks in case they were needed to haul the items that they would take. They were in a rented wagon that was parked behind the house and out of sight. James had stored all of the gems in his clothing and the walking stick and knew that they would be safe until he had a chance to hide them on board the ship on night watch. They drank some more.

By midafternoon the men heard a noise and the cook entered the house with the market items for the evening meal. She was an older dark woman with a noticeable limp. James had not bothered to get to know her because he knew her fate at the time of their meeting. There was somewhat of a language barrier between them anyway. James sat in the kitchen area not helping her in her struggle with the items she was carrying. It would be easier for Pete if her hands were full and she was unable to defend herself. As she entered the kitchen Pete sprang from behind the door and came up behind her driving his knife up under her ribs while encircling her throat with his arm to hold her. The knife was about ten inches long and he had inserted it to the hilt in an upward motion. When he reached the hilt he twisted it to the right a half turn and then withdrew it and stabbed again. He felt her tighten and struggle just a little. He felt the wind leave her lungs and then the relaxing of her body. He knew that she would live a little while longer in agony and laid her on her back to watch the life slip away. Pete had always enjoyed surveying his work and watching the horror on their faces and the questioning of the eyes. James felt nothing at all---just another part of the plan coming together and a piece of the plan being completed. It was strange how he could be so sensitive about his plight and what happened in his family but not have any feelings about the grief and chaos that he wrought in his new life upon others in his quest for revenge.

It is long thought that each man has a soul. Men of this sort have either lost theirs or never had one to begin with. There are evil things that walk this world and we will all come face to face with these living demons. We might simply pass them by on the street but we might find ourselves facing them like the cook. We might not recognize them until it is too late. The point is that we cannot assume nor are we meant to understand the existence of these soulless men and woman or why they permeate our lives and the world in general. It is an advantage to accept that they will eventually and inevitably cross our paths and learn to recognize these enemies early on in normal daily interactions. This gives us a better chance of surviving the encounters.

Pete retrieved one of the trunks and opened it. They loaded the cook into it and slammed it shut and returned it to the wagon. James cleaned up the blood and disarray so there would be no evidence of the disturbance when the man returned to the residence. James put on the meal and started it cooking. Pete and James loaded the boxes from under the bed onto the wagon and covered all of the cargo with a large tarp. They moved another trunk into the undergrowth near the house for later use. Pete spent some time going through the house and deciding what additional things he would liberate before they left for the office. He found some pistols, a sword and cutlass that he would take. He found some trinkets that he would most likely use as gifts to ply women in foreign ports and some cash and coin.

There was a noise at the door and James was startled. The man had come home early and Pete was still in the house. James went to the door and distracted him with a cup of tea allowing Pete to escape out the back door and into the yard. Pete had taken some of the articles that he had planned to steal. He thought it would be a good idea to move some of the things out now so it would shorten the time after the initiation of the plan. This was a mistake.

James came into the kitchen and the man followed him. James was acting somewhat nervous and the man began to question him as to how the day went. He noticed that the cook was not at her station and questioned James.

"It is certainly not like Marita to miss a day. Have you heard from her today?" asked the man.

James quickly replied "I thought I heard her here earlier but I was in the other room. When I came to the kitchen she was not here."

"Where did the market items come from then? Did you go to the market?" asked the man

"No I have been here all day." replied James

"Then she must have been here as these items were not here when I left the house. It is odd behavior that she would not talk to you and tell you she was leaving?" the man said to James a little more alarmed. "Something seems out of place!"

"I don't know why she would come and go without telling me, sir! I hardly know her or her habits!" James shot back.

"Maybe not! I do expect that you would make it your business to run the household in a way that these things would not be a mystery!" the man replied.

James was not in the mood to be accused of anything or under suspicion. He knew the timing of the events were critical and there was a risk to having to take an action too soon! "I will remember that and try to do better!" he replied on edge.

"I hope dinner will not be delayed. In the meantime I will go to Marita's house and get to the bottom of this" stated the man.

"The meal will be finished in minutes. It would be better that you ate before it has gone to ruin. Maybe you could go after we are finished." countered James

"I am concerned of her health or condition sir, do you have no compassion?" shot back the man. "We will eat and then we will both go in search of her!" he commanded.

James knew that this would expose their plan. They would have to complete their deeds with an earlier time frame. He would have to get word to Pete of the problem and he would have to be very careful not to be caught. The man's mood had turned sullen. While James was finishing the meal the man disappeared into the house. James could hear mumbles and scraping and furniture being moved. He tried once to find the man and spy on him to see if he had possibly missed any of the valuables that were in abundance in the house but could not leave the food cooking for fear of burning it. He took the opportunity to signal Pete to the back entrance and alerted him of the man's state of agitation and the possibility that he suspected something was amiss. Pete wanted to move immediately to end it and move on but James convinced him that a raucous was not in their best interest to get the maximum reward from the plan. He would simply feed him, ply him with alcohol and as he slept they would initiate the events that would make them rich and get them back aboard ship as planned. Fortunately the man had not checked the trunks under the bed to find that they were missing. James kept interrupting his search with chores and distractions until finally they settled into the seats around the kitchen for the food. James served it generously with a bottle of wine and later after dinner brandy and then a stiff drink. The man's mood mellowed greatly and he decided that he would stop by Marita's house on the way to the office the following morning. As he was reading his Bible he drifted off to sleep. Pete entered the back room on James's signal and they moved towards the sleeping man. Pete approached from his front and James had moved in behind him. Pete had his knife out and began the attack. As he approached he tripped over the wine glass the man had sat on the floor in front of him and the noise startled him. He rose from the chair quickly and his hand reached under his coat. Pete had not totally recovered but scrambled to get his footing and continue his attack. The man drew a pistol and leveled it at Pete and fired striking him in the shoulder and spinning him around to the ground. He started to move forward but felt a sudden sharp pain in his back and James came down hard with the dagger from the walking stick and pierced the man right below the neck in his back. The dagger dug in and did its gory duty. James twisted the dagger for maximum damage and Pete had recovered and brought his knife across the man's throat slicing cleanly through the carotid artery causing a bloody fountain to come forth splattering the floor, walls and himself with the gooey red gushes. Pete seemed to have a small smile turn the corner of his lips even in the pain he must have felt. James caught the man and laid him back into the chair. He rushed out to the bushes and recovered the second trunk and with Pete's limited help loaded the man into it and drug it out the door. James retrieved the wagon now and moved it close to the back door of the house. They loaded the rest of the items on their list and the two trunks. He knew that if anyone entered the house at this point the blood would be a giveaway that foul play that had transpired there. He quickly took the oil lamps and poured the oil all around the room and throughout the house. He would burn the house to cover the evidence and keep the locals busy fighting the fire while they plundered the office of the man on the other side of town. They would have no choice but to turn out every man, woman and child to fight the blaze. If allowed to burn it would quickly spread to the wooden structures throughout the city and burn unhindered until it burned itself out. There would be no time for anyone to think that there was foul play or that the plan was still underway.

Pete was distracted with the wound he received so James was able to easily hide the jewels that he would keep for himself. They finished loading and took the wagon towards the office to collect the articles that James had found on his visit there. He would allow the gems from the office to go into the split in order to deflect any suspicion from Pete. The expected treasures would be accounted for in the final take. He felt that there would be about one hour in the office and was prepared to deal with anyone that would be there if anyone had lingered behind. He was happy to see that the office lights were off and it appeared deserted. They pulled the wagon to the back of the office in the alley and James dismounted and took the bundle of keys he had taken from the man. It took just a few minutes to find the correct key and gain entry. Pete followed. He was in extreme pain by this time and noticeably favoring his arm and shoulder. James pointed out quickly what needed to be loaded and the big issue would be moving the gold. James had to unload some of the gold and then reload it into the wagon. When this was completed he spread the oil from the lamps on the floor and again ignited it into a consuming ball of flame. As the first pops of the fire began to take hold they were astride the wagon and heading for the docks. Pete was passed out by this time from blood loss and needed medical care. James could not have cared less about the man's survival but knew that he would have to keep him alive long enough to get the place on the crew---after that it didn't matter what outcome befell Pete. In fact, James felt if he acted it out correctly he could appear to be in charge through Pete's stupor and trust. He would certainly try to sell this to the crew as they arrived. As he pulled up to the ship he came to a fast stop. James shouted "You men! Come here and help with this wagon and the Captain! Don't dally, he is ill!"

The first man down the gang plank was the biggest and as usual would be the test that James would face. James was aware of it and that the crew would be watching. Survival of the fittest is what sea life was all about. The man sauntered up to James and said "What makes you think you can be giving orders? You are the slave!"

"I have the authority of the Captain to issue these orders and I tell you again---get the Captain on board and this wagon unloaded into the Captains quarters. Get his wound looked at immediately" shouted James. The man hesitated and stared into James's eyes. They locked their gazes and James anticipated the big man's next move.

The big man said "I don't think we will be taking orders from a slave!" The big man reached across to grab him. James ducked low and retrieved the dagger from the head of the walking stick. He took a large slice behind the man's knee in the soft tissue severing the cartilage and ligaments and making this leg useless for life. The man went down like a large sack of potatoes and was writhing in pain. James was over the man with the dagger to his throat as he landed and ordered the crew to care for the Captain and unload the wagon as he had previously ordered. He looked at the big man and said "You bloomin' idiot! Did you not think that my orders were reasonable? The Captain was here to hear them and disagree if this was not what he wanted done! Now you are no good to the crew or yourself. You will not be going to sea with us!"

The big man shouted "You can't do that, I am the first mate!"

James said "…and you have had your last sail" as he cleanly sliced the dagger across the man's throat knowing that he would put on a bloody and impressive show for the crew. He gurgled and struggled then lay very still. James shouted "Pick him up and take him on board we will dispose of the body at sea!" The men scrambled down to the dock and hoisted the big man on board.

Pete was taken to his quarters and the ship's doctor went to his side. The ball was still in the wound and it had shattered the collar bone and a part of the scapula. The tissue damage was extensive as these guns shot a large caliber round. Getting the ball out would not be a problem and they gave Pete many rounds of rum getting him ready for the surgery. He would be awake when the cutting was going on and would have to bear the pain with the help of more rum. There was a large entry hole but the exit damage was three times worse. A huge chunk of flesh and bone was missing and the doctor could not close the wound. He cauterized the bleeding with a large heated knife burning the bleeding areas so they would clot. He packed the wound with clean bandages and poured some rot gut whiskey onto them to cleanse the wound. James had seen this type of wound before and the outcomes had not been good. Adding the filthy conditions of the ship it was likely that the wound would become infected. If that happened death was certain. The danger was always infection. James explained that they could not leave him behind and ordered them to make sail as soon as the wagon load of items was aboard and stowed in Pete's quarters. This they accomplished in short order with many hands. The glow from the fire at the man's house could be seen in the distance and the town had emptied to fight that fire. The flames could spread quickly if not contained and engulf many more structures. The flames from the man's office were visible now also and the response was being formed. The diversion was a good one and no one would miss the ship leaving port or even remember them being there for days now.

Pete would recover as long as there was no infection. They would have to keep the wound clean and freshly dressed but at this point it was becoming beneficial to James for Pete to succumb to his wound. He was positioned to take over the ship if Pete died. This was the best chance he would have as Pete would be unconscious and unable to countermand the orders given by James. Nor could he alert the crew that he had not given James any authority to act. James was aware that this would be the fifth death at his hands if you did not count his wife; Ann. He was keenly aware that this would not be his last murder and this gave him a perverse thrill. The ship slipped out of port and into the sea. They were out of harm's way now and the sails were fully opened and moving the ship at a good clip on its way back to the Irish Sea. They could not know of what lay ahead for them there.

James called a meeting of the crew and established that he would run the ship until the Captain recovered telling them that this was on the Captain's authority. They took the big man and tossed his body overboard where they knew the sharks would feast. James led them to the two trunks with the man and Marita's bodies in them and had them thrown overboard and weighted in the open sea. He had survived the misadventure now and had positioned himself to return to England with the ability to strike a blow at his enemies. He was not aware that his enemies in his absence had been preparing for just such a battle.

Peter's Return to Society

Things had been falling into place for Peter. His clientele had increased and he had hired some apprentices in his accounting firm. Peter was a hard taskmaster and expected his workers to keep the same lifestyle that he himself kept. This lifestyle was to get up, eat a large breakfast, go to the office, eat a large lunch work until dark and return home for a large dinner with aperitifs afterwards. His workers could not afford the large meals or drinks however. Peter's weight had quickly blossomed and he was approximately three hundred pounds at this point in his life. He was sedentary in his work and got little exercise except his mind and fingers on the pen and ledgers. His personal habits were slipping and he had a disheveled look to him. He had to have his clothes made special to fit his large frame as none were available to him in his size in the normal course of business.

Peter fashioned himself as a good catch for some woman and felt a need to have a son. It would be the end of the Ambrose line if he failed at this endeavor. He felt like it was his destiny to restart the family. He had a need to return his family to their past standing that Ann had so cherished. Unfortunately with his weight issues and slovenly personal habits no local girls were finding him desirable for marriage. This did not bother Peter in the least. A bride could be purchased if necessary and this seemed to suit his needs much better than a local girl. With a purchased bride it was more of an employer/employee relationship instead of having to deal with the emotions of a real relationship. This he felt would avoid the pitfalls of marriage that he had seen with his mother and father. He would be the leader of the household and people would follow his commands, including his wife, whoever that might be. He contracted a matchmaker to make the arrangements for a wife. He set out her physical features including hair length and color, eye color, religion, cultural background, education and ethnicity. Not so strangely this woman strongly resembled Katherine Houghton Henshaw in appearance. Other than his mother she was the only woman he had ever really known. When this was all complete and reviewed by the close circle of consultants he kept around him the woman he had custom designed acted much like Ann on paper. The one exception would be her subservience to him. He had created a hybrid of the two most dominant women he had known. Peter was clear that the marriage consultant check for mental illness in the family of the bride before presenting her to him for marriage. In any form, Peter would bring the women to the house and have her stay there until he decided on the one to be his bride and the mother of his son. In his mind the woman would not be much more than a surrogate and a nanny. This suited his demeanor and expectations of the relationship. The overwhelming task now would be to find a woman who would have him or a family willing to sell their daughter off in such a way. During the troubling times with political upheaval brewing between Parliament and the King it was not hard to find the latter. Peter was determined to have for his wife a subservient woman that would not ever rise up and reign over him in the way his own mother had administered their household. A woman like his mother in this respect would simply not do. Rather, the woman he sought would be patient without being seen, heard or wanting to speak her mind and yet be competent with the household and marital duties required of her. Peter wanted a son to carry on the family and to this end he entered into this quest.

After several months and several introductions Peter was introduced to Ann Johnson. She was known by her friends as simply Annie. She was from a lower station of society but not so low to be considered a commoner. She had no misconceptions of her duties or the social climbing tendencies and pressures that came from Peter's mother and her family. There was what seemed to be a comfortable ambiance in her presence. Annie wanted children and security. From her family history security had always been illusive and she was willing to shoulder many adverse things in life to achieve this one personal wish. She was not physically attracted to Peter but knew that sex and motherhood with him would be a part of the bargain. Peter was not the romantic type and this duty would be more of a business arrangement than a personal need. She was pleasant, intelligent and willing to keep the peace even if it meant being subservient within tolerance. Annie was not a natural beauty like Katherine Houghton but to Peter he was making his own match and he knew what qualities and habits he would accept. In many ways this was like hiring an apprentice or worker and he approached it in the same way. Annie and Peter spent time together over the next several months. Annie felt fortunate and appreciated Peter's intelligence. She was put off by his demanding nature and his appearance but in the end she made her own compromises to achieve her ultimate goals. An arrangement was made and Peter and Annie were 'wed' in a small civil ceremony with no guests in the summer of 1636. Peter was moving forward in his life and after the original adjustment period it was back to business as usual. Peter was now just twenty-two years old but had his business in good shape and was legitimately making his way. It seemed that the influence and shadows of his mother and father had been cast away and there was a level of acceptance in the local society. Peter was happier than he had been in some time and consciously sparred with himself to give up his vendetta against the Henshaw family. It was a pivotal time and Peter struggled with the decision. When he thought he had it decided the past and the hatreds would creep back into his brain and he would begin the process all over again in a cyclical thought pattern that lasted for months. There were social invitations that now came that had been withheld. Annie was a very likable woman and she enjoyed the social life. Peter was still Peter and did not mix well in these circumstances but he would venture out with Annie's urging to fulfill his own obligations to the family. It does not mean that he liked or felt comfortable about it. Inevitably the circumstances of the past would raise their ghosts at these affairs and Peter would feel the old rumblings of the negative feelings that these issues brought to light. Charles noticed that Peter was ambiguous. He should be very happy but there was always a dark cloud around him. Annie picked up his spirit but a fog always entered after these social get-togethers ended. He would become moody, short-tempered and depressed. It was not from missing his father---he most likely hated his father for many reasons. He still had the dual identity issues with his mother---the one of the nurturing and loving mother and the other the monster who did such evil things in the name of society and mental illness. All of it had its impact and all of it still stirred inside of Peter in a dark and unpredictable way. An all-encompassing fear arose in Peter that he would eventually sink into the mire of mental illness and that there was nothing he could do to escape his fate. It was bred into his very being.

Within months of the marriage Annie announced that she was with child and the preparations for its birth began. The house was a whirlwind of change. The rooms were painted, a nursery room was selected and outfitted for the baby's arrival and the areas around the house were trimmed and cleaned up. The house had gone into a mild state of disrepair during the period of Peter's return from school and his marriage to Annie. Charles had urged him to keep the work on the house current but Peter had no real flair for anything that took him from his ledgers. It was apparent to all that Annie had a knack for this work and threw herself into it with gusto. The appearance of the house and its lawn and garden's now exceeded its appearance when Ann was alive. The environment had a light and breezy air when Peter was away and even when Peter was home he only dampened the glow that Annie put forward in minor details like a passing cloud casting a brief shadow on the ground. Peter found this brightness and happiness to make him uneasy and suspicious of how it could happen. He wondered if there was someone else in Annie's life or if she would take his money and betray him in the future. All of the paranoid ramblings of the mental illness that had consumed his mother were beginning to peek out of the corners of his mind now and it frightened him back into the dark recesses of those thoughts and his helplessness in those old times. The need to lash out at something to rectify the injustices of the past had never left him. He was barely able to contain it. He knew that there would be a time and a place that he would find his own vengeance and he just needed to be patient. For at least this time Annie and the pending delivery of an Ambrose heir could not fail to brighten his life to some degree. These were the mood fluctuations that Charles, Annie and friends were seeing and they did not know what to make of them.

Henry, Sea Captain

Henry was feeling the call to the sea. The first few outings were orientation and the crew hazed him like any other sailor even though he partially owned the fleet. Henry would have had it no other way. He felt to lead men you had to have a full range of experience and earn his own respect. He set about to perform every duty on the ship from the lowest of the ship hands to the highest duties of Captain. The differences in the two Captains from which he had learned his skills were dramatic and he would be different than both of them. Roger was a true pirate and therefore approached his task with no sense of humanity or fear of the outcome. It was all or nothing and it was a foregone conclusion that he would not live to be an old man. Captain

Robertson started his career on a merchant ship, signed on to a Pirate ship and then found middle ground as a contracted privateer. Henry saw himself as more of a Naval Captain for the protection and honest use of the sea. He fashioned himself as the enemy of the pirates; who would murder, steal and abduct innocent people like cattle. Captain Robertson would operate under the rules of his charter with the Henshaw family and Roger would constantly be the black sheep of this group; knowing the rules of the charter but always stretching them to his advantage. One thing for sure was that he had no need for abduction or slavery under his current duties so the darkest of his arts were kept in check.

Henry's first battle was a short one. Captain Robertson's ship found a pirate vessel at anchor and attempted to move into gun range of it. The ship was small, nimble and fast and anticipated the moves in a professional manner. Knowing they were outgunned and outmanned the ship simply hoisted anchor and fled. Several volleys of cannon fire were dispelled after it and at least one hit scored but it did not damage the ship sufficiently to slow it down. There was no boarding of the vessel or hand to hand combat in this encounter. Pursuit was inevitable but it was known that the smaller ship would make its getaway by its speed differential alone. Not far into the pursuit and ship entered a fog bank and disappeared. The crew was anxious because this was the first chance to accumulate the plunder that they all would split---they had come up empty.

The second encounter went much better. The pirates were on a ship much like Captain Robertson's ship. Robertson was seasoned however in the ways of the sea and had guns well stocked and ready for battle. It is probable that there was not a ship in the Irish Sea as heavily gunned or manned as this ship. In a standing battle it would be difficult to defeat. They kept the guns stowed and covered and flew a merchant flag to draw the pirates into gun range and at the proper time they would unveil their true identity when it was too late to disengage and flee.

Henry thought this to be brilliant and a learning experience. The pirate ship fired its first volley across the bow of the ship warning it to stop and be boarded. The pirates must have thought they had found easy prey. This was becoming a rarity for them as even true merchant ships were arming themselves. They sailed in closer and Captain Robertson was on deck in his full glory. The ship even feigned fright and chaos in order to fool the attackers into a sense of security and surprise. The pirates came along side and anchored. Henry estimated twenty four guns on the ship and a crew of around one hundred and twenty five men. This stood in comparison to fifty plus guns and a crew of three hundred and fifty aboard Robertson's ship. These assets were kept hidden behind the ramparts that had gun ports that could be flipped open quickly. Behind these ramparts the gun crews were standing in ready and the cannon was loaded. The marines were assembled and squatted in hiding. Robertson allowed the pirates to send three boarding parties into the water of some sixty men—almost half of their crew. They would be easy targets on their way across the water to board. They would allow them to get half way between the two ships before Robertson would spring his plan into action. All was silent and hidden until that time. The boarding boats for the marines were covered with sail material but ready to launch as soon as the boarding party from the pirates ship was dealt with in the isolated waters between the two ships. Robertson knew that the crew left aboard the pirate ship would not be able to man only about one third of their guns that were facing the battle field or about four working guns that would be firing against at least twenty-five in the return volleys aimed at their gun emplacements. Even with a full crew they would have been outgunned 25 to 12. Make no mistake—four guns were still dangerous and deadly but with their crew extended and the realization of the overwhelming fire power the pirates might surrender or turn and run---but they would not be fast enough in this attack because of Robertson's planning. These pirates were aware that their death was imminent whether it came in the battle or after capture in the gallows. Most likely they would fight to their deaths. Robertson would not allow Henry to go on the first wave of attackers and risk injury and displeasure with his employers. He would board on the second wave and Captain the boat back to harbor after it was taken if it was not sunk in the action. Realistically that was to be the last option as the boat needed to be afloat to claim their rewards. The pirates in the landing boats had just crossed the half-way point and were completely committed and exposed on the open water. The trip back to their own ship at this point would take longer than completing the mission and attacking the ship as they would have to turn their boats to the broadside to retreat. This would be suicide. The marine sharpshooters on deck and the cannon would have a turkey shoot. Even though it was unlikely that any of them would ever reach the ship alive they were committed.

Suddenly there were flashes of motion all up and down the port side of the ship. The cannon doors were opened and the assault boats uncovered and the launching process was underway to board the pirate vessel. The sharpshooters took aim on the individual boat captains on the landing party and fired. The three boats rocked with the shots and the respective leaders fell dead. Six cannon focused on the landing boats along with the Marine's long guns to stop them before they reached the ship or could return any substantial fire. The other cannon fired the first volleys at the ship itself. There were two direct hits on deck and various short and long shots. The pirates were taken by surprise. They turned their guns and the gun crews started to load for return fire. The second volley obliterated two of the remaining four gun crews on the ship and the threat was nullified. The pirates volleyed with the two working guns and one shot was short and the other hit the deck. Two sailors were killed and one had a leg completely severed by the cannon ball. The second rounds were of grape shot which sprayed shrapnel in a wide area when the round exploded taking out any person within its range. This tactic was in preparation for the boarding parties and to eliminate as many guns and personnel as possible reducing the damage to the crew and ships assets and eliminating much of the resistance to boarding. The grape was totally effective on the pirates in the landing boats and they lay dead in the water and spread around the boats in various gory poses. Some were missing arms and some legs others were not recognizable as a human being and most considered the remains as fish food at this point. Any pirates still living would be killed and tossed into the sea. The boats would be recovered and taken back to the ship when it was secured. The outcome of the battle was no longer in doubt---the body count was the question mark! Would any surrender or would they fight to their death? One of the critical points of this attack was the speed of the boarding parties to get on board the opponents ship. The first wave launched in unison with the first volleys of cannon and by the time they passed the pirate landing parties they found the opposition all dead. The remaining crew on the pirate ship was thinking about revenge instead of escape and wanted to get some rounds off to do some damage; which they did. By the time they realized they should have spent their efforts in setting sail it was too late. They worked feverishly after the second volley from their guns to raise sail and move away but this took time and the first assault boats were already pulling along the side and throwing their grappling hooks and ropes. This was an intricate dance of sorts as the men on the ropes were at their most vulnerable. The first up the ropes were the most aggressive and accomplished fighters and those waiting below trained their guns at the ramparts. If an unlucky enemy peered over the side to attempt to stop or slow the boarding the guns below would roar and the fine red mist would erupt over the side. This was a good way to thin out the defending force but also a risk.

By the time the first boarding party was completely aboard there was a force of fourteen pirates to try to repel them. They were greatly overmatched and by the time Henry boarded with the second boarding party they had the last five cornered on the bow rails. The Captain laid down his sword and surrendered which caused a large whoop from the landing party on their conquest. No sooner had the celebration begun when the Captain and his men dropped to the ground and out of their boots came pistols. The Captain aimed at Captain Robertson but the shot never came. Henry had fired and caught the man in the forehead just above the right eye and almost a quarter of his skull was blown away with the shot. Two of the remaining four got their shots away and two of the first party went to the ground wounded. One was gut shot which probably meant death and the other was wounded in the right shoulder. He would be dropped at the next port as he would not be able to perform his duties and there was no room for waste aboard ship. Henry fired his second pistol killing a second pirate who had fired his round at the men. He was now considered blooded in battle and this was a large step for a man at sea. He was accepted now as one of them and the Captain owed him a debt of gratitude that could never be forgotten. The price that Henry paid on this trip and those to follow is to have to question his beliefs, ethics and Christian upbringing and reconcile it with the killing and depravity he saw aboard ship and the pirate's lifestyle. Fortunately the bible had plenty of passages about war, killing, and the lifestyle that he found himself wrapped into on board the ships of sea.

Henry, by 1633 had developed his own strategies. He would captain the flag ship but surround it with faster smaller ships to allow him to surround and engage any pirate ship in force. If they stood to fight they could center fire from all sides. If they decided to raise anchor and flee their speed could be matched and they would be hunted down. By developing different battle strategies and a system of communications between the ships the flotilla would be a formidable foe in the Irish Sea against the pirates. At times Henry's command was joined by Captain Robertson or Roger for short periods and many discussions were had about this strategy and new plans developed. One of these plans was in ship design. Henry wanted a ship that was faster than anything at sea and could be armed sufficiently to fire strategically on the pirates in flight. The objective would be to take the ship but if this was not practical then to engage it, damage it or slow it long enough for help to overtake the battle and make the capture. Several plans were drawn up and sent to William at the ship docks. There were prototypes under construction and being tested at all times. Those that did not fit the bill were sold to merchants who wanted a ship with defenses for their own merchant purposes and these ships could certainly accomplish that goal. On his visits from the sea the talk always turned to ship building and improvements along with updates on the family and the businesses and the political climate of England.

John Henshaw: The Irishman!

John Henshaw had quietly made his way through life in the shadow of William and Henry. William was the focus of the family as the eldest son. Now with Henry turning into the flamboyant man of the sea there was little talk of John's contributions. John had presented the family with the first child of the next generation. Henry had never married and William and Katherine had delayed their entry into parenthood to a later more sane time if one ever came.

The years in Ireland were bittersweet. John and the family were well liked and well thought of in their business and personal lives. John was torn about the treatment of the Irish by the English monarchs in the past and to the present time. There were many military engagements and King Charles kept contingents of troops at his disposal to put down insurrection. The monarchy had long provoked the Irish so they could take their land from them and award it to friends of the crown. By design the Irish were known for their hot tempers and passionate lifestyle. It made it an easy task to provoke them into altercations. This played right into the King's trap. John was torn as the Henshaw ships were engaged in bringing the English troops and supplies into Ireland but he knew that if they refused that Charles would simply confiscate the ships or find another way. John hoped that by bringing passage he would learn of the intent of the troops and hopefully bring about a peace that would stop the killing and raping of the Irish kingdom.

John had mirrored the family businesses that were active in Liverpool in Ireland. He put them in to the ports of Belfast and Dublin and throughout Ulster. John was very much the counterpart of William in Ireland and quickly becoming his equal. John had his own set of strengths. His mind was quite analytical and his problem-solving skills were better than Williams. He devised many of the business ideas that were instituted to improve the businesses and keep them at the forefront of their markets. He was a shrewd businessman and had the knack for negotiations and the making and sealing of agreements. To this end he used the talents in business. These same talents were in his wife's family and the community as a whole on a more personal basis.

Religion had not been taken lightly in Ireland. Predominantly Roman Catholic they were constantly at odds with the King's movement to unite the three kingdoms under one religion and based predominantly on the Protestant Church of England. The Catholics had a hard time with England because of the political visions of the Popes of this time and the violent history of Catholicism in the three kingdoms. It was a hopeful sign to the Irish when Charles entertained an envoy from the Pope, the first in over 150 years, but this was soon diminished by the treatment of the Irish and the occupation and theft of their personal rights and property. The rest of non-Catholic of the United Kingdom's saw it as the opposite and a threat to their personal freedoms.

These misgivings sometimes intruded on John's peaceful life that he so desired. He promoted an atmosphere of tolerance and this was the way their relationship operated except in those periods where the King stirred the pot, so to speak, and created more mistrust or created incidents to provoke Ireland. The Irish were intelligent enough to use the conflict between Scotland and England to their own advantage and they negotiated religious concessions from the King for their pledge to fight for the Royalists. This too had John and the family at odds as the Henshaws and Houghtons were leaning to the Parliamentary side of the conflict. The Irish, to their credit, probably leaned towards the Parliamentary side of the issues too but had to weigh their options to improve their own lot in life. As it all stood the Irish would take arms against William and Evan if war broke out and they were called to the service of the King. Receiving concessions for religious freedom was at the top of the Irish list. John was a politician in his own way and kept a low profile when the subject came to his ear. It was business as usual other than this.

The frequent trips to Liverpool aboard ship had given John a good background as a sailor. Rather than fall back into a role as a passenger on these journeys, John would work as crew and spend the down time speaking and questioning the various Captains and crew members about life at sea. He could easily see the draw that it had on Henry. The brothers knew that any war would surely come to Liverpool because of the importance of the port and its ability to supply a standing army or the King's need to cross Irish troops into England. It was a rare time that the troop movements were aimed at England instead of Ireland but the lull in hostilities was a fine thing for the Irish. Flagging the ships under Ireland's flag seemed like a good decision as the political scene was heating up with the unrest in England and Scotland coming to a head.

Trade between the kingdoms was brisk and with new international ports opening the import and export business was booming. The various businesses in Liverpool and Ireland were all successful at this point and those that were associated with them from the most menial worker to the managers were prospering. King Charles continued to find creative ways to rob the common man of his earnings but overall the situation was positive. John was a family man and his wife and child centered his life and kept him from taking sail as Henry had done. Sometimes he envied Henry but then would consider the trade-off he had made and felt that the scales more than tipped in the favor of his decision to stay on land.

The Family Way

William was away from home more and more in the late 30s and early 40s. This in its own way had an impact on the decision to have a family. When he would return from his travels there would be a passionate interlude between Katherine and William as a celebration of their time together. Children at this time were out of the question but very much desired by both. There was always the shifting timeline of when the situation to bring children into the world would be right. "When I get the business stabilized", "When the political climate settles", "When I am able to be home more often" were all excuses to put off the family. William was a workaholic and the realization would have to set in that nothing was going to change and that the decision would have to be made to have children no matter the circumstance or the time for family would simply pass them by. Children were in the plan----just not now.

James Ainsworth/Ambrose

The ship had been to sea for approaching one week since they had made their escape from Algiers. They left the town in dire straits with fires in both ends of town and the firefighting resources stretched to their limits. The plan had enabled the ship to slip out of port unsuspected and unmolested into open sea. So far James had usurped the power of Pete as he lay in a state of unconsciousness due to his wounds from the man's pistol. The wound was festering and infected. Pete's fever was high and he was in and out of consciousness. James would have to act fast and enlist the services of the new first mate that he had appointed. He would have to make a bargain with the man to declare himself Captain when Pete passed on. It was not if he died any longer but simply when it would happen. James spoke with Pete when he would swim into the real world and trained him to reply "You're the Captain now" when prodded with a set of questions. It would begin with a question about his life at sea and progress to his appointment to Captain of this ship. James's plan was to whisper these things into Pete's ear and his response to the questions "What did the Captain say when you were given your commission?" would bring about the response "You're the Captain now!" would be repeated over and over. On the night watch James brought the first mate, named Chaz into the Captain's quarters for a discussion. He told him of the Captain's condition and his impending doom. He then told him that Pete was in and out of consciousness and had asked that he assume the role of Captain of the ship upon his death. He would need someone to corroborate his wishes and that the first mate would certainly be the party for this epiphany. Chaz was at first hesitant. James said that it would be well worth his time and that his appointment to first mate on a permanent basis would be rewarded for his loyalty with a bigger share in the ships plunder and additional privileges and benefits on board ship and in port. Chaz was quiet for a moment while he let the weight of this statement sink in to his thoughts. Chaz was not stupid. He knew however that he did not possess the sharp mind that it would take to command a ship and survive for very long at sea and in battle. He pictured himself as the head of a ship but there was always that area of his consciousness that whispered he could not do this job and it was this whisper that came to him with his agreement to join James in his coup for control of this ship. After all, James did seem like the type of mind that would not only make the ship successful at plundering other ships and coastal towns but would be able to use his wits to allow for the survival of his ship and crew in tough times. Chaz agreed to be the source and James went to work. He told Chaz that he would have to whisper into the Captains ear as he was having trouble with his hearing and he did not want to risk their conversations being overheard by any other crew. He went through his trained monkey scenario with the Captain and got the desired result. Chaz heard clearly as the Captain said to James "You are the Captain now!" At this point James had no need for Pete and the sooner his demise the better. Later on that night James administered a lethal dose of poison to Pete and by morning he had his own ship.

Since leaving port they had been sailing in tandem with the Captain who had taken his ship and put him in bondage from the Irish Sea to Algiers. This Captain had underestimated him and was unaware of the happenings between Pete and James. James was astride a formidable ship now with fifty cannon and a crew of three hundred and fifty men. The pirate Captain was on board his Corsair with twenty four cannons and one hundred and fifty men. James would have to act quickly while the element of surprise still existed. Once the pirate Captain had discovered the disadvantage in guns and men that he faced he would certainly nullify the threat. He would most likely replace James with a Captain of his choice and James was not willing to give an inch of his ill-gotten gains. The only way to gain the support of his crew against their old Captain was to give the appearance that they were under assault by their former ship and crew. They would need to defend themselves against some of their old shipmates who were now their rivals and enemies. James was an expert at manipulation and immediately began planting the seeds of mutiny about the ship. Initially he passed a story purportedly told to him by Pete that the Captain had a history of cheating his crews out of their shares at the end of the journeys. This was not totally untrue. The Captain did cheat as was the nature of most pirates. It was the threat to life and limb that was added by James, through the silent voice of Pete that set the crews imaginations on fire. The crew was three hundred and fifty men and only about fifty of those had come from the mother ship of the pirate Captain. James would have to grow his support base in the new sailors and began his attack there in the mind before it would become bloody on the deck. The vocal leaders from the old crew would have to be discredited or disposed of entirely to make this work. The body count accredited to James would add many men before this work was done!

During one of the earlier assaults on a merchant ship the Corsair moved in position between James's ship and the merchant ship twice and made it impossible for the ship's guns to fire on its victim or to mount a boarding party. The Corsair fired its cannon and boarded the ship claiming it's booty for the Corsair. The talk amongst the crew on James's ship centered on the Captain of the Corsair failing to yield in the attack or giving them a share the plunder. The momentum was building and James continued to flood the rumor market with tales of distrust and deceit. He had to be creative in his stories and had to source them from old crew members that he had known. Even at this point the crew aboard ship that had served with the Captain could not verify nor dispute the stories and when asked could only state that they did not know either way. Eventually there were stories that the crew on board that had originally manned the Corsair were targets of the Captain's wrath and divided off from the rest for retribution at the proper time. James increased the rum rations so that drunkenness amplified the stories and created a whirlwind of emotion among the crew aimed squarely at the pirate Captain. Eventually during another battle the Corsair again sailed between the ship and its prey and the gun crews this time did not stop firing. At the onset William could see that they were not aiming at the Corsair but there were several near misses as large plumes of water from the cannon rose and splashed the Corsairs deck. James was startled when he trained his spyglass on the decks of the Corsair finding the Pirate Captain and saw him waving his hands frantically and pointing at the ship. He spied the gun crews on the port loading and aiming their rounds at his own ship. He waited; knowing that he would have to suffer incoming fire before turning the firepower of the ship onto the Corsair. This inbound fire would stir the men to action and verify that the rumors of the pirate Captain were true. It only took minutes. Seven guns fired from the port side of the Corsair. Five rounds landed harmlessly in the water just short of the ship but two rounds hit the ship; one damaging the rigging and one landing on deck and decimating three sailors. A cry went up and the cannon crews were already loaded. The Corsair had rowed much closer than they had wanted and were trying to make a turn away from the ship when twenty five cannons opened up on it from starboard. Due to the closeness of the Corsair it took many direct hits but the first volley of hits engulfed the Captain in a ball of smoke and flame. The gun crews in their ire had targeted his command and the officers of the ship were vaporized where they stood. The Corsair was heavily damaged and was listing to port. The screams of the rowers below decks could be heard. Some were terribly injured and some were trying to tear from their chains knowing the ship was doomed and on its way to the bottom. The cannon reloaded and fired another deadly volley tearing into the Corsairs side and opening large wounds that were quickly filling with sea water. In less than fifteen minutes the Corsair and crew had slipped below the surface and disappeared. There were still some deck crew foundering in the water but they were to be left to their own devices or drown. The merchant ship had made for the high seas but James took up pursuit. The crew chanting him on and singing their sea songs at the top of their lungs in a feverish state as the sinking of the ship and the pursuit of the merchant ship had brought their emotions to a bloody pitch. On this day they would not be denied and they would be particularly bloody with the crew and passengers in their agitated state. James set back and allowed the atrocities to go on knowing that this crew had now bonded under his leadership and his self-appointment of Captain of the ship was solidified for as long as he survived. He now had a loyal following but his command would be bloodier than most. He stood in the Captains perch and focused on the far horizon. "Set sail for Ireland and be quick about it Mates!" he shouted.

The Situation of 1638

The decade of the 1630s was coming to an end. It had seen the death of Sir Thomas and Marjorie Henshaw, the marriages of William Henshaw and Katherine Houghton, John and Mary Henshaw and Peter and Annie Ambrose. It had seen the development of the Henshaw businesses and the acclimation of the brothers into them. It had seen the advent of the shipping business and Henry's attachment to the sea. It saw Ellen Henshaw marry John Harrison. This time had also witnessed the dark side of humanity with the murder of Sir Thomas Henshaw by James Ambrose/Ainsworth. It had seen the disgrace of Ann Ambrose and her insanity and demise in the asylum. It had witnessed the capture of James by pirates and his murderous ways to escape them. Politically it had seen a relative time of peace in England change to a volatile condition pitting King Charles I against Parliament and the Scottish Covenanters. It was a time of deceit and upheaval and a time for the Henshaw family to protect themselves and their interests which was partially accomplished by basing their interests in Ireland. It was a risky proposition as the Irish were being drawn into the upcoming conflict on the side of the King with the promises of new freedoms and rights for their religious beliefs and personal dignity. Things were shaping up for war and the King and Parliament were calling their armies to quarter. The Henshaw family had one bargaining chip and it was a large one. With their fleet patrolling the Irish Sea the pirates were lessening their attacks and abductions. The King found this to be helpful by allowing him to commit his Naval capital elsewhere and to lessen the threat of outside interference and troubles in the face of his internal conflicts. In the near future he would invade Scotland setting off the Bishop's Wars and then a long period of three civil wars in England itself dividing the country and cities into choosing one side or the other.

James Ambrose Ainsworth:

As Captain of his own pirate ship he had set sail from Algiers in late 1636. The pirates meandered up the coast of Italy and Spain resupplying and perfecting their terror tactics on their way. As 1638 dawned James was approaching the Irish Sea and his focus was on creating as much havoc as possible to gain a name befitting his bloody command. He was blissfully unaware that the situation in the Irish Sea had drastically changed in his years away and had only heard scuttlebutt in the ports of call where the pirates could debark for a few days of land and fun. He considered the stories to be completely out of proportion to the situation he would be facing knowing the easy ways of the sea when he departed. He had heard some stories of Henry Henshaw as Captain of one of these opposing ships and was delighted at this news.

William and Katherine Henshaw:

Family plans were still on hold approaching 1638. William was active with his father in law in the political debates of the time. Liverpool was in an uproar and the Mayor of Liverpool was firmly on the side of the King in his disputes with Parliament and the Puritans. Evan Houghton was a huge voice in opposition. His family tree claimed another Evan Houghton who two generations prior was the Mayor of Liverpool himself and this was well known to its citizens. It was an awkward situation as most of the citizens of Liverpool leaned against the current Mayor's position and favored the Parliamentarians. For the time being the point of conflict rested firmly in Scotland with the issues of the church being forced to alter their religious ceremonies and traditions by Archbishop Laud. These same changes had been forced into the Church of England over the last few years with a less than favorable reception. The dreaded thoughts that Charles I was leading England back into the control of Rome and the Roman Catholics was a constant threat. Land rights and religious freedoms were hot topics and there simply was no way that land owners and Protestants could accept the rule of Charles I on either issue. It was seen as a way for Parliament and thus, the subjects of the King, to get concessions or some control. They set their sights to reshuffle the doctrine of the exclusive power of Kings. Charles had blundered already and Parliament seized on it to coerce agreements and Archbishop Laud's quest was shaping up to be another confrontation for Charles against his subjects and the three Kingdoms. William, through his business, military and personal contacts was firmly in support of the Parliamentary forces and was aware that Liverpool would be a strategic holding for either side at some point. Most of the family was now in Ireland except for William and his family and Ellen and her husband. The central control of the Liverpool businesses was shifted to Dublin and Belfast making them in essence Irish companies and a sea away from the influence of Charles I. William and his brothers knew that in the realm of the Irish Sea that their Naval flotilla would rival the ships of the King if he chose to confront them or attempt confiscation. The Parliamentarians made note of the formidable force under the shipping company's control. William knew that he would face battle before this conflict found its inevitable end.

John and Ellen Henshaw Harrison:

William had told John and Ellen to prepare for departure to Ireland for their safety during the upcoming troubles and in early 1638 they made the port in Belfast. They would not return unless needed or an end to the conflict and safety at home was assured. John continued in his work with the companies and reported directly to William. John and Ellen remained childless through this time. It was determined that John Harrison would head up the English businesses and John Henshaw would take care of the Irish side and assume the responsibility at the head of the family if anything were to happen to William. This would continue until or if an heir were born to William and Katherine.

Peter and Annie Ambrose:

Life trudged on for Peter. Annie was a different sort. She lit up a room with her bright personality and charmed the harshest person in the room. She was a caring person and a hands-on mother. There was a nanny but the duties and experience was shared between the two. Annie wanted to be a part of her son's life and be there when he cried, walked, talked and became more and more of a man. Joshua was a bright boy and was becoming attached to Annie and indifferent to Peter. Peter for his part remembered his mother and how close the relationship was with Ann. He could not fathom the bond between Annie and Joshua because he could not separate his flawed history of motherhood with the genuine thing. He brooded, doubted, worried and became jealous of the natural love between mother and son. It was what he had wanted with his own mother----it was not what he had received. He saw the mother/son relationship as a threat to his own power over the two of them and did not like it.

Ironically, Annie had achieved the social acceptance that had existed in Ann's fantasy life but never came to reality. Annie, in contrast, was well liked, generous and in demand as a friend. Peter accepted this social status as a duty but loathed the social interaction as a reality. If this was the life his mother had followed then things might have ended differently. It was also partially because of his awkwardness at this social vocation that fed this weakness. The more successful Annie was with her communal duties the more Peter would have to endure. Over time Peter was developing an animosity towards Annie because she effortlessly achieved what her mother had toiled at and failed to achieve in her lifetime. He envied the position that Joshua had in his mother's affections and it wormed its way into Peter's being like a parasite in his family life. Peter's success in the business world continued to flourish but he too felt the winds of conflict coming to Liverpool. His business was not of the sort that could be uprooted and based in Ireland like William had done. His was a service business with a fixed clientele and he knew it would suffer with the fortunes of war.

Captain Henry Henshaw:

Henry had taken to the sea with great success. His apprenticeship under the two old Captains had been a quick study and with the help of William's military tactics and some common sense the use of his flotilla of ships to press an attack on pirates in the area had become very successful. During his first two years at sea with his crews and ships he was personally responsible for the capture of five pirate ships and the sinking of another seven. He had eliminated some twenty-five hundred pirates from this Earth and apprehended another three hundred that were turned over to the King's authorities for trial and probable hanging. The Irish Sea had become dangerous for pirates and several had moved on to areas less protected. There was however a substantial number of pirates and ships who by nature took up the challenge and stayed in the area along with others who were just entering the waters without knowing of its dangers.

Henry loved the sea and found his duty to be a Godly one with benefits to the family, its employees and any who would take to sea in the area for their livelihood. There were adverse effects also. The longer that Henry was at sea the more his conscience and soul tolerated things that he would not have been able to reconcile into his structure of religion and morals from his earlier life. He felt he was becoming Godless like those that surrounded and his enemies. It bothered him that he was responsible for massive deaths even if they were deserved. He worried about his soul. He worried about the loss of innocence in his new world where he saw a dark side of the human spirit that most would never know or understand. He did not have to worry that he was thought of as a hero to the crown and those who counted on the sea for a living or transportation; this was a given. Instead he wondered how he would ever be able to settle down. Would any woman ever accept him with all of the blood on his hands and the mysteries of how he would be finally judged? The church had a way of accepting what they would normally call sin if it benefited them in any way. This certainly was the case here. But Henry had begun to doubt the church and looked more towards his personal relationship with God and wondered if his actions would be as readily accepted when his time would come. He feared his judgment but knew that he must continue. He knew that he was destined to a life of a bachelor and because of his beliefs he did not carouse or take prostitutes as the other sailors under him did. He was sacrificing his happiness and future for his love of the sea and his understanding that his mission was necessary. In affect his bride was the sea and he would follow the path of many of the ancient mariners who came before him.

James Ambrose/Ainsworth

James return to the Irish Sea could hardly go unnoticed. He knew that Henry was Captain of his own ship and making the pirate life miserable in the area. It was his decided action to attack as much shipping as possible in the most outlandish ways so that his reputation and escapades would be the topic of discussion in the ports of call. In this way he hoped to draw Henry out to sea in pursuit of the most discussed pirate in the area to take his prize. James smiled in the anticipation of his crew taking on and killing Henry's ship and crew. The first of the confrontations would not take long. James bore down on the seas just outside the Liverpool harbor. It was not a wise move for a pirate but for James it was just what he wanted to get an expected result. The word spread quickly of the brash pirate who had stationed himself to attack Liverpool shipping just outside of the port. Henry heard of this situation almost as it happened. He called his crews together to answer the challenge. From his spyglass James could see the activity aboard the ships and knew he would soon be at Henry in battle. First he would sneak into port and visit his son. He wished to tell him of his plans for Henry Henshaw.

Peter Ambrose Accounting House in Liverpool

Peter was hard at work in his office with the door closed. Those who worked there knew that this was a sign meaning he was not wanting to be disturbed or distracted from his work. The amount of time that he spent in solitude was increasing and his employees were forced at times to blunder through work on which they needed his guidance to complete for fear of his wrath. Peter heard the bell on the door from the street ringing but knew that his receptionist would handle any walk-in. He heard a loud commotion and was becoming annoyed. Shortly thereafter came a knock on his inner door. He knew that those in the office were aware the meaning of the door being closed. He was not to be disturbed and if they interrupted him they would suffer their fate. Peter pulled open the door and shouted to the woman "What is it! I wish to be left alone to complete my work!"

The woman said "There is a man in the office who demands

to see you! He will not identify himself and he has threatened several of us already. We do not know what to do!"

Peter said "I will handle this! You would do well to take notes of this encounter so that you may handle them yourself. It is what you are paid for you know!" With that he walked into the main office and found a man standing there. He was obviously in disguise and that usually was a good sign that this was not the sort to associate with in your business. Peter shouted "I am not in the market to buy your goods nor to provide you with charity. If these are your purposes you may turn around and leave before I have you put out."

The man replied "Aye---ye would; would you? I doubt any of this bunch would be up for the job! We have things to discuss that is best done in private so will you take me to your office or should I find it myself!" With that he walked past an open-mouthed Peter and found his way to the inner-sanctum of Peter's world. Peter did not appreciate it one bit. He followed the man and entered his office and slammed the door behind them. He said "You sir do not barge into my office without an appointment. Now what is your business and then get out!"

The man now looked intently into Peter's eyes. He said "Do ye' not recognize your own father!"

Peter was shocked. He felt a pang of familiarity when first meeting the man but so much had changed and James did not look anything like he did at their last meeting. He said "My father! This is a joke. You didn't want to be my father when you had the chance. I suspect that you are here for a hand out and that will not be coming. You robbed my inheritance when you left. All I have I have made for myself. You have not been a part of it!"

James said "You are right about that but it is not a hand-out I am after. I have plenty of my own. In fact I would like to store some of it in your safe hands." With that he produced the bags of diamonds and precious stones and tossed them one by one on Peter's desk.

Peter was shocked but then it dawned on him "These must be a part of your other life and I imagine you did little work in mining them. Who did you steal these from father?"

James replied "It doesn't really matter does it. It will never be found out in this lifetime and I might need them for some insurance. I do not want my current business partners to have access to them. You see me laddy that I am the Captain of me own ship now. I have set up business just outside of port and will be lookin' to engage Captain Henry Henshaw in the near future! I will tear him from limb to limb when I find him!"

Peter said "You should think this through! Henry does not travel alone. When he takes to sea he has several ships with him and they have been very successful in ridding the local waters of your kind!"

James hissed "Well, It seems like you have crossed over to their side sonny boy. I would have never expected it from you!"

Peter said "Of this you could not be more in error. I have my own plans to settle those scores but your problems are of your own making and not theirs. You are a fraud and a murderer and you have done me no favors in my own life!"

James said "Nonetheless, I plan for there to be one less after we engage in the waters of the Irish Sea! Don't worry, I no longer carry the Ambrose name. I use a new name for a new life. I will be back for my stones sometime. Consider them a gift if I fail in my mission!" With that he left!

Peter was shaking and angry. His father was now a highwayman of the sea: A common pirate! If he had heard the stories correctly he was a very bloody one at that. This could not be good for his standing in the community. At least he was not using his own name to discredit him further if he was found out. Someone would surely recognize him if they brought him to justice. This could not happen to him. He had struggled for so long to put this behind him. He would have to watch what developed carefully and then do what he must to protect himself.

Captain Henry Henshaw on Board "The Falcon"

He had heard the rumblings on the docks. There was a cocky pirate who anchored just off the coast outside of the Liverpool port and was violently attacking ships. It was reported that they took no captives. They killed them all in gruesome ways and left the ships adrift in the waters so they could be found. Those that boarded the ships were sickened by what they saw there. To complicate things further many of the victims were local sailors, business men, women and children. They all met the same grizzly fates in very creative and sick ways. Henry felt that it was a challenge directly thrown at him from a personal level. He had angered many in their community and knew that this could be an elaborate set up to eliminate him from hindering their ability to operate and plunder the shipping lanes. Henry was partially correct. He sent two fast riders to Heysham and Barmouth, the closest ports to the north and south of Liverpool, with a message to his Captains anchored in those ports. The message was a call to aid and a detailed plan of attack on the pirate ship causing the damage. Shipping was embargoed in port to stop the carnage in the meantime. They had no argument from those that would leave port. The matter would come to a head within a few days. Henry also sent a message to William of the nature of the attacks and the plan to end them.

James Ambrose/Ainsworth

He hung on the docks and visited his old haunts. He looked up his woman but she had moved on to ply her trade elsewhere. The rumor was that she had found another man, much like James had been that would keep her and give her a good life in exchange for her womanly gifts. He could have expected no less from her if he was attached to any type of reality. James had long ago departed that world. James, as always, failed to understand life's realities and believed that the woman was devoted to him for life and would wait for his return in celibacy. He did not understand that these women of the docks were much like him and the only loyalty in them was for their own benefits and comforts. When James lost it all and left the woman quickly moved to another beneficial situation without a thought of James except to say what a failure he was. This too had come to his ears on a drunken evening.

One other thing came to his ears. He was recognized by one of his old cronies from the day he had his rooms there. The man was no threat and quickly told James of the plans that were awaiting him when he took back to sea. This man was an employee in the shipyards of the Henshaws. There was much talk while they worked and he had overheard a discussion between William and John Harrison of Henry's plan. James was pleased and invited the man to his room at the Inn. He suggested they take a short cut through the alley so they could arrive to their cups quicker. They spoke of the old times as they cornered into the alley. They walked about fifty steps and the man spoke no more. James decapitated him in the alley and took the head with him so there could be no identification. He turned at the Mersey River and heaved the head into the flowing muddy waters. He smiled as it sank. He could not risk the man getting too free with his words in his drunken condition at the local pubs. He went back to his dinghy and rowed back to his boat hidden in the darkness and fog. He had one advantage with the embargo. He knew that any ship approaching would be considered an enemy and he would fire without provocation.

The Ports of Heysham and Barmouth

Ironically, when the messages arrived at Heysham and Barmouth Henry's old acquaintances were in each of the ports. Captain Robertson read the message at Heysham about the time Roger was reading it at Barmouth. They immediately raised anchor and sailed for their rendezvous. With them sailed three smaller ships that could achieve great speed although carrying fewer guns and crew. The two captains sent them ahead to enter the waters and engage the ship at the earliest possible time. They would not be far behind. Both of the Captains had transferred their flags to the newest of the ships leaving the boatyard. Even with their size the speed was not terribly slower than the smaller sleek ships. The enemy would soon be engaged.

Captain Henry Henshaw on Board "The Falcon"

Henry awaited the return of the rider's to acknowledge the contact with the ships on the nearby ports. This he had just received. He ordered the crew to raise anchor and started tacking out to sea. He knew that the ships were on their way long before the riders could have made their way back to port. He did not know who was in port but each of the ships had worked together before and could anticipate the others movements and strategy. He would be pleasantly surprised at those answering the call. His current ship was "The Falcon" It was the newest of the efforts in ship design between he a William and very capable at sea and deadly.

James Ambrose/Ainsworth

James felt no threat. In fact his previous conquests had been so easy that he had lulled himself into a false security and sense of invincibility. His drunkenness probably aided his confidence. He had reconnoitered the mouth of Liverpool harbor and mapped out his plan for Henry. He found an overgrown entrance to a small deep water bay. He was not trying to hide. In fact he wanted an audience to witness a show of his bravery to those ashore as he ended the life of Henry Henshaw. It in part was why he had picked the place to make his stand this close to shore. The pirates prepared for battle and felt they could not lose. James sighted the first of the boats from Barmouth approaching the entrance to Liverpool. From this distance the ship appeared to be a large ship. This was in part from the design of the ship. Each of these small ships was rigged to look like its full sized mates. Looking through the spyglass would then give the impression that the ship was farther out to sea than it truly was because of its size on the horizon. James thought that he had Henry in his sights and pulled anchor and set sail from the safety of the bay. He could not understand the line of approach as he expected Henry's ship to approach from the opposite way. He felt that somehow Henry had left port and gotten out to sea unnoticed. It was of no consequence since he was now approaching for battle. It was then that he realized that the approaching ship was within gun range and that its batteries had opened fire to their broadside. He set his guns to return fire but they had great difficulty finding the range. It still had not struck James that he was fighting a miniature ship. Things would only get worse for him. He scanned the Liverpool approach and found another ship approaching from the port. He was now confused and froze in his tracks trying to make sense of it all. He was still scanning the horizon when he sighted five more ships coming at him. Further out he saw the two full size ships carrying Captain Robertson and Roger's flags. It was then that he could compare the sizes and relative distances and noticed that those ships closing on him were smaller ships that carried great speed. He knew now he did not have the option of calling off the engagement and fleeing back to sea. He failed to recognize that Henry's ship was not a miniature and was bearing down on him. James cannon opened fire on any ship within gun range but the speed and maneuverability of these smaller ships made their guns miss their marks. James was screaming at the top of his lungs to fire and make hits. The ships gunnery crews were in disarray and were not able to figure their range and direction. They were disoriented by the size, speed and distance of this menagerie of ships that looked alike through their spyglasses but were very different in reality. James suddenly got the idea that Henry's ship would be the one leaving the Liverpool port and turned to take him on. All cannons were ordered to fire on that single ship and they did.

Captain Henry Henshaw on Board "The Falcon"

Henry had sighted the enemy ship from a good distance. He probably made contact long before they noticed him. The pirates were having fits with the smaller and faster ships that had been

thrown at them in the initial attack. He recognized on his perimeters the flags of Captain Robertson and Roger and knew that the pirate ship was in for it today. He had heard the cannon batteries let go from the pirates. At first they fired on the initial sighting of the approaching ship but now they had focused their fire on Henry's own ship. There seemed to be a personal aspect to this battle. It would make sense later that they would fire on the ship leaving from Liverpool if this conjecture was correct. Henry brought the ship to stern to make it a smaller target and waited for the other ships to close in for the kill. The pirates were heavily armed and the cannon fire was coming in great waves. Henry thought it strange that a seasoned crew was having such a time finding its range. They took a few hits in the initial bombardment but damage and injuries were considered minor. They had sailed closer to the pirates and Henry had trained his spyglass on the bridge of the pirate ship. He first noticed the chaos of the officers and the crew. He thought this was a good sign in a battle to have your enemy so confused and especially when they were greatly outnumbered. He trained his glass on the Captain and he was shocked. He recognized that the ship's Captain was none other than James Ambrose or whatever he called himself these days. Henry tried to signal to the others but could not make contact in the heat of battle. The pirates were surrounded by six of the smaller ships and taking fire from all. Captain Robertson and Roger were beginning their own runs to maneuver to the pirate's broadside and set the landing boats to their gory work. Henry turned his ship to expose the 25-gun cannonade and his crews opened their bombardment of the ship. The pirates were taking many hits and it was becoming apparent that they would lose their ship if not their lives in the bombardment. The advantage they now had was their proximity to shore. They would not be afloat in open water and had an escape path if they could get there. The first mate turned to James for direction but James was gone. He did not have time to look for him in these battle conditions and started to give commands. It was about this time that the ships found their range and the cannonballs smacked at the hull and decks. The noise was overwhelming and there was a musical beat to the explosions. It did not take long for the ship to be reduced to a pile of splinters and those that could dove to the port side facing land and hoped to reach the beach before the sharpshooters could get into position to do their bloody work. As the ships bore in to finish the survivors off James dragged himself onto the beach and without hesitation made his escape into the foliage behind and out of sight. There he would rest and then make his way back into Liverpool to take inventory and revise his plans.

Captain Henry Henshaw on Board "The Falcon"

The ships did there mop up duties and several were pulled from the water to be hung later. They searched and searched but the Captain of the pirate ship was nowhere to be found. Captain Robertson boarded "The Falcon" and was later joined by Roger. They saw Henry in quite a state. He was angry and upset and they could not understand why. They had completely vanquished their enemy in a decisive fashion. There were rumors of large stores of gems and gold on board the sinking ship. In these shallow waters it meant that a salvage operation could recover a large amount of it or all of it. Roger said "Why so glum in the face after a great battle and victory?"

Henry looked to his friends and said "I was in close enough to spy the helm. The Captain of this boat is the same man who murdered by father. I don't know what name he uses but he was James Ambrose, the father of Peter Ambrose, the accountant. Both men stood quietly. Captain Robertson said "Well, it is likely that he went down with his ship so you can close that book. His story is told!"

Henry said "Not so! I picked up the first mate. Before he met his maker he told me that his Captain had abandoned them and made his escape to shore with the first incoming volleys. He saw him make the tree line in good health. He is on the loose and must be found. I must get back in port and warn William. He will be looking for him to murder him!"

Roger said "You go, we will finish here. We will divide the booty with you as it was your sighting!"

Henry said "No---you take it all and divide it. I ask that for my share you have your crews join into the search for this man. I will return to Liverpool. His son is there and I would bet he will eventually show his face at his office." With that he turned his ship and went back to port.

The Docks of Liverpool. "The Falcon's" Berth

Henry knew there was no time to waste. He dispatched a rider to Sheriff Stratford and Judge Wickford. He sent another rider to find William. While he was waiting he decided to go by Peter Ambrose office to see if he had seen his father. He did not believe that James would bypass Liverpool without seeing Peter. He took his pistols and a long knife hidden in his waistcoat. Since sighting James Ambrose he had known that the family was not safe until he was dealt with in a way that resolved his crimes. He knew that he would be cautious and checking every door and alley before crossing it. He walked briskly but alertly to Peter's office. When he arrived he peaked through the glass to see if he could spot anything suspicious. The office was in place and the workers busy. Nothing seemed out of place. He opened the door and entered. He was immediately greeted by the receptionist. They were acquainted so he exchanged pleasantries with her. He engaged her in conversation and started to draw her out. He asked "Have you seen anyone out of place or strange come to the office lately?" She looked around and the room went quiet. They were all suddenly listening intently.

She said "Funny thing that you would mention that. Just yesterday we were visited by a quite rude man. No one knew him but he was quite pushy."

Henry asked "Did Peter know the man?"

She said "He didn't at first but when the man left he seemed to know who he was. He was rather upset by it all. Strangely he smiled when he left and returned to his office whistling."

Henry said "Could I speak with Peter?"

She said in a whisper "His door is closed so you can't go in. This man broke into his office and we have all been told if we bother him again when his door is closed he will fire the lot of us! So I would have to say no! I hope you understand."

Henry thought a moment and it came to him that he probably already knew all he needed to know. James had been here, that was obvious, but what was his business and what did Peter know of it? He knew that confronting Peter would harvest no results. He asked the woman to contact him if the man came back. She said that she would but he could not tell Peter that she was responsible. With this promise Henry left the offices and made his way back to the ship.

A dark shadow stood in the darkness of the alleyway across the street in hiding. James stood watching him leave Peter's office wearing his disguise that he had used to kill Henry's father. It wasn't the exact disguise but looked similar to it. He had to steal some clothes left out to dry because his clothes were soaking wet and torn in several places. He needed to get some of his gems so he had money in his pocket. With enough he could still accomplish his goals. He stuck to the shadows and followed Henry back to his ship. Foot traffic was heavy on the docks. James did not have the opportunity he needed so he slunk back into the shadows and moved to a hiding place nearby. He was hungry, cold and angry but he knew he was close to one of his objectives.

Captain Henry Henshaw
He was certain that he had been followed from Peter's office. He had stopped several times and made sure to stay in public places and move with the crowds. He was also sure that this had to be James Ambrose or someone acting in his behalf. It could not have been Peter. In his corpulent state even small walks about town would stress his body and stamina. He rode his carriage to all engagements. His appearance would make him stand out. He would stay armed and on alert. The crew was off in the town celebrating their victory over James's ship and he found himself utterly alone on board "The Falcon". It had been a long day and he had little sleep the night before arranging the assault. He drank a cup of wine and went to his log to record the day's activities. He found himself yawning quite a lot and felt his eyelids becoming heavy. He fought the feeling hoping that some

of the crew would return soon so he could sleep with a watch on guard. The rider's had not yet returned with the Sheriff and the Judge. William had not responded yet either but with all of his duties he could be hard to locate. He drifted off to sleep.

William Henshaw at Wavertree Hall

William was alerted of a rider approaching quickly. He dressed and went to the portico to greet him. As the rider came near he recognized him as a man who worked on the docks. The rider pulled up and dismounted handing his reigns to the doorman. He walked to William and handed him the message from Henry. William was shocked. He felt angry, violated and wished to find his own revenge. William told the stables to ready his horse and told the messenger to await his readiness and they would ride together to Henry. William went to his room and holstered his pistols and put on his sword and battle gear. He quickly mounted his horse and was away.

The Stockade in Liverpool

The second rider had found his mark. Both Sheriff Stratford and Judge Wickford were conducting business of the King at the stockade at this time. The Rider found the Judge first and gave him the letter from Henry. The two addressees read it together and were astounded. They knew that Henry was in grave danger. The two mounted their horses and gathered a few constables and set off to the docks.

James Ambrose/Ainsworth

He had crept onto the docks in his disguise. His face was covered and he knew how to blend in to this environment. He got close enough to "The Falcon" to see that most lights were extinguished. The watch light on the deck burned brightly to light the gangplank. He noticed a light in the Captains quarters. All else was quiet. He crept forward after watching for a while.

His mind filled with all of the pas hate. His hatred rose to a climax and he made his decision to make his first attack now. Fueling this was the loss of his ship and all of those riches he had stashed on it. Because of his old enemy he had again lost everything. He left the shadows and crept stealthily up the gangplank. Once on deck he could make his approach to the Henry's cabin in the shadows but he knew through intuition that he must move quickly now. He was against the wall outside of Henry's door. As he started to leave the shadows and be exposed in the light he heard a loud noise on the wharf below. A man shouted "Ahoy! Is everything all right on board?" The man waited. He was the dock guard who made his regular rounds around this time. James was sure that this was not out of the ordinary and slipped into the shadows once more. If the guard came aboard he would be forced to take his life. After a few moments with no answer the guard started off mumbling "They must all be in town I suppose! I wish I were with them. I could use a pint!" With that he made his way back to the docks. James waited until he was sure the man was gone and moved to Henry's door. He pushed it open quietly and could not believe his luck. Henry lay with his head on his desk in deep sleep. He drew his long knife and moved stealthily forward. There is something in a man that alerts him of the presence of evil. Apparently Henry had this sense come upon him and he slowly raised his head and rubbed his eyes to clear his vision. Before he could regain his senses James struck. The knife did its work and cut Henry's throat cleanly. There was a spray of blood that soaked James and splattered the walls and pooled on the floor. James bathed in it to his delight. Henry had but minutes to live but James wished for him to know who had sent him to meet his father and raised his head with a fistful of his hair so they were eye to eye. He said "So, two down and three to go. You took from me and I will take from you until your family no longer walks on this Earth." With that he made his escape.

"The Falcon "

Judge Wickford and Sheriff Stratford arrived shortly after James had crept from the dock. They could not have missed James by but a few minutes. They ran to "The Falcon" and knew they were too late. The ship was empty and ghostlike. Henry's cabin door was askew. They knew what they would find but were still shocked at the bloody reception they received. Henry was still alive at this point and told them "Peter's office---he has been there. He will go back! Find him!" With that he took a deep breath and it was his last. They looked around the cabin for any clues but found none. They heard the approach from the docks and went outside to see William running to the ship. They walked down the gangplank and stopped him there. He looked deep into their eyes and shook their heads no. William understood. He was devastated and inconsolable. The Judge spoke "William, you do not want to see your brother in this state. We will care for the body. We will sound an alert for James Ambrose. He will be coming for you next or another member of your family."

William said "They are not here for the most part. John and Ellen have left for Ireland. Katherine is here with me but the house is well guarded and on alert. John and Mary and the baby are also in Ireland. We will find him and end him once and for all!"

The Judge said "Henry told us before he died that he had been to Peter's office and that he would return there. We will watch the office until he returns. That is where we will find him. I imagine it will not be long before he goes there."

William said "Then that is where you will find me in waiting!" He returned to his horse and rode off in the direction of Peter's offices. William stabled his horse nearby and walked to the office. He dismounted and checked his weapons. When all was in readiness he paused for a moment. He knew that in his heart he wanted to take this man's life. He knew that in reality it is what was destined to happen if he found him. Much like Henry he had to reconcile his coming action with his God and found that the God promoted by the Church of England to not rise to the occasion. He knew that there was something missing in the Church. It had become a political faction more than a religious one. It sought all things that the greedy men of power sought. They only wished riches, power, prestige and the easy life. This is not what was taught in his bible and he knew that Jesus had lived a life of poverty for the most part. Sir Thomas and Marjorie had passed a sense of charity to William and his brothers and sister. He felt it deeply and could only see evil on those that sought these things for personal benefit. He would have to ponder his relationship with God and religion another time. It was dangerous for his mind to wander so with James Ambrose on the loose. He took up a position where he could watch the rear entrance to the business. He was sure that James would not enter through the front with the sure knowledge that many were in search of him for retribution and arrest. His wait was not long. A hooded figure appeared from the shadows moving with stealth. He made a direct line to the rear door of the Peter's office and tried its handle. It did not move. Showing little patience he threw his shoulder into the door and William could hear the wood splinter. The door could now come open. The man entered and pushed the door closed behind him. With the sill shattered the door gapped back partially open. William crept to the door with his pistols drawn and ready for battle. He pushed the door open. He heard a loud pop and the wood splintered on the door sending splinters of wood in all directions. He ducked back to cover as he heard a second pop from a pistol. The wood erupted once more. A third pop came in close proximity to the second one. Something was not right. James could be carrying a third pistol but that would be unusual. The wood in the door had not splintered on the third shot meaning it was directed elsewhere. He realized that there could be another occupant of the office and with James there they could be in danger. He crouched low and entered the room diving behind the cabinets that held financial files near the door. All was quiet. There was no pop and the room remained still. There was a thick smell of gunpowder in the air. The room was clouded with its smoke. William got his bearings in the dark and moved out of cover. He expected to hear a shot but the silence was deafening and out of place. He moved forward towards Peter's office and tripped over something in the aisle. He fell hard with a thump and knew that his position would be exposed if he was in the sights of the assassin. He tried to scamper to his feet but was entangled in some way with what lay in his path. He tried to throw it off but focused on a bloody hand that clutched at his waistcoat. The hand held a bloody long knife and even in its weakened state was trying to stab at him. He grabbed the hand and dislodged the knife. He was looking into the face of the devil when he could focus. James Ambrose lay on the ground in a pool of his own blood. He said "It has long been my desire to end your life. I have gotten two of you Henshaw vermin but it appears that my mission will not be accomplished. I thought I had raised a worthless boy but it appears he has surprised us all!" With that he breathed his last. There was a whimpering coming from Peter's office. William entered into the dimly lighted area. Peter sat at his desk with his head down and his hands covering his face. His pistols lay before him with smoke still wafting from the barrels.

Peter Ambrose

Peter was startled in his sleep. He slept at the office this night as he had since his visit from James a few days before. He did not leave the office and had food brought in to him by his employees. He had an arrangement with a local cook to bring him his meals but any additional food he had to arrange himself. This he put on his employees who would be required to check on him from time to time to meet his every need. This night had begun in a normal enough way. He had heard the scuttlebutt in the office about the battle outside of port and its outcome. He knew that the ship that went to the bottom was the ship of his father. He also knew that more likely than not James had escaped the fighting and would soon reappear to collect his jewels. Peter had other ideas for them. When James ran off he had stripped the estate of all means of support. Peter really never understood and Charles had kept the estate in operation. He was grateful that he had. Now these jewels of his father's had landed in his keeping and they were of a much greater value than what he had stolen from the estate years before. He had no intention of parting with them and that would be a matter of dispute when he saw his father again. Because the stash was with him he knew that he would see him once more. With the sinking of his ship he knew that this meeting would happen very soon now. He would need money to make his escape from the gallows and this would bring him to Peter's office. He would leave without his jewels and if there was a dispute he would leave without his life. Peter had vowed this in his mother's name.

He had been awakened by the door splintering. He knew it would be his father and picked up his pistols and hid them on his lap below the top of his desk so they were concealed from view and waited. His nerves were starting to take over because he had never killed a man and this man purported to be his father. He was uneasy about the delay. James should have entered his office but had still not appeared in the doorway. He would not shoot him right off. He wanted to hear what he had to say. He might be able to use it later as a defense. He also had some things he wanted to tell James before sending him to Hell. He was startled to hear the first pistol shot and ducked down behind his desk. There was noise in the outer office. He decided to go investigate and see what the situation was. As he reached his door a second blast lit up the room and he could see his father in the flash firing towards the door at something. He wasted no time and fired his pistols point blank into James chest. He fired both pistols at once and there was only one report from both pistols but much louder than James's shots. He fell to the ground. Peter just turned and went blankly to his desk and sat down. He did not look or speak to James. He placed the pistols in front of him on the desk and put his face in his hands. This is how William would find him. Underneath his hands Peter had the beginning of a smile on his face knowing that he was a wealthy man at the expense of James who had once left him to ruin. He would play the role of a distraught son who had accidentally killed his father thinking him to be a burglar. He cried out loud when William entered the room to comfort him.

Sheriff Stratford, Judge Wickford and their Constables.

As they gathered their forces and dispersed them to areas of the town to search for James Ambrose they made their way to Peter's office. They wished to survey the area for James and make contact with Peter to notify him of the day's events. They knew that he often slept at his office and had heard that he had been doing so for days since hearing of James possible return. They found this strange but did rule out the possibility of a contact between the two early on. They were nearing the offices and heard a pistol shot being fired. They spurred their horses to a gallop and rushed to the office. They were sure that this would be the source of the shot. They pulled up their horses and tied them off to the rail. They rushed to the alley as the second and third shots were fired. They ducked down and pulled their arms. They moved quietly to the door which they found ajar. They entered slowly with the arms drawn. They moved through the darkness where they found a faint light coming from the door to Peter's own office. They fired their lantern and were rewarded with the sight of James bloody body lying in the floor. They moved forward and slowly entered the office. William was there with Peter. William called them outside and left Peter to his emotions. William told the story as he had seen it and that Peter himself had fired the fatal shots. Later it would be known that Peter had fired two shots into his father's body but nothing would be made of it. Peter apparently had played his part to perfection. There would be many condolences and many would see Peter as a hero to rid the world of such an awful presence. None knew that Peter's own motives had been much like his fathers'. Greed, power and revenge had once again molded the Ambrose family history and another generation became acquainted with murder and deceit. Peter felt no remorse and basked in the glory this secret murder had brought to him. The community reaction to him was positive in all aspects and it seemed to bring closure to the ill feelings of the community towards Peter. He had accomplished much more than he had set out to do.

Henshaw Hall Graveyard
Henry was laid to rest next to his father and mother. The graves had been plotted to reflect the rights to passage. Below the graves of Sir Thomas and Marjorie were eight grave plots. This would allow for the four children and their spouses. Henry would never have a companion in his heavenly universe but had done much good during his lifetime and his rewards were sure in heaven even though he had questioned his actions during his lifetime. The family turned out to yet another funeral at the hands of James Ambrose. It would be their last at James hands but not at the hands of the Ambrose family. This poisoned relationship with the Ambrose family continued in blissful ignorance unaware of the true intentions of Peter Ambrose for their future.

Raising of the King's Army
The Bishop's War
Bishop Laud now made his move towards bringing Scotland

into religious compliance. This was the next logical step in his conversion of the United Kingdom to the Church of England. Ireland was strongly Catholic and a much tougher nut to crack. Bringing Scotland under his control would make the battles with Ireland much easier. So with the changes in the church in place in England he took the next step; the Kingdom of Scotland. Scotland had its own traditions in its churches. They had allowed some of Laud's changes to be installed into their churches merely to keep peace between the nations. They were an Episcopacy, although begrudgingly, and wished to be left to their own beliefs and traditions. This would not suit Laud's agenda. They saw this as a direct attack on their religious traditions and freedoms. King Charles remained silent and Laud took this as a vote of confidence and moved quickly to implant the changes under threat of force. It started to unravel when Laud introduced and mandated the use of the Anglican Book of Common Prayer into the Scottish Churches. There was immediate reaction to the order and in 1637 riots broke out in Scotland in protest of the dictates. In February of 1638 the Scottish National Covenant met and drafted a document described as a 'loyal protest' rejecting Episcopacy and the infringement of their religious freedoms. The document covered many things but stipulated in particular that the changes had not been approved by the free Parliaments of the General Assembly of the Church of Scotland. Charles thought that he had found a technicality with this argument to force Scotland into submission. Since they wanted to put the issue to their Parliament and the General Assembly of the Church of Scotland Charles forced the issue and summoned the General Assembly to meet in November of 1638. The issues had time to fester between February and November and the Scottish defense of their position became steadfast. He had again misjudged the situation—a feature that was becoming commonplace in his reign. He had blundered politically by allowing so much time to pass between the action and the reaction. Charles encountered a radical mood in the General Assembly and things could not have gone worse. Charles goal was to force the changes into the church and to have complete compliance to his wishes. He felt by his summons that the General Assembly had no option but to accept his "Book of Common Prayer" and the Episcopacy that he had established. What he received was a vote to reject the book and a declaration that the office of Bishop (the basis of Episcopacy) was unlawful. Charles was in a state of apoplexy by the complete rejection of his church and by extension his rights as King. Since he could not force the church to voluntarily submit to the changes he demanded for the Assembly to rescind its orders. Charles turned to another of his Chief Advisers and summoned Sir Thomas Wentworth from his position in Ireland. Charles had appointed Wentworth (1st Viscount Wentworth) to Ireland in the post of Lord Deputy of Ireland during a time of trouble there. Wentworth had appeased the Irish and raised significant revenue for the King from his negotiations. It was Charles belief that he could do the same in Scotland. This too was a failure as the time for diplomacy with the Scots had passed and the bad taste of Charles's own brand of negotiations cast a dark shadow on the process. The political state of Scotland was now in complete revolt and Wentworth could not control the situation.

The Assembly, of course, refused Charles order. The stage was now set. Charles returned to England and began raising an army. The Scottish also began raising an army that would be known as the Scottish Covenanters from the Scottish Covenant who had originally protested to Charles on the issues in dispute.

The Call to War

William was finding it more and more difficult to support the King in his quests. His old military unit was torn in their own support for the King. Charles had put out the call to raise the army against Scotland but the unit and the area were leaning to the side of Parliament and the Scottish Covenanters. William could not in conscience go to battle against a force that was fighting for his own beliefs and personal welfare. Word finally came down that if pressed into service the unit would fight with Parliament. In this case they would stay home and not join forces with Charles against the Scottish unless Parliament raised their own army to dispute the issue internally. Support for Charles in the South and East was waning and when he took to the field he was in a much weakened state. Many units failed to mobilize and join the attack. Some would only act if the Scots attacked their home areas and then only in defense of their property and families not in the name of the King.

It was this uncertainty that caused William to withdraw and focus on the family, businesses and the shipping concerns. With Henry's death William wanted time to re-evaluate his relationship with his God. For a long time he had questioned the teaching of the Church of England and it's Earthly agendas. Many of the things he had seen from his King and the Church did not reconcile with his understanding of the bible stories of his youth or the teaching of his parents. This was further complicated by his association with Evan Houghton, who was a noted "Roundhead" and a supporter of the church. "Roundhead" was a derogatory term given to Parliamentary supporters. Evan had been imprisoned and issued fines from the King for his outspoken resistance to the King's policies. William had learned that Evan had been questioning his church more and more with each of Laud's changes in its being. He had begun to investigate other religious alternatives and discussed his doubts with William openly. William was no longer in the military. William knew that at some point the ships might be a valuable resource to whichever side the Henshaw Family would support in the upcoming conflicts. In this event John would take over the business interests while William protected their properties and families in England and Ireland. They found themselves firmly in a predicament that had yet to play out to any certain end.

The End of Peace

Many potential conflicts were now entering the area and were beginning to crowd each other in Liverpool and the Irish Sea.

First: The Barbary Pirates were still very active in the area even though there was now an effective deterrent.

Second: James Ambrose/Ainsworth, with the death of this bitter enemy some peace was found.

Third: Political and religious turmoil had again raised its head and conflict with Scotland is inevitable. Armies were being raised and it was believed that the fight would be in the North of England as historically dictated. The King had enlisted Irish forces with the promises of religious freedoms. It would be a true civil war with much at stake. Eventually the Parliamentary forces would join with the Scottish Covenanters to divide England even further. Liverpool would be pivotal in the battles in the East and North of England. The division in Liverpool was problematic. The Mayor's support of the King and his Royalists Army initially gave them the run of the city. In direct conflict the citizen's support of the Parliamentarians was by a wide majority. This established a situation in government that was not representative of it citizens and was supported by very few subjects on this issue in the area. The word was not good in Northern England. Charles had taken his army, what it was, north and fought to a standstill. Neither side could claim victory but the Scottish by default were considered the winners of the conflict as Charles and Archbishop Laud had failed to overturn the rejection of Laud's religious edicts and Scotland had declared and proven to all that their Parliament was a substantial part of ruling Scotland and that the King would have to accept their challenge. They would not blindly follow the monarchy simply because they claimed dominion over them. Charles had felt the same defeats in his dealings with the British Parliament and there too had to concede some of the King's powers to Parliament in settlement of his blunders. He would rather have kept the power in the seat of the

King. In some ways his past failures had invigorated both the Scottish and Irish Kingdoms to claim additional powers for themselves. The Irish made their claim through a negotiation that pledged to help the King in his battles against the Scots and Parliament and the Scottish claimed theirs by standing firm against him.

Fourth: Peter Ambrose, although not a definitive threat to the Henshaws at this time would soon face his past and his growing hatred. He was with a loving and personable woman, in Annie, who had exceeded the wildest hopes for the Ambrose family. On a personal basis Annie was successful and accepted with open arms into the local circles with reservations about the rest of the family. Annie's child was still open to interpretation and young Joshua was the biggest question mark. He was moody and similar to his father. Peter had taken an interest in Joshua and undertook to indoctrinate the boy into the family way including his hatreds. This interest from Peter and his heritage was having a predictable effect on Joshua. Annie felt the undercurrents and did her best to offset the stories that were spewing forth from Peter to Joshua but in the end there was little she could do in the family structure and the etiquette rules of her time. She had to be obedient and stay in the background on such matters. With the reign of Peter Ambrose beginning over the family the darkness was rising to another level. Peter's sudden wealth did nothing to dampen his desires.

These were the things facing the Henshaw family during this time. History will tell us that this was the beginning of a spiral into Civil War and strife for the next 30 plus years in the three Kingdoms. Many would feel the stress and many would feel the loss of possessions, religious freedom, personal freedoms and human life.

Charles I, King of England, arrived at the Scottish border with his forces in the spring of 1639. The battles commenced and continued until the spring of 1640. Like Villiers in the French campaigns, Charles army did not deliver a decisive blow and retreated with the results still in question. Scotland offered Charles a truce to allow him to retreat and save him from humiliation. The conflict, known as the Bishop's War came to a conclusion with the Pacification of Berwick. The truce proved temporary when Charles again took to the field. This ill-fated renewal of hostilities ended with the utter defeat of Charles and his forces in the summer of 1640 and the Covenanters went on to capture Newcastle. The defeat pressed Charles into capitulation on the issue and he agreed not to interfere in Scottish religious freedoms. He could have simply negotiated to a satisfactory compromise between the two with no military intervention and saved face on the issues. With Laud leading the reformation of the church there was simply no way of toning down his rhetoric. Scotland required that Charles repay them for the war-expenses incurred due to Charles invasion of their Kingdom. Charles left the field for a second time in disgrace.

Recall of the English Parliament
Charles came home with a mind towards vengeance. He had made a peace that only he knew would be temporary. He was already developing a plan to suppress what he considered a rebellion in Scotland. Because of his disputes with Parliament the same monetary problems were still plaguing him. His need for revenues and capital were worse than ever. This had to be addressed and the only way for this to be cured was to call Parliament into session. He did this in 1640 with the idea of convening a simple session of Parliament and demanding that they collect the taxes and grant his yearly authorization to collect his customs from the ports. He could not have been more mistaken. This Parliament was newly elected and led by John Pym, the Puritan. Emboldened by the rebellion in Scotland and its outcome the Parliamentarians found this to be an opportune time for discussing the old grievances and press the King for

concessions to strengthen the powers of the Parliament and further deplete those of the King. The first order of business was Parliament's stand against another invasion of Scotland. Charles had absorbed a devastating political blow with his defeat and his ego had taken an equal defeat. Parliament's advice fell on deaf ears and Charles was angry that they would stand against his wishes. He declared this to be a lèse-majesté (offence against the ruler) and dissolved Parliament within weeks of it convening with no relief of his financial situation. This was termed in history as the 'Short Parliament'. Charles again raised an army and went to Scotland. This was without the support of Parliament which left him underfunded, undersupplied and outmanned for such a campaign. He was still a party to the Truce at Berwick but paid it no heed. It was disastrous for Charles. The Scots crushed Charles forces and drove him back into England. They took this momentum to invade England and occupied Northumberland and Durham. In fact almost all of the North of England was occupied by the Scottish forces. This was now the third devastating defeat for Charles in a decade. Adding to Charles's problems was a term in the surrender requiring him to pay £850 per day to keep the Scots from advancing. The terms were simple—pay the money each day or the Scots would simply pillage the north and take what they were owed while burning the cities and towns of Northern England. Scotland took notice of Parliament backing a "no war" policy before their dissolution. The Parliamentarians and the Covenanters were becoming fast allies through the actions of King Charles.

All this put Charles in a desperate financial position. As King of Scots, he had to find money to pay the Scottish army in England to avoid further assaults on the kingdom. As King of England, he had to find money to pay and equip an English army to defend England and drive the Scots out of the North. His means of raising English revenue without an English Parliament fell critically short of achieving his goals. Against this backdrop and according to advice from the Magnum Concilium Charles finally called the British Parliament into session in November of 1640 from a very weak position and was ripe for the inevitable assault on the powers of the King. The Magnum Concilium was a meeting of the House of Lords. Without the House of Commons it was not considered a legitimate Parliament. It would be akin to the US senate meeting and governing the country without the House of Representatives. Under the demands of Parliament and the subjects of the King it was clear that the entire Parliament must now be called or total revolt was a likely outcome.

The Long Parliament

The Puritan led Parliament felt the wave of change as it convened in 1640. Charles naively believed that it would be business as usual and would address the collection of taxes and the mandate to collect customs revenue. He did not foresee the widespread visions that Parliament had for enlarging their own powers and making the King accountable to them. With Pym and Hampden taking the lead Parliament became another less bloody but just as significant battleground. The Parliamentarians knew that the King would have to cave to their demands due to the weak political and military position that he had put himself into at this time. Parliament wasted no time and passed laws rapidly and forced them on the King. They included laws:

- They required Parliament to convene no less than every three years without being summoned by the King
- The King could not levy any tax without the consent of Parliament.
- Parliament gained control over the King's Ministers
- The King would no longer have the prerogative of the King to dissolve Parliament without their permission even if it was in session over the three years

To soften the blow the Parliament included a provision that all adults in the Kingdom sign an oath of allegiance to Charles. This Parliament was to be known as the "Long Parliament".

Parliament was not through with Charles. Remembering the power of Weston as an adviser earlier they now went after Charles current financial troubleshooter, Sir Thomas Wentworth, 1st Earl of Strafford. He was arrested and imprisoned in the Tower of London. Pym claimed that statements made by Wentworth were worded to demonstrate a readiness to campaign against the kingdom. They claimed that this readiness was aimed at England itself when most likely Wentworth was referring to the kingdom of Scotland and the conflict there. It was to the advantage of Pym to keep the rhetoric flowing and hot against the crown. He knew that it was probable that the outcome of the case would not conclude in the guilty verdict. A Bill of Attainder was used to arrest and imprison Wentworth. This device did not require a legal burden of proof but did require the King's approval. Charles was now on familiar ground with Parliament remembering the outcome of the business with his friend Villiers. His anger had not diminished and would not serve him well in this political battle. Charles refused to approve the Bill of Attainder and there was a standoff. Wentworth himself understood the ramifications of the conflict and personally asked Charles to approve the Bill knowing that it would surely mean his death. He believed that this would head off the spectacle of war looming before him. He was executed under this belief in May of 1641.

Wentworth had limited the scope of the King's decision in the struggle with Parliament. He did not consider that his death would have other repercussions. He had made many promises to the Irish in his position there before Charles sent him to Scotland. Now the Irish Catholics feared that there would be a backlash of Protestant power as a result of Parliaments new found powers. The Irish did not wait and went on the offensive and chaos ensued. Because of the back room agreements made by Wentworth with the King's approval in the early 1630s the public sentiment promoted by the Puritans and Protestants in essence stated that the current uprising in Ireland was with Charles support. Now the Protestants again felt threatened and felt that Charles was taking England down a path to Catholicism in a short matter of time.

Charles had found himself in an all too familiar circumstance and his ego and temper again brought on ill-advised action. In part to avenge the death of Wentworth Charles assembled 400 soldiers and marched to the House of Commons to attempt the arrest of five members of Parliament for treason. Parliament knew of the action in advance and the five were placed in the security of Parliament. Charles summoned William Lenthall the Speaker of the House of Commons and inquired about the whereabouts of the five members. Lenthall replied in a face to face response to Charles "May it please your Majesty, I have neither eyes to see nor tongue to speak in this place but as the House is pleased to direct me whose servant I am here." Charles was publicly embarrassed again and making it worse was the premise that Lenthall was accountable to Parliament and not the King. In his haste and embitterment Charles let this go unchallenged. Charles had made a fool of himself again and this time in front of the entire sitting Parliament and his subjects reinforcing the political victories of Parliament in this round with the King.

Local grievances

By 1642 Charles's escapades had deteriorated the support of the monarchy within the Kingdoms. The North of England was already in Scottish hands and Charles errors and misjudgments continued to polarize otherwise loyal citizens. Along with his programs to raise needed capital by selling influence was the King's imposition of drainage schemes in the Fens. These schemes had trickle down affects to the livelihood of thousands of people in the area and their protests fell of the King's deaf ears. His popularity fading and anger towards him reaching a crescendo the sides were being drawn up with certainty. Eastern England now was solidly in the camp of the Parliamentarian forces which included Liverpool, Toxteth Park and Siddington where the Henshaw family resided. The North of England was in the hands of the Scots leaving little support for the King in the remaining areas. This support brought notable military and political figures to the aid of Parliament such as the Earl of Manchester and Oliver Cromwell. They would play a large role in the upcoming conflict.

Wavertree Hall

William and Katherine shared a passionate life in their bedroom during their times that it was possible to be alone and together. Usually this would be at times that William could return home from his travels and obligations. It was during one of these returns to Katherine that she became pregnant in the latter part of 1641. In the late spring of 1642 William and Katherine were rewarded with the first son born into the Henshaw family. The baby was healthy and they named him Joshua from the bible. This name was chosen because Joshua had led his nation from bondage to freedom and from Egypt to the Promised Land. It was hoped that Joshua could do the same for those in England under the rule of an unethical King. He was their pride and joy and the heir apparent to the Henshaw family name and coat of arms just as William had been with Sir Thomas. William wanted so much to be home with his wife and son but could not curtail his travels and responsibilities. Whenever the opportunity arose he would stay and work from home. This was a rare opportunity however. William was a loving father and husband. All that he did was for his family, not only his immediate family, but the families of his brothers and sister. It was his vision to maintain, nurture and expand the family holdings so that the future generations would live in a grand lifestyle and carry on and honor the family name and its heritage. He was thrilled that he had finally become a father and the family unit was now complete. Not that it was finished, just all of the parts were in place now and the family had its heir. This relieved the family of the provision in the Stanley will to redistribute the Henshaw estate if there were no heirs to inherit down this line. As Joshua grew and was beginning to walk Katherine had another surprise for William. She was again pregnant and was to bear another son, Daniel, in the summer of 1644. The selection of the name Daniel darkly reflected the reminder of the fall of Babylon which the Roundheads used as an example to liken to the practice of history of Catholicism in the Kingdoms. William and Katherine were ecstatic but it would be short lived.

__Family History:__
__Daniel and Joshua Henshaw were born in Lancashire, England. They were born either at Toxteth Park or Wavertree about 2 to 3 miles east of Liverpool.__

William, by this time had been relieved of his military duties at his request because the political climate was tense. He would serve as one of the local militia as did all able bodied men in times of threat. The Royalists and the Parliamentarians with their standards and armies raised attacked and the feared hostilities had finally broken out. Liverpool and its surrounding areas found itself in internal conflict. It's Mayor's and the citizen's priorities remained at odds. Many of the citizens were finally driven away from King Charles by his policies and those of his closest advisers including Bishop Laud and the King's own wife who now acted in a role as his advisor. His schemes to raise funds by any and all means were inherently unfair to his subjects and pushed them farther and farther from their loyalty to the crown and into the hopeful world that the Parliamentarians were promising with a victory in this conflict. At the very least there would be some representation for the common man instead of being forced to live with the decisions of the King and the Royal family with all of its corruption and political favoritism. The thought of King as God was being replaced by the hope for freedom from tyranny and freedom of religious choice. Charles without knowing it or at least recognizing it was becoming his own worst enemy and alienating his subjects into open rebellion. He had completely lost touch with his subjects and only acted on what was good for himself or the Monarchy. At any time there could have been dialogue and compromise to end the conflict before it came to its inevitable dark conclusion. Men of conscience chose their sides. Most decisions were made based on which side of the conflict would best reflect benefits to the individual making the decisions. Those that were currently receiving favors from the Royalists would choose to continue this course; while those that found themselves on the other side of the question would choose to go with the changes that the Parliamentarians promised. The Scottish question was also a factor for both sides. The open revolt to Bishop Laud's changes in the church had come to war. All of the north of England would be affected.

William had evacuated his brothers and their families to their holdings in Ireland. It was now time for Katherine and his family to move to safer surroundings. Their goodbyes were hard as William did not get to spend enough time with his child or his wife under normal conditions. He loved them very much and was a devoted father and husband. With Katherine pregnant he knew she must seek shelter away from Liverpool until the hostilities had passed. He felt a deep responsibility as head of the family to his brothers and sister and the interests of his community which tore at him in all directions in these troubled times. There was fear and trepidation in every household about the journeys their loved ones must take for their safety. Katherine would join the rest of the family in Ireland for the duration of the upcoming civil wars. Both knew that the leaders of opposition and their families would be at risk from many enemies.

William and Evan were looked upon to be leaders in the upcoming conflict. Because of their military service, community standing and land holdings the outcome of the war could be either good for them or devastating to their businesses, land and families. Their choices were easy to make. Some others had to weigh their options more carefully. There were those that were at great risk of ruin if they chose the wrong side. This created a problem. The resources of the city, at least those in control of the Mayor would be at the use of the Royalists and opposed to the wishes of the majority of its citizens. The Royalists would also use Liverpool to bring the Irish fighters across the sea to join their cause to fight for the King. The local militia was now called up and it fell to the Henshaws and the Houghtons to organize the defense of Liverpool. The defense was complicated with the Royalist occupation and the constant march of troops from Ireland in allegiance with the King through the city. The militia allowed the troops to operate unhindered hoping that the hostilities would not visit upon them or their loved ones. During the month of May of 1643 Liverpool fell to Parliamentarian soldiers and they took control of the town. This occupation stemmed from the tradition of support given the King by the local government officials and the knowledge that it would have adverse effects to the lives of those who did not support the Kings views. Not all of the cities and towns supported the Royalists however and broke tradition. Parliament had anticipated the actions of the King and appointed many of their ranks as Mayors, Governors and to other important offices in these areas. After the taking of Liverpool by the Parliamentary forces; ditches were dug with earth ramparts erected around Liverpool in defense of the inevitable Royalist counter-attack. Liverpool's defenses were bolstered by soldiers from the Parliamentary army. In June 1644

Prince Rupert led a Royalist army to attempt and re-capture Liverpool. Rupert was a glory-seeker and wanted to acquire his fame and fortune during this conflict. He was considered to be a rebel who decided his own agendas and based on the outcomes of his conquests his reputation and fortune would be made. This painted him in a positive light and would enable him to procure later favors, offices and promotions for himself. He did not see Liverpool as a glorious conquest and most likely would have preferred moving to larger and more important battles that would make his reputation much stronger. He described the town as a 'mere crow's nest which a parcel of boys could take'. He was required to engage and take the city by the King and could not avoid the conflict. William and Evan had built their defenses well and held the church and Liverpool Castle which overlooked the Mersey River and the bay. They knew that Rupert had much success in raiding nearby cities and that they were at a severe disadvantage in numbers. William said "Evan! We are in danger here but we have given our forces their best chance. Holding the high ground and being entrenched changes the odds greatly although they are still not in our favor. Prince Rupert commands many soldiers and cavalry. In our present circumstance the cavalry is neutralized and for each of our soldiers that is entrenched or behind walls and in the earthworks at the castle or church we are equal to ten of theirs. It will then come to our own valor to carry or lose the day. We did not invite the fight but the fight came to us nonetheless and we will live or die with pride!" Evan looked at William and gave him a pat on the back.

He said, "I fear it will be the latter but we will do it with pride. You take the Castle with half our men. I will stay in the church with the other half. If they breach our position here we will retreat to the castle for our last stand. It will be an honor to fight with you! Your father would be proud!"

Prince Rupert attacked the city with no hesitation. The battles were vicious but the forces in the city were well prepared and well organized. Rupert was not used to defeat and marched upon the 'crow's nest' with supreme confidence. To his surprise he did not gain the upper hand. The first attacks were repulsed. The forces that held the city were ecstatic but knew that the battle was far from over. Then news was received in Liverpool that the Parliamentary forces were ordered to move to join in the battle for York many miles away. It was long thought that the forces that held York would control the north of England and such an important prize took precedent over any other battle. Lord Fairfax broke the news in the afternoon that he was to abandon the battle and regroup near York. He knew the outcome at Liverpool was doomed and those left to defend Liverpool were in danger of being wiped out to the last man. Nonetheless he had his orders and had no choice but to follow them. They could make a stand here and take Prince Rupert or most likely they would meet him again at York or nearby. The withdrawal in essence only delayed the major battle with Rupert and sacrificed those fighting here to his wrath and fame. The Royalists attacks on Liverpool were resisted fiercely by the townspeople and militia. Sir William and Evan divided their forces in the Castle and the Church and put up an excellent fight. Evan's forces were in the Church. He felt that the church, although more exposed, would be the first line of defense. William and Sir Thomas in their military discussions long ago had felt that any opposing forces might find the siege of the church to cause some hesitation and divisiveness. Rupert's Cavalry first attacked and decimated the forces outside in the earthworks that they had prepared. The remaining forces retreated into the church and from his viewpoint William could see that Evan was leading that action. The lancers then made their attack and forced down the door to the church. The battle was at hand. Rupert's cavalry now engaged the earthworks at the Castle. William joined the battle at its early stages and slew many of the cavalry on his horse,

Soldier, given to him by his father for such an encounter. They both performed brilliantly and William could feel his father riding with him on his shoulder. The church was now overrun and the remaining forces were fighting their way towards the castle and its safety. William could make out Evan's figure as he battled his way up the embankment. William broke ranks and galloped towards Evan. He pulled him onto his mount and road back to the lines at the castle. They were both distressed to see fresh lancers joining the fray below and many legions of soldiers in reserve. They gathered their remaining forces and retreated into the castle. They brought up the gate and made their stand. This maneuver cost the militia many more of its numbers. As they were being overrun in their retreat many were slaughtered and unable to put up much of a fight while in retreat and facing the overwhelming numbers against them. Rupert laid siege to the castle at this point. As night fell there was no decision in the battle but the odds were overwhelmingly in Rupert's favor. Rupert raised his standards and set his battle lines for an all-out attack. The fighting was intense and Rupert was repelled many times. With each failure his anger grew. With the Parliamentary troops fighting at their side they managed to repel Rupert and at the end of the day his forces were camped at the position from which he made his first attacks. The militia stayed on watch on the castle ramparts. The Royalist troops then sacked the town outside of the embattlements of the castle. All in its defense were forced to watch as their houses and businesses were robbed and burned. Some watched as their wives and children were taken into captivity and came to the understanding that they may never see each other again. They knew that the best answer to their enemy was to fight them ferociously and defeat them to regain their loved ones and exact a revenge on those who attacked their homes. If this could not be accomplished than they would take as many of Rupert's forces with them to their deaths as possible weakening him for future battles. There would be no surrender.

The Parliamentary troops left by sea in the cover of darkness leaving the people of Liverpool to defend their town themselves.

Evan and William sat by the fire trying to get some rest. Both had injuries but none serious. Evan said "I don't believe that we will be leaving this castle or see another moon on this Earth William. Rupert is merciless and most likely angry at being delayed with us. It is said he did not think much of the taking of Liverpool. He would have preferred a bigger prize. With our defense holding his anger grows. He will be all out for victory on the morn. It will be our last."

William thought for a while and said "Well, so be it then. I would have liked to have seen my son grow and the birth of our next child. I would like to be able to say goodbye. It is the lot of the soldier to forego those things in many instances. We will fight the glorious battle and we will have a heroic death if that is what God wishes!"

Evan simply replied "Aye, It is so!"

As morning broke William woke to loud drumbeats and chanting from Rupert's forces gathered outside the walls of the castle. The militia had reoccupied the church and Earthworks at that location. Rupert would be starting his attack with no gains. The difference would be the absence of the Parliamentary forces that had bolstered the defense the day before. William knew that Evan would want to be at the church but he believed that he should stay in the castle. Evan would hear none of it and said he would begin the fighting where he had the day before. The battle unfolded much the same. The Earthworks around the Church were attacked and they again fell to the cavalry. The Church had been weakened. Entry was much easier this time and this happened early in the fighting. There was one difference. Evan knew they had substantially less force to defend the church. He ordered powder kegs to be placed by the Church doors where the breach had occurred. These were fused and set to blow with the lighting of the fuse. Evan's forces put up a stiff resistance. Rupert was getting impatient and he did what Evan had planned for him to do. He sent a large force to storm the Church. Evan had the doors barricaded so that it would take many men against a few to gain entry. The forces stacked up at the door and many were ready to gain their entry. Evan called for the majority of the force to withdraw to the Castle Earthworks and kept a small and mobile force with him. They started to dismantle the barricades and weakened them to make them easier to breach. With that he sent the rest of the force scurrying to their next positions up the hill. He stayed alone waiting for Rupert's men to enter. This did not take long. Their tempers ran high and they entered the church in a blood frenzy. Evan waited and when he thought he had the maximum amount of the enemy inside the walls and he could wait no longer he lit the fuses. Those inside were too busy celebrating the breach that they did not notice the burning fuses. Evan made his escape through a basement opening and hustled up the hill. He was confronted by a few cavalry that were in pursuit of the escaping forces. They came eye to eye with Evan making his way to the Earthworks. As they slowly recognized him as being one of the leaders from the day before they turned and went for him. They were met by William and Soldier with a small force before they could get to him. They were quickly dispatched and for the second time William pulled Evan onto his horse. Their eyes silently met with the knowledge that this would be the end. He took him back to the castle. They were pursued by another charge of cavalry that was closing on them as they reached the opened gate to the castle. They quickly dismounted and jumped to the defense of the gate as it was pulled closed and barricaded. The fighting was intense. Those inside were always at an advantage because no matter how large the attacking force they had to funnel down to single or double file at the gate to make entry. As they were struck down the bodies of the dead or dying created another obstacle to entry. Rupert was losing many of his cavalry in this attempt to gain entrance. There was a loud explosion in the church and it almost blew it apart. There were many loud screams. Several of Rupert's men ran from the Church in flames. Others just lay dead or in agony with injuries that would prevent them from ever fighting another battle if they survived. Those battling for entrance to the castle fell silent as they watched the conflagration. Rupert temporarily called a retreat to regroup his forces. Eventually the bodies were cleared enough for the gate to close and latch shut. He was angry that he had to continue to lose a large amount of his men in this effort. It weakened his force to take what he considered an objective that made no difference in the outcome of the war. He knew in fact that these people were not hindering the passage of troops and supplies through the port. This was a useless and costly battle and its losses to both sides were wasted.

The next charge was fueled by the anger as a result of the explosion and the decimation of the forces in that assault. These enemies had lost friends and probably family members and were driven by revenge. Rupert came to the field with over ten thousand men and would leave with many dead and others wounded beyond fighting. His anger and impatience grew each minute without a victory. Evan and William split their forces on the wall to defend the castle. They could see over the ramparts that Rupert was bringing up his cannon pieces to bombard the wall. Evan with his forces had taken a position. William was at the gate. As the bombardment started the militia crouched down to minimize their exposure to the fire. Rupert's sharpshooters and archers took aim and joined the siege. These had little affect and caused only a few casualties. The main damage was the crack that started in the wall near Evan's defensive position. Both men saw it and realized its importance. Evan moved his forces to intercept the charge if the wall came down. The bombardment continued. Large chunks of the upper wall were breaking off and falling inward. Those positioned there had to abandon the area in fear of injuries from the falling debris. There were batteries firing on the gate to breach it but that was a much more difficult egress into the castle. Suddenly all of the cannon were focused on the spot in the weakened wall. The firing intensified and in short order a breach opened a wide gap giving access to the inside court. It was not large as Rupert had hoped and could be defended as at the gate. All assaulting this breach would have to taper down to single file and the defenders would have an easy time of it. This was not to be however. Rupert had learned that lesson and continued the salvos against the wall until the breach opened wider and wider to accommodate a large force entering the castle at this point. Then the firing stopped and the world went silent. Again Evan and William's eyes met. They gave a simple nod and turned to their duties knowing that short of a miracle their defense would soon be over.

William could hear shouted orders from Rupert forming up his units. They would make their charge at any time. They would have some open field to traverse and this was their best chance to bring down as many as they could before they arrived at the gaping hole in the wall. The sharpshooters and archers climbed the ramparts and took aim. The cannons were loaded with grape shells and readied to blunt the attack. There was a loud shout from Rupert and then the chants from his men bringing their emotions and anger to a fevered pitch. One man broke the line and started his charge and the others seeing this followed behind. The militia opened fire and the archers found their marks. The cannon did their damage but nothing could stop the inevitable outcome of this assault. Evan took his dragoons, lancers and cavalry into the breach and fought valiantly. The forces at the gate were not as vicious. As the enemy poured into the courtyard William gave his command to his second and mounted Soldier to join with Evan. He had no more mounted when he saw a lancer come at Evan from behind. He did not see him until too late and was struck in the shoulder with its point. The lancer twisted and tugged to do maximum damage and to make sure that Evan would fight no more. To his surprise and in great pain Evan pivoted with his pistol in hand the fired creating a large hole right above the lancers right eye. The scene from behind was much different. The back of the lancers head erupted into a bright red spray and pieces of skull and brain matter flew out at great velocity. Some of the remainder of his head tumbled to the ground in a bloody heap. Evan was still standing but was bleeding profusely. William was at a full gallop. Evan continued to fight but the loud noise from his pistol and the bloody display had drawn attention to him. He was soon surrounded by several of the lancers and they charged him and ran their weapons into him with a viciousness that William had known in only one man in his life. Evan went down in great pain and agony. The lancers were now trying to torture his last moments and William would have none of that and charged them. He fired his pistols taking two of the attackers to the ground. He pulled his sword and quickly brought down another two. They quickly regrouped and surrounded him much like they surrounded Evan and the attack had the same results. They did not injure Soldier as he would make a wonderful prize for Prince Rupert. William fell. He was facing the opened eyes of Evan Houghton who was still conscious and breathing but his life's force was slipping from him quickly. He reached his hand out to William and said in a whisper "Let us join Sir Thomas and Henry my son!" With that they looked into each other's eyes and nodded to each other once again before the final assaults on their body achieved their end. With the fall of Evan and William the battle was soon over. There were victory celebrations and Prince Rupert occupied the city. He occupied the city for 18 days and then moved out leaving it to join more important battles to lift the siege of York.

Parliamentarian forces under Sir John Moore eventually retook the town on the next day. Liverpool would not come under attack for the duration of the war. There was business as usual as those who had fled filtered back into the city. The destruction was cleaned up and the losses counted. Businesses were reopened with whatever products could be salvaged. The shelves would be restocked quickly with incoming cargoes and the vendors from the countryside would return to the open markets. The bodies were collected and plans were made for their internment. A message was sent to Wavertree Hall to inform Helen Parker Houghton of the death of her husband and son in law. It would be left to her to make the arrangements and to get the information to those waiting in Ireland.

William was killed fighting at the side of Evan Houghton, his father-in-law at the storming of Liverpool in 1644 (during the English Civil Wars) while fighting against King Charles I. Evan Houghton also died in the action.

Wavertree Hall, Helen Parker Houghton

Helen had stayed cloistered in her home. The servants were armed and Evan had hired some mercenary soldiers to protect her and the property. The hostilities passed and Wavertree had not been molested in any way. With it laying three miles from town it was thought to be secure enough. Helen sat in her parlor in darkness and quiet. Tears came easily. She could not eat as she had no appetite. She could not sleep for worry for Evan and William. She thought that her daughter was most likely in the same state. On the first day of battle she could hear the cannonade. It was loud and lasted for long periods throughout that first day of fighting. She had hoped against hope that they were able to run off the enemy. She was aware that the force that they would meet was a large one and the battle would be in doubt. Early the following morning the cannons began again. The walls rattled and she could hear horses, carriages and wagons on the road hurrying to the battle or away from it. She knew the second day of fighting was not a good omen for the forces entrenched in Liverpool. They would weaken with each day of battle and those who wished to take the city would grow stronger. She longed for word of the battle and that Evan and William were safe. The battle continued and her fears rose. This would continue throughout the day and then all fell silent. It was an eerie silence. Her God had deserted her and did not seem to be in the area. There were no calls from the birds and the movements on the road had slowed and all of the traffic was going into the town. She hoped to go into town as soon as she could but Evan's orders were for her to stay at Wavertree and safe. He would come to her if he was able. The sun was setting when she heard the sound of hooves coming down the lane to the house. She opened the door hoping to see Evan and knowing that anything less would be bringing bad news. She heard the doorman outside greet the rider but it was not Evan or William's voice that she heard. It was Sheriff Stratford and his tone was dire. She opened the door and knew what news he brought before he spoke. She had to hear the words spoken though to know it was real. Afterwards she collapsed into the Sheriffs arms and she was helped inside. They brought her tea and a bottle of good spirits to put in it. With the doctors busy with the carnage they could not expect him to come for their care. The servants took this upon themselves and the only medicine they had to calm her was the spirits. Helen did not partake normally but this was not a normal situation. She drank what was placed before her and retired to the parlor and closed the door to compose herself to begin dealing with her grief. Before she retired she wrote out a message to be dispatched to Ellen and Katherine in England with the news of the battle and its outcomes.

Once in the room she fell to her thoughts. Rupert did not want to fight in Liverpool. There was no hindrance to troop movement or supplies to either side of the conflict. The death and destruction in the end allowed Rupert eighteen days of camp in Liverpool before moving on. From what she knew of the battle and the facts surrounding it there was no justification for the death and destruction that had visited them here. The deaths were meaningless and had no purpose in the war from either side. Liverpool could have easily been bypassed and there would be no change to the results of the conflict. It was now as it had been before the bloodshed. It was hard to lose two honorable men for no apparent reason. She thought of all of the others who had died there too. Only a short list of the local casualties had been circulated but it was growing each day. She know those that had died in Rupert's service had left their own families in the same state as those from Liverpool. She questioned her God. She questioned her King. She questioned each of those who made these life and death decisions that affected so many lives so deeply without consequences to themselves. It was easy to send men to their deaths if there was no threat to those in power. She prayed that those that had a hand in these deaths would meet their own fates before the conflict ended. It was so unnecessary that the greed and lust for power had cost so many so dearly.

The next morning she would make the arrangements for the bodies and the burials once again.

Katherine Houghton Henshaw

The word was received a week after their deaths. She read the message in privacy and called John to come to her rooms. Joshua was an energetic boy who was approaching his second birthday. He had come into a world of so much hope and promise. She was deep into her pregnancy for their second son. He would be another son who would not know his father because of the evils of war, religion and greed. Before sending for John she took some time to herself. The cook had taken Joshua to the kitchen for some special treats when she noticed that the news had been bad. Katherine, much like her mother, composed herself after a short period of mourning and praying for William's deliverance to his heavenly rewards. She prepared to meet with the family and announce the news and join with them for a memorial service before departing for Liverpool. The family and the doctors advised her against travel at this late time in her pregnancy but she could not bear William being alone at this time. She needed to be there. She needed to go to his grave and mourn him properly. She would not feel it was real until this was done. John agreed to accompany her to Liverpool to pay his respects. He needed to organize the businesses in Liverpool and inventory their losses and damages in order to make the transition with the death of both William and Henry in short order. Mary and Eleanor would stay behind until he was surer of what he would find there. Katherine packed the bags for Joshua and herself and met John on the docks. They would take the first ship to cross to England from the boatyard. They did not have to wait long. Captain Robertson had come to port as soon as he heard the news knowing that she would need transportation. He had lost two of his bosses and his dear friends now in a short period of time. He struggled with those who believed in God. He knew that a God would have spared these three good men if he truly existed. This reinforced his atheism and he would point this out whenever questioned about his peculiar belief in the future. They set sail within an hour of Katherine's appearance on the dock. He was able to load the ship with enough trade to make the crossing profitable for all involved. It would take two days to get to port in Liverpool.

Wavertree Hall

Katherine arrived into Liverpool in the late evening hours on the second day. She took a room at the Inn near Peter Ambrose's office. It was a better part of town and Captain Robertson said that it had little damage from the siege. She needed to rest after the crossing. They hit an angry sea which delayed their passage and tossed the ship on large swells. Katherine sailed well but in her current condition felt ill most of the way. She was grateful to get back on land. She sent a messenger to her mother announcing their arrival and their plans. She also asked the she make contact with the doctor to see of his availability. The baby would not wait long now to come into this evil world. With these things done she put Joshua to bed and fell fast asleep. They slept well into the morning hours.

Helen was beginning to feel worry again. She had expected Katherine and Joshua in the early morning. The clock was sweeping towards noon now and she had not yet appeared at the Hall. She began to make plans to locate her and go to her to check her condition. As she made the arrangements for the trip into Liverpool the doorman announced the arrival of a carriage at the gate. She was relieved to see Joshua sitting with the driver and having a time of it imagining he was driving the team. As they arrived the doorman helped Katherine from the carriage and into the house. She looked drawn and pale. She announced that she had felt the first of many pains that would follow leading to the birth of her second child. Katherine had a midwife staying at the house and they sent for Dr. Anderson who had birthed all of the Henshaw children now for many years. The midwife took control until the doctor's arrival. Fortunately he had planned to check in with Helen that morning and was not far up the Liverpool Road when the rider found him. He whipped his team and sped to Katherine's aid. Helen met him at the door and apologized for demanding his time with so many for him to care for since the battle and all of the casualties he was personally dealing with at the time. Katherine's birth could not have come at a worse time. Dr. Anderson said "Truthfully my lady! It is a pleasure to do this duty after caring so much for the gore of battle. This at least reminds us that our God does good things too!"

Katherine's labor would be long. She struggled through the night and it was very emotional doing it all alone now. Of course her mother was there and she could feel William and her father in the room but she still could not help but feel utterly alone. It made the pain and the struggle of this little one even more difficult. At last in the early morning hours the baby wriggled his way free and took his first breath into his new world. He howled into the cold night like a lone wolf. He was quieted by his mother's breast. Joshua was awakened from the noise and came to meet his new brother before returning to his sleep. Helen felt a hopeful moment in the face of all of the adversity. Katherine pondered about what to name him. She thought of her father and her husband. Either name would work but she felt that using one would dishonor the other. Like Joshua she turned to the bible and came to the name of Daniel. In her despair she found the verses related to the fall of Babylon and Daniel came into her mind and it seemed to fit the times and the situation. Daniel was born just a few weeks after his father died. He would not know him as a man. The other man that would have had a positive influence on the boys had also died on the same day in that same place. She would do this alone. She had no feelings for any other man and her life had revolved around William almost from its beginning. She knew there would never be another in her heart or mind.

Peter Ambrose

Peter did not join in the fighting. He stayed at his home and acted much in the same way as Helen did during the battles with two noted exceptions. First he hired a small army to protect his office and property. He wanted to be secure and make sure that the gems he had in his possession were not confiscated in the sacking of the town. With armed guards at the office those sacking Liverpool did not see the need to delay their looting and moved on to other targets. They knew that with the time constraints involved they would not get to every building and home anyway. Second, he hired riders to go back and forth between the battle and his home to keep him informed as to which side was in control and the outcome of the battle. This pivoted back and forth for two days but in the end it could not have turned out with a better result for Peter. He secretly celebrated the deaths of Evan and William and drank himself into a stupor. Annie tried to enter his room several times during this period and was rebuffed. She found Peter's behavior to be very strange with the sad news of the deaths of many of their friends and acquaintances. She did not infringe on his privacy further. She spent her time huddled with Joshua and comforting his fear during the battle. Annie knew that Peter was acting different in his dealings with others. His treatment of her was degrading to near abuse. So far he had limited his behavior to mental abuse but she was sure if she would have insisted on staying with him in his room that it could have been physical. He was even more detached from her, his friends and clients. She believed at one time that this was not possible but it had proven to be true.

Peter woke up late in the day from his night of drinking and celebrating. As his senses returned he was in a thoughtful mood. With William dead there was nothing impeding his path to Katherine. That is except Annie. He wished he had never met her now. He could not have foreseen this outcome. Since he had the Henshaw businesses as a client it would not be out of line for him to make a call to her and pass it off as a business call to take care of necessary paper work and accounting due to the changed circumstances. This was not entirely untrue. His motives were really the only dirty business.

Katherine Henshaw

The trip had worn her down. The hard labor and the care of her newborn had fatigued her beyond her abilities. Helen was glad to take on the duties so Katherine could recover and get rested. It helped her to heal and to forget the dark events that had surrounded her. She reveled in Joshua's constant jabbering and wondered at his imagination. The baby was demanding but slept through the night and would be considered very well behaved for a new born. Katherine was feeling overwhelmed and anxious that she had not visited William and Evan's gravesites. She felt that she was betraying their memories. If she was thinking clearly she would know that they would have told her to rest and recover but she had to find her own closure to their deaths. Joshua asked to see his father every day. Katherine did not know how to approach the subject with a two year old and had not felt up to it as of yet. Her hormones would not settle for some time and this would heighten her emotional state. She just did not know if she could control herself to do this. It was an unneeded worry for her. Helen brought Joshua in for a visit. He said "Mommy! Daddy is sleeping with grandpa and his Daddy now. He has a nice place under a big tree and he is in heaven with God. Grandma took me to see him. He is happy now!"

Katherine looked to Helen "He is happy Joshua. He is in heaven and is looking down at us every minute. He will always be with us."

Joshua said "I know! Grandma, can I go play now?"

Helen said "Yes, if your mother says so!"

Katherine nodded and off he went! She said "Thank you mother! I did not know if I had the strength to get through that. I am glad that you are strong. I have so many things to address and don't know how to get started. I want to go to the graves as soon as the doctor will approve of it! I will need to see John, Peter Ambrose and those of our managers that are left from the battle. I am the heir to all that William and I had. I will have to act as such."

Helen said "Yes you are the heir but these things will keep until your health returns to you! Now get your rest and don't worry about a thing!" She pulled the door shut and Katherine was fast asleep in minutes.

Katherine Henshaw and Helen Houghton

The baby was now stronger and able to travel. Katherine was up and moving about some but not completely back to full health. She could not bear to wait any longer and begged Helen to bring the carriage and take her to her husband's and father's graves so she could say her good-byes to them. Helen gave in with the agreement to have the doctor accompany her there. Katherine, Helen, Dr. Anderson and Joshua made the trip and like Joshua had described their final rest would be under a beautiful tree with limbs opening forth like the welcoming arms of God. She decorated the graves with beautiful flowers. She spent time in silent prayer at each grave. Unknown to the others she spent some time in discussion with both. She was telling them of Daniel and the outcome of the battles to date. She laid out to them the future plans she was making for their holdings and families and hoped they would approve. With that they remounted the carriage and started back to the house. There was once again a hooded figure lurking in the woods.

Peter Ambrose

Peter had made himself scarce at home since the death of William. They felt this change in his offices also. He spent time away from the office and at these times nobody knew where to find him. Peter had found other things of interest and he had found himself thinking of another time and another place. He drifted back to his time in the woods following Katherine and hoping against hope that he could satisfy his mother's wishes to turn her emotions from William and on to himself. Now there was no William to deal with and he again returned to this world. He was much bolder at this age and he would be more direct with Katherine. He now had his wealth and standing of his own. He did not think he would fail. He thought that Annie could simply be dismissed as he would any other unneeded employee. He had never loved her. She had fared well and served her purpose to him. He would support her life so she would have no complaints. Peter was making another plan and would put it into action soon. His mother and father would finally be proud of him when he pulled it together. He would also take William's own children into his world now. He would be sure to make their lives miserable. They would be the heirs and arms bearers for these two hated families. He could humiliate and dispirit them making them look as nothing more than a commoner before he destroyed them completely and with them the line of the Henshaw family.

Wavertree Hall: A meeting with Judge Wickford, Henry Brisby, John Henshaw and Sheriff Stratford.

Katherine and Helen greeted them at the door. Judge Wickford, Henry Brisby, John Henshaw and Sheriff Stratford came to Wavertree when things allowed to discuss what would happen with the estate and to follow up on their well-being. They entered and tea was served. There was polite conversation before getting on to the more serious issues. The men were not sure how the ladies would react to discussing these topics. It was generally thought in this time that women were the weaker sex and had little stomach for these types of things. It would soon be apparent that the women of this family did not meet this mold. After the tea the talk started in earnest.

Judge Wickford started the conversation "Ladies! We wanted to meet with you because with the passing of Evan and William Katherine becomes the heir to the Henshaw and Houghton holdings. These will of course pass to Joshua in time but he is not of sufficient age to hold these properties now. With the Civil War undecided there is much to discuss and plan. With William and Evan siding against the King there could be a backlash if the King should prevail in the fighting. We pray that this will not happen. Even if this does not happen when the King retains his throne he will be heavily in debt and will be looking to raise revenues for his debts and tributes to those that fought against him or their survivors. We will need to protect your properties and estate so it does not go into the coffers of the King."

John said "Our Arms are ancient and recently re-assigned to the family. Along with that attaches our property and the property awarded to our ancestors in Ireland. Those should be safe enough for the present. It is the other movable valuables that we must protect. Our fixtures and stocks in our homes and businesses will be at risk."

Henry Brisby spoke up "We can protect many of those things. Some should be placed in security or moved to Ireland for the present. We can establish an inter-vivos trust for the family's holdings which will separate them from any attacks on the family as a whole. We will name a trustee for this trust who will administer the trust as it stands. It is suggested that there be several trustees named that will be succeeding trustees after the original is deceased or otherwise unable to perform the duties of trustee due to ill health or mental capacity. It seems prudent with the passing of William and Evan to do this. It is especially important if Charles remains on the throne after the conflict is over."

Living trusts, as a species of **trusts**, have been around since the 1600s, a creature invented by English solicitors and blessed by the **Chancery** Courts of old England, who applied a species of law called **Equity**. The **inter vivos** trust, the solicitors successfully proposed, excises specific property from a living person and sets it separate and apart, to be managed as a separate, financial entity (the separate entity aspect of a living trust is not unlike the independent legal being given to a **corporation**, a distinct yet similar creation of the law which was developing at the same time in England).

http://www.duhaime.org/LegalResources/ElderLawWillsTrustsEstates/LawArticle-1286/The-Living-Trust-Inter-Vivos-Trust-Trust-Information-You-Can-Use.aspx

Katherine said "I will bow to your wisdom gentlemen. Of course, my mother, John and I would like to discuss it all and get back to you. Could you tell me how quickly we would need to complete this trust idea?"

Brisby said "The sooner the better but with all that is at stake it is prudent for you to discuss this with John and your mother.

It will affect her also. We will give you a few days and then return to you. If you decide earlier just send a courier to us. I will take the liberty of drafting the documents so they are in waiting if you decide. With that they were served tea and exchanged pleasantries. There was so much to do in the meantime."

There were many meetings and discussions that evening and the next day. As the day was closing and the sun retiring from the sky a carriage made its way up to the path to Wavertree Hall. Katherine had expected no one and especially at this hour of the day. Helen confirmed that she did not expect visitors. The carriage was met by the livery boys and as the door was opened they saw the portly frame of Peter Ambrose disengaging from the small carriage door. He was dressed in his finest with everything polished from head to toe. Katherine could only believe that he was of the opinion that there was some sort of social gathering at the estate by mistake. She thought that she could cut short the visit but knew it was acceptable to offer tea and foodstuffs to a guest. She met Peter at the door and said "Peter, You are all dressed for the evening. I hope that you were not expecting a social event. We have nothing scheduled. We are in complete disarray and have worn ourselves out just trying to keep up."

Peter said "Actually I have come to make a social call. I did not expect a party nor want one. We will need to sit down at some future time to go over the holdings and their condition. I have some papers that will need to be signed at the very least tonight. May we go inside please?"

Katherine was put off. She did not know what to make of the visit and maybe the papers were important enough to make the trip. She decided to persevere and took him to the parlor. Instead of getting out papers and talking business Peter began by saying "It is so different out here with all of the gentlemen of the residence gone. I am sure that you two ladies can take care of things with some help." He paused "It is also the first time that we have been in our old childhood places. It is just the two of us now. These woods carried many memories for me. I am sure that you have many memories also." Katherine was feeling uneasy and Helen squirmed in her seat. Peter noticed and hurried along with this conversation. It was a savior for him at the point of the conversation that tea and cake were served. He was able to collect his thoughts and measure the reactions he had seen to what he had said so far. He felt that it was not going well but assigned the blame to the women being in an emotional state and tired from their meetings and arrangements. He decided he had better get the papers he had drafted signed so he could leave with his business complete if he did not get the reception that he wished for from this meeting. He would try to speak to Katherine again after they were rested and their emotional states returned to normal. The business papers could not wait. He wanted them signed while they were distracted and would not read them through. He had carefully crafted these papers to his benefit.

Katherine served the tea and they all sat down. There was a nice plate of cakes and fruits for the three of them. Peter took a plate and loaded it to the edges and began eating. Crumbs fell down his nice clothes and onto the floor. He continued to talk as his mouth was chewing making his words seem garbled and far away. It was hard for Katherine to focus on the conversation anyway because her mind was on so many other things. Finally she said "Peter, you said you had some papers that needed to be signed?"

Peter said "Yes, Indeed I do!" he opened his valise and pulled out a stack of papers. He had put the trust papers near the bottom of the stack. Many were simply papers that needed to be signed for taxes and various business filings. By getting her in a rhythm signing the papers he knew that the chances of her reading them would be diminished. He laid them down and gave the explanation that these were just standard papers for the estate and businesses but they could not wait any longer to be signed and sent off to their proper places. Katherine performed like a trained dog. She signed and signed and grew less interested with each paper passed under her nose for signing. When they got to the trust papers she paused. She said "Peter, Mr. Brisby was drafting the trust. Has he spoken to you?"

Peter replied "Yes, we spoke on the street not two days ago." This was not a lie but it surely stretched the truth. He had spoken to Brisby two days ago and the topic of the trust was never discussed. Peter took it to mean that they had taken him from the loop of knowledge of what was going on with the estate. He also thought that maybe Katherine had requested that he be terminated from his duties with the Henshaw family in light of all of the recent crimes at the hands of his family. Brisby had said his greetings and Peter had responded. That, in his mind, answered Katherine's question. Yes, they had spoken!

She started to read it but her eyes were sore and burning from crying and sleepless nights. Eventually she raised her eyes and took a deep breath and signed the document.

She said "Is there anything else Peter?"

Peter said "Yes, there are some matters that I would like to discuss with you in private if we could?"

Katherine looked to Helen. She was very tired and started to drift off. She said "Mother, Peter would like to have further discussions but it does not require your presence. Please go to bed and get your rest, I will follow when we conclude our talk!"

Helen said "Oh! Then I will retire. I am quite tired and do not know what I could add to the discussions. I will take my leave, Good Night Katherine, Peter!" With that she walked uneasily to the door and up the stairwell to her room.

Peter sat for a moment drinking his tea and enjoying the rest of the cake. Katherine waited not wanting to be a bad host. Finally Peter began "It is somewhat of a journey through our past as we reflect on all that has happened. When we were kids things were simple. The three of us would sometimes play in the woods.

Do you remember?"

Katherine said "Yes I do remember those times fondly." She did not want to bring up the day of the troubles between Peter and William that started the downfall of his family.

Peter said "My mother was always sure that we would be married. She was only doing her motherly duties. It is a shame the way it all turned out for her and father. They both could picture the joining of the two houses and all of the happiness that it could bring. She made it her life you know."

Katherine said "When I was young I did not follow these things. It was clear from and early time in my life that I would be with William. I never questioned it nor had reason to believe that what my mother and Marjorie Henshaw spoke about was not to my best interest."

Peter said "I do not intimate that it was. I have often thought about what might have been in my life if you had followed my mother's wishes is all. Did you ever think about that?

Katherine, trying to be polite answered "Peter, at that age I was not thinking at all about boys let alone matches. I was unaware of all of these things until I was called into the Parlor and questioned by Judge Wickford and Henry Brisby. I can only say it caught me off my guard and that I had no idea of the pressures you were put under. If I had anything to do with that I am sorry!"

Peter said "Well, you did not directly have any part in the goings on. Now we find ourselves alone in this world for the first time since our childhoods. My parents are gone, your father has passed. William's parents and William and Henry are passed and it is just us that have survived." He paused here and took a sip of tea for affect. "Katherine, maybe I should again broach the subject that my mother believed. There is a chance now for us to join our houses and see if my mother's vision was a correct one!"

Katherine was feeling very uncomfortable and the path this conversation was taking. She replied "Peter, you are a married man with a child."

Peter replied "Annie is nothing to me but a necessary surrogate needed to carry on the family name. We were married in a civil ceremony and not in the church for this reason. She can be sent away. I will take care of her needs. Of course, Joshua would stay with me"

Katherine was now shocked and angered but she tried to keep her temper. "Peter! That is not a thing to be said or considered. Annie has been a devoted wife to you and a good mother to Joshua. You cannot be so calloused as to cast her away without another thought to it!"

Peter replied "I could if there was a chance for the two of us. She was always second choice and will forever remain that in my mind."

Katherine replied. "Peter, if what you are asking for is for me to affirm a love to you or to diminish my life with William you are greatly mistaken. From my earliest memories it was always William that was my destiny and even now there can be no other. I will not marry again. I will not taint the good works of Annie either. She is a good woman and you must focus your attentions on her and your son."

Peter was angry and his face was showing red. He said "There is nothing stopping you from saying yes. In fact, you need me to help with your holdings and raising your sons. They need a man about that will teach them about the things of life. Being married will protect you from the King's whims of women holding land and businesses. I would be good for you!"

Katherine had heard quite enough. She replied to Peter "The trust papers will do just that. Henry Brisby explained that all to me. As for your estate, if you look closely at the deeds you will find that my father purchased the Ambrose estate shortly after your mother passed away and your father disappeared to save it from the King and keep you in it. He did this for your own good will and life. He paid for your schooling and oversaw all of the estate otherwise you would have lost it shortly thereafter. You can bring nothing to the house that I do not already control. I find it offensive that you would speak this way to me on all of these subjects and diminish my role as a woman and in a time of great sorrow. It is best that you leave this house now. I am becoming angry and I do not wish to engage you in that state!"

Peter was shocked. Until now he had believed that he was the heir to his father's estate. He had not questioned it before. He did not know if what Katherine said was true but before he could respond he would need to do his due diligence and search the land records for its truth. He said "Then, good evening Katherine, I will file the papers on the morn and we will speak again when you have come to your senses." He was angry and gritted his teeth with every word. He called for his carriage and struggled with his body to get to his feet. An avalanche of cake crumbs fell to the floor. Katherine noticed several tea stains on his white shirt and clothes. She found him disgusting. Peter turned and said "It is of no matter what you think. You will see!" With that he left.

Katherine called the servants to clean the mess. She poured herself a cup of tea and sat by the fire for a long while. Peter's presence had brought back many old memories. It brought the good memories of her childhood, her father and William. It brought the unpleasant ones of the incident with Peter, Ann, James and the murders of Henry and Sir Thomas. It finally brought back her grief at the loss of William. She finally fell asleep in her chair and never made it to her bed that night. She drifted off with a feeling of vulnerability that had not been there before.

The Offices of Henry Brisby

Katherine continued to feel uneasy about Peter's visit. She made an appointment with Henry Brisby to discuss the events of his visit. At the very least she could determine if they had spoken and if Peter was acting on the authority of Henry as he had claimed. Henry and Judge Wickford now seemed to her to be the two men that she could trust in her life and had long been counsel to her mother, father and William. She arrived a bit early. She did not like to be late or kept waiting and extended this courtesy to those she had dealings with in her capacities.

She entered Henry's offices and her mind was going in many directions. She had failed to notice that she was being followed. There was a presence just out of her periphery that she failed to notice. In fact there were two. Peter had hired a man to shadow any movements that Katherine might make. He wanted to know what she was doing at all times. He wanted to gather any information he could that might help him to force the relationship since it had gone so badly the previous night at Wavertree Hall. With the trust in hand he had more cards to place on the table when the time was right. Peter himself had risen early and called for his carriage. He left without explanation to his employees and simply said that he would return. He went directly to the hall of records at the Court of the Chancery to determine if what Katherine had said were true.

The other set of eyes were Annie's. She understood her position in the household and knew of Peter's feelings. She did not have feelings for Peter on that hand. She did however love her son and wanted to see that he was not ruined by Peter's bitterness and hatred. She was aware that Peter's only love was of Katherine. She needed to know what had happened the night before. Peter was sullen and angry that morning and had dismissed her and Joshua angrily. She would wait and find a proper time that she could approach Katherine and have a discussion with her and warn her of his intentions. It was unfortunate that she did not know them all. From her interactions with William and Katherine she was very impressed. They had always treated her as a friend and fairly in society. She would wait all day if she had to.

Katherine was welcomed in to Henry's office. She was surprised to see Judge Wickford there also. Henry began the discussion "Katherine, I was pleased to see that you made an appointment. I hope you do not mind that Allen sits with us!" Allen was Judge Wickford's given name. She felt embraced by the warmness of this under the circumstances. Henry said "I have drawn up the trust as we discussed and there will need to be some of the details discussed to complete it to your liking. Is that all right with you?"

Katherine was speechless. Henry said "Is something wrong? Have I offended you?"

Katherine gathered herself now. She said "I am surprised. I did not come here about the trust. Indeed I thought it was settled. I came to discuss the meeting that I had with Peter Ambrose and Wavertree yesterday afternoon and into the evening. He came unannounced and forced an invitation to sit in the parlor. He had brought a packet of papers that he stated needed to be signed right away. I settled in to this task and came upon the Document of Trust near the end of the stack. I questioned him on this and told him that you were preparing the trust. His reply was that he had spoken to you on these issues. I was tired and ready for sleep at this time and questioned it no further. In fact, Peter has never brought harm to my family so there is no need for distrust. I finished with the papers and Peter did not want to leave. I sent mother to her bed as she could not hold her eyes open any longer. I felt the same but could not be a bad host. After mother retired Peter broached a very unsettling topic. He wanted to extend a matrimonial proposal to me. I told him he was a married man and I had no interest in remarrying for the rest of my life. I told him that I was devoted to William and would remain so. He responded by saying that he could send Annie away. He harped again and again on joining the two houses. I finally told him that the house of Ambrose had been purchased by my father many years ago so he could continue to live there and be taken care of until he was of age. I told him his only other option was to lose the estate all together because of the state of affairs that his father left it in. His face turned red and his hands were shaking. I did not know that he was unaware of the state of his inheritance. When I told him there would be no marriage I felt he would jump at me. He left the house then but made some disturbing comments about the conversation. I feel that he had made a threat but it was only a feeling. He probably just lost his temper as he has always done."

Brisby looked at her and knew she was shaken from the visit from Peter. He said "First, Allen and I will visit Peter and obtain a copy of The Declaration of Trust. He should have prepared a copy for you. He is not a barrister however and was acting out of his scope of knowledge and authority. We will discuss that matter of his estate with him. We will also discuss his approach on the subject of relationship with you. You should not be bothered with it further. The matter of the trust however is troubling. We will get the trust papers finished today and filed to the Chancery. Would you mind signing the signature page while they are finishing the transcript? Once they are on file they will take precedence to any paper that Peter could hold."

Katherine said "I am a bit overwhelmed here. I have so much to do and research to maintain the properties and the businesses for the family and Joshua now is heir to a large estate. He will need to be schooled in these businesses just as his father was. It will take some time obviously. Joshua is two years old almost. Daniel has just come in to this troubled world. It will be many years before either will be ready to run the businesses. In the meantime John will run the bulk of the estate and keep me informed as to the problems and benefits of each."

Judge Wickford stated "Katherine. You may call me Allen. We have been friends a long time now and have been through so much. So many things have happened that it is important to stay sharp. All types of criminals and thieves come to prey on the weak. Peter's behavior was out of line. His dismissal of Annie is a point of concern. With his family background we worry as to his intentions towards your family. What you tell us of your meeting is disconcerting but we will get to the bottom of it. Allow us to research these matters and inform you of our findings!"

Katherine said "I would like nothing more. At this time I am simply not up to it all. I will continue to focus on my education with the family businesses and holdings. Please update me with no delay on any new information that you find!"

With that the meeting ended. Without a clear understanding of the consequences the meeting established another critical decision in Katherine and the family's lives.

Annie Ambrose

Annie was brought to attention as she heard the doorbell chime across the street. She spied Katherine exiting the office of Henry Brisby followed by Judge Wickford. They said their goodbyes and Katherine started off to do her shopping before returning home. Annie hurried from her hiding place to catch up to her. As she closed the distance she called out "Katherine! I was hoping to find you here. I have wanted to pass along my condolences at your loss."

Katherine said "Hello Annie. Thank you, it has been hard. I am pleased to see you. I hear so much about you and we have not had the chance to get to know each other. I have some shopping to do. Would you care to accompany me?"

Annie said "I would love to. Where are we off to next?"

Catherine said that she was looking for a suitable memorial for the graves of her husband and father and that would be the first stop. She also needed to buy some clothing for herself and her boys and visit the market for foodstuffs. Annie was ecstatic. Katherine was proving to be the lady she had heard that she was from those who moved in their circles in Liverpool. Annie said "I know that you grew up with my husband and that you are probably closer to him than anyone. He sometimes puts people off but he is a good man I think."

Katherine did not want to tell her about the meeting she had just had with Peter the night before. She genuinely liked Annie though. She would approach their friendship on a personal level and keep it between the two of them without bringing Peter's erratic behavior and their family histories together. Katherine said "Annie, the past is just too painful to think about right now but I am very glad to meet you. Maybe we can just keep things in the present and the future."

Annie was just as happy to avoid the past and the subject of Peter and his family's behavior in the past and keep it behind them also. She knew though that her mission was to warn Katherine. She worried that her meeting with Katherine would be strained because of this but it turned out that neither woman wanted to dwell in the past. A good friendship was beginning. For Katherine's part she felt protective of Annie after what she had learned. For Annie's part she needed a friend to help her overcome the disappointment of being married to such a man as Peter Ambrose. This meeting would be a turning point for both women. As they walked up the street they were shadowed by Peter's man. He tried to get close enough to hear the conversation. Annie decided that she would keep the warning to herself for now and continue to monitor Peter's behavior. She would protect Katherine if a danger became eminent.

The Office of Peter Ambrose

Peter had a busy day. He first went to the Chancery and filed the Trust papers. He knew he had to be the first to file the papers. Being that there were no illegalities in them and they were properly signed would make them hard to overturn with no proof of incompetence or fraud. He then went to the Hall of Records to research the history of the various deeds to the Ambrose Estate. To his angst he found what Katherine had told him to be true. His anger rose in his throat until he could not swallow and felt like he could not breathe. He felt like his body was radiating intense heat. His stomach was anxious and he wanted to strike out at someone or something. He did not want to show his hand now. There would be some arguments with Judge Wickford and Henry Brisby but he will appease them. Once that was done they really had no choice but to let the trust stand. It would take great amounts of time and money to overturn it with Katherine's signature in place. He felt betrayed and defrauded by the various people that he trusted. Charles had to know. The very person who had seen him through his hard times and had been brought back to run his household had to be aware of the fact that the property was sold out from under him without consulting him or even giving the courtesy of knowing what they were doing. There would be revenge for this act. He would find some way to recover his property and make those responsible for this injustice pay for their deeds. He returned to his office in the late morning. He told his staff that he did not want to be interrupted unless a man named Willie came to see him. With that he slammed the door.

A few minutes later and derelict entered the office. He was filthy and wore tattered clothes. He wore a large hat pulled down over his face and wore a long beard. He walked to the receptionist and asked for Peter. The receptionist looked him up and down and try to measure whether or not she wanted to jeopardize her job for the likes of this man. She said "Mr. Ambrose has left strict orders that he is not to be disturbed Mr. ????"

The man answered "Willy, the name is Willy and that is all ye need to know!"

She was startled at what business this man had with Peter but she knew that she had to put him through. She was long aware that Peter had contacts in the shady areas of life. She told him to wait at her desk and went to Peter's door and knocked. He shouted "I told you not to bother me!"

She replied "Sir, a Mr. Willy is here to see you. You said to make you aware if he were to come in. Peter yelled "Send him in!"

She returned to her desk and led "Willy" to Peter's office and opened the door. She watched him stroll in and walk straight to the liquor shelf and pour himself a double shot of expensive Brandy. Peter just sat there. He looked at the receptionist and said "That is all, you are not needed here!" He dismissed her with the wave of his hand and she closed the door and left the room. She did linger outside of the door to make sure that everything was all right but she overheard more than she could fathom in the next few minutes.

Willy got right to business "I followed the lady all day. She went right to Brisby's office first thing this morning. The judge was there too. I tried to get close enough to hear them but the access to the window was blocked. She was there about two hours so I imagine they had quite a talk. She spent the rest of the day picking grave memorials for the two. She also bought clothing and market."

Peter said "That is hardly worth the Brandy let alone all that I pay you!"

Willy said "That isn't all and you aren't going to like this at all. The lady was joined by your Annie as she left Brisby's office and she stayed with her all day long until she left town for home. They looked like they were becoming good friends and confidantes. That cannot be good for you."

Peter's voice rose and he said "It is left to me as to what is good for me or not! You will not take that tone with me sir! Keep up your work and you will be paid just as you were when my father was in town. You know better than to get loose with your mouth so keep that drinking under control. If I find you to be a threat you will not be around long to tell your tales. Do you understand that sir?"

Willy said "Yes Sir! You pay well even though I take all the risk but you have been fair overall so I will not expose you!"

Peter said "Then our talk is finished and you will be on your way. Here is your pay and stay out of the bars!"

The man took the money and rushed to the door to leave. The receptionist heard his footsteps and retreated quickly to her desk.

Shortly after Willy left the office the door chimes were once again heard. The receptionist looked up and was astounded to see Henry Brisby, Judge Wickford and Sheriff Stratford approaching her desk. They approached her and said "We wish to speak to Peter. Is he in?"

The receptionist did not know what to do. Peter had made it clear that he was not to be disturbed but she could not deny men of this standing. She did not know how Peter would react if she went to his door once again but she was caught now in the middle and had no choice. She said loudly so everyone could hear. "Yes he is in! He has asked not to be disturbed however!" Then she whispered "He will fire me if I disturb him and I cannot afford to lose my job. If you will all just force your way by me and allow me to resist I would greatly appreciate it!"

Sheriff Stratford said "That would be a privilege." and the drama started to play out. He pushed by her stating that they would not be denied an audience with Peter. They were important men and had come all this way for all to hear. She protested and backed towards Peter's door. Her voice rose in protest until Peter's office door was thrown open and his voice boomed out. He said what is going on out there! His face paled as he cleared the door frame and saw who was coming his way. He wished to escape and not be drawn into the conversation at this time. He was not as prepared as he wished to be for the confrontation. Then his mind seemed to calm. He had done all he needed to do and he had the upper hand. He would play it if needed.

The Sheriff said "Peter we need to speak to you about your visit to Katherine."

Peter said "I don't know what you are talking about. I conducted some business with her as I am engaged to do by her husband. This now falls to her and I had to get signatures to file her papers. That is all! Of course you know that I have to keep my dealings with my clients confidential."

Brisby almost exploded "How dare you stand and lie to our faces. We know that you took papers to establish a trust to Katherine and intimated that we had spoken on this subject. We both know that you misrepresented that to her and we have had no such discussion! What do say you to that sir?"

Peter stood strong "The question was "Have you spoken to Henry Brisby?" and the answer was that yes I had. We spoke not more than two days ago."

Brisby said "That was hardly the answer to the question she asked you and boarders of fraud Peter!"

Peter said "Nonetheless she had the opportunity to read the papers and chose to sign them. She also had the option to withhold her signature on any one of them. The trust was filed in the Chancery this very morning and is a matter of record."

Brisby responded "I want to see a copy of that document and all of the others that you took to Katherine."

Peter said "Once again that is a matter of confidentiality that I cannot breach."

Brisby said "You did not provide her with copies of the documents and surely you feel the responsibility to her to do that."

Peter said "No sir I do not! If she has any questions on the documents she can come to me directly to get her answers. I certainly owe no explanations to you gentleman by any means."

Judge Wickford stepped in "Peter, I had hoped that it would not come to this. I had hoped that you would rise above your past and be a good man. We must assume that there is more evil afoot in this matter. We will be looking into it and we will have our answers. You surely filed a copy of the papers with the Chancery and I will get that by court order"

Peter stood back and said "You—all of you in this room have no right to call anyone a fraud. You have lied to me all of these years. Charles, Katherine and all of you have stolen my inheritance and kept me in the dark all of these years. You have the backbone to stand here and tell me I am dishonest!" He was red in the face and shaking now. The men looked at each other.

The Judge spoke "Peter, your father stripped all cash and valuables from your estate when he fled after murdering Sir Thomas. The options were not good. If we did not sell the property it would have been seized by the King for taxes and you would have nothing. The deal was struck for your benefit so you could continue to live in the residence, get your education and move on with your life in relative comfort. If these men and Evan Houghton would not have stood up you would have been an orphan and sent to the streets. All in all you were treated more than fairly. Evan even paid more for the property than it was worth in the market. He paid for your education, the maintenance and operation of the estate and holdings and you were allowed to live in luxury for a token each year. You could not have had a better outcome."

Peter said "Well I am of age now and I want to buy it all back."

Brisby said "The property is not for sale! Evan has invested substantial sums over the years improving the properties, building the herds and making improvements to the farm ground. That money could not be recovered by sale and you have no way of earning enough money to even afford the market price if it were for sale!"

Peter was now in a hard place. He could not admit to his new found wealth without admitting to his complicity in Henry's and his father's murders. He had also failed to pay the taxes on his wealth. He had yet to be able to determine value. The stones and gold would have to be appraised secretly to even know the value of his wealth. He said "You are right! I will have to find another way to get my property back! I believe that I already have that in motion now! If you gentlemen will kindly leave now I will get back to my menial work!" With that he went back into his office and slammed the door. The three men looked at each other and their concern for Katherine grew.

Peter Ambrose

Peter was still shaken that he could be kept in the dark about his own affairs for so long. He had found indisputable proof that it was all true. He understood what they had told him but was still angry. He believed that if the problem was brought to him that he could have found a way to save the estate. He did not know how or where he would have gotten the funds but knew he would have figured it out. The buffoons who had handled it were most likely looking to lift his inheritance from him. It made no matter. Peter's plan had given him his method of again obtaining his property plus much, much, more. Peter knew that there would be questions about the trust. He had allowed for as much. The actual trust that Katherine had signed was an irrevocable trust. The properties could not be withdrawn from it now that it was filed. Peter, himself, was listed as the trustee for Joshua and Daniel Henshaw. Katherine and Helen would continue to reside and operate the estate and businesses but Peter had the powers within the trust to end this at will. He did not want to rock the boat and tip his plan too early though and would let it all play out until the time was right. He knew that there would be an inquiry into the trust. To sooth the ire of the judge, Sheriff and Henry Brisby he had filed two separate Trust documents. The real document and another greatly watered down version that would be similar to the one that Brisby would have drafted. He then bribed the document keeper to pass the lesser of the two to anyone making the request. When the three inquirers acquired their copy by court order they would see the less volatile of the two documents. They would never know the other existed until he sprung the trap. There were still many things to do before this would happen. If Katherine would wed him none of this would be necessary. He would have the

Ambrose Estate restored to him and all of the Henshaw holdings would come under his control. He would be granted the arms for both families since his family lacked their own. These were, after all, just women and had no business with this kind of power or wealth. He had set his affairs just right to capitalize on them as soon as there was a weakness. He had the backing of the Stanley family because of the provisions of the old will. His own son would then become the rightful heir instead of William's oldest son to make things even better if that were possible in his mind.

Henry Brisby

Henry sent his clerk to the Hall of Records with Judge Wickford's order for the papers filed by Peter Ambrose. He returned with the copies much later. The man who worked in the records was a very nervous man and seemed incompetent in his duties as the clerk. They all knew him and felt that his behavior to be off somehow. Henry immediately set to review the records that were retrieved. On their face they appeared to be normal business filings for the most part. The trust document seemed in order in an almost generic sense. The reaction they all got from Peter was very defensive and the document he was looking at did not require such a harsh reaction. He would discuss his findings with the judge as soon as they met up again. There were inconsistencies in the events that were taking place but he could not put his finger on them.

Wavertree Hall

Word had come from Henry Brisby that the papers shed no light into the high vitriol of her meeting with Peter or the reception they had received at his offices. He had to assume that this was Peter being Peter. For now there would be no worry about the papers with so much else to accomplish in such a short time. She did not believe that Peter would stop his advances even though she had made it clear they were unwanted and would ultimately end in another failure for him. In spite of Henry's report she felt uneasy about Peter and his motives. His reaction to finding out about the sale of his father's property in order to save it was of concern. He seemed like a volcano ready to erupt. This same temper in the Ambrose family had already caused her so much grief. Since there was not much to do about it she would focus on the positive and move forward in her duties. She would stay close to John but would have to deal with most of the Liverpool side of things since John would return to Ireland and his family. Katherine decided to work at the things she could control herself and put off those that she couldn't. This would be sensible for the time being with so much to do. She would delegate the issues with Peter to Brisby for now.

Henry Brisby

Henry decided that a deeper look into the actions of Peter Ambrose was warranted. It reaped an unexpected result. Fortunately, under the current situation it would not be a problem but the potential for later problems under specific circumstances should be addressed. It was through Margaret Stanley that Royal blood entered into the line of the Houghtons. Margaret Stanley, or rather, her marriage settlements, would be the utter destruction of the Houghton line if certain conditions existed. The old Stanley family line (Earls of Derby) became extinct in 1735. The earldom reverted to Henry Stanley, of Bickerstaffe, Margaret Stanley's father. Margaret Stanley and Richard Houghton were married in 1585. Both sides of this pairing brought considerable wealth and holdings to it. Richard Houghton's father, Evan Houghton, seated him at Wavertree Hall. He was then endowed with Penketh Hall, and 107 acres of land in or near the city of Liverpool. It was in her marriage settlements dated October 8th, twenty-seventh year of Elizabeth that the potential problem arose. The settlements stipulated that should the issue of the marriage fail, the property should revert to the "right heirs." This meant that the holdings would not move forward but rather backwards overturning the path of inheritance. These properties would be returned to the original legal heir or their respective families. Simply, the Stanley's would have the lands fall back under their control rather than to the Houghton and Henshaw heirs. This seemed harmless enough on its face as long as William and Katherine produced a legitimate heir to the line. The marriage of Robert Houghton and Marjorie Stanley produced only one child, Evan Houghton. The marriage of Evan Houghton and Helen Parker also produced only one child, Katherine. With her marriage to William Henshaw the lineage was safe for another generation. The "right heirs" were lining up for their payout as William and Katherine lingered in their marriage with no children and thus no heirs after twelve years of marriage. In 1642 this speculation ended with the birth of Joshua and two years later with the birth of Daniel. The anticipation of the "Right Heirs" should have ended there. There is speculation that it did not.

Brisby conjectured on the possibilities and tried to look at it from all sides. He spoke to Allen Wickford, John and Katherine about it. The facts of the current situation were that it made little difference in this generation or the next as the proper heirs were in place. Only the death of Katherine, Joshua and Daniel would alter that outcome. The issue was put aside for the time being and would only be revisited if the need would arise. God willing it would not.

Katherine Houghton

The years trudged on. Katherine was busy with the children and learning the issues of the businesses and running the estate. She was quite capable and was competent in her tasks in a short time. Her mother helped with the boys. Kathrine would have had a much harder time of it without her mother's help. They lived a life as normal as could be expected under all of the dark circumstances. This part of their lives all intertwined perfectly and the boys continued to grow.

Katherine was constantly dodging the advances of Peter Ambrose. He continued his stalking of Katherine and seemed to truly believe that he would wear her down and bend her will to his desires. Katherine knew that this would never happen and the more he pursued her, the more disgusted she became with him. She avoided him whenever and wherever she could. When she had to meet with him she was accompanied by one of the men. She never allowed herself to be alone. She observed that after each rejection Peter would become sullen and angry but kept his temper for the most part. Soon after there would be some issue with the estates and she suspected that he was at fault. They were not large issues and could more correctly be labeled as annoying. Yet there was a threatening hue to these responses. Sheriff Stratford, at the urging of Judge Wickford, assigned one of his men as an unknown security guard who followed her whenever she left Wavertree.

She continued to build her friendship with Annie and it blossomed. Annie spent much of her time at Wavertree Hall and continued to watch over the situation between her husband and Katherine in secret. This greatly angered Peter. Katherine did not want to cause trouble in their marriage. Annie told her that there was nothing that she could do to improve or destroy the sham of a marriage. At times Katherine would notice bruises on Annie's arms and face. Annie made attempts to cover them but everyone knew how she had acquired them. Peter himself seemed proud of this behavior and obviously saw nothing wrong with it. Annie persevered.

The boys continued their growth and entered into the educational process. They went to a local school because Katherine could not bear to be apart from them. Peter's own son, Joshua, was in their school but he was a few years their elder. He took pleasure in bullying the boys and inflicting pain and trouble on them. He was verbally and physically abusive to them and was called to the Dean many times for his behavior against the brothers. Peter was proud of this behavior and reinforced it to Joshua. Joshua so wanted to please his father that he continued to find more and unique ways to continue his father's will. Peter in this way fostered the painful and dark history between the two families. Annie tried to step into the issue and paid a price from both father and son. Peter did not discipline Joshua for attacking Annie. He felt it was a man's prerogative to exact this type of punishment on a noncomplying female.

Peter Ambrose's Office

Willy slunk through the alleys in the early morning chill. He had information that would be worth some silver from Peter and he could not wait to pass it along and collect his fee. His alcohol needs had increased and he needed a bottle. The office had not yet opened but he knew that Peter was spending most nights there. He staggered through the cold to the rear door. Peter had told him not to be seen at the office. He hammered on the door and then went to Peter's window and tapped loudly on it. Finally Peter's angry red face appeared in the glass. He motioned him to the back door and met him there. He quickly took him to the office and slammed the door. He said "Be quick about your business before the workers arrive!"

Willy said "I have done your business and I need a drink." He walked to the bottle and Peter stopped him.

Peter said "I have told you I do not like you falling into a drunken state. You are constantly drunk and that puts me at risk. A drunkard tells too many tales and I cannot afford what you know to be made public!"

Willy said "You worry too much! Do you want the information or not?"

Peter shook his head yes but knew that he would have to find another man of Willy's unique talents to take over the duties soon. This would not go well for Willy but Peter considered him expendable.

Willy said "Your missus was with the Henshaw woman again. This is becoming a regular thing. Not that that matters but I did get close and heard the conversation. They were discussing you in very unflattering ways. She was complaining about being beaten by both you and young Joshua among many things and as it is with women folk the information will be passed from ear to ear. It will ruin you in the community if this happens."

Peter said "If it reduces the amount of these social nightmares that I must attend then the more power to her."

Willy said "That is not all. Miz Katherine seems to think that you had a hand in the murder of Sir Thomas and harbored your father afterwards to aid in his escape. She paints a pretty picture she does. She also suspects that you have committed some sort of fraud upon her but she as of yet has not figgered it out. She has people looking into it though. This friendship can cause you many problems I am afraid!"

Peter handed him a full bottle of cheap whiskey. He gave him a few coins and sent him on his way. He would handle him later that night. He had to stop the flow of information from Annie to Katherine. It was not the right time for his plan to be exposed. That time was coming but it was not yet its time. He locked his office and walked to the livery. He told the coachman to take him home.

The Ambrose Estate

Annie was feeling good with her new friendship and some moral support. Peter spent little time at home and this made her world more tolerable and secure. She heard a buzz among the servants and went to the door to see Peter's Carriage enter their path from the road at a fast clip. She felt a foreboding and went to her room. Peter arrived and the household felt his mood and stayed out of his path. He called for breakfast and brandy. They scurried around and prepared it as quickly as possible and set it down in front of him hoping that he did not feel the wait was too long. He took up his fork and took a bite. He spit the food out across the table and started shouting and cursing. He picked up his plates and threw them at the servers and they retreated into the kitchen. The cook would not dare show his face. Peter asked for the whereabouts of Annie. Nobody wanted to answer but finally the butler said that she had retired to her room. Peter stormed up the steps to the sleeping quarters and beat against her door. She did not answer but inside she was shaking from fear. Peter finally put his shoulder to the door breaking its casing and slamming it open. He bellowed "You ungrateful Bitch! You disrespect me with that Henshaw woman. What have you told her? You will tell me! What have you learned from your meetings? I know all about them. Did she tell you that I wanted to marry her? That I would make you disappear if that was what was necessary. I would you know! You mean nothing to me you bitch!"

Annie tried to angle her way to the door during his tirade and had almost reached it when she felt her hair being tugged and being drug back into the room. Peter slammed the door and the shouting continued. The servants had gathered in the hallway fearing that he would kill her. They did not dare intervene. There was loud crashing and the sound of skin to skin. This went on for some time. Finally the broken door was thrown open and Peter walked out in a sort of arrogant swagger. He ordered his carriage and more food for the trip back to town. The servants scurried to meet his needs. They could not check on Annie until he had left the residence. They were in fear. The sound was void and all was deathly quiet behind the door. The doorman watched until he was sure that Peter had left the premises and then gave the signal to the others. They entered Annie's room and found her in a bloody heap. Her face was swollen already to a point that her eyes were shut. Her mouth was a bloody mass where her lips had split and blood oozed from her nose. It was most likely broken. They could not determine her other injuries but they knew they were severe. She should not be moved but if Peter returned he would surely finish the work he had started. They had to get her from the house. They did not know where to take her. Annie was in and out of consciousness. They told her she needed to be moved away from Peter's reach. She only asked for Katherine over and over. They knew it would not be safe to bring Katherine there so they loaded the wagon and set out for Wavertree Hall. They hoped they would find refuge there also.

Wavertree Hall

Katherine had been having a busy day. She had just returned from Liverpool and more meetings with Brisby, John and the various managers in charge of the family interests. She was not yet as good as William was at her duties but it would come in time. On the road home they were forced off the side of the road by a speeding carriage. Katherine identified it quickly as Peter Ambrose's carriage. She was only glad that it was headed the opposite direction from her. When she arrived back to her home she had set with the boys and they had their lunch and then the nannies took them for their lessons. Katherine was settling in to read the business reports and do her studies from the books she had identified that would help her to better understand the functions of business and the specific operations of their own products. She had been at her books about 30 minutes when there was a commotion outside. She glanced through the window and saw a wagon and several others in front of the house. One of the servants, Katherine considered a healer had crawled into the wagon and was busy administering to someone inside. Katherine abandoned her books and rushed to the front of the house. She asked what had happened and the doorman said "Missus Katherine, It is Missus Annie and she is in a bad way!" Katherine rushed to the wagon and looked inside. She was shocked at the scene. She ordered them to bring her inside and took her to a spare bedroom. She chose it because the bed was comfortable and it was close to the washroom and stairs with easy access in and out of the room. She sent a rider for Dr. Anderson and told the servants to get hot water and towels in a basin. They carried Annie to the room and Katherine immediately went to work. She cleaned her face of blood to better see her injuries. She undressed her and checked over her chest and then her extremities looking for deformities and bruising. She found all of these things and feared that she was bleeding inside. She cleaned all open wounds and dressed them. She did not give her any medication as she remained for the most part unconscious. She knew that Dr. Anderson would want to evaluate her before ingesting any drug. Katherine had worked in the hospital tending to the soldiers after she was recovered. Soldiers were constantly being brought from the fields of the ongoing war to be cared for in Liverpool away from the fighting. Katherine had learned much of the medical treatments for various wounds and was able to identify and diagnose most injuries. With Annie she worried of internal bleeding and the mysteries of severe head injuries.

Dr. Anderson came within the hour. He praised the care that Katherine had given and had much the same concerns as she had. Dr. Anderson gave her a dose of Laudanum. She would sleep now for many hours. Katherine assigned the servant with medical training to sit with her to monitor her until she recovered. She would be assigned day and night until she was out of danger. Katherine would spell her so she could get her rest. Dr. Anderson asked what had happened to her and Katherine brought him up to date with what she knew. She sent a rider for the Sheriff. They both met with the staff of the Ambrose house after this was done to obtain the full story. The staff told Katherine that they did not know what they would do. They could not return to the Ambrose house for fear of punishment much worse than Annie had received and even after that they would be dismissed from their service. They had nowhere to go. Katherine had her servants make up quarters for those who had fled. She did not know what she would do about them just yet but she would find a place for them within the Henshaw/ Houghton holdings or within the community. It was Annie's health and their security that would need her attention just now.

As the preparations were being made to house the Ambrose staff were underway Sheriff Stratford was greeted at the door. He gave his hat and coat and was escorted into the study for tea. Katherine was notified of his arrival and gave her instructions and placed the butler in charge of the work. She checked her appearance and made her way down the stairs. She greeted Sheriff Stratford and they sat for tea. Katherine said "Sheriff, I know that you have been given the immediate facts but I must stress how serious this has become. Annie was brought here by the Ambrose staff. They are in fear of returning and are sure they will be dismissed from their employment for helping her. Annie has severe injuries and is sedated. Dr. Anderson is attending her and we have a twenty four hour watch on her as she sleeps. We hope there are no internal or head injuries that we have missed. Her face is unrecognizable and will get much worse before it gets better. We fear for her survival at this point in time. Of course she will stay with me until we can decide what must be done.

Sheriff Stratford said "Peter's behavior is deteriorating. I am afraid it is also having its effects on young Joshua. I have heard reports of the young boy striking his mother. This pattern seems to repeat through each generation of the Ambrose family. I do not know under current law what we can do. Keeping her here for now is best. I must stress to you that you are not Peter's favorite person since you have not accepted his will and cowed down to him. He does not like women of power and intelligence. Add to that the histories between your families and it is a volatile situation. I will meet with the Judge and we will pay Peter a visit. He will know something is askew when he hears that his staff has deserted him en masse. He will not be happy to see us. Where is young Joshua if I may ask?"

Katherine said "That I do not know! He could still be at the Ambrose house. I am not sure if anyone stayed behind so he could be alone. I know that Peter is not there. His carriage ran us off the road on my earlier return from Liverpool. I would suggest that you pay a visit to the house to see to his welfare."

The Sheriff said "You are probably correct. I will take him to his father at his offices if he is there. That will reduce the chances of him coming here after his son! I will send a messenger if there is anything that you will need to know before we can get back here."

Katherine said "I appreciate that! I will have the gentlemen from Ambrose to take up a watch around the house since there are no duties for them as yet."

They finished their tea and Sheriff Stratford turned his horse in the direction of the Ambrose house for yet another family crisis.

Annie continued to rest. She cried out in pain at regular intervals. It is good she was sedated so she would not remember most of it. The outlook for her was not good. She was an exceptional person. She was fair and courteous to her staff and this is probably what had saved her if she indeed did survive her injuries. The staff's love of her and hatred of Peter made the effort necessary to them. Katherine had to make sure that they would be rewarded for their heroism.

Office of Peter Ambrose

Peter came back to Liverpool in and angry mood. He felt avenged from the disloyalty of his wife. He felt a sense of pride to show the world he was a man and took care of his manly duties. In these times there was a certain mindset that allowed this behavior. This was the basis for Peter taking these actions knowing that there would be little or no consequence for his attack. He had been cloistered in his offices for several hours when the receptionist knocked on the door to announce the presence of Judge Wickford and Sheriff Stratford. He was quite put off by it and would have waved them away if he could.

They entered his office and were greeted by an inebriated visage. With his bulk his instability of foot was almost threatening in itself. Sheriff Stratford addressed Peter "You sir are a bully of women and an unbearable drunk. We have come to discuss your attack upon youy wife!"

Peter said "It is the business of my house and none of yours. I will not answer your questions and will not waste my time explaining a man and his duties to the likes of you two. I take care of my business myself!"

The Judge stood and said "There are other repercussions to your actions other than a law. Society will not suffer you any longer and your business could suffer."

Peter laughed loudly. He shouted at them with his foul breath "I don't care about society, I never have and having to see the fat bloated faces of you and your crowd sickens me on a regular basis. As far as business is concerned, I have all the coin I will need for a long time. I was giving thought of shutting the business down anyways so I did not have to see any of you twits in the future."

Sheriff Stratford stood for a minute. He knew that his temper was on its threshold now. He looked at the Judge and he nodded in the affirmative. The Judge moved to the door and threw the bolt locking it. Sheriff Stratford took out his brass knuckles and his Billy club and went to work. He struck Peter hard to the face and watched the surprise and pain ripple through the rolls of fat. Peter yelled "You get out of my office. You can't do this. I will have you arrested and you will lose your positions!"

The Sheriff landed another blow cutting him off in midsentence with a squeal of pain. The office staff had gathered outside the door and listened with great pleasure. They knew that if none of them came to his aid they would be dismissed. They, like their counterparts at the Ambrose house, did not care and would stand in solidarity when Peter would wake from his beating and have the wherewithal to confront them. They might add to the beating before leaving. After a long and painful session the door bolts were slid open and the men walked out. They looked to the staff and said. He will not die. Leave him to feel the pain. His household staff has exiled themselves to Wavertree. I am sure that you would all be welcomed if you feel insecure about Peter's vengeance. You should continue your work until and if you are dismissed.

The workers went back to work. At the end of the day they locked up and left. No one checked on the well-being of Peter. Many debated whether or not they would report to work the following morning. Many had no choice. Once outside of the office they organized themselves and decided to assemble at Wavertree Hall until the threat had passed. Katherine would have to prepare more sleeping quarters and accommodations. The Judge and Sheriff were aware of the decision and sent supplies and food ahead of them to help with the crisis.

Peter began to stir somewhere around midnight. Reality returned to him in waves. He hurt all over and knew that he had injuries. He called for help but no one came. He slowly sat up but the pain made it difficult. His vision was blurry. He touched his face to find it swollen and sore. There was blood on his fingers and he knew he must look terrible. He scooted to his desk and used it as a crutch to pull himself to his feet. It hurt to move. He shuffled his feet to the door and opened it. He started to shout for his receptionist but when he opened his mouth a sharp pain emanated from his jaw. He felt it and knew it was broken. He continued to shuffle into the work area only to find it empty. He was angry that no one was around. The clock chimed midnight and he knew it was late. It was an unwritten rule that somebody stay through the evening hours to run errands and see to his wants and needs in a form of slavery that Peter enjoyed very much. He had not eaten and was hungry. He went to his toilet to clean up. He looked in his mirror and was shocked at his appearance. He could not go to the pub to get his meal. He would be laughed at and ridiculed. He went to the back door of the office and found a vagrant in his alley searching through the trash. He called to him but kept his face covered. The man came to him carefully fully knowing the nature of this man. Peter said "I need you to go to the pub and get me my dinner! I will pay you well and you can get some food yourself!" This was very unlike Peter but food was an important part of his life.

The man said "I am very hungry. I have heared of what you done! I think you might get your food yourself. I would rather go hungry than help a sad man like yourself. It looks like someone gave you what you deserved."

Peter was shocked. He said "What do you know of what I have done! It is none of your business how a real man keeps his woman in line."

The man said "Well, that might well be but I don't have to agree with it. I imagine if you waddle yer fat arse down to the pub you will get another thumpin!" With that he left the alley with Peter's temper fuming. Another man passed the alley and saw Peter. He yelled "You lowest dog of humanity. Do you want a fair fight? I would enjoy givin' you a good thrashing after what you did to that fine lady of yours." Peter quickly ducked into the door just as a large rock struck the casing by his head. He slammed and locked his door. There would be no food for him tonight and sleep would be difficult with all of the pain he was in. He would make sure his staff would pay for their neglect of his needs in the morning!

Wavertree Hall
Katherine had all of the arrangements made for the staff of the Ambrose house when a single rider came down the drive. He was

a messenger from the Sheriff. He dismounted and went to the door. Inside the approach of a rider had caused a stir and Katherine met him at the door. The message from the Judge told her that the staff from Peter's office was en route to Wavertree Hall. He was sending bedding, food and supplies to help out. They would not return to Peter's employ. He would clear it all up for her when he arrived later in the evening. Katherine called the Ambrose staff together and had them make further arrangements for the arrival of even more guests.

Sheriff Stratford and Judge Wickford arrived a few hours after the messenger and escorted a wagon load of supplies. They dismounted and told Katherine that they should expect the office staff in the next few minutes as they had passed them on the road. They updated her on the status of Peter Ambrose and asked about Annie. Katherine told them that Annie was still being medicated so the issue was still hour by hour. They felt she would recover now but did not know what the short term and long term damages would be. It was sure that arrangements would have to be made for a permanent move for her safety. Katherine had already decided that she would be a permanent resident of Wavertree Hall. It would be nice to have a friend that she could spend time with and provide company. Annie would be able to help with the boys. Sadly, she had probably seen the last of her own child.

Judge Wickford started the conversation "We will need to plan for these people. Peter will make their lives miserable. I have had a thought. The financial records in the offices are the property of Peter's clients. Peter seems to have no fear of losing his clients or business and I can already predict he will lose most of those that have made his business if not all of them. Is there any room in your buildings for an office Katherine?"

Katherine thought a while. She replied "I can set some temporary space and find permanent space after that if needed."

The Judge looked at the Sheriff knowing what was coming

next. He said "Katherine this is what we need. I have the core of the business that will arrive here shortly. Peter's receptionist managed the business for the most part. Peter did work on ledgers but his place would be easily filled with a new hire. My proposal is to set these people into their own business to compete with Peter, their former employer, if he decides to continue. He has stated he did not. I think it will work. All of his current clients will be looking for someone to take over their accounts and who better than those that already know them. We will make this happen tonight and move forward tomorrow. We will place a sign walker in front of Peter's office with security for them in place. It is not likely that Peter is up for another fight at this early time. He could use a weapon though. I will meet with the staff to tell them our plan. If you can give me the address to deliver the files from Peter's office I will have them moved there. As Sheriff I am seizing the records to protect the citizen's privacy. Just tell me where to move them. "

Katherine was excited. There would be a reward for these good people who stood up for Annie. There would be many more outcomes to his behavior that would let Peter know their feelings for him over the next week. She did not know how he would survive but it was clear that he had some plan in mind. His reactions were not at all what had been expected from all that had recently happened. It was likely he had a second source of wealth that gave him this relief to act out the way he had. They all needed to be careful.

The Office of Peter Ambrose

Peter awoke to loud noises outside of his office. He got up painfully and walked to the door of his office. He heard noises of banging, scraping and grunting. Someone was shouting orders. He heard the door chimes ring many times. He did not want to be seen by others until he had healed some but he feared that the situation was getting away from him. He dressed and threw open the doors to the office. To his surprise he found Judge Wickford and the Sheriff in charge of dismantling his office. He shouted "What is the meaning of this trespass and what is my staff doing?"

The Judge said "There you are Peter. I am glad you are up. I have a court order here to remove all records and files from your office and I needed to serve you properly. You there! Make sure that these are taken. Not one file is to be left inside these walls! You understand I am sure that your business here is over. These people are no longer on your staff. They are new businessmen. They will be taking over these accounts. The privacy and security of the documents is of primary importance to your former clients and the court felt it necessary to secure them at this time."

Peter was infuriated. He started towards the Judge but Sheriff Stratford stepped into his path. He said "Come, come Peter! I am sure you have not forgotten our last meeting. If you have just looked in the mirror I am sure you would remember. I would be glad to give you a proper reminder if that is not enough!" Peter backed down.

He yelled "You will be hearing from my counsel!" and returned to his office and slammed the door. The workers stepped up their pace. They did not want to be around this man any longer than needed. Their work was completed in short order and Peter's business was reduced to several empty desks and file cabinets. He was left alone in his office.

Much later, when he was sure everyone was gone he made his way into the outer office. There were no workers and the place had been stripped down to the empty chairs. He was now sure that his attack on Annie had been met with an unanticipated result. He had lost his business and it could not be recovered. He did not know where Annie and the others were but he suspected that she only had one friend that she could turn to in times of trouble and that would be Katherine. The Henshaws had again been a party to his failures in life and his anger grew. Peter was startled as a large brick shattered the window and landed at his feet. He heard angry, taunting voices outside and retreated once again to his office and barricaded himself inside. He quickly packed his things. He disguised himself as best that he could. It was hard to disguise his now 400 pound frame. He snuck through the back door and headed for the livery to regain his carriage. To his dismay, the carriage had been commandeered to move files by the Sheriff. There was only an old mule left in the stables so he took it and headed out. As he went through the streets he was recognized immediately. They laughed and humiliated him. They threw garbage and rotten produce at him striking him several times. There were rocks and other things in the mix. The older boys ran along his side attacking him with sticks and other things they would find about the streets. He finally broke out of town. The mule would not move any faster but those in pursuit had tired of their games and returned to what they were doing.

Peter moved along the road and past Wavertree. He noticed guards posted at the gates and recognized several of them as his staff at the office and the Ambrose house. They glared at him and invited him to attempt to enter the grounds. He continued on as they stared at him with pity and disbelief. They had all seen the immense damage that he had inflicted on Annie and felt he could never be repaid. Peter did not know what to expect at his house but knew with what he had seen it would not be the same.

As he rode into Ambrose house he was angry. He would send the mule back to the livery with the stable boys. They could walk back. He would get some food and no one would deny him without serious repercussions. He got to the front of the house and there was no one there to take the mule. He called out! He shouted now! No one came. His broken jaw caused him much pain. He knew it would be difficult to eat. He tied the mule and went to the door. The doorman was not at his station either. He would be punished. He went to the kitchen bellowing out his orders for food only to be met with silence. He looked around and no one could be found. He went up the stairs to Annie's room with the intentions of giving her another beating for causing all of the atrocities that had been visited upon him but he found her room empty also. He went to Joshua's room and found him asleep. He woke him and asked him to explain the conditions. Joshua said "Judge Wickford and the Sheriff have been here. The staff took mother away for care. She was in a bad way. I do not know where they took her but I suspect to be with Katherine. They all left and did not return. I don't believe that they plan on coming back!"

Peter said "It is of little consequence. There are many beggars out there that need the work. They are all dismissed. They will starve in the streets and I will not raise a hand to help them!"

Joshua said "Father, who will take care of things. We have no servants. I have eaten bread and cheese but it will soon be bad and I don't know how to make these things. Do you?"

Peter said "I am not a cook! I will hire a new staff!"

Joshua said "Who will work for you after all of this?"

Peter slapped him across his face and said "You will never talk to your father that way! Now you go get me some of that bread and cheese and something to drink! We will make do!"

After gorging himself on the food he retired to his room and slept the bigger part of two days as his huge frame began its healing process.

Wavertree Hall

Katherine had become the leader she needed to be. They relocated Peter's business into a waterfront office that she had arranged to purchase. The receptionist would act as the office manager and all of the workers would split the profits of the business and receive their normal salaries so as not to disrupt their families. The staff from the Ambrose house was split up. Some were employed at Wavertree and some were found employment elsewhere. Katherine was always in need of farm help so she moved those in this field into those positions. Those with the livestock were kept. Katherine expanded the herds to accommodate the workers. She also bought some good horse stock and increased the business in this area. All in all the downfall of Peter Ambrose was a good thing for all of those that were displaced by it. Katherine had consulted with her advisors and an eviction notice was prepared for Peter and Joshua to leave the Ambrose Estate to protect the investment there and to recover its assets before they could be sold or destroyed. No one believed that Peter was not capable of this and more now that his true self had been exposed for what it was.

Annie had woken up about two weeks after the beating. She was slowly improving but walked with a limp and her vision was not good. She was forgetful and seemed to be slower of wit. She had constant and severe headaches. Dr. Anderson said this was to be expected and that some of these issues would improve but others would not. Only time would tell how full her recovery would be. Katherine and all of those that knew Annie were pleased at each small step she made towards healing. They also blamed Peter and he was an outcast at this point. He stayed sequestered at Ambrose House until his eviction was forced upon him. Then he and Joshua relocated to his offices in town. He was able to find workers but had to go far away to engage them. Nobody in the immediate area would work for him even if they were starving. His reputation grew and was now common knowledge. Those that did work for him were of questionable backgrounds and heritage. He could never sleep well at night knowing that they might slit his throat for a shilling. Ambrose House had again passed to a dark and dismal time. Katherine left things as they were at the house. She had evicted Peter but had no animosity. She was concerned about Peter and his sanity and the welfare of Joshua. Peter somehow remained at an unreal level of amusement and the reasons were only known to him.

It was now late in the decade of the 1640s. The century would soon pass its halfway point. The Civil Wars still boiled throughout the country and showed no signs of abating. Charles I was convicted of High Treason and beheaded on January 30, 1649. This ended the first English Civil war and brought Oliver Cromwell to power. There would be more civil unrest over religion and the vacant throne. For at least a few years there would be no declared war.

The time passed quickly now. The boys were growing. Joshua was now eight years of age and Daniel would be seven. Annie had become a part of the household and seemed much like an Aunt to the boys. Her presence allowed Katherine the freedom to run the family holdings with her framework of managers and family. Helen helped with the household and had made good friends with Annie. John was overseeing the family interests in Ireland and lived in Ulster. Ellen and John Harrison helped immensely with the English businesses.

Katherine was a striking figure and many suitors came to her wishing her hand. She turned them all away. Peter kept a quiet watch on the situation but knew that he would never have her. As with things that went against Peter she became as powerful an enemy in his mind and William and Thomas before her. She represented the Henshaw family and was his natural foe. He watched and he waited. He had his trap and he would spring it when the time was right. He was not a man of patience and if things did not meet his schedule he would take steps to hurry them up. He would have the hand of God reach out to help him along in his current quest.

Wavertree Hall

It was in the spring of the sixth year following the deaths of William and Evan. The winter had been harsh and the early spring had been cold. As was the normal in England, it was very damp and rainy. Helen had first come to the kitchen to help prepare the food. She was pale and shaky and looked feverish. Katherine was concerned and asked on her health. Helen said she had caught a chill and was suffering from influenza. She said that it would pass. Over the next few days her fever grew and she took to the bed. Dr. Anderson was called and gave her medication. It had little effect and he began to search for other inflictions. Her breathing became labored and she began to cough until her throat was inflamed and talking was painful and strained. Katherine took a bedside vigil and it was on the tenth night that Helen Parker joined her husband for eternity. Katherine felt that she was totally alone in the world now to raise her sons. She accepted the heavy burden of watching over the welfare of so many until her boys were educated, grown and could take over their legacy and their position in society. Peter made another ill-timed attempt to force Katherine's hand and she reacted to him with finality. He shuddered and she feared that he would strike her but she stood her ground and told him to never broach the subject with her again. She knew she had hurt his feelings but he was simply not taking no for an answer.

The following spring had been much like the one before. It was again miserable with rain, cold and dampness. It had been a miserable winter. It was just cold enough to make things uncomfortable. It did not get cold enough to make the hard freeze that would bring a fresh start to the Earth by killing off all things evil in its icy grasp. They lived in festering muddy conditions. The city would be clogged with waste and human excrement. When the temperatures changed science took over and a noxious sort of goo festered and grew with all of its germs and diseases. Being a port town, Liverpool would be susceptive to the import of the ship's rodent passengers. Several port cities were already in the grip of the Plague that had decimated European populations for years. As the ships landed from these ports and the rodents disembarked to find food the plague went with them. In a short time an outbreak would hit Liverpool. As the first cases were reported Katherine sent the boys to stay with John in Ulster. She would be busy. With her medical training she was enlisted by Dr. Anderson as a nurse to minister to the sick. They took all precautions but those that took care of the ill were regularly and closely exposed to the disease. Annie stayed at Wavertree and ran the household. Word came to her that Katherine had caught the fever and that she was to stay at Wavertree to care for the house and the boys if worse came to worse. By staying at Wavertree Annie would not be exposed to the disease. Katherine reasoned that if she did not recover the boys would need her. Henry Brisby would see them through. Judge Wickford would support him. Katherine battled the disease bravely but could not overcome it. She died shortly after the first symptoms appeared. All told over two hundred souls met their demise at the hands of this deadly disease. Katherine was one of them. To prevent the spread of the disease the bodies were mass buried in a grave on Sickmans Lane which is today Addison Street.

Peter had heard the rumors of Katherine's illness. He did not leave his quarters during the outbreak fearing the disease. He did send some of his workers from time to time to collect the news of Katherine's health. He was elated when the news came of her death. His plan would soon be coming to light and there would be no stopping him this time.

Annie sent word to John in Ireland. He returned to Wavertree with the boys as quickly as he could. The boys were old enough now to understand that they had lost both of their parents and were considered orphans. They called Henry Brisby to come for counsel. Henry appeared within two hours of the summons. He told them the details of what he knew of the existing trust. He reviewed the claims of the Stanley family against the holding but they were of no consequence because of the standing of the boys as the rightful heirs. They proceeded on those presumptions. Within a short time they would know they had been caught in the plot hatched by Peter Ambrose.

The Ambrose House

Peter had been planning for several years now. He would finally see his property returned to him and so much more. He would get his final revenge on Annie who figured prominently in the plans for the Henshaw estate and the care of its heirs. He went to his files and pulled out the copies of the legal documents he would need. First found were the trust papers naming himself as trustee for the estate. The second was the last Will and Testament of Katherine Henshaw. There would be debate on these documents but Peter had been careful in their filing to assure that these "hidden" documents would carry the weight of legal scrutiny and supersede any others.

Peter had been in contact with Richard Mather. Mather was ordained as a Puritan minister in 1620 and was stripped of the title in 1634. In 1635 he left for the Massachusetts colony. He established a family there and a church. He had many children including Cotton Mather a Puritan who was prominently involved in the Salem Witch Trials. Peter had no interest in any of these religious vocations. He was only interested in finding a man of such integrity that would act as his co-conspirator to spirit the Henshaw sons far away from Liverpool to enable him to access and control their inheritance as he saw fit. For this Richard Mather would be paid a tidy fee for the transport and upkeep of the boys to a minimal level in Massachusetts while keeping the nature of this business confidential. An acknowledgement of this deal at any time during Mather's life would have set the record straight and allowed the boys to retain the family's properties. This good Christian man, for all of his life, was involved in the crimes of abduction, fraud and the breaking of the commandments in front of his God.

The following extract from a letter written by Mr. F. W. Henshaw, of Montreal, Canada, will show the estimate placed upon the Rev. Richard Mather by the Henshaw family : " My belief is that he was in collusion with the wretch, Ambrose, in defrauding the two boys — Henshaws. His silence as to their history, which he unquestionably knew all about, is strong enough evidence of his complicity in the dastardly act."

Peter waited for a short period of time. He sent his watchers out to report back on the movements and actions of Judge Wickford, Henry Brisby and Sheriff Stratford. With the arrival of John Henshaw and the boys from England there was a meeting set to discuss the future for the Henshaw boys and how the Estate would be supervised until the age of adulthood. The meeting would be held at the office of Henry Brisby in Liverpool beginning at 9 am that following Wednesday. Peter would be ready.

The Office of Henry Brisby: 9:00 am

Everyone had arrived and the meeting was called to order. The boys were there but at their age they would not understand the proceedings. Annie, John Henshaw, Ellen and John Harrison and the others thought that this meeting would be short and put down a plan that they all expected. Shortly after the meeting had begun there was a disturbance outside. Henry left the room and returned at gunpoint. Peter Ambrose strode into the room in the company of his hired hands. All of them armed with pistols and sword. Peter was wearing a glowing grin. He said "I did not want my business here interrupted thus my escort. Mr. Brisby, the papers I will leave have already been presented and approved in the court in London by my counsel. They are binding. I will give you some days to verify the facts. In seven days I will take control of the Henshaw estate as signed and verified by Katherine Henshaw some years ago. To make the passing less ugly I will staff the houses with my own people so those in employ will need to vacate by that time. That will include my unfaithful wife who should vacate immediately. The boys are to be taken to Wavertree and left in the care of my staff. All others who would attempt entry to the properties will be considered trespassers. I think that concludes my business here! Seven days is what you have. You will find all in order!" With that they backed out the door and left.

The room was silent. Annie spoke "Can he do this sir? Were you aware of the papers?"

Brisby replied "No! I was not. I went to the clerk of the court and was given what was purported as all of the papers filed by Ambrose under court order."

The Sheriff said "I will be heading to the court for an explanation immediately." He left for the clerk's office.

They continued their meeting although in a somewhat feverish state. The Sheriff returned from his mission at length and entered the room. "I have word my lords! At first it was not forthcoming but I found my own way to loosen the lips. The clerk and those of his employ were bribed by Peter Ambrose to keep the secret. The papers that were received were legitimate but they failed to respond to us on the second level of papers filed that day by Mr. Ambrose. By law those were the ones that held the force and not the ruse passed on to Mr. Brisby. It is true that Peter Ambrose is in control of the Henshaw and Houghton estates and in control of both Joshua and Daniel as their guardian!"

The Judge broke in and said "We can fight it in the courts and win. I will take a lot of time to overturn such a thing. In the meantime I am afraid that Mr. Ambrose will do his damage and exact his revenge! I will start immediately. Annie you must vacate Wavertree as quickly as possible for your own safety. Pass the word to those from the Ambrose staff to do the same. He will have at them now!"

The Ambrose House – 7 Days Later

Peter was overseeing the loading of wagons. He would seat himself at Wavertree Hall to make the point of his conquest. He was all smiles. He told Joshua that he too would make the move. He would leave Ambrose House for good. They would continue to maintain the house, livestock and grounds but there would be so much more to do. He had accumulated a force of mercenaries to make sure his will would be done. He would not be bullied by the Judge or Sheriff any further. He did not care what the community thought of him. He just knew that he had avenged his father's and mother's deaths and failed wishes. They would be proud of him if they were here. At daybreak they started up the road to Wavertree Hall and met no resistance.

He called the staff to order and dismissed them all. He brought his own staff to the house and had hired additional staff for Ambrose House. The boys were there and were ordered to their rooms and separated from each other. Annie had fled and was staying at Judge Wickford's residence. She would later divorce Peter Ambrose and marry Sheriff Stratford. They would do their best to have this travesty overturned but with all of the turmoil in the Kingdom it would be hard to accomplish anything in the courts. Peter was aware of this and would waste no time in making his moves. He dispatched a letter to Richard Mather in the Massachusetts Colony. He hoped to hear back within the year. He knew what the answer would be because he had made the deal with Mather back in the time of his immigration. He knew that the Massachusetts Bay Colony was a hard place. They needed funds and they needed labor. Peter would send both. The boys would provide a regular income to Mather and he could put them to labor for whatever they were worth. In essence he would send them into a sort of religious slavery at the height of Puritanism in the colony. Until then he would keep the boys locked in their rooms and out of the public eye. He did not allow any of the family or Annie to visit with them. They were completely isolated on their own. Peter sent his man to the docks to check for his response from Mather daily after a few months. He really had no idea how long it would take. A year had passed and the boys were kept like criminals in solitary confinement. He did not allow them time together. At first they were both defiant.

For each act of defiance they paid a very real and physical response. As time went on they both dealt with it differently. Joshua's anger was undiminished and he lashed out any chance he would get. He would never accept what Peter Ambrose had done and would fight it to his death. Daniel was the same way at first. After a while though he did what was necessary to accept what he had been dealt. He knew that these things were out of his hands and there was nothing he could do but pray and hope that those outside were working to get the issue resolved in some way. It was not abnormal in these times for inhuman treatment by the government or the church. He could only live on faith and this he did.

It was in the late fall that the reply came back from the colonies. Robert Mather would agree to take the boys and collect the fee that had been negotiated from Peter Ambrose in their previous meeting. Peter was happy. He knew life would be easier with the boys out of the country and out of his life for good. He had planned this for a while. He would put the story out that the boys had been sent off to school in London. To avoid any questions he would add to the story that they had been away since shortly after Peter took control of Wavertree Hall. He would have time then to devise a story as to why they would not return to Liverpool after the time had passed for the completion of their school. He had to devise a story for the Stanley family to explain why they would not be receiving the lands back from the estate that they had expected. Peter was good at defrauding people now and this would be of little concern.

Peter booked passage for the boys for the following spring. He knew that the passage would not be good in winter and he needed to show that he had acted responsibly if his plan was found out. The Captain wasn't pleased to have young boys on board the ship and especially two who could not take care of themselves. The confinement and scant food had weakened them. They had wilted from inactivity and malnutrition. He negotiated extra funds from Peter to compensate for the extra care they would be on the crossing. For the months leading up to the voyage the boy's diet was improved. They put on some weight and they were given some work to do to build their muscles. They would be rousted from their beds in the middle of the night and taken to the stables to muck stalls and stack hay so they would not be seen by the public in passing. They were never allowed to be in contact with each other or to speak. Then when the sun began to rise they were hustled back to their rooms.

There came a day that Peter was visited by a man at Wavertree. He was obviously a sailor and was dirty and smelled foul. Peter was very glad to see him. He told him that the ship was in port. They would unload and reload the ship's cargo and be ready to depart for the colonies. They would hope to take to sea in a fortnight. Peter said the boys would be ready. The sailor demanded half of the payment up front and that their belongings would be delivered in advance so that they would only have to board the boys before setting off. As soon as he knew they were off to sea and that there were no witnesses he would start passing his school story.

The Office of Henry Brisby

Henry had been hard at work. Those that had taken the bribes from Peter were now under the thumb of Judge Wickford. The Sheriff continued to patrol near Wavertree Hall to see what could be seen. The gates were under guard and it seemed as though it was a military fort or prison there. Henry had filed several court pleadings to overturn the trust and will in the boys favor. He was met with more requests for information and a defensive posture by the courts. He knew he was fighting an uphill battle. He worked hard but now they found themselves battling a man that had unlimited wealth at this disposal. They were sure that more bribes were being paid to make the process more difficult. Peter could delay this process forever it seemed.

Wavertree Hall

It was a dark and moonless night. The boys had been fed early and their food spiked with a sedative. They were fast asleep when the men came for them. They were tied and hooded and moved in the darkness to a wagon and covered with blankets. The wagon was loaded with hay and the center left open where the boys were placed. Their journey had begun. They pulled out onto the road after midnight. There were several of Peter's mercenaries traveling with the wagon. Sheriff Stratford was camped in the woods near the road and saw the procession. He mounted his horse to follow. As he entered the road he was accosted and surrounded by another group of horsemen that impeded him from following. He tried to move around them but found himself in the crosshairs of their pistols. He was being confined to the road and not allowed to pass. He knew this had to be Peter's big move but he could do nothing about it. He went back to the trees to gather his gear and devise a plan to get by the guard. He feared it was too late already.

The Docks of Liverpool

The wagon pulled up to the docks. Two bundles were unloaded from the hay wagon and hustled on board. When they got them on board they were unwrapped from these bindings and buckets of water thrown on them to wake them. The Captain wanted to be sure that the boys were alive and healthy to make the trip as negotiated. He knew that in many of these crossing there would be a certain amount of death and disease. Young boys of this age starting out ill would not make the trip. He inspected the boys like cattle and then nodded. The wagon pulled away and the Captain shouted "Cast Off, lift anchor and get us into the harbor boys!" There was a flurry of motion. The boys were still groggy from the drugs but moved to the railing as the ship achieved the harbor. They looked back and recognized their fathers businesses on the wharf. They saw many of their family's ships flying different colors. The flags carried a dominant letter A in the center. They looked at each other. They had both grown since they last saw each other. They shivered in the cold and Joshua put his arms around his younger brother for warmth. They stayed at the rail until Liverpool was out of site. They knew that something life changing had just occurred.

And so their journey had begun. Brisby, Stratford, Annie, John all continued to work to restore the boys to power over their inheritance but they were unaware of the developments and thought them to be in schooling in London. No one heard from them and no one had seen them for some time at their departure. In truth they only had Peter Ambrose's word on their circumstances and his word had proven untrustworthy on so many occasions already. It seemed that all was lost. During the following years the plague had struck London. Word was passed by Peter Ambrose that the boys had caught it and succumbed to it just as their mother had done earlier. This seemed to close the book on the brothers and the quest for justice. Only Peter Ambrose and Richard Mather would know the truth now. The boys would be too far away to defend their position and everyone believed them deceased.

Excerpts from the Will of Peter Ambrose found in the N.E.H. & G.Register Vol. XLVIL July 1893, Page 394.

Peter Ambrose of Toxteth, Lancashire, gen, 22 December 1653, proved 10January 1653. Has the following bequest's. Also my will and mind is and I hereby give and bequeath to Joshua and Daniel Henshawe, late sons of William Henshawe, late of Toxteth aforesaid deceased, who are now in New England, so much money as shall make up what hath " ben " by me laid forth for them and expended for them for their voyage to New England and otherwise, the sum of thirty pounds, to be paid them at such time as they shall have attained fullage and shall give a sufficient discharge for the whole thirty pounds.

To Joshua Ambrose my elder son that capital as called Wautree House or Wautree Hall.

www.ingramcontent.com/pod-product-compliance
Lightning Source LLC
Chambersburg PA
CBHW060233100726
47907CB00003B/617